FROM FIELD TO FURNACE

FROM FIELD TO FURNACE

The Story of One Family's Journey into the Industrial Revolution

MARILYN FREEMAN

Spellbrooktales

ISBN: 9781739688097

First Printing, 2023

Preface

In the heart of 18th-century Shropshire, a profound metamorphosis sweeps through the lives of the Bangham family, capturing the essence of an era marked by radical change. "From Field to Furnace" is a compelling historical novel that delves into the lives of ordinary people navigating the tumultuous waters of the Industrial Revolution, a pivotal period that reshaped society and human existence.

As the world witnesses the advent of technological marvels, like the revolutionary use of coal in iron production, the Bangham family becomes the embodiment of an epoch in transition. The story unfurls against the backdrop of an agrarian society on the cusp of transformation into an industrial powerhouse, exploring the intricate shifts in work, family dynamics, and societal norms.

This novel immerses readers in the lives of the Bangham family, offering a personal lens through which to witness the grand tapestry of history. We follow their journey from the tranquil enclaves of Bangham's Wood to the bustling industrial settlements of the Severn Gorge, where the relentless demands of the Darby ironworks reshape their existence. The central question of whether Joseph Bangham and his kin foresaw the profound impact they would have on the world through their toil at the furnace underscores the magnitude of the Industrial Revolution. It prompts reflection on the consequences of technological advancement and the enduring uncertainty it brings.

Spanning the years from 1713 to 1766, "From Field to Furnace" invites readers to intimately engage with the complexities of the Bangham family's joys and sorrows, grounding the historical context in relatable emotions. The Severn Gorge, renowned as the 'cradle of the Industrial Revolution,' vividly comes to life, painting a rich backdrop of the period's environment and atmosphere.

The narrative acquires moral and ethical dimensions as it explores 18th-century England's often brutal justice system. The Bangham family's encounters with the law offer glimpses into the harrowing world of prisoner transportation to America and the desperate plight of its enslaved people, hinting at the nascent anti-slavery movement.

"From Field to Furnace" is a riveting and enlightening historical novel that not only imparts knowledge about a pivotal era but also touches upon timeless themes of human experience, progress, and its consequences. A tale equally engaging for history enthusiasts, family saga devotees, and those intrigued by the human facets of industrialization.

NB: The book is in two parts, Part One being 'Coalbrookdale' which was previously published as a standalone novel, and 'Riding the Tides' which brings the story of the Bangham family in the Severn Gorge up to the year 1766.

PART ONE

COALBROOKDALE

1713

Chapter 1

Spring had arrived early in the Severn Gorge and the hedge-rows were bursting with birdsong. Joe Bangham strode along the track from his home in Bangham's Wood at the bottom of Benthall Edge, down to the bridge over the River Severn at Buildwas. He noticed the river was high, after the rain which had swept along the Gorge the day before. Crossing the river, he turned right, along the north bank, then after a mile or so, took the track running beside the Coalbrookdale stream.

He had heard the ironworks were taking on new men. On visits to Madeley on market days, there had been talk of Mr Darby building another furnace at his works in Coalbrookdale and that he would need more workers. Apparently, he was paying eight shillings a week, which was more than Joe could earn as a farm labourer even when there was work, which was intermittent. It was said that the jobs at the works weren't permanent and couldn't be guaranteed, but Joe felt that even if he could do a few weeks in the year, it would be a great boost to the family's finances. So, he was determined to try his luck, and as he walked along the track towards the works, was feeling hopeful. He was eighteen years old, strong, and ambitious. He was at an age when anything seems possible, and he exuded an air of optimism that was infectious. He was certain Mr Darby would take him on.

As he walked along the track up the steep sided valley, the sound of industry grew louder. He passed the forges and the foundries, which were surrounded by stacks of iron pigs, the raw material from which they produced their various wares. Here, was all noise of metal on metal and the shouts of men trying to make themselves heard above the din. As he walked further on, the bulk of the furnace came into view. He could smell the smoke and fumes and hear the sound of the stone being tipped into the mouth of the furnace, and the rumble of another load being wheeled across the bridge to be next in line. He stood for some moments, transfixed by the noise and the smell and the sight of the bright golden red light issuing from the mouth at the base of the structure, with sparks flying in all directions. He was used to the sounds and sights of the woodlands and meadows where he had lived and toiled all his life. Obviously, he had seen many small furnaces over the years, but this was something completely different. As he watched and listened, he began to understand more fully, the extent of the change that was coming.

He noticed a gentleman, full bearded and rather better dressed than the rest of the men, standing to one side, also observing the scene. He immediately recognised him as Mr Darby. He had seen him several times in Madeley, on market days. Taking a deep breath and standing tall, Joe strode up to him and, removing his cap, asked if he could speak with him. Mr Darby smiled, and Joe introduced himself, offering his hand. Mr Darby seemed a little taken aback but nonetheless, shook Joe's hand warmly.

'What can I do for you, Joe Bangham,' he asked, with a wry smile.

'Well sir,' said Joe, 'I wonder if you might have any work? I had heard you were taking on more men.'

'Oh, you did, did you? Well, I might be. What work have you done before?'

'I've worked the land sin' I was eight-year old, and my family make charcoal in t'wood under Benthall Edge.' Joe replied, 'But I'm strong an' fit, an' willing to do what's needed Sir.'

Mr Darby asked him what he knew about making iron. Joe replied that at the moment he didn't know very much, although his family had supplied several furnaces in the area with charcoal for producing brass and iron over the years. He assured Mr Darby he was willing to learn and wasn't afraid of hard work.

'Well Joe,' Mr Darby explained, 'I am minded to give you a try, but as I'm sure you know, this work is not guaranteed. Some weeks, particularly in the summer, we produce no iron, maybe because there is no rain to fill the pool, or maybe because we just don't have the orders.'

'I understand sir, but I believe this to be t'future of mekkin' iron and I want to be a part on it.'

Mr Darby nodded thoughtfully, then smiled and agreed he could start the following Monday. The work was to be from six in the morning, until six in the evening when the furnace was blowing. He would also be expected to work night shifts as needed. He would start on six shillings a week until he had gained some experience and then Mr Darby said he would look at it again. The usual rate for an experienced worker was eight shillings a week. Joe was happy and grateful to be given the chance to prove himself.

'I won't let thee down, Mr Darby,' he said, offering his hand, which Mr Darby took, once again with a wry smile, thinking that there was something appealing about this young man. Of course, time will tell he thought, let's see how he performs when his real work begins.

Joe turned and walked briskly away down the valley. He was excited. For the first time in his life, he could see new horizons opening up before him. For as long as he could remember, all that was ahead of him were days of toil in the fields, interspersed with long nights camping by a clamp in the woods. Now he had the opportunity to become part of a bigger future, part of the change he was certain was coming to the world.

For decades, the Bangham family had been supplying furnaces up and down the Gorge with charcoal for smelting iron. From what he'd heard about the events at the Darby Works, the demand for their charcoal may well be about to decline. Apparently, Mr Darby had much improved his way of making iron for casting, and new ways of working were coming to the Gorge. The making of iron would no longer rely on coppicing and producing charcoal. Joe had long since realised the limits of this endeavour, which relied on growing trees, of necessity a slow business. Mr Darby used coal instead of charcoal to make his iron. Joe instinctively knew that the family's reliance on making and selling charcoal was going to have to change, and he could be an instrument of that change, rather than resisting it. To a young man such as he, it felt exciting. This was the future. As we can imagine, his father was not too pleased with the prospect of his eldest son going to work for Darby, the man who was showing the world that charcoal was no longer needed in the production of iron.

Of course, Joe understood his father's reluctance. To produce a clamp of charcoal needed two people to camp out in the woods for five days and nights on end, to tend the fire. If the fire got out of control, becoming too hot, the product was ruined. If he went to work at the Darby works, it would mean that Will, his younger brother would have to work with his father during the 'burn', leaving only the youngest brother Richard available for a second clamp, which without him, would be impossible, and the family would be limited to producing one clamp at a time.

Joe had long realised that sustaining the growing family on agricultural labourers' wages was impossible. Even with the charcoal burning, it didn't bring in enough to feed and clothe them all. Times were hard at home after his mother's death, with eight children, the youngest being just one year old. Walter, his father, had done his best, but losing his wife had hit him hard. Two of Joe's sisters had had to go into service up at the Hall, and as the boys grew up, they each, in their turn, were apprenticed for seven years to the Benthall farm and then eventually helped Walter with the coppicing and charcoal burning. As Joe climbed up towards Banghams Wood he was sure he had done the right thing by seeking work with the Darby's although he wasn't convinced his father would think the same.

It was with some trepidation that he now approached the Bangham home which was a stone-built house with a turf roof. It had originally been built as a squatter's cottage by his grandparents many decades earlier. At the time, in order to claim squatters' rights, it had to be constructed within one night, with four walls and a roof, to qualify as being finished. Since then, the Bangham family had been coppicing in this wood, and over the years it had become known as 'Banghams Wood.' In the beginning, the house had just one room, but over the years, the family had added another two rooms above, a wash house, a hog pen, and a separate privy. Other families had arrived and built their squatter cottages, and it became a hamlet, and a water pump was installed, to be shared by all the families.

The Banghams' cottage was sparsely furnished with little beyond the beds, a table, several stools, an old trunk, and a few rustic chairs. Years ago, his mother had made bedspreads and rugs out of old rags which gave it a cosy feel. The log fire blazing brightly in the hearth was the main source of light. Candles were expensive and only lit when the last of the daylight had gone. His sister Elizabeth had a stew-pot cooking above the fire, which was emitting a wonderful aroma as Joe entered, reminding him just how hungry he was.

No one spoke as he came in. There was an awkward silence. They all knew where he'd been of course, and they also knew what their father, Walter, who was sitting in one of the chairs by the fire, felt about that. Joe took off his coat and cap and hung them behind the door.

'Well,' he said, 'Is none of ye going to ask 'ow I got on?'

'We can see how thee got on,' Walter retorted, 'by that look on thy face.'

'In case any of thee wants to know, I start next Monday.'

Still, no one spoke, all eyes now on Walter.

'Look father, I know thee aren't happy about this, but 'tis the future thee knows, an' we need to be part on it. With this new way of mekkin' iron, a big part of our market for charcoal will go, I'm sure on it.'

'And in the meantime?!' Walter shouted, 'How are we supposed to feed ourselves? Did Darby say thee'd have work every week?'

'Well, nay, it might be a bit up and down like,' Joe replied.

'There thee are then, what are we meant to do when 'ee can't give thee work? Stop eatin' fer a week or two?'

'Well, we can carry on with the charcoal as well, there's still a market for it at the moment.'

'Thee means me and father can, while thee goes off chasing thy dreams,' interjected Will, who was becoming irritated by Joe's assumption that the charcoal burning could go on as before, trapping him even further in his life of toil.

'An' how are we meant to do that when we won't know from week to week whether thee'll be around to 'elp?' Walter went on loudly.

'Me, father 'n Richard'll never run two clamps when thee are called away to thy precious Darby's!' interjected Will.

You could hear a pin drop. Joe looked crestfallen and the others all kept quiet for fear of making Walter even more angry.

'Look father,' Joe said finally, 'I'll work harder than I ever worked afore. I'll make sure I bring in enough to top up what we might lose from cutting back on the farming an' charcoal. I just want a chance to give us all a better future.'

'So, the past ain't good enough for thee now, I suppose!' Walter responded angrily.

'Please, father, that's not what I meant. I know you've always done yer best for us. You and ma, when she was here, God rest her soul, but times are changing, an' we need to be part on it. I can do this, father. I can make life better for all on us. Just trust me.'

'Well, I don't seem to have much option, do I?' said Walter now. He felt and looked visibly smaller. He knew that some of his authority was ebbing away to the next generation. Joe was young and capable, and deep-down Walter knew he was right. The family had to move on if it was going to survive and Joe was the one who would lead the way. He would still have Will to help him carry on with the charcoal, unless, that is, he decided to desert him too. Will, for his part, sat broodingly gazing into the fire. He would have liked to carry on with the conversation, but Walter's capitulation cut the ground from under him, and he too had no option but to accept it, albeit grudgingly. He couldn't help feeling that Joe was somehow deserting the family, leaving him to carry the greater part of the burden.

Still, no one else spoke. They were all aware that something important just happened. After a few minutes Elizabeth got up and laid the table for supper. She lit the candles and then ladled the stew from the pot into each bowl, placed the loaf of bread she'd made earlier in the middle of the table and told them all to sit down for their supper. It was eaten largely in silence.

The family was somewhat depleted now that both Margaret and Abigail were away in service at the Hall. Walter sat at one end of the table, and Elizabeth, his eldest daughter at the other, where her mother had once been seated. Elizabeth was well past the first flush of youth, being thirty-two last birthday. After her mother died, she realised she would have to take on the roles of mother to the little ones and house-keeper for her father. Her own dreams of getting married and having a home of her own had to be sacrificed on the altar of keeping the family together. Joe's brother Will sat next to his father. The genetic connection was obvious. They both had broad shoulders, heavy brows, and a large nose. Still brooding, he knew, once Joe had left, he would have to assume respon-sibility for the family should anything happen to Walter, who wasn't getting any younger. His future would be tied to this family come what may, and he couldn't afford the luxury of dreaming of a different one, unlike his brother, Joe.

Martha sat next to Elizabeth. Dear Martha, Joe thought, glancing at her now. Martha was one of those people blessed with a sunny disposition, but not much in the way of rea-soning power. She was thirty years old but never seemed to grow up somehow. Of course, she was always willing to help Elizabeth with the chores, particularly looking after their old horse, Ned. Her favourite jobs though, were feeding the hog and cleaning out the pen, which was just as well, as no one else seemed keen. Often, she could be found searching the woods for snails to give the hog as a special treat, and which the beast always crunched with gusto. Service would never be for Martha though, and she would remain in the family home. All the family loved her dearly and were very protective of her.

Dorothy was a pretty, bright, eleven-year old. Like Joe, she was always ready for something new. Margaret had brought a few books discarded by the family up at the Hall, and Dorothy would spend hours pouring over the pictures and trying to understand the lettering that went with them. By the time she was eight, she had grasped the concept of reading. If only she could get some schooling, thought Joe, she could go far in the world. Maybe he could do something about that if all went well at the Darby works. He had heard that soon there might be a Charity School in Buildwas. Maybe he could help to send her there.

Sitting opposite Joe was Richard, the youngest of the boys. At fifteen he was still half man, half boy. He was as bright as Dorothy and had never had the chance of an education either. However, he was strong and willing, and maybe, thought Joe, he'll be able to follow in my footsteps in Coalbrookdale.

Elizabeth broke the silence to tell them all that she had seen Margaret at the market today and she had said she would be coming home for a visit on Sunday. Margaret was twenty-eight and had been in service up at the Hall for twelve years, working her way up to chambermaid. When Abigail was fourteen, Margaret had secured her a position as a scullery maid. They were both allowed to come home to visit the family on one Sunday a month, but of course, hardly ever on the same day. Walter beamed at the news. Margaret had always been the apple of his eye, being the spitting image of her mother.

Thus, the mood in the Bangham household lifted and when the table had been cleared, Martha popped out to the pig pen to feed the scraps to Archie, this year's pig. The family settled down to an hour or two in front of the fire until it was time for bed. After taking turns to visit the privy and having a quick swill in the bowl of water brought from the pump, they all prepared for bed. Will, Joe and Richard slept with Walter in the main bedroom. Martha and Dorothy shared the smaller room with Elizabeth.

Chapter 2

Sunday was the one day the whole family tried to avoid work if possible. Of course, if they were in the middle of a 'burn', whoever was tending it had to stay in the temporary shelter erected in the woods beside the clamp and couldn't join the rest of the family. This Sunday, however, they were all there and excited at the prospect of Margaret's visit. She always brought news of the comings and goings at the Hall, and from the wider world. They had many visitors from further afield, and the news of the day always managed to percolate down to the servants, and thence to the Banghams. There were often a few sweet treats that cook gave Margaret for the family and she herself often brought a little something from the market or tobacco for her father, who enjoyed a pipe beside the fire when the day's work was done.

She arrived in the early afternoon, with a basket full of various titbits as usual. Everyone gave her a great welcome of course, and then they all settled down around the fire to hear her news. She soon picked up the rather strained atmosphere and asked her father what was wrong.

'You'd better ask Joe,' he snapped.

Margaret turned to look at her brother.

'What have you been up to now our Joe?' she quizzed.

'Nothing! I haven't been 'up to' anythin'. It's just that father's none too pleased that I've got a job working at the Darby Works. I start tomorrow.'

'Well, that's good, isn't it?' Margaret said, 'The family could do with the money, after all.'

'Father doesn't seem to think so.'

'Father?' Margaret said quizzically.

'Well, I'm sorry if I'm bein' daft, but I don't like the idea of one of us workin' with the Darbys, making iron by burnin' coke instead of our charcoal!'

'Oh I know father, but it is said, this new way of ironmaking will bring great change, and surely it's better to be part of it than be left behind by it?'

Realising that he was outnumbered on this issue, he changed the subject, asking Margaret what had been going on at the Hall. She told them that things had settled down now, with the new master. It had all been a bit difficult after the old man died a year or so ago, but things were much better now. The new master and his wife liked to entertain, which obviously meant a lot more work for the servants, but she had to admit, it was a much happier place. The mistress was considerate of the servants, was a good manager, and things were running smoothly, which was more than could be said for matters further afield. There was news of riots in the streets and mobs attacking chapels up and down the land. Everyone was grateful she reported, that this unrest hadn't reached the Severn Gorge as yet. She wasn't quite sure what it was all about, but she did know it concerned religion, and people called 'dissenters.

Dorothy, who had been quiet until now, piped up.

'What are we, father?'

'We aren't much of anythin' right now,' Walter responded. 'Mind, way back we was known as Hoogenots or some such. I remember my father tellin' us that 'is father, my grandfather, had crossed the sea from France.'

'Why?' asked Dorothy, as always, in pursuit of the whole story.

'Because, so he said, they weren't allowed to go to a church accordin' to what they believed like.'

'So does that make us the same as these 'dissenters' then. Does that mean they'll attack us too?'

'Enough!' exclaimed Will, 'Your imagination's far too active our Dotty. No one's going to attack us!'

'How's our Abigail doin',' Elizabeth enquired. Elizabeth had a soft spot for Abigail. They had become very close after their mother died. Abigail was easy to understand, always being an uncomplicated, obedient child, unlike Dorothy, who had much more definite ideas of her own and was often challenging of Elizabeth's authority.

Margaret assured her that Abigail seemed to have settled in well and was doing a good job. She hoped to be home for a visit in two weeks' time, but in the meantime sent them all her love. They chatted on, while Elizabeth prepared the Sunday tea. She had asked Walter to slaughter one of the older chickens as a special treat to cook along with the rabbit he'd caught, as Margaret was coming home. They had been boiling in the pot over the fire along with vegetables from the plot outside. Elizabeth jointed and shared out the meat, serving it up with vegetables piled high and they all enjoyed a hearty meal.

When they had finished, Walter settled down in front of the fire, filling his pipe from the twist of tobacco Margaret had brought for him, feeling content with most of his family around him for once. Soon, Margaret noticed the light was fading outside and announced she must be getting back to the Hall. Joe immediately offered to walk back with her. He was grateful that she at least, hadn't dismissed his decision to work for the Darby's as a 'daft idea', as his father had called it. He was eager to talk to her about it all, and the excitement he felt at this chance to change his future. She had done it, after all. Working in service had its advantages as well as drawbacks, and at least she had escaped the fate which loomed for Elizabeth and Martha.

She was happy to accept his offer and after she had said her farewells to the rest of the family they set off for the Hall. Joe took the lantern as it was now getting quite dark. They strolled arm in arm down the track then clambered up the steep slope of Benthall Edge, chatting easily about this and that. Eventually Joe asked,

'Margaret, do you really think I'm doing the right thing, workin' for Darby?'

'I do Joe,' she reassured him. 'There are big changes afoot, and I see and hear about them all the time, but you have to understand that father doesn't see it. He's spent all these years farm-working, coppicing and making charcoal, and probably thought it would go on this way forever.'

'I know. it's hard for him to understand, but I thought Will would.'

'Will can't allow himself to, Joe. He knows that father will need him for the charcoal as long as he's able to carry on with it. He probably resents that you're free to choose your own path.'

'Aye, you're probably right, I hadn't thought of it like that. Well, I'll just have to make sure I make a success of it then, for all us sakes,' Joe asserted.

'I know you will, our Joe. Come 'ere and give your big sister a hug.'

They had arrived at the gate to the Estate and now they hugged each other, Joe saying,

'Thanks our Margaret, I knew you'd understand if anyone would.'

With that, they reluctantly parted and went their own ways and holding the lantern high, Joe made his way back down through the woods then along the track, thinking about to-morrow and the new path his life was about to take.

Joe arrived early in Coalbrookdale the next morning. He had woken early, eager to get started on this new life. As he approached the works, he joined several workmen also walking up the lane towards the furnace. Some said 'Mornin' and others just nodded in greeting. The thought crossed Joe's mind that he would soon know these men. They would become part of his life.

The furnace now loomed up ahead of them and he noticed a man who had an air of authority standing to the side of it and assumed this might be the person who would be his 'maister' here. He was obviously right in this assumption, as the man suddenly raised his voice, so that all could hear him and said,

'Mornin' all! First of all, Bangham here is having a try with us. I want you Bamforth, to show him the ropes. Understood?'

'Aye sir, that I will, Mr Newton sir' replied Bamforth, touching the peak of his cap.

Joe nodded at Bamforth and moved to stand nearer to him. He knew Bamforth vaguely. He assumed he lived in the cottage down at the end of the track, where it joined the road up to Madeley. He had seen him a few times, coming or going along the road when making his way up to market. They exchanged nods but spoke no words as Mr Newton had continued to give the day's instructions to the men.

Some of them were told to go and tend the limekilns which were ranged at the other side of the site, beyond the furnace. Joe and Bamforth, along with two others were given the job of charging the furnace, one man was to deal with the bellows, and the last two were to deal with running off the iron. Joe wasn't sure what any of this meant as yet but knew that he soon would.

When Mr Newton had finished speaking, the men dispersed across the site. Bamforth introduced himself as Fred and motioned to Joe to follow him up the steps to the platform behind the furnace. Joe noticed three piles, one of limestone, one of coke and one of ironstone. Bamforth said.

'Right lad, let's see what you're made on.'

So began the Banghams' long association with the Darbys of Coalbrookdale. The work was hard, and the days were long, but as they passed, Joe grew in strength and over time it became easier. The hardest part of his day was the long walk home at its ending, and he promised himself that one day he would build his own cottage in Dale Coppice so as to be near to his work.

Life in the Bangham household settled down to its new routine. When there was no farm work, Walter and Will worked at the coppicing and when they had gathered enough fuel would set a clamp. As the burning process took around five days and nights, they took turns at sleeping in their makeshift shelter or watching the clamp. In the daytime one of them might go home for food or a bit of rest. Once the charcoal was ready and nicely cooled, they would load up the cart and with Ned between the shafts would take it to sell at the market or deliver to their various regular customers up and down the Gorge. Without Joe's involvement, all this kept the two men pretty busy.

Richard, having no one to partner him in setting a second clamp, had taken to doing more work on the home farm at the Hall. This suited him well. He enjoyed being out in the fields and whenever he had the chance, loved to get involved with the horses. Moses, the horseman, had noticed Richard's affinity to them and the way they responded well to him. Thinking that he might make a good horseman with a bit of instruction, he had taken it upon himself to encourage Richard's interest. He let him help with the grooming and bedding down whenever other duties allowed.

Elizabeth, helped by Martha, had her hands full with the cooking, washing, cleaning, and tending the vegetable plot, which is where most of their food came from, supplemented by the odd chicken, rabbits, and the hog when it was slaughtered once a year. Of course, there was always something to darn or repair. Margaret often brought discarded clothes from the Hall which Elizabeth repaired or refashioned into clothes for the family.

Washing took a whole day by the time she'd fired up the tub in the scullery, filled it with buckets of water from the pump and got it hot enough to make a difference to the state of the men's clothes. Joe's were always full of limestone and coke dust, Walter's and Will's were covered in charcoal and Richard's in horse muck. Thankfully, they didn't change them too often. Still, it was always satisfying to peg them out on the clothesline and see them flapping in the breeze. She would often see Rose from the next cottage doing the same on washday which was usually on a Monday. They would have a chat, mostly about family news or what was going on up at the Hall.

There were four more cottages in this small woodland community, arranged in a rough semi-circle and Rose and Alf Bottoms with their three youngsters, Alf, Tommy, and Jess, lived next door. Alf worked at the quarry on Benthall Edge. Next to them were the old couple Mary and Eddie Grove. They'd lived here all their married life and raised their four children in their little cottage. They had all flown the coop now. Eddie did a bit of gardening for the Hall, which along with the odd rabbit he managed to snare, just about kept them fed. The neighbours helped them out whenever they could. Elizabeth always made sure they got a few joints each time the hog was butchered.

Next to the Groves were the Foresters. Tom also worked up at the limestone quarry, and Ella was kept busy with her two little ones, Charlie, and Freddie, and with the housekeeping. They were a nice young couple in their twenties. Ella loved to grow vegetables and their little plot always had something ready to harvest. She would also share a crop with Mary and

Eddie if she had anything to spare. She was pregnant with their third child, so there would soon be another resident in their little community.

At the end of the row lived Arthur Green, on his own now, since his wife Jane had died a couple of years ago in childbirth, along with their third child. It was so sad. They had been a devoted couple with two children aged four and six, far too young to lose their mother. Arthur was a labourer on the farm and was finding it hard to be father and mother to Freddie and Eliza, who were now six and eight. Of course, he had to work to bring in the food, and so the children were left alone most of the day. Elizabeth and the other women looked out for them when their father was at work, particularly old Mary, who was always ready to share whatever she had with them if they were hungry. She would take them foraging in the woods for blackberries or elderberries whenever they were in season, or hunt for mushrooms or wild onions. The children loved her dearly.

So this is how, like so many others in the Gorge, this tiny community rubbed along together, just helping each other to get by.

Chapter 3

Harvest time came early to Benthall Edge that year. There had been plenty of rain to grow the wheat and plenty of sun to ripen it. There was much work available for the few weeks of harvest. Joe was still largely laid off from the works because the furnace was closed down for the summer. He had been given some labouring work on the construction of the new furnace, which the Company was building further down the valley towards the Severn. However, the work was intermittent, and he was glad to make up his wages by working at the Hall farm along with Richard, Will, and Walter, scything the wheat, and then stacking and tying the sheaves.

Once the harvest was in, the women and children of the hamlet went to work gleaning any ears of wheat that had been missed by the men. They did well that year, and when they had pooled all their gleanings together were amazed to see they had several sacks full. Elizabeth and the other women spent several days threshing the wheat to extract the grain and then grinding it into flour, which was divided up between the households according to the number of mouths to be fed.

During the first week of September, the furnace at the works was charged and blown in, and Joe settled down to regular day shifts once more. Mr Darby had told Mr Newton that he was pleased with how Joe was doing and instructed him to pay him the full eight shillings a week he had promised. This was great news and even Walter had to admit that the extra money would come in handy. Mr Newton told Joe the new furnace would soon be ready for blowing in when it might be necessary to introduce a night shift. There would be extra money for anyone willing to take it on, and he asked Joe if he would be interested. Joe didn't hesitate, and readily agreed.

In October, Walter judged that the hog was fattened up enough for slaughter, and Old Ted, the pig killer, was sent for. He had been performing this job, up and down the Gorge for decades. Martha of course was upset at the prospect of Archie being killed, but she had known it would happen, as it always did. Pork was, after all, the family's main source of meat.

Old Ted was a blacksmith during the day, so the slaughtering had to be done at night. He arrived at dusk and erected a tripod of poles about eight feet high from which Archie would be suspended once it had been cleanly and skilfully despatched. The animal was hung by its hind legs and the blood allowed to drain away to improve the quality of the meat. The scene was illuminated by several torches and presented quite a spectacle, enjoyed by all the adult residents of the hamlet and also by any of the children who could peer unnoticed from their bedroom windows. Martha had grown fond of Archie and couldn't bear to watch.

Once the blood had drained away and the carcass singed using the torches, Old Ted butchered the beast into joints. Nothing was wasted and the next day, Elizabeth set about placing the hams and sides of bacon in salted water, set the lard to dry out and thoroughly rinsed the chitterlings before frying them up for tea. The day after that, the joints were hung against the wall at the side of the fire to dry.

On the following Sunday, Margaret and Abigail got special permission to come home for the 'pig feast', and for once, the whole family were together. After waking early, Walter had lit the bread oven and Elizabeth and Martha had prepared cakes and pork pies which went in, along with a huge joint of pork, and the potatoes. It was a happy day in the Bangham household and for once, there were no arguments. It was good to have everyone together. One of those memorable days for any family.

Joe noticed that Abigail, now sixteen, was growing into a pretty young woman. She had a ready smile and a kind nature and Joe worried that she might easily be taken advantage of. After tea, he and Richard took the lanterns and walked Margaret and Abigail back to the Hall. Walking ahead with Margaret, Joe quietly mentioned his concerns to her, and she assured him that she would keep an eye on Abigail, who was walking some ten paces behind with Richard.

Returning to the hamlet, Richard and Joe took advantage of a rare opportunity to enjoy some conversation. Joe asked if Richard would like to come to work for the Darby's, as if he fancied it, he was sure he could get him on, as the new furnace was soon to be blown in. Much to Joe's disappointment, Richard told him there was no way on earth he would leave working on the land to work in that noisy, hot, dirty, and smelly place. Besides, he said, he hoped to be the horseman at the farm one day.

'But there's more money to be had up at the works than ye'll ever get on the farm,' Joe said.

'Well, our Joe,' Richard replied, 'money ain't everything.'

Joe couldn't really argue with that, and they continued their walk home in silence.

When they arrived at the cottage, Elizabeth had made some posset, and they all sat down to enjoy a piece of the cake brought by Margaret and spent a companiable hour in reflection on the day. The larder and their bellies were full. Life for the Banghams seemed good, and they took a moment to enjoy it. However, as so often happens in life, things were about to change.

When Joe got home from the works the next day, he could see that Elizabeth was upset about something.

'What's to do our Liz?' he asked.

'I just bin round to Arthur's,' she said, 'an' I don't like what I just seen.'

'Why, what's wrong?'

'It's the little uns. Oh Joe, I think it's measles! They've got terrible fevers, both on 'em, and that red rash our Abigail had, d'ye remember?' she went on.

'Oh I do, an' she was so poorly with it. We nearly lost 'er! Is there owt we can do to help poor Arthur, him being on his own, an all.'

'Well, I've just made some basil and ginger tea with a bit of honey in it, fer the fever, and I've said I'll go over after tea an' see what I can do.'

'Right, well tell 'im, if there's owt he needs, just to let on.'

Elizabeth had boiled some bacon in the pot with vegetables for tea, and as soon as Will and Walter came in, served it up. They were all shocked at the news, Dorothy of course wanting to know what measles was.

'Well, I 'ope you don't find out,' Joe told her, 'it's none too pleasant if you catch it.'

'Have you 'ad it?' Dorothy went on.

'We all have, apart from you, so you keep well away from that cottage, d'ye 'ear me!' Walter interjected sharply.

As soon as she had served up the supper for the family, Elizabeth threw her shawl around her shoulders and picked up the jug of basil tea. Telling them she didn't know how long she'd be, so not to wait up for her, she strode out into the night.

Matters at the Green's house were not at all good. Eliza, the eldest at eight years old seemed the worse of the two. She had a raging fever and bright red spots all over her body and even on her face. Elizabeth was very worried about her. Her brother Jimmy didn't seem quite so bad, but he was definitely hot, and the spots were redder than they had been when she'd called in earlier.

Poor Arthur was in a terrible state. When he saw the look on Elizabeth's face as she checked Eliza, he said quietly, his eyes full of fear,

'Ah can't lose 'em Liz, not after, you know ....'

'And nor shall you,' Elizabeth replied earnestly, 'not if I have 'owt to do with it!'

She set about sponging the children down with calamine lotion. The room was hot, and she told Arthur to damp down the fire a bit. She poured two cups of the basil infusion and handed one to Arthur to give to Jimmy, while she propped Eliza up against her arm and coaxed her to take some. Then she gave both children a cupful of water and settled them back down.

'Have you eaten anythin' Arthur?' she asked him.

'Nay, I couldn't fancy anythin',' he replied.

'Well I'll fix you some bread and drippin', and then ye should try an' get some rest. You've still got to work tomorrow.'

'I con't leave 'em Liz,' he retorted.

'I'll stay fer a few hours, they're all fed an' watered back 'ome, so they'll do fer awhile and I told 'em not to wait up.'

Elizabeth made some supper and they both sat by the fire, just talking quietly for an hour or so, then after kissing the children, Arthur went to his bed, asking her to wake him in a few hours. After dozing for about an hour, Elizabeth woke with a start. Eliza had cried out and as Elizabeth felt her forehead, she was very concerned. The calamine and the basil brew hadn't seemed to do much to cool her down. She gave her some more of the infusion and sponged her down again, but she continued to be restless, tossing her head around and then she seemed to be hallucinating. Her eyes were wide open, but she didn't seem to recognise Elizabeth. She was calling out for her mother, reaching out her arms and pleading for her help.

'Hush child,' Elizabeth said, and stroked her hair, as maybe her mother had once done, and that seemed to calm her a little. Jimmy, meanwhile, was sleeping peacefully, and he wasn't quite so hot.

It must have been about two in the morning when things reached a climax. Eliza's fever had worsened, and she grew more and more restless. She was pouring in sweat and looked white, although the spots seemed redder than ever. Elizabeth woke Arthur, telling him that it looked like things were coming to a head. He ran down the stairs and fell down beside Eliza, grasping her hand and putting it to his lips.

'Thee cannat leave me, Eliza,' he whispered, with tears now coursing down his face.

'Father,' she whispered, suddenly lucid. 'Ma's come fer me,' she said, with a sweet smile on her lips, and then her face relaxed, her eyes glazed over, and she was gone.

Arthur was distraught. He let out such an unearthly moan, the whole hamlet must have heard it, and anyone who did, would have known what it meant. Young Jimmy had woken up and was crying now. Elizabeth went to him and 'clipped him up' to her breast to comfort him.

'Hush now little man,' she said.

'Why is father mekkin' that noise,' he asked, 'why is he cryin'? Is Eliza alright?'

'I'm so sorry,' Elizabeth replied to him, 'Eliza has gone to be with yer Ma.'

'Noo!' he cried, 'I want to go too! Father, I want to go too!'

Arthur dragged himself away from his daughter and turned to Jimmy.

'Nay lad,' he told him 'I need thee 'ere,' and took him from Elizabeth's arms, hugging him as if he might break him.

Elizabeth tended gently to the little body, carefully washing her, brushing her hair, and placing her in a clean nightdress. Then she covered her with a sheet and turned her attention to the living. Jimmy was a little better and seemed to be over the worst. He was sitting on Arthur's knee and hugging him tightly. They were both rung out and Elizabeth persuaded Arthur to go to his bed, suggesting that he take Jimmy with him. They both needed the comfort each would bring to the other.

Elizabeth told Arthur she would come over at first light to check on Jimmy again, and to help him with the arrangements. He knew what she meant but gave no comment. She made sure the fire was damped down and then quietly left the sad little home.

She crossed the clearing to her own home, thinking how sad it was for Arthur, losing not only his wife but his beloved daughter too. Life could be so cruel she thought to herself. He didn't deserve such grief. She also realised how lucky they had been as a family, that they had managed to raise all their young ones to adulthood, all except Dorothy, who wasn't yet an adult, but was nearly so.

Rather than wake the others, she took a drink of ale, then rested in the chair for what was left of the night. After dozing for what seemed like half an hour or so, she heard Joe moving around upstairs, getting ready to go to work. She roused herself and poured him some ale and made him some bread and dripping. Joe clattered down the stairs and swung round the door jamb into the room. He was surprised to see his sister up at this hour, but then he remembered where she had gone to, last night.

''Have ye bin up all night our Liz?' he asked, ''Ow are things over at Arthur's?'

'Oh Joe,' Elizabeth replied, fighting back the tears, 'It's young Eliza. The measles took 'er in the early hours.'

'Oh no!' Joe cried, 'Not young Eliza! She be such a sweet child.'

'Arthur's distraught Joe. First Jane and now Eliza. Tis so sad!'

'D'ye think he'd want me to call in at Johnson's on my way to the works?'

As she refilled his cup, she replied,

'Well, I don't want to rush things our Joe, thanks anyway, but he'll need to move at 'is own pace. Anyhow, I'd best get over there, I said I'd help 'im get on with the arrangements.'

'Aye, of course. Well, tell 'im if there's owt' I can do, just let us know.'

'Aye, that I will, our Joe,' Elizabeth replied then picking up her shawl went out into the chilly October morning.

As Elizabeth made her way across the clearing, the thought occurred to her that she would need to let Rose know what had happened as soon as she could, they would need to keep an eye on their little ones, and keep them inside, away from Jimmy. She knew how quickly measles could rip through a community and it wasn't fussed who it took as it passed by. She just hoped to God that it wasn't already too late.

It was cold inside Arthur's cottage. He obviously couldn't have much of a fire for the moment and there was just a small one in the hearth. Just big enough to boil a kettle. Once the undertaker had been and little Eliza had been dealt with, they would take her upstairs until it was time for the funeral. Elizabeth made a pot of herb tea and then called up the narrow stairs to see if Arthur was awake. After a few minutes he came down. He looked terrible. His eyes were red-rimmed and his face white. He had obviously not been able to get much sleep.

'Mornin' Liz,' he said, 'I can't believe my little Eliza's gone.'

He went over to where Eliza was lying beneath the sheet and lifted the topmost edge. At the sight of her sweet little face, he broke into heaving sobs once more. Elizabeth went over to him and put her arm across his shoulders to offer him some comfort. They stood like that for some minutes until his sobbing subsided. Elizabeth led him gently over to the chair in front of the fire, then poured him a cup of the herb tea.

Then without a word, she went quietly up the stairs to check on Jimmy and was relieved to find him sleeping peacefully. His fever had abated, and he had obviously passed the climax. He would survive.

'When you're ready Arthur, we'll need to get in touch with Johnson,' she said quietly.

'Aye I know,' Arthur replied.

Johnson was the carpenter who lived down in Buildwas. He also doubled as the local undertaker and he would come up to measure the body and then make the coffin, which would be a plain deal wood affair but adequate to the task.

'D'ye want me to ask Will to pop down fer ye? He's just in the wood building a clamp with Walter, but I know he could spare an hour to nip down to Buildwas.'

'Aye,' Arthur responded quietly, like a man in a dream, 'if thee thinks he wouldn't mind.'

'Right, well I'll pop o'er to our house, I might just catch Richard afore he leaves, an' he can take a message to Will straight away.'

Arthur just nodded and carried on staring at the fire.

Elizabeth walked home quickly and was glad to see that Richard was still there. He already knew what had happened because he'd seen Joe before he left for work.

'It's a bad do Liz,' he said sadly.

'Aye, it is so,' she replied, and then asked him if he would find Will in the coppice and ask him to fetch Johnson.

He readily agreed and left shortly afterwards. Elizabeth decided she'd better do the rounds with the news and was soon knocking on Rose's door. Of course, she was shocked to hear about Eliza and immediately checked her little ones, but for the moment all seemed well. Then Elizabeth thought she had better let the Groves know. Mary and Eddie had treated the children as their own since Jane had died. They were devastated, Mary bursting into tears. Eddie put his arms around her in comfort and Elizabeth left them like that, to continue on her sad mission. Next door she found that Tom had already left for his work at the quarry, but Ella was devastated as well as desperately worried for her own two, Charlie and Freddie. She told Elizabeth Freddie had seemed a bit under the weather for a day or two, and when she checked him, he did seem a little bit hot.

'Well, best they both stay inside where ye can keep a close eye on 'em,' Elizabeth told her, 'Ye can't be too careful with measles.'

'Aye, I will that,' Ella replied.

Elizabeth went back into Arthur's cottage to find him sitting exactly as she'd left him.

She was full of fear now. If Ella's two came down with it, it would be more than likely Rose's would as well. After all, they would have all been playing together nearly every day. She was fervently hoping that all the adults would have already had it. She had seen what it could do to adults who had never caught it as children. Of course, she realised, Dorothy was very much at risk as well, and that terrified her.

'I've sent our Will to fetch Johnson, Arthur. 'E should be 'ere pretty soon. Will ye have her buried with Jane,' she asked gently.

Arthur dropped his head into his hands, saying,

'Oh God, I cannat bear it.'

'Ye can and ye will,' Elizabeth assured him quietly, placing a hand on his shoulder.

Just then there was a knock on the door. It was Johnson, and Elizabeth invited him in.

He took his cap off, then said to Arthur,

'I'm right sorry for thy loss, this is a bad do.'

He asked Arthur if he could carry Eliza upstairs where it was cooler, or would he like him to do it? Arthur suddenly sprung up, saying.

'If anyone's goin' to carry 'er it'll be me,' and proceeded to pick her up. With tears streaming down his face he made his way upstairs and laid her gently on the bed. He picked Jimmy up out of the other bed and took him downstairs. Elizabeth helped Johnson to lay Ella out properly. Then Johnson set about his work, which basically just meant wrapping her in a woollen shroud then measuring little Eliza's body so that he could make a coffin. When he went downstairs, he asked Arthur if she was to be buried with her mother. Arthur could do no more than nod.

'Right, well, you leave it to me. I'll be back tomorrow with the coffin and in the meantime, I'll arrange for the funeral to be the day after, if that's alright with thee.'

Again, Arthur nodded in agreement and Johnson left.

The next few days were busy ones for Elizabeth. She took it upon herself to look after Arthur and Jimmy, feeding them as well as her own. Ella's Freddie did go down with it, and then Charlie. Somehow, Rose's three managed to avoid catching it and she kept them inside the house for weeks, just in case.

Young Eliza's funeral was a sad affair. As the autumn winds swirled the fallen leaves around them, Will, Joe, Walter and Alf carried the little coffin down the hill, with Arthur, Jimmy, Mary, and Eddie, herself, and Martha walking behind. Tom and Ella were busy caring for Freddie and Charlie, and Rose and Alf didn't go for fear of passing something on to their youngsters. Elizabeth felt that Dorothy would be safer at home as well, much to her annoyance because she'd never been to a funeral and was desperate to go.

The little procession slowly made its way to the bridge over the Severn, turning left towards Buildwas and the burial ground at the ancient church. The vicar said a few words and a prayer or two and everyone threw a handful of dirt on the coffin. Elizabeth stood beside Arthur and steadied him as he leant so far over the grave, she was afraid he was going to throw himself in with his little girl. It was heart-breaking to see and hear his grief.

The next couple of weeks were touch and go with Charlie and Freddie, but eventually they recovered, apart from some loss of hearing in Freddie's right ear. Thankfully, none of Rose's three got it and nor did Dorothy.

Chapter 4

The hamlet slowly returned to its usual routine, but Elizabeth continued to look out for Arthur and Jimmy, making sure they were eating properly, and along with Mary, seeing to their washing. She had to admit she was quite drawn to Arthur. He often wore a helpless expression, as if he had no idea how he had ended up in the situation in which he now found himself. This had awakened her mothering instincts, and she couldn't do enough for him, or Jimmy for that matter. This wasn't lost on her menfolk back home. Walter in particular sometimes seemed a little impatient with her when his meal wasn't ready because she'd been distracted by helping Arthur and Jimmy out. Elizabeth never rose to the bait. I've done enough for that lot over the years, she would say to herself, it won't do them any harm to wait a bit now and then. December brought the first snows of winter to the hamlet, but no more than a dusting, just a hint of what was to come. More of a problem was the icy wind which seemed to find its way through every nook and cranny in the old cottages. Rags were pushed into gaps round windows and doors, in a vain attempt to keep it out.

Joe had settled in well to the work at the Company. He was a good worker and was earning the respect of his workmates and bosses alike. He had agreed to move over to the new furnace when it was blown in, which would be in the New Year. For months there had been a lot of talk among the men about the riots taking place up and down the country against the new protestant King George and the Whigs. Rioters were attacking the homes and businesses of anyone who was not High Church. They were aware that the Darby's were Quakers of course, as were quite a few of the men themselves and there was much apprehension in case the Shrewsbury mob who had been attacking dissenters, as they called them, might find their way into the Gorge. Joe himself wasn't religious although he knew that his family was descended from the Huguenots of France and had affiliated to the Church of England when they arrived in the country. He wasn't quite sure where all this left him as far as religion was concerned but he knew very well that if it came to a test, his loyalties would be with his employer, Mr Darby, who he knew to be a good and fair man.

Winter arrived in earnest a couple of weeks before Christmas. A blizzard had blown along the Gorge from the east overnight, and when the hamlet dwellers opened their doors in the morning, the world was white and silent. The snow had formed into huge drifts sweeping up from the ground and reaching to the roof of the privy. It was laying several feet deep, right across the clearing.

There would be no coppicing for Will and Walter today, thought Elizabeth, which would be just as well as there would be plenty of work to do around the hamlet. Joe set out for work as usual, hoping he would be able to get through the snow drifts. However, when he reached the track leading down to the bridge, he realised it was going to be impossible for him to get through. The snow had drifted across the track from hedge to hedge. It was completely impassable. He retraced his steps to the hamlet and then decided to try another route. If he cut through the copse under Benthall Edge, maybe he could take the track down beside the incline plane the quarrymen used to send their limestone down to the wharf. When he arrived back at the cottage, Arthur was just delivering Jimmy for Elizabeth to look after while he made his way over to the quarry to see whether they had any work for him, as farm work would be impossible in the snow.

As the two men walked together, they were fairly silent as they negotiated their way along the track which was cloaked in snow and difficult to make out. As they went along, Joe was thinking how much he liked Arthur.

'How are ye doin'?' he asked Arthur.

'Oh ye know, it's hard, being father and mother too. I often think, if Janey had still bin around, she would have seen that summat was up with our Eliza, afore she got properly poorly like.'

'You mustn't blame yourself, Arthur. Everyone knows you did your best.'

'Well, it just don't feel like it, an' that's the truth Joe. But I dunna know what I'd have done without Liz these past months. She's bin me rock!'

'Aye, I know man, she's a good lass, our Liz.'

Arthur was a decent sort, thought Joe. He'd had so much tragedy to deal with and yet it hadn't made him bitter. He had noticed that Elizabeth rather liked Arthur too. Well, she deserved some love and happiness and a life of her own. She'd spent every waking hour since his mother died, caring for others. It would give him great pleasure to see her settled with a family of her own, and it sounded like Arthur was pretty keen as well.

They emerged from the coppice and in front of them was the incline plane, not that they could actually see it, as it was covered in snow. However, the track which ran down the lee side of it had been sheltered from the wind somewhat and the snow hadn't drifted across it. Joe decided he would be able to make his way down to the river this way and said goodbye to Arthur as he set off down the track. Once down at the river, he turned left and made his way to the bridge.

The snow on the north side of the Gorge didn't seem any-where near as deep. It must be the way the wind was blowing, thought Joe, grateful that he could now stride out up the valley, and he would still only be a few minutes late for work. When he arrived at the furnace, he could see there seemed to be fewer men than usual. Obviously, some of them had not been able to get through the snow. However, the furnace still needed to be loaded, even though there were few men to do the work and Joe got straight to it.

The snow lay around for a week or so, and then just as it was beginning to thaw, a hard frost set in, freezing the wet sur-face solid, making walking treacherous. Icicles began to form, hanging down from the cottage eves like daggers, threatening to fall on anyone who banged the door shut. The children of the hamlet had a wonderful time of course, sliding around and playing with a 'sledge' old Eddie had made for them. A week later the thaw set in.

Christmas 1714 brought a couple of days respite from work and on Christmas Day, Elizabeth prepared a veritable feast of pork, apple sauce, potatoes, and vegetables. Everyone brought something to the feast as well, and Eddie brought a flagon of beer he'd been brewing for weeks. Ella, now heavily pregnant, had made some tiny pink sugar mice for the children, Arthur brought a bag of apples he'd been storing since harvest time, and Rose had made some ginger biscuits. Of course, everyone had to bring their own stool or chair to sit on and it was quite a crush to fit everyone inside Walter's living room, but it was all the merrier for that. Eddie had brought his old fiddle and to the delight of all, the day was rounded off with singing.

It was late when they all reluctantly decided it was time to leave. They had full bellies for once and were happy to be part of this little community in Banghams Wood. They felt content to look forward to the year ahead, with the exception of Arthur of course, who had found the day particularly hard, watching the other children playing around and wishing his Eliza had been there with them.

Elizabeth was up early the next morning. There was a lot of clearing up to do after the previous day's revelry. It had been good though, she reflected, to see everyone enjoying themselves together for once. Of course, it had been hard for Arthur, and she had felt for him. Young Jimmy as well, seemed very quiet at times, obviously unsure where he fitted in to things without his big sister around.

Margaret and Abigail would be coming down from the hall in the afternoon. This was one of the rare days when they were allowed to visit their own family after the busy Christmas Day at the Hall. They arrived about midday with a box of sweet-meats for the family to enjoy and cook had been generous with the leftovers from the Christmas Day feast at the Hall and had given Margaret enough food to provide the Bangham family with a hearty meal, which they thoroughly enjoyed, particularly the rich fruit cake, not being something they saw very often. It was lovely for Walter to have all his children around him for once.

Margaret entertained them all by telling them about the Christmas festivities up at the Hall, the mountains of food, the house full of guests, and the music and dancing. Dorothy sat at her feet, eyes shining as her imagination ran riot. The rest of the family showed varying degrees of interest. Will wasn't interested in the least. The way he saw it, he could never aspire to such a life of luxury, so why would he want to hear about it? It only made him even more discontented with his lot.

Finally, it was time for Abigail and Margaret to leave, and as always, Joe was the first to volunteer to walk them home. There was still quite a bit of frozen snow around and it took them longer than usual to reach the gate into the estate. Joe said how great it had been to see them both together, for once. They all embraced warmly and went their separate ways. By the time Joe got home, the family were all preparing for bed and as he had an early start the next day, he did the same.

The following day, as she did every day, Elizabeth was crossing the clearing to Arthur's to check whether they needed anything, she noticed Ella going out to the privy. From the look of her, she thought, Ella won't be long now, her time must be coming up. Elizabeth would need to be ready to help deliver her baby as she had done with so many of the others. Mary would help too, of course. She had seen many babies brought into the world and had had four of her own, so unlike Elizabeth had personal experience of the pain that must inevitably precede every birth.

So it was, that three days later Elizabeth was preparing for bed when there was a loud knocking on the door. It was Tom, as she expected.

'Liz, can you come? Ella's waters have broken. 'Tis time.'

Grabbing her shawl and throwing it around her shoulders, she picked up the bag she had already prepared, containing the things she might need.

'Aye lad, c'mon, let's go,' she quickly replied.

She told the rest of the family not to wait up for her then followed Tom out into the darkness. Ella was upstairs and Elizabeth could hear that the pain must be getting bad. She was wailing loudly, and Elizabeth immediately went up to her after instructing Tom to bring some hot water from the pan on the trivet. Ella was standing, bent almost double and holding on to the bed. Every couple of minutes she tensed and cried out in pain. Elizabeth managed to persuade her to get on to the bed so that she could see where things had got to. At that minute Mary turned up. She had heard Ella's cries across the clearing and knew what it meant. As Elizabeth checked the progress of the baby, Mary held Ella's hand and between contractions, wiped her brow with a damp cloth.

The baby was taking quite a while to emerge, and Elizabeth was getting rather worried. Ella was tiring now, and she was worried she wouldn't have the strength to push when the time was right. Then, after one particularly strong contraction, she could see the baby's head. With the next contraction she told Ella to push as hard as she could, and the baby flopped out into her waiting hands. It was a little boy. She was concerned he wasn't breathing and started to rub his little body and flick the soles of his feet to stimulate him. After a minute or so, she was relieved to see him open his eyes and start to cry loudly. Having tied the birth cord in two places with string, Elizabeth quickly cut the cord with her scissors. Mary had been tending to matters while Elizabeth had been dealing with the baby and was awaiting the arrival of the afterbirth, which appeared after another contraction. Elizabeth sponged the little one clean then wrapped him in his blanket and offered him to Ella.

'It's a grand lad,' Elizabeth told her, and Ella reached out her arms to receive her son, with tears streaming down her face. Tom ran into the room and dropped down beside his wife and child, and mother and father beamed with happiness, heads together, gazing down on this tiny soul that would share their lives.

Elizabeth tidied up, then she and Mary left them in peace as Ella put the child to her breast. As they came out of the bedroom, two little heads were poking out of the doorway to the other room wanting to know if they had a brother or sister. Elizabeth said that they'd better go and ask their mother and father, and held the door open for them to join their parents. Charlie and Freddie burst through the doorway and gathered round their mother, staring in wonder at their little brother, who was to be called Benjamin.

Downstairs, Mary made a jug of herb tea, took cups up to Tom and Ella and then poured drinks for Elizabeth and herself. They put another log on the fire then settled down to enjoy their well-earned drinks. So, another life had successfully made its entrance into their little community and as they sat, they wondered aloud what kind of a life the little one would have. Mary hoped it would be an easier one than she and Eddie had lived.

Chapter 5

Winter dragged on through January and February, with more snow and frost making life harder than ever in the little community in Bangham's wood. There was little farm work to be had and Walter and Will had no choice but to carry on with the coppicing and charcoal burning to bring some money in, but camping out in the woods for five days and nights in the middle of winter took its toll, particularly on Walter. At the end of February he had a particularly bad bout of bronchitis, which they were all afraid might be consumption as they called it, but which today we would call tuberculosis. As it was, after a few days rest in bed, and a week or so in front of the fire, he slowly recovered, much to the relief of all.

Joe managed to keep working all through the bad weather, bringing in much needed money for the family. He observed that things were changing rapidly in Coalbrookdale. The new furnace was now working at full capacity and the workforce had more than doubled. Carts were coming and going when the snow allowed, bringing raw materials, and taking away the pig iron to various foundries and finished goods down to the wharf to be shipped down the Severn to Bristol and beyond. It was bustling with activity and Joe enjoyed being part of it. It was hard work, of course, but it was exciting, especially when, on rare occasions, when they were a man short, he was asked to help out with drawing off the iron from the furnace.

Joe could see that the business was prospering as he admired the grand new house Mr Darby was building a little further up the valley. He was a good man though, and he worked hard, even alongside his men when needed. He was constantly experimenting with different mixes of raw materials to improve the quality of the iron they were producing. He was greatly respected by the men and whenever there was talk in the ale houses about 'dissenters' his workmen would always speak out in his defence. So far, the Gorge had escaped the riots that were still raging around the country, although there had been talk about trouble in Shrewsbury, when a mob had attacked a dissenters' chapel.

One morning when Joe arrived at the works, Fred Bamforth was in an agitated state and told him that a riotous mob had been seen by Tom, one of the men who came from a small hamlet to the north of Coalbrookdale, making its way down from Shrewsbury, intent on attacking Mr Darby's works. Tom said he had seen their torches in the distance and heard their angry cries. He had hurried down to the works to warn them.

Mr Newton had sent a message to the Justice of the Peace in Much Wenlock to come to read the riot act. Mr Darby was sent for and was soon standing on the steps of the furnace, calling to the men to use restraint. He wanted no violence, he told them. However, he realised that the mob had to be confronted if the works was to be saved.

Mr Newton told him they would try to hold up the mob until the Justice of the Peace arrived. He quickly called all the men from the forge, the foundry, and the furnaces together and told them to gather in the lane to block the way, to prevent the mob from reaching the works. No one dissented, as they all knew that by defending the works, they were defending their own livelihoods. If the works was destroyed, they would all be destitute.

Each man picked up whatever he could use to defend himself, then they formed up in a line four deep across the lane and awaited the arrival of the mob. It was still fairly dark, being around seven o'clock in the morning, and they could see the lights of the torches approaching as the mob made its way down the hill towards them. The shouts of 'Down with George!' and 'Down with Dissenters!' rang out.

Joe had picked up an iron bar. Predictably he planted himself firmly in the front row of the Coalbrookdale men and waited for the onslaught. As it happened, the 'mob' turned out to be rather fewer in number than the men defending the works. There were maybe twenty or so, with at least sixty Darby men standing their ground, armed with iron bars and hammers and anything else that they had been able to pick up along the way, and making rather more noise than the rioters.

The mob halted about thirty yards from the Coalbrookdale men. Several of their number, seeing that they were so obviously outnumbered, and by a crowd of men considerably stronger and probably tougher than they were, first faltered and then began to turn around and start running back the way they had come. When Joe saw this, he shouted, 'Come on men!' and led the charge to chase the mob away. It was a rout, and in minutes the rioters had disappeared over the brow of the hill, heading back towards Shrewsbury. The men who had chased them off strode back towards the works and as they approached, a cheer went up. As he had led the charge, Joe became the hero of the hour, and Mr Darby thanked him personally for his loyalty and his courage at seeing off the mob. A message was sent to tell the Justice of the Peace that his services were not needed on this occasion and the men returned to their work, relieved that violence had been avoided.

As often happens in a close community such as this, word of the events spread around the district, from one neighbour to the next, growing more notable with each telling. By the time word reached the Hall, the story was that Joe Bangham had led the charge to see off the mob, and when Margaret arrived at the Banghams house the following Sunday, she was full of it. Joe wasn't at home, as he was working an extra shift at the furnace as they were short-handed.

Even before she took her coat and hat off, she said to Elizabeth,

'Our Joe's the talk of the valley, who'd have thought it?!'

She proceeded to relate the current version of the story, of how Joe Bangham had charged the mob single-handedly and saved the Darby works, and how he was now famous for his heroic stand against the rioters.

Joe himself hadn't said much about it during the week, so what Margaret had to say came as a bit of a surprise to them all. Everyone was greatly impressed, particularly Dorothy, and proud of their brother. Everyone, except Will of course, who, jealous as ever of Joe, said he didn't believe a word of it and that it was all an exaggeration. He was right, of course, but no one chose to believe him, as they would rather bask in the reflected glory of Joe's considerably enhanced reputation.

The next week, twelve hour shifts were brought in. Joe was asked if he still wanted to work night shifts at the new furnace as it was now fully functional and producing good quality pig iron. He knew it would be hard, and not easy to fit in with the rest of the family's routine, but the money was better, and he welcomed the chance to take on more responsibility. He would be in charge of loading up the furnace and would have an assistant working under him. The pay would be twelve shillings a week. He gladly accepted and started the following week. The shift was from six in the evening to six in the morning.

He was right that this proved rather inconvenient for the rest of the family, particularly at mealtimes, which didn't please Elizabeth, who liked to keep to a routine. Still, they all realised that the extra money Joe would be bringing in would certainly be a boost to the family finances, and so they began to work around it. Actually, once she got into the rhythm of it, Elizabeth decided that she quite liked having Joe around in the afternoons. She made tea for the family for about four thirty so that they could all eat together before Joe set off to the works. Will was a bit resentful because it meant that if he was working on the farm, whereas before they would all have waited for him to get home, now he had to eat his meal on his own, later in the evening. Typical, he thought, everything has to revolve around Joe, the hero of the Valley, these days. This just added to his brooding resentment of his older brother.

Although Joe settled into his night shift pattern, he was thinking more and more that he ought to start planning to build his own house in Dale Coppice. It would be so much more convenient. Of course, he would still help out with the family's finances. He began to think how he could broach the subject with Walter, who he knew would see it as just one more betrayal of the family, and goodness knows what Will would think of the idea. He thought he would speak to Margaret first, the next time she came to visit. She would understand and would perhaps give him some support when he told the rest of them. So he filed the idea at the back of his mind for the moment.

Meanwhile, Elizabeth was spending more and more time with Arthur and Jimmy. Whenever her work was done at home, and everyone was fed, she would go over to Arthur's and once Jimmy was in bed, they would spend a pleasant evening in front of the fire, just talking quietly. They discovered they had a lot in common in the way they felt about things. They were both kind and gentle souls, always ready to help anyone. Neither of them was particularly ambitious. They were just content to live as comfortably as possible, without extravagance, which was just as well, as there wasn't much of that in Banghams Wood. It was perhaps inevitable that their relationship fairly soon developed into more than just friendship and it became apparent to them both that they needed to be married, and one day in April, Arthur quietly proposed to Elizabeth. She was delighted. She had long since abandoned the idea that she would ever get married, but Arthur had changed all that. She wanted this more than anything in the world. She had fallen deeply in love with Arthur and had grown very fond of Jimmy too. The next evening after tea, Arthur crossed the clearing to speak to Walter. He knew it would be difficult for him. He supposed that he had thought Elizabeth would always be around to keep house for him. How would he react to the thought that she would be leaving?

Actually, when he asked Walter if he would give them his blessing, he didn't seem shocked at all. Arthur guessed correctly that it had been pretty obvious to everyone the way things were going. Elizabeth had been spending so much time with him that they would all have been more surprised if it had come to nothing. No one was sure how things were going to work out though. They doubted whether Martha would be up to keeping house and cooking and so on. Of course, although Dorothy was still young, she would be able to help Martha out with many of the chores. In any case, they reasoned, Elizabeth would be just across the clearing if she was needed.

Of course, at this point, they had no idea of Joe's plans to build his own house on the other side of the Gorge. When he came home the next morning, Elizabeth was full of her news. Joe wasn't unduly surprised, but he did realise that perhaps he would have to postpone his plans for a while, until things at home had settled down and they could all see how things worked out with Martha. They would all undoubtedly need some support with Elizabeth no longer living in the house.

It was a beautiful day in May, when Arthur and Elizabeth made their way down to the Holy Trinity Church in Buildwas to make their vows. The apple and may blossoms and pussy willows were out on the trees and the track was lined with bluebells, daisies, and wild violets. Margaret had brought a lovely yellow dress which was surplus to requirements from the Hall, and Elizabeth had altered it until it fitted her perfectly. She wore a headdress of wildflowers and carried a posy of the same in her hands. With help from Martha and Dorothy, Joe had decked out the cart, even securing a few flowers to old Ned's bridle. Elizabeth and Walter sat on the cart arm in arm, and with Will holding the reins they led the procession down the track. It was a proud day for Walter, and he only wished Elizabeth's mother could have been there to see their eldest daughter married to Arthur. He was a good man and Walter knew he would look after her, as best as he could. They would never be rich, but Walter was sure they would be happy together.

Arthur and the rest of the family and neighbours followed them down to Buildwas. The sun sparkled on the river as they crossed the bridge, and the whole Gorge looked particularly lovely in the sunshine. The service in the church was short but adequate to the task in hand, and the couple emerged as happy as any couple should be on their wedding day. A wedding breakfast had been prepared by the women of the hamlet and was laid out in Walter's living room for when they returned from the church. All agreed that it had been a wonderful day and finally, Arthur and Elizabeth left to return to the Green's house to begin their life together.

Young Jimmy stayed with Mary and Eddie for a couple of days, while the newlyweds enjoyed a short honeymoon. Elizabeth moved her things into Arthur's cottage the next day and their married life began. Things in the Bangham house seemed very strange to everyone without Elizabeth organising them all. It took a few weeks to get into some sort of routine. Martha did her best but did need quite a bit of support from the others. Dorothy was good at reminding her what needed doing and when, particularly with regard to the cooking. Of course, Elizabeth was literally only yards away if anyone was in any doubt about anything. For her part Elizabeth threw herself into organising their own cottage, which had been without a woman in it for three years. It needed a good 'bottoming' as she told Arthur. She soon had everything clean and shipshape. Then she started on the vegetable patch which had also been rather neglected. Having Elizabeth around certainly suited Arthur. Everyone remarked how cheerful he now was, which, given the tragedies he'd had to endure was a tribute to Elizabeth's good care.

Will and Walter found extra work on the farm with the lambing and spring planting, and after that was over, went back to the coppicing and charcoal burning. Richard was getting more involved with the horses. Old Moses was finding things harder these days. He was plagued with rheumatism caused by a lifetime spent outdoors in all weathers and was only too happy for Richard to give him a hand. Alf and Tom were very busy at the limestone quarry. It seemed that the Coalbrookdale Ironworks had an insatiable appetite for the stuff, and there always seemed to be another cart at the bottom of the incline plane, waiting to be filled.

Over at the Works, Joe was in his element, organising his shift at the new furnace. There had been a few teething troubles with the furnace but by April 1716 it was going well. He found he was good at making sure that all went as it should, and he kept the furnace topped up and blowing well. As well as doing his own job, he was always ready to help his workmates out, and he had earned their respect as well as that of his employer. Of course, things didn't always go smoothly. As in any industrial environment at that time, there were accidents, particularly when the commodity being produced was molten metal. Joe was just finishing his shift one day when, as the men down at the mouth of the furnace were pulling the plug to run off the first batch of the day, there was a sudden surge of energy and molten iron shot out and struck Bill, one of the workmen, on his arm. He screamed out in agony and Joe was the first man to reach him. He was horrified to see that the metal had gone clean through the man's left arm. Bill continued to scream as Joe picked him up bodily and removed him to a safe distance where Mr Newton was calling out for someone to fetch the surgeon.

They carried him out of the furnace building and over to the clerk's office, where he was placed on a blanket on the floor awaiting the arrival of the surgeon from Madeley. Joe was shocked to see the extent of damage inflicted by the molten metal and he understood more clearly than ever, how it had to be treated with the utmost respect. The next evening when Joe came on for his shift, he learned that Bill had had the lower part of his arm amputated as the wound was too extensive for it to heal safely. It would be a long recovery and of course, he would no longer be able to work at the furnace, but it was said that Mr Darby would find him a job that he could do, once he was well enough.

The spring and early summer of 1716 were quite dry, and the furnaces had to be blown out in June as the water in the pools became dangerously low. They couldn't risk it being so low that it couldn't turn the water wheels to work the bellows at the furnaces. This meant that Joe was without work for three months. He helped Will and Walter with the coppicing and with Richard's help when he wasn't at the farm, they were able to burn a couple of extra clamps and build up their charcoal stocks. Walter was very pleased to have Joe around more often, particularly as he was feeling rather tired these days. The bronchitis he'd suffered in the winter had taken more out of him than he liked to admit.

Arthur and Elizabeth had settled into married life. Young Jimmy adored Elizabeth, who gave him plenty of love and affection, which he had sorely missed since the death of his mother. It was no surprise to anyone when, in September, Elizabeth joyfully announced that she was expecting a child. Another new life was soon to make its appearance in Banghams Wood.

Will's resentment at what he perceived as Joe's desertion in going off to work for Darby, hadn't diminished over the months. In fact, if anything, it had grown. Even though Joe was able to help out during the summer, Will knew that come the autumn, he would be off again, working nights for Darby, leaving him to toil in the woods with his father who seemed to be growing weaker with every passing year. He would have to bear the increased load alone, whereas he had always expected that he and Joe would take over once Walter was no longer able to do the work. He was worried what would happen when that time came. He couldn't work the charcoal burns alone, and Richard was getting more and more involved with the horses up at the estate. He knew that he would never leave his beloved horses to join him in the charcoal business. In any case, even though he would never admit it to Joe, Will knew that the demand for the product would be diminishing over time. There was no guarantee that it would be a viable business in the future.

Would he, could he, contemplate crossing the valley to work for Darby? He thought not, after all he'd said to Joe about that. There was always the quarry, but that was back-breaking work, even harder than what he was doing now, and the pay was poor. The thought occurred to him that perhaps he could seek work on one of the Severn trows that carried goods and people to and from Gloucester. This was an altogether more exciting prospect and he determined to explore the possibilities when the time came.

In the meantime, he and Walter carried on as usual, coppicing and then burning when there was no farm work to be had. This year there had been plenty of that, as the harvest had been good, and the wet weather held off until all the crops were safely gathered in. Grudgingly, he had to admit that Joe had pulled his weight in that direction, and it had been good to be working with him again. He wished he would give up the works and come back permanently, but sadly, he knew that wasn't going to happen.

Ella's baby, Benjamin, was thriving and in fact, all the children in the hamlet seemed to be enjoying a healthy spell after the traumatic events of the previous year. However, everyone had noticed that Eddie was in declining health. He was looking older. He was stooping slightly and walking more slowly with each month that passed. Mary mentioned it to Elizabeth one day when they were hanging out the washing. She could see the decline in him. Nothing she could put her finger on, just a general 'gooin doon 'ill', as she said. Of course, she knew that if anything happened to Eddie, without any income at all, she couldn't survive on her own. She supposed she would have to rely on the parish, unless one of her children were to take her in. Neither prospect pleased her. She and Eddie had always been independent. They hadn't asked anyone for anything, and she didn't want to start now. In reality of course, she would have little choice in the matter if she wanted to survive at all. So, it was with some trepidation that the hamlet viewed the oncoming winter. No one said anything to Walter or Eddie, but they all knew that a harsh winter could bring danger to them both.

By the end of September Joe was back on permanent nights at the new furnace. The daily trek across the valley and back was just as onerous and he was more determined than ever to build himself a house in Dale Coppice. He decided that he would do just that, after spending this one last winter living in Banghams Wood. It was obvious to Joe that there were plenty of orders coming into the business. They were casting pigs more or less constantly, but also bellied pots, many of which were shipped off down the Severn to Bristol. From there it was said that they were sent all around the country, mainly by sea to other ports around the coast, and even to countries over the oceans.

Chapter 6

1717: As it happened the winter wasn't as harsh as the previous one. The snow, when it came, lasted only a week or two and then melted away. It was, however, a pretty dreary time. There was plenty of rain which made the trackways inches deep in mud. Delivering the charcoal with old Ned pulling the cart was difficult to say the least. The weather was generally wet and damp with plenty of fog. It was an altogether miserable season, only punctuated by Christmas, which everyone determined to make the most of, as usual.

As they had all feared, in late February, Walter went down once again with a bad cold which rapidly turned to bronchitis and this time progressed to pneumonia. Within a week he developed a high fever, and they all knew what it meant. Margaret and Abigail were sent for, and as he struggled for breath, all his children gathered around him to say their goodbyes. He knew exactly what was happening to him, he had watched his father going the same way. He told them all not to be sad. He would be going to be with his beloved Jane. On the 12th day of March 1717, Walter Bangham took his last breath.

Once more, on the following Sunday, a sad little procession made its way to the burial ground. Because of the condition of the trackway, the coffin had to be carried by the men, Joe, Will, Richard, Arthur, Tom, and Alf, which was no easy task and more than once they had to pick their way through the mud. Somehow, they made it and after a short service in the chapel, Walter was laid to rest.

For some weeks, the family found it hard. Walter had always been at the centre of their world and without his influence they all seemed to lose direction for a while. As when any pivotal member of a family passes on, there was a certain amount of adjusting of roles. Will, although not the eldest, still tried to take on the leadership role. While this was accepted by Richard and Dorothy and of course, Martha, it certainly wasn't by Joe, Elizabeth, Margaret, and Abigail, who had all, each in their own way, already 'left' the family. This brought tensions as you would expect, particularly between Joe and Will, further exacerbating the rift between them.

Will was very worried. Without Walter he could no longer produce charcoal, and as yet, he had not decided what else he would do to bring in some money. Tom and Alf, who worked full time at the quarry, offered to help him get a place there as they were busy at the moment supplying limestone to the Darbys, among others. Although this was something he wasn't keen to do long term, he decided that at the moment he had little choice and agreed to work there, if they would have him. So, after some fifty years, charcoal production ended in Banghams Wood. It was the end of an era, and change was indeed coming to the Gorge.

Elizabeth went into premature labour shortly after Walter's death. She had been working hard to support the Bangham household as well as her own and had probably done too much, precipitating the early onset of labour about four weeks before her due time. However, helped by the other women, the baby was safely delivered. It was a little girl weighing just six pounds, but she seemed healthy enough. They called her Jane, after Elizabeth's mother, of course. Arthur was overjoyed at having another little girl. She could never replace Eliza, but he would love her just as much.

The river of course was high all through that winter, making navigation more difficult, which in turn meant that on occasion raw materials from the south, bound for the furnaces, were late arriving, and the wharf filled up with goods waiting to be transported in the opposite direction. Everyone battled on as best they could and somehow the furnaces were kept going. The men saw little of Mr Darby. It was rumoured that he was unwell, although no one knew exactly what was wrong with him. A general air of apprehension grew. There was no natural heir to the business ready to take over from him. His son, also Abraham, was still a child. During breaks, the men often wondered among themselves, what would become of the works, and therefore their jobs, should anything happen to Mr Darby. Joe was optimistic as usual, assuring anyone who would listen that 'Somebody'll take it over, just thee wait an' see.'

Spring came in early after the reasonably mild if wet winter. Arthur and Elizabeth were happy with their little family. There was plenty of work at the quarry with the increasing activities over at the Darby works. It seemed they could never take enough limestone to keep the furnaces running. Elizabeth, having once accepted that she would never be a mother, was entranced by her little girl but was sad that Walter hadn't lived long enough to meet his grandchild. She and the rest of the women worked hard in the garden plots, hoeing and planting to ensure a good supply of vegetables for the year.

It was the Sunday before Easter that Abigail came home for a visit. Elizabeth thought it odd that she came to her house first, rather than going home, but when she came in, she could see immediately that something was wrong. Abigail was pale and looked worried and Elizabeth noticed a thickening around her waist, which immediately rang alarm bells. When Elizabeth quietly asked her what was wrong, she broke down in tears saying that she thought she was going to have a baby. Elizabeth asked her who the father was, but she steadfastly refused to say. Knowing what a temper he had, Abigail was terrified of how Will would react. She knew he wouldn't take kindly to having to keep her and a baby, as well as Martha and Dorothy.

Elizabeth was shocked but not entirely surprised. There were always men around ready to take advantage of an innocent young girl. Of course, they were never around to face up to the consequences. She wasn't looking forward to telling Will about this. She hoped he wouldn't take out his anger on Abigail. She decided that she would first talk to Joe to work out some plan as to what could be done. Abigail would now have to leave service at the Hall and come back to live in the hamlet, which would mean another two mouths to feed without any extra money coming in. She told Abigail to say nothing to Will until she'd had a chance to speak with Joe and she was obviously relieved to leave it in Elizabeth's hands for the moment. Abigail spent the afternoon with Elizabeth, not wanting to show herself to Will in case he suspected something. As she was leaving, she decided to pop her head in the door, intending just to say hello before setting off back to the Hall.

However, Will had been disappointed that she had been home and not come across the clearing to see him earlier, and told her to come in for a minute to warm herself at the fire before setting off back to the Hall. As she entered the room, he could see she was moving awkwardly with her back to him. He'd seen women move like that before when they had something to hide, and he asked her,

'Have you got something to tell me, our Abigail?'

Never any good at telling lies, she looked down at the ground and said,

'I'm sorry our Will, I didn't mean for it to happen.' and started to cry.

'No! Abigail! Not you! You're nobbut a child still! Who did this? Tell me Abigail, who did this to ye?'

Abigail said nothing, still crying and shaking her head violently.

'It's no use Abigail, ye'll have to tell me. He must be made to pay for what he's done. Was it one o' them toffs up at the Hall?'

Will was shouting now. Elizabeth heard him across the clearing and came running over.

She burst into the cottage and scooped Abigail up in her arms.

'Leave her alone Will!' she shouted. 'She's not telling us and that's that. What's done is done and we'll all just have to make the best on it!'

'Well, I won't be leaving it there – I want to know who did this. She's still a child. I'm going to be asking around and one way or another I'll find out and when I do, he'll be sorry he'd been born.'

When Abigail had calmed down, Elizabeth walked her back to the Hall, telling her not to worry, and to leave Will to her. She would make him see sense.

Will had managed to get work at the quarry, although he didn't enjoy it one bit. He had been used to working for himself and wasn't used to being given orders. Unlike Joe, he found this particularly difficult, and he never bothered to hide his displeasure, which did not endear him to his employers. However, they were busy and needed the labour, so they had put up with his surly attitude, for the time being at least. He was now more determined than ever to find work on one of the Severn trows as soon as he could. He knew that with the increased activity over at the Darby works, there were more boats than ever coming and going along the river and he had heard they were always looking for deck hands. Before that though, he mused as he worked, he had something else to deal with. He wasn't going to let the matter of Abigail's ruin, as he saw it, drop, before he'd found out who was responsible.

Will was still at the quarry on the day following Abigail's visit as Elizabeth went across the clearing to speak to Joe as she had promised. He was shocked, of course, and angry, but not with Abigail. It was as he had feared all along. She was altogether too pretty and good natured to be overlooked by a predatory man, and there were plenty of them about. Elizabeth told him Will had taken it badly and was determined to find out who had put her in the family way. Joe told Elizabeth to give him time to think about what could be done. He told her he had some ideas about his own future and maybe in some way he would be able to help Abigail as well, and that was how it was left for the time being. As for Will, Joe knew he could be hot-headed and wasn't one to let this drop. He feared what he would do if he ever did find out who the father was.

Of course, Joe had long intended to build himself a house in Dale Coppice and as he walked across to the works that evening, he was beginning to see how he might also help Abigail out. Once the baby was born, she could come and live with him. She could keep house for him, and he would provide a home for her and her child. However, he was a bit concerned that when he left Banghams Wood, he wouldn't be there to keep an eye on Martha. She was such an innocent and had always looked to Joe for support. Will didn't have much patience with her unfortunately. He also had an idea that Will had an intention of seeking work on one of the trows and may be away from the house for days on end. Still, he determined to discuss his idea with Elizabeth the next day.

After much deliberation over the next few days, the two of them, along with Arthur, came up with a plan. All they needed now was to convince Will that it would be the best solution all round. The idea was that once Joe and Abigail left the hamlet, Elizabeth, Arthur, and the children could move across to the Banghams house with Martha. Will, Richard and Dorothy would then move into Arthur's house which was the smaller of the two. That way, Martha would be looked after, and Dorothy was now old enough to keep house for her two brothers.

The following Sunday, Liz and Joe sat down with Will and told him about Joe's plan to build a house in Dale Coppice. At first, he didn't listen to the rest of their idea, about Abigail and the baby going to live with Joe, because all he could think about was that with Joe gone, he would be trapped again, unable to escape the family responsibilities once more. Of course, he knew that Martha couldn't be left on her own while he went off down the river. So when they finally managed to explain that he and Richard could go and live with Dorothy in Arthur's place, it came as a relief. If he was away, Richard and Dorothy would be fine on their own.

So it was agreed that Abigail would stay with Will until after the baby was born, at which time, Joe would move into his own house, and Abigail and the baby would join him. The rest of the plan could then be implemented. It seemed like a good solution all round, and when Abigail next came to visit, she was delighted. Joe had always been her favourite. By the end of April, her condition became more obvious, and she had to leave her position at the Hall and return to the hamlet.

In the meantime, Will had been making enquiries among the farmhands and quarry men and now had a good idea who had made Abigail pregnant. There was an under-butler called James Furlong, who it was well known couldn't keep his hands to himself whenever there was a young lass around. When Margaret came down one Sunday, Will asked her outright whether it was him. Although she denied it, she looked very uncomfortable and wouldn't meet his gaze.

She realised that he hadn't believed her.

'Leave it Will,' she pleaded. 'Nothing good can come of you getting involved now.'

'Leave it?!! Nay, I canna leave it! I won't let him get away with it.'

No-one said anything else for fear of making matters worse, but they all exchanged worried glances, fearing what Will would do next.

They didn't have long to wait. Will came in late from the quarry on the Tuesday evening in an agitated state and Dorothy, who never missed a thing asked him what was wrong. He snapped at her that nothing was wrong, and she should mind her own business. At that, she made some excuse to go over to Elizabeth and Arthur's house and told her that something was wrong with Will.

When Elizabeth confronted him, she could see the fear in his eyes, and he admitted that he'd sorted that bastard out once and for all. She immediately knew what he meant.

'Oh my God Will, what have you done!?' she exclaimed.

'I just give 'im what 'e deserved our Liz. I guarantee 'e won't be touching no more lasses.'

Elizabeth sent Dorothy and Martha across to her own house while she tried to get out of Will exactly what had happened.

Eventually he admitted that he'd been up to the Hall and seen James making his way back to the kitchen from the privy. He'd confronted him, saying he knew it was he that had put Abigail in the family way and what was he going to do about it. James had replied that if he hadn't done it someone else would have, as Abigail was rather too free with her favours.

'I couldn't let him say such things about our Abigail, could I?' he said. 'I just had to hit him. I struck him hard on the jaw and he fell backwards. He went down like a felled tree, and as he landed his head struck the edge of the paving stone. I swear I didn't mean to kill him Lizzie! Just to let him know he couldn't get away with it.'

'You mean you actually killed him, our Will?!' she said with a look of horror on her face.

'Aye,' he replied, 'well, I think so. He never moved after anyhow.'

'Oh God! Will, you'll have to get away from here or they'll string you up, for sure!'

Will looked full of fear and indecision.

'What must I do, our Liz? Where can I go?'

Elizabeth thought for a moment and then said,

'Did anyone see you do it?'

'I don't think so,' he said quietly.

'Then your best chance is the river! You must get down to the river and hope to God there's a trow ready to leave for Bristol. It's a big place and you'll be able to lose yourself there, or even work your passage to America. I've got a bit put by and you'll have to pay your passage on the trow. You must get away before anyone adds two and two together and comes looking for you.'

'Oh Sis, how can I leave you all like this?' he pleaded.

'Well, if you don't want to swing on the end of a rope, you don't have a choice. Get some things together while I go and find what money I can spare, and neither of us must tell any of the others what's gone on. The least they know the better.'

Will threw his clothes in a bag and after quickly eating some bread and dripping and taking a swig of ale he was ready to leave when Elizabeth came back with the few coins she'd managed to find.

'Now go, Will, quickly, before they come lookin' for ye. If they do, I'll try to send them off on a wild goose chase to give you a bit more time, but hurry now and hope to God there's a ship ready to leave straight away.'

Will hesitated for a moment, completely horrified at what he'd done and how in a second his life had changed forever. Then he said,

'I'm so sorry Liz, to be going like this. Will you all be alright without me?'

'Too late to think about that now,' she said. 'The main thing is you need to get away and right now! Don't look back our

Will. God protect you.' and with that, she gave him a fierce hug and pushed him out of the door before the emotion of the moment caught up with her and she broke down in tears.

Will ran down the track to the Buildwas bridge then along the north side of the river to the wharf, where to his relief, there was a trow that looked as though it was just finishing loading pig iron, probably bound for Bristol. After a quick word with the captain and the exchange of a few coins he settled himself down in a corner of the deck, making himself as inconspicuous as possible. Within the hour, the trow pulled away from the wharf and Will Bangham was leaving the Severn Gorge, maybe forever.

Elizabeth calmed herself down and then went over to her cottage. They were all full of questions, of course, and she did her best to hide what had gone on but they all, with the exception of Martha, had a good idea. When she said that she wasn't able to tell them anything, in the end they accepted that. It didn't take long of course, for them all to realise that Will had gone, and once news got around about James the under-butler being attacked, they soon worked out for themselves that he'd had no choice but to leave Banghams Wood and would probably never be able to return.

Joe was angry with him for being so stupid and doing such an evil thing as to attempt to kill a man. No man had the right to take another's life. As it turned out, James wasn't in fact dead, although he didn't regain consciousness for two days and there had been some doubt as to whether he would survive. Well, now Will had made his bed he'd have to lie in it, thought Joe. This of course gave them all plenty to think about. With one of the main providers gone from the Bangham household, there would have to be changes sooner than they had anticipated.

As it happened, Richard was now working full time with the horses up at the Hall and Moses had said that it was time he retired. He had told Richard that he would speak to the master to see if he would take him on as the horse man. The master agreed as he'd seen the way Richard had handled the horses. It would mean a room above the stables for Richard, so as to be on hand should the horses need any attention. Since Abigail had left the Hall, there was a vacancy for a scullery maid, and it was decided that Margaret should ask if they would take Dorothy on. She was horrified, until they told her that perhaps she might get a chance to learn to read, as there were plenty of books around at the Hall.

That was settled then, once Joe had built his house in Dale Coppice, Arthur and Elizabeth would move across the clearing into the Bangham place with their two and Martha. There were plenty of people looking for somewhere to live, with the growth of the Darby Works and the Quarry, so perhaps their own cottage could be let out for a few pence a week which would help with the family budget.

They did all miss Will of course, coming so soon after Walter's death as well. The Bangham family was now somewhat depleted, and soon there would be no Banghams as such, left in Banghams Wood.

Chapter 7

At the works, what they had all feared, came to pass on May 5th. Mr Darby finally lost his two-year battle with illness and passed away. This was of course sad in itself, but more than that, the men now worried what would become of their jobs. The funeral was a simple affair as Quaker rituals tended to be, but the men and their families lined the road to Dale End with their caps removed and heads bowed as the coffin was carried on the horse drawn wagon. It was taken along the road to Madeley, across the river and up the steep slope to the Quaker Burial Ground at Broseley. Joe had remained at the works until mid-morning, in order to pay his respects. He was sad to watch the funeral of Mr Darby, the man who had given him his chance and always treated him fairly. It was heart-breaking to see Abraham, his young son, at just six years old, fighting back the tears and trying to be a man for his mother's sake, riding in the carriage behind the coffin with his mother and the other children.

Over the next few weeks there was much speculation about what was to happen to the works. By now there were scores of men, working either in the foundries or the furnaces; many families around the Gorge directly dependent on the Darby works, and also many more in the coal mines and quarries which supplied their raw materials. The whole district held its breath until it became known that a Bristol Merchant, Thomas Goldney and Mrs Darby's son-in-law Richard Ford were to take over the running of the business. Joe was pleased to hear that one of Mrs Darby's relations, a Mr Joshua Sergeant had taken it upon himself to look after the interests of the Darby children. Joe would not have been pleased to hear that they had been totally disinherited because of their father's early death.

For a while, little changed at the works but as the weeks went by Joe noticed that the place was taking on a more organised air. Richard Ford managed the day-to-day business of the works, and he was obviously determined to make his mark on the place. Joe had to confess that things had been a bit lax for the last few months of Mr Darby's illness. Mr Ford called all the men together and explained that although he was a fair man, he did expect a full day's work for a full day's pay and that there were many men in the Gorge and beyond who would be only too willing to take the place of any man not prepared to work hard. Well, Joe thought, I suppose he has to start as he means to go on, if the business is to survive and prosper, which after all is in everyone's interest.

The range of goods was increased, and all manner of cast iron domestic utensils were now being produced at the furnaces. Quantities of kettles, skillets, cooking pots and smoothing irons were being shipped down the Severn to Bristol or loaded on to carts to be taken by road to Shrewsbury or further afield, even, Joe had heard, as far as Manchester.

Abigail seemed happy enough now that she felt her future would be secure with Joe. He made enquiries among the men at the Works about finding a plot in Dale Coppice. A few of them, John Spencer, Ed Boden, and Will Lloyd had already built their squatter cottages there and were pleased that Joe intended to join their settlement. As they said, there was strength in numbers and neighbour could help neighbour in time of trouble. They all offered to help Joe raise his house when the time came. Abigail's baby was due in the autumn, so Joe intended to use the summer to get his house built and ready for when the baby arrived.

Elizabeth spent any spare time she had, getting the Bangham house ship-shape for the time when her family would move into it. Little Jane was thriving. She was a bonny baby, who reminded her of Abigail when she was little, and reminded Arthur of Eliza. They both loved her dearly.

Things weren't going so well with Mary and Eddie. He seemed to be growing weaker and looking older with each passing week, although no one could really put a finger on what was wrong with him. He didn't seem to be in any pain, at least none that he admitted to. However, in the second week of June he took a turn for the worse, suffering a huge loss of blood. He took to his bed and there he stayed for several weeks with Mary catering for his every need, until one morning when she left him for a few minutes to bring him a drink of water, he quietly slipped away. After 40 years of marriage and four children raised safely to adulthood with Eddie, Mary was understandably distraught. Ella and Rose helped her to lay him out and Mr Johnson was sent for. Young Jimmy was inconsolable. He had been very close to Eddie, who had spent a lot of time with him, particularly since Eliza had gone, and Elizabeth did her best to comfort him. Poor child she thought, he must feel that everyone he loves is taken from him.

Two days later another sad procession made its way down the track to the Buildwas burial ground at Holy Trinity. Mary's children all came, and her eldest daughter Susan insisted that she should go and live with her and her family in Madeley Wood. She didn't object. She had long since come to terms with the fact that she would never manage on her own without any income, and she and Eddie had never had the means to save anything. Susan stayed with her for a few days to pack up her belongings. With old Ned in harness on the cart, the men of the hamlet loaded them up and with Susan and Mary sitting at the front, with Joe, they set off down the track towards the Buildwas bridge. Everyone had gathered to watch them leave and there were quite a few tears to be seen. Mary had been a good neighbour to them all and she would be sadly missed.

It had been a fairly dry spring in 1717 in the Gorge and the reservoirs which fed the wheel that powered the bellows at the furnaces were so depleted by the beginning of June that, much to the annoyance of Mr Ford, both the furnaces had to be blown out. The furnace men, including Joe, were laid off. There was some maintenance work to do on the structure of the furnaces but by the end of June that was all finished.

Mr Newton told the men that unless he could find them the odd bit of work in the ironworks or the foundry, which had reasonable stocks of pig iron and plenty of orders, there would be no more work until the reservoirs filled up again. Joe decided it was time to put his plan into action and went with the other men to choose the plot upon which he would build his house. It took him the best part of a month to amass the lumps of stone, and the timber he would need. It was decided that the house raising would be undertaken on the first weekend in July.

The Banghams Wood men came across, and Elizabeth and the other women had made food for them to bring with them. They began the work early one day and with the help of the Dale Coppice men, John, Ed, and Arthur, worked into the small hours building the simple structure that would qualify as a squatter's cottage. By the time dawn was breaking it was all but finished. Four walls and a turf roof stood where none had been before. Joe had his house. The Banghams Wood men set off wearily down the track to their homes, with the exception of Joe, who wouldn't leave his house that night. John's wife Susan brought him a hot drink and some bread, for which he was mightily grateful. Then after heartily thanking everyone who had helped him raise his house, he threw himself down to rest on a blanket on the ground.

He fell into an exhausted sleep and was woken up at about nine o'clock by the sound of children playing. He rose and washed at the pump, and John emerged from his cottage to invite him to come in for a bit of breakfast. He gratefully accepted although he knew they would have precious little for themselves at the moment, with John being laid off from work for the summer. There was porridge and a little honey, and a swill of ale and Joe felt all the better for it and ready to begin his day's work. He intended to make and fit the door and window frame to his cottage, to keep out the wind and rain before the weather turned. Richard came over every few days with some food for him as he wouldn't risk leaving the cottage empty in case someone else should decide to take up residence. The other Dale Coppice residents also shared what they could with him.

It took him a further four weeks hard work to get his cottage into a truly habitable state. He did manage to do a few labouring jobs down at the Works which helped him to buy the few things he needed from Madeley Wood market. He made a couple of beds, one for himself and one for Abigail. In time, he would add another couple of rooms to the cottage, but it would suffice for the time being. In fact, it was looking quite cosy by the time he brought Abigail across the Gorge to take a look at what would soon be her new home. She was delighted with it. In a couple of months' time, she would be moving in with Joe and her baby and she was happy.

Joe settled into his new home and found his neighbours to be pleasant enough. John and Susan Spencer lived in the cottage next to his with their children Elizabeth who was about eighteen and Tom, sixteen. They had lived in Dale Coppice for ten years or so, John working for the Darby company as well as doing some farm labouring whenever he needed to. Ed Boden and his wife Mary with their three were in the next cottage along, and in the far cottage were Will and Margaret Lloyd, a young couple who hadn't been married very long and as yet had no children.

August turned out to be wet and the reservoirs started to fill up again. By the beginning of September 1717, Mr Ford judged it to be safe to blow in the furnaces. When Joe turned up for work, Mr Newton took him to one side and said that one of the furnacemen had finally been forced to stop working due to ill health. This meant they were a man short, and he wanted Joe to take his place. He would be working permanently in the hearth of the furnace, which Joe knew would be hard and dangerous work, but Mr Newton said it would mean working days now and he would still be paid twelve shillings a week. Given that he would soon have Abigail and the baby to feed and clothe, he readily agreed to the move. It would make life easier for Abigail if he was working days and all in all, he felt it was a good move.

The furnaces were soon in full production again, and busier than ever. Orders had poured in over the summer months and they were working flat out to fulfil them. Joe felt satisfied he had achieved his aim of moving across to Dale Coppice and life was easier without the daily trek to and fro across the Gorge at each end of his shift. He did miss his sisters and Richard of course but couldn't really say the same about Will. Of course he did wonder what had become of him. Bristol was a gateway to the wider world, and it was quite possible that he was right now on his way to the New World. Perhaps they would never know. What Will didn't know though, was that James had recovered from the attack, and in fact, he couldn't remember a thing about what had happened and therefore was unable to point the finger at Will. Of course, people had their suspicions, as he had disappeared the very next day, but no proof, and had Will chosen to come back he would probably have got away with it. As it was, the family just had to accept that their brother was gone, most likely forever.

In Banghams Wood, life had taken up its new rhythm after Walter's death and Joe's departure. Abigail had continued to live there for the time being, until after the baby was born, when she would move across the valley to join Joe. Martha, with Dorothy's help, was coping surprisingly well at keeping house for Abigail and Richard. Elizabeth and Arthur were struggling a little financially, but Elizabeth was a good manager, and they were happy enough. Baby Jane was thriving, and Jimmy seemed to be getting over the loss of Eliza and Eddie and had started to play more with the other children of the hamlet.

Eddie and Mary's house stood empty for a good three months, then one evening at the beginning of October, a new family arrived, piled along with their belongings on the top of a cart, pulled up the track from Buildwas bridge by an old cart-horse. They arrived without notice and initially, the current residents of the hamlet were rather resentful of the intrusion. This was a tight knit community where shared joys and trage-dies over the years had bound them together. They had jointly endured hardships and deprivations, experienced each other's bereavements and joyous occasions alike. They felt that the arrival of a family of strangers in their midst would be bound to cause disruption, maybe even some realignment of loyalties. They surveyed the family and the pile of belongings on the cart with curiosity of course, trying to judge what manner of people they were.

The man looked to be in his thirties, and his wife about the same. Their clothes suggested that this move was a downward step for them, as did some of the items piled on the cart. The furniture was definitely not homemade and there seemed rather a lot of it. There were several bundles which looked to contain clothes or household linen and baskets full of kitchen utensils and earthenware pots. The children, one boy and one girl, were scrubbed clean with their hair topped with smart hats, and wearing clothes that would have been at home up at the Hall.

As it happened, this had been one of the rare dry days that autumn, but as they pulled up the cart, it began to rain and Arthur, Tom and Alf all offered to help unload their belongings. As they did so, they chatted to the newcomers, and it appeared that they had come from Madeley Wood. They were Benjamin and Dorothea Blake, and the children were David and Susan. Apparently, they were related to Mary, who had leased them the cottage. Apart from that, they discovered little about the reason for the apparent lowering of their station in life. No doubt, they thought, this would become clear over the days and weeks ahead.

Arthur took it upon himself to point out a few of the basic rules of living in the hamlet, explaining that the pump was for the use of all. They would be made welcome as long as they were considerate of the other residents, keeping their little plot tidy and their children under control and not bothering anyone else. Benjamin Blake assured Arthur that their only wish was to settle peaceably in the hamlet and be good neighbours to one and all. With that, everyone left them alone to settle into their new home. Elizabeth dropped by later that evening with some bread in case they had not brought any with them. They were very grateful and thanked her for her kindness.

As the days went by their story began to unfold. One day Dorothea was chatting to Elizabeth as she tended her vegetable plot, and she explained that Benjamin had owned a trow on the river and had been doing good trade for the past ten years. Then tragedy had struck. Down in Gloucester docks there had been a collision and the trow, along with all its cargo had sunk. Benjamin had lost his means of making a living and the loss of the cargo had also cost him much of his savings as he had to recompense his customer in order to at least preserve his reputation. He hoped to get a new barge to rebuild his business, but in the meantime the family had had to give up their rented home in Madeley Wood and Dorothea's aunt Mary had kindly suggested they take her cottage until they could get back on their feet.

Elizabeth felt sorry for their bad luck, and she liked Dorothea. They immediately struck up a friendship which was to last many decades, even though their lives would grow apart once again before too long.

By the beginning of November, everything was ready for Abigail and the baby in Dale Coppice. Joe had added another bedroom for the two of them and furnished it with a bed and a cot for the baby. It was on the 4th of November that Abigail called out for Elizabeth in the night, saying that the baby was coming. She laboured for twelve hours, and Elizabeth could see that it was a big baby. Abigail was quite small and slim, and it was hard going for her. Finally, at 2 o'clock the following day, Michael was born. He was a fine healthy baby with a shock of ginger hair, and Abigail was delighted with him. She stayed with Elizabeth and Arthur for three weeks before Richard took her and the baby in the cart over to Joe's cottage. Elizabeth was upset to see them go. She had enjoyed having Abigail around. They had always been close, but they had grown even closer over the last few months. Still, she knew it was for the best. She and Joe would soon make a good home for young Michael

Chapter 8

1718: Abigail and Michael soon settled in with Joe. She was grateful to him for taking them in and worked hard to create a comfortable home for them all. Her experience as a scullery maid and helping Elizabeth with the vegetable plot and the cooking, had equipped her well for the running of a home, despite her youth. She did find it hard though, to get used to the noise from the works, which never stopped. Day and night there was the roar of the furnaces, the hammers of the foundry and the men shouting to one another in the distance, trying to make themselves heard over the din. She noticed the air was full of soot from the furnaces and any clothes left out on the line more than a day were covered in it.

More than once, in spite of what had eventually happened to her at the hands of Furlong, she remembered fondly, the quiet, ordered days of life up at the Hall, and even in the hamlet in Banghams Wood. Still, she thought, she wouldn't want to go back into a life in service, where as a scullery maid, she had been at the beck and call of everyone. At least, living with Joe she was free to organise her day as she wished. She loved Michael, in spite of the way he'd been conceived. However, she was sad that what had happened to her had in the end resulted in Will having to leave Banghams Wood. Although she was touched that he had tried to avenge her, she did feel guilty that she had been the cause of his disappearance from the family.

She soon made friends with Elizabeth Spencer, who, although she was a little older than Abigail, seemed pleased to have another young woman in the hamlet to talk to. Abigail suspected that there was a little more to it than that though. She had seen the way Elizabeth looked at Joe and made any excuse she could think of to pop into Abigail and Joe's cottage whenever he was at home. For his part, she wasn't sure whether he'd noticed or not. It was infuriating. He seemed completely absorbed in what was going on at the works. His new job on the furnace floor was hard and he came home completely worn out. Abigail determined she would say something to him about Elizabeth soon. He needed to open his eyes, he wasn't getting any younger himself, she mused. He was going on twenty-two now, which to Abigail, seemed ancient.

By mid-December Joe decided it was time to visit Banghams Wood to see how Elizabeth and Arthur were faring. Since Will had left, Arthur had taken on the role of head of the family. Of course, Richard was now living over the stables at the Hall and Dorothy was in service, so there was only Martha and his own family to look after. He was a good man and Joe didn't doubt that he would fulfil the role, but he did want to put his mind at rest regarding Elizabeth. He knew she would be missing him and Will and the others and he wanted to see her before the winter weather made visiting Banghams Wood nigh on impossible.

He crossed the valley on the following Sunday. Although Abigail would have loved to see Elizabeth, she didn't go with him because she wouldn't risk young Michael's health by exposing him to the weather. It was cold, and a wet westerly was blowing up the Gorge as Joe crossed the Buildwas bridge. He hadn't seen the family since Abigail had moved across to his place several weeks earlier and he was eager to listen to all their news. When he entered the cottage door, Elizabeth shrieked with delight at the sight of her favourite brother.

'Eee Joe! Y'are a sight for sore eyes!' she exclaimed, declaring that she'd greatly missed him, then added, 'I never expected you today, but you'll eat with us? There's plenty to go round. It's a pity Margaret won't be coming; it was only last week she was here.'

'That's a shame,' Joe declared, 'I was hoping I might see her, or Dorothy, but never mind, it's good to see you and Arthur and the little ones. How've they been?'

'They're both fine reet now, thanks,' Elizabeth assured him, adding 'How's our Abigail and Michael?'

Joe reassured her that they were both in good health and settling down to life in Dale Coppice. He told her that Abigail had made friends with Elizabeth Spencer, who lived with her family in the cottage next door. Something about the way he spoke, gave her a clue that perhaps it wasn't only Abigail who had made friends with Elizabeth Spencer, but she said nothing, storing the information away for future reference.

It was good to see Elizabeth back in the Bangham family home. They had moved in shortly after Abigail left and the place was looking cosy and well ordered, just as Joe would have expected. The smell emanating from the cooking pot suspended over the fire was teasing his taste buds into life as he settled down on the settle, opposite Arthur at the hearth. They chatted amicably while Elizabeth busied herself with feeding little Jane. It turned out that a family had moved into Arthur's old place. Thomas Baker had been taken on at the quarry a month earlier and had been looking for a place for his wife, Laura and his two young children, to move into. Arthur said he had seemed to be a good worker and he offered him his house at a rent of a shilling a week, which he had gratefully accepted, and the family had moved in almost immediately.

Joe asked how the Blake family were settling in since they had moved into Mary and Eddie's old place. Arthur said they kept themselves to themselves most of the time. Apparently,

Benjamin was trying to finance another trow so that he could start up his haulage business on the Severn again, so Arthur didn't think they would be with them for very long. Elizabeth seemed to be friendly with Dorothea though, and they often helped one another out with chores around the hamlet. Arthur said he had wondered whether to talk to Benjamin about perhaps working for him on his trow if he finally restarted his business. Joe said it sounded like a good idea given there would certainly be plenty of river work in the future, the way the Darby works was growing, with raw materials and finished goods being sent up and down the Severn several times a day.

Elizabeth declared that dinner was ready, serving up a ladleful of the meat and vegetables onto each plate, and they all sat round the table to eat. As they ate, Joe enquired about the goings on at the Hall. Had Richard and Dorothy settled in up there? How was Margaret? Had there been any rumours about why Will had left Banghams Wood?

Elizabeth told him they were all fine. Dotty had taken well to life at the Hall. She was a bright girl and was already well thought of, or so Margaret had told them. In fact, one of the maids who had had a little education was teaching her to read, and she was loving every minute! Richard was thoroughly enjoying caring for the horses, and it was obvious he wouldn't want to be doing anything else. As for Will, Margaret said she hadn't heard anything. After all, no one at the Hall knew anything about Will and she wasn't about to enlighten them. Elizabeth had said nothing to the others about his assault on James until she'd heard that he wasn't dead and was fully recovered. When she had told Margaret about it, she said it was what she had suspected all along.

Joe stayed for another hour after supper and then declared he must be on his way. He said his goodbyes, gave his sister a hug and set off towards the river. It was dark now but there was a full moon, and he was easily able to pick his way down the familiar track to the bridge, enjoying the night sounds he had known all his life. An owl hooted some way off, to be answered by one closer to hand. The cry of an infant fox looking for its mother sounded off to the left followed by rustling in the undergrowth as no doubt she answered its call. It had been good to catch up with Elizabeth and to see the old place again. After all, he had been born and grown up in the cottage in the wood that bore his name, and his new place didn't quite feel like home to him yet.

On the other side of the river, as he walked up the lane beside the brook, the noise of the foundry and the hammers in the forge grew louder and the air became thick with fumes from the furnaces. Normally he didn't notice it, but now, after visiting Banghams Wood, in contrast to the peace and fragrancy of that place, the noise and the smell of Dale Coppice assaulted his senses. Still, this was a small price to pay, he thought to himself, for the steady work and good pay he received from the Works.

As the days grew shorter and winter tightened its grip in Dale Coppice, its inhabitants prepared for the harsh conditions which would inevitably soon arrive. The woodpiles were replenished, and any gaps around windows and doors were sealed against the winter winds. The hog had been killed, butchered, and shared out in the hamlet according to the number of mouths to be fed. This year, Joe had been allocated his share even though he and Abigail had just arrived. This was a measure of the respect in which he was held among the Coalbrookdale men. They knew that he would more than earn his share in the months and years ahead.

Christmas in Dale Coppice seemed strange to Joe and Abigail. It was the first time either of them had spent it away from Banghams Wood and the rest of the family. Not that there was much of the family left there, Joe mused, as he was clearing out the hearth to set it again to cook their meal on Christmas

Day. Abigail had prepared chicken, ham, and vegetables to go into the pot, which was soon bubbling away over the fire. After they had finished supper there was a knock on the door and when Joe opened it Elizabeth Spencer was standing there, and shyly said that her mother had sent her round to see if he and Abigail would like to come over for a drink of ale as they were having a bit of a party, it being Christmas and all.

Abigail smiled as she watched Joe's face turn pink, which told her she had been right all along, he did have a soft spot for Elizabeth. Of course, he was happy to accept the invitation. Without hesitation he threw his coat on and donned his cap. He damped down the fire and Abigail picked Michael up, wrapping her shawl around the baby and herself, and they followed Elizabeth back to the cottage next door. The whole Spencer family made them welcome, and their first Christmas in Dale Coppice turned out to be every bit as enjoyable as any they had had in Banghams Wood. This was particularly true for Joe and Elizabeth. It was obvious to everyone that there was an attraction between them and from that day they were seldom apart, except when Joe was at the furnace.

The winter turned out to be as harsh as anyone could remember. The snow scurried around the clearing in Dale Coppice, drifting into huge mounds against the cottage walls until it reached the eaves and could grow no higher. Each morning the residents of the cottages had to dig their way out of their doorways. It was the end of February before the last of the snows had melted away and the March winds began to blow along the Gorge. Birdsong once again competed for attention against the constant drumming of the hammers in the forge, and the trees began to burst into life once more.

As 1719 wore on, demand for the domestic goods being manufactured at the Darby Works continued to grow. Joe was now skilled at iron making, experienced in judging when any adjustment of ingredients was needed to ensure a good product. The Coalbrookdale Company was developing a reputation for the quality of its goods and shipments were being sent far afield. Joe was always proud to hear that Coalbrookdale products were finding their way into homes and businesses up and down the land and even to the Americas!

Whenever he got the chance, he would chat to the hauliers to find out where the shipments were heading. He was particularly interested to talk to the Bristol hauliers, conscious that they were a link to an outside world he would probably never himself see. One such merchant was Solomon White. He owned his own Severn Trow and plied his trade constantly between the Gorge and the port of Gloucester where goods would be trans-shipped to be taken on to Bristol. One day in early March, he sought Joe out to give him a letter which he said he had been given by a man who asked him to deliver it to Joe personally, even though it was addressed to Elizabeth Green. Joe guessed that it might be from Will. They hadn't heard from him since he had left Banghams Wood.

As the letter was addressed to Elizabeth, Joe decided he must go over to Banghams Wood on Sunday to deliver it to his sister. To be fair, it wasn't much use Joe opening it himself as he couldn't read. Nor could Will for that matter. He must have paid a letter writer to draft it for him. The following Sunday, Abigail and Michael crossed the Gorge with Joe, to visit Elizabeth and Arthur. Perhaps Margaret or Dorothy might be there and if they couldn't read it, maybe they would know someone up at the Hall who would be able to decipher it for the family.

As it happened, neither Margaret nor Dorothy was at Elizabeth's that Sunday, much to Joe's disappointment. He immediately gave Elizabeth the letter which he told her had probably come from Will. She opened it carefully, almost reverently, as though it was a thing of wonder.

'Well, there's a lot of writing here Joe,' she said, 'but it might as well just be a load of scribbles, as I can't decipher it and I don't know anybody round here as can.'

'Well I do!' declared Arthur, 'Benjamin Blake is your man! He's sure to be able to read and write, nobody can run a business the way he has without learning their letters.'

'You're right Arthur! Benjamin will be able to read it. Will you go across and ask him if he would mind coming over to read it to us all, Arthur?'

Arthur gladly agreed and disappeared across the clearing to speak to Benjamin Blake, who returned with him after about ten minutes or so. He took the letter and with all the family seated round, full of anticipation, he began to read:

Dear Liz and all,

I want to let you know that I am in good health and trust this letter finds you all the same. I have been working at the Bristol Docks since I arrived here. The work is hard but no harder than I'm used to. I have met people from all over the world, here in Bristol. I hear stories of all kinds of wild places and the animals that live there. I've heard that over the ocean, in the Americas, a man can make his fortune. There is land to be had that a man can call his own. No greedy landowners there. They call it a land of opportunity Liz, and I am moved to go there myself. By the time you receive this letter, I will be aboard the Matilda, halfway across the ocean, bound for America. One day I will return with a fortune for all of us to share Liz. Please do not worry about me. I am happy now that I am bound for a new life in a new world.

God bless you all,

Your loving brother, Will

After Benjamin had finished reading, all were silent, as they took in the news that their brother was at that very moment on a ship somewhere in the middle of the great ocean, sailing to the other side of the world. Elizabeth broke the silence as she spoke softly,

'Oh our Will, whatever will become of you?' then turned to Arthur and buried her face in his shoulder, weeping quietly for the loss of her brother. Joe thanked Benjamin for reading it to them and took the letter from him. Benjamin said he was glad he'd been able to help, saying he was sorry it had been such upsetting news for them all, then took his leave.

Joe wasn't sure what he was feeling. He was angry at Will for getting himself in the situation of having to leave home through his recklessness, but he was relieved that at least it sounded as though he was following his dream. He knew Will had always wanted to explore the world beyond the Gorge and now he had his chance. He turned his attention to Elizabeth, trying to console her, saying that at least Will seemed in good health and fine spirits as he set out on his adventure.

'It's what he always wanted our Liz, you know that,' he said quietly, 'to get away from this place and see something of the world. Well now he has his wish, and we must try to be glad for him.'

'I know you're right Joe, we must try, but it's hard and we all know we may never see him again.'

The conversation about Will ended abruptly as young Michael decided he was hungry and exercised his lungs to let everyone know it.

'Lordy Abigail!' Elizabeth exclaimed, 'that's a hearty cry! You've got a strong lad there and no mistake!'

'I know Liz,' Abigail agreed, 'when he's hungry he certainly leaves me with no doubt about it,' as she sat down by the fire and put him to her breast.

'Well I'd best get the rest of us fed an' all,' Elizabeth declared, and set about preparing the vegetables to add to the rabbit Arthur had caught that morning, which was already cooking in the pot.

While they waited for the meal to cook, Joe asked Arthur what news he had of Benjamin Blake's plan to set himself up with a new business. Arthur said he had spoken to Benjamin only last week and he said he hoped to have his new boat within the next month or so. He also said he had asked Benjamin if there would be any jobs going. Benjamin had told him that he would certainly be taking men on and if Arthur was interested, he would be happy to keep him in mind. He did stress that the work was hard, but Arthur had insisted that it couldn't be any harder work than what he had endured for years on the land and then up at the stone quarry, and he had told Benjamin that he definitely wished to give it a try. Joe told Arthur that the Darby works was taking on new men all the time, and if he liked he would ask for him. Arthur thanked him but said that he would really rather try his luck on the river than work at the ironworks with all the fumes and dirt it threw out. When the wind blew from the north, it was now even finding its way across the river and into Banghams Wood!

The smell emanating from the cooking pot, told Elizabeth that supper was ready to serve, and she told them all to sit at the table while she filled their bowls. As it was still early in the year, and the days short, as soon as they had finished, Joe announced that he and Abigail must be making their way home to Dale Coppice. Elizabeth said that the afternoon had gone all too quickly and that they must come back soon, hopefully when Margaret or Dorothy was visiting. Joe promised that they would. In fact, now that the worst of the winter was over, perhaps they could visit more often, he told her.

With that, Abigail wrapped her shawl tightly around herself and Michael, and she and Joe said their goodbyes and set off down the track to the bridge. The light was fading fast, but Joe knew every twist and turn of the track, he'd trudged it often enough after all. Fifteen minutes later they had reached the bridge, just in time to see a barge loaded up with coal passing underneath it, heading for the wharf downstream. The river was high, as it usually was at this time of year and a brisk breeze had blown up. Looking down at the black water swirling around in the wake of the barge, Abigail shivered and said,

'I do wish Arthur wasn't set on going on the river Joe. I heard only yesterday about a boat that got sunk down towards Bridgnorth way, and seven men died. It seems to me once the river takes them there's only one end.'

'I know,' Joe replied, 'but we live in a dangerous world Abigail and accidents can happen anywhere, whether it's in a quarry or on a river. Don't worry, Arthur will take good care, with Liz and the children waiting for him back home.'

This seemed to settle Abigail's mind and she declared that they had better hurry home now as Michael would soon need feeding again. As they walked back up the hill to Dale Coppice, Abigail was deep in thought. She had long since realised, before Joe himself did, that he and Elizabeth were meant for each other. She knew it wouldn't be long before they were betrothed. What she wondered, would happen to her and little Michael? Would Joe still want her to live in Dale Coppice with them after they were married? Still, this wasn't something she could talk to him about until he had got round to asking Elizabeth to marry him. Men were so infuriatingly slow sometimes she mused.

So, no one was surprised when Joe and Elizabeth announced that they were to be married. They had hardly been out of each other's sight since Joe and Abigail had settled into the hamlet. Joe extended his house, adding another bedroom and a brewhouse, determined to make it fit for his new wife. So it was, that one beautiful June morning, two processions wended their way to Holy Trinity at Buildwas. Joe and Elizabeth strode hand in hand down the track by the brook, followed by John and Susan Spencer and Abigail and Michael. Joe glanced lovingly at his bride to be. He thought she had never looked lovelier, in a white dress with a blue shawl around her shoulders. She wore a wreath of wildflowers around her golden curls and carried a posy of daisies in her hand. As they neared the Buildwas Bridge, they met the Banghams cart as it crossed the river, pulled by Ned with Elizabeth and Arthur with the children, and the rest of the family all piled on top.

The service was short, the main event, and indeed the purpose, was the reciting of the marriage vows and the signing of the register in the presence of the witnesses. Afterwards, Joe lifted Elizabeth up onto the wagon and climbed up beside her. Richard took the reins and led the procession along the riverside and up the hill to Dale Coppice for the celebration. Elizabeth and Arthur had brought a roasted hog joint and a barrel of ale to contribute to the meal, and the Spencers provided the rest. It was a fine sunny day and tables were set up in the clearing for the wedding guests. A fine feast was laid out and afterwards one of the men brought out his fiddle and dancing soon commenced. Later, on the cart on the way back home to Banghams Wood, Elizabeth remarked to Arthur that it had been 'a reet fine do!' and she was glad that Joe and Elizabeth had been given a day to remember. She was sure they would 'mek a go on' it' she declared, and Arthur nodded in agreement. This was to be old Ned's last duty, as old age finally took its toll and a month after the wedding he died in his sleep. The family all grieved for him of course, he had served them well for over eighteen years.

Joe and Elizabeth settled down to married life and within a year she was pregnant with their first child. However, it was an ill-fated pregnancy which failed at the seven-month mark. When the child was delivered it was a poor little mite who could never have lived to see the world. Elizabeth and Joe were devastated, and it was a year or so before they were ready to try again. Eventually try they did, and before long Elizabeth was pregnant again. To their delight, on 26th May 1724 a beautiful little girl, who they named Elizabeth after her mother, was born. She had her mother's blue eyes and golden hair but was unmistakeably a Bangham.

Chapter 9

1724: The last few years had been busy ones in and around Dale Coppice. Each month would bring more newcomers. Often, they would be relatives of one or other of the families already settled in the hamlet, but occasionally complete strangers would turn up, determined to find work in the valley. Its reputation for being a hive of industry had now spread far and wide and acted like a magnet for families with no other means of earning a living.

The men who had founded the settlement became leaders of the group, and as needed, they called a meeting so they could all agree the rules by which Dale Coppice would be run. Everyone knew that in some of the settlements around the Gorge there was much rowdiness, drunken behaviour and even debauchery, particularly among the newcomers, and they were determined to keep Dale Coppice a fit place to live and bring up their families. Of course, everyone who worked at the Darby Works also knew that the owners wouldn't tolerate any drunkenness among their work force. The work was far too dangerous for that, and in any case the Darbys were Quakers who were renowned for their sobriety.

So there were now ten households in Dale Coppice. Six of the families were dependent on the Darby Works for their livelihoods. The other men worked either at the quarries or the mines thereabouts. The women tended their vegetable patches and looked after the hogs, which were owned communally and when they were slaughtered the meat was shared out between the families according to their need. In the last couple of summers when water had been short and the furnaces were blown out, some of the men had found work repairing the furnaces ready for the next season, or in the foundry. When without work, Joe and some of the men kept busy coppicing and building a couple of clamps to produce some charcoal, which was still needed in other furnaces and for domestic use around the gorge. It wasn't as lucrative as working at the furnace, but it served to keep their families fed.

At the works there had also been much change. As well as bellied pots and other domestic items, the Darby's had occasionally produced steam engine cylinders. Joe was always excited to be involved in the casting of parts for steam engines. He was bright enough to understand that these machines were indeed going to bring great change to the world. So far, while the engines were fixed to the ground, they had been used to pump water out of the mine workings, or at the pitheads, to raise and lower the cages down to the coal seam. Now there was sometimes talk of engines that would be able to turn wheels set on tracks. Wooden rails were already used in the valley to carry coal and stone from the mines and quarries, using a wagon hauled by a team of horses. The idea of placing a steam engine on a wagon to drive wheels which ran along tracks didn't seem too far-fetched to anyone with a scintilla of imagination, and Joe had plenty. However, it was to be many decades until these developments came about, and Joe Bangham would never live to see them. In the meantime, the Coalbrookdale works continued to cast parts for the Newcomen engine, and the men took great pride in their work, becoming famous for the quality of their workmanship.

Abigail had asked Joe and Liz whether they minded having her share their home, but both of them told her that she could stay with them as long as she wanted to. Nevertheless, she did dream that one day, she might have a home of her own. Since Liz had moved in, it hadn't felt like her place anymore, and Abigail felt that she had to defer to her in matters to do with the household, as she was Joe's wife and it was, after all, his house. Nevertheless, she did her best to help Liz with the chores and generally felt she earned her keep.

Arthur had been working the barges for the past two years now. Benjamin Blake, now Owner Blake, had been as good as his word and had given Arthur a job on his trow. Arthur loved the work, hard as it was. At least he could see something of the world outside the Gorge. They sailed the Blake vessel, the Oriel, an upstream trow, down river as far as the Gloucester Docks, when they had to tranship the cargo to larger vessels, or downstream trows, for the second part of its journey to Bristol and the wide world beyond. Then they would reload the Oriel with goods bound for the Gorge, or sometimes, Shrewsbury. The boat would then be hauled back upriver against the flow, with the help of gangs of bow haulers based in pubs along the riverbank.

Elizabeth still wasn't too keen on Arthur working the river. He was away for days on end and she constantly worried that one day, he wouldn't return. She had lived by the Severn all her life and she knew its moods. It could be calm, gently flowing along when the level was low in the summer months, but when the north westerly drove sheets of rain along the valley, or the snows of winter melted too quickly, it could rapidly turn into a raging torrent as it forced its way through the narrow gorge. She had heard enough tragic tales of men and boats lost on the river to know that however careful a man was, no matter how well he could swim, the river showed no mercy. Once the fast-flowing water of the river in flood took them, few men could resist the pull of its currents. Still, she had to admit that he was earning good money. Owner Blake valued his diligence and reliability and paid him accordingly. She just prayed that God would protect Arthur. It was all she could do.

The winter was harsh that year. Snow piled high along the tracks, thawing slightly, then freezing overnight, making moving around treacherous. Joe was thankful that he only had the relatively short distance from the hamlet to the works to cover, remembering the winter of 1715, when he'd had to battle his way through the snow and ice from Banghams Wood, across the Gorge to the works. Liz had turned out to be a wonderful mother and a capable homemaker, and they were ecstatically happy now that they had their beautiful baby girl. That winter there was always a good fire with a pot bubbling away when he arrived home, tired and hungry from his day's work at the furnace and the trudge back through the snow.

It was at the end of February 1725 that the snow which had turned to layer upon layer of ice over the long winter months, began to melt. The rate of melting brought alarm and dread around the Gorge. Everyone wanted to see the end of it of course, but not like this. They knew that if it melted too quickly the river wouldn't cope with the volume of water tumbling down the valley sides, not just in the Gorge, but all the way upriver to its source in the Welsh hills. Arthur was away on the Oriel taking a cargo of iron goods downriver to Gloucester. Elizabeth judged they should be on their way back upriver in the next few days and prayed to God that they would stay put in Gloucester until the worst of the floodwater had passed. As predicted, by the third day of the thaw, with rain now pouring down hastening the melting of the remaining snow, the river had turned into a raging torrent, almost reaching the top of the arch of Buildwas Bridge. The wharf was packed with boats waiting for the flood to subside before making the hazardous journey downriver. No boats had arrived upstream for two days and there was much concern among the owners and bargees' families alike. Still, there was nothing to be done except to sit tight and wait for the water level to fall.

Elizabeth was beside herself with worry. As she glanced at Jimmy and Jane playing by the fire, she felt sick to her stomach with the thought that they may no longer have a father, or she a husband. By the end of the third day after she had hardly slept for two nights, she was desperate to find out if there was any news. She felt completely isolated in Banghams Wood. The Blakes had moved out over a year ago now that they owned their new boat and their finances had improved. Their house had been occupied by another quarryman and his family, who would know nothing of what might be happening down on the river. The next day, the rain had stopped, and the snow and ice were all gone. She left the children with Martha while she trudged down the now muddy track to the bridge to see if she could find out what was happening. She was horrified at the sight of the river, which was still far too high, just managing to find its way under the Buildwas Bridge. Making her way along the north side of the river, towards the wharf, her heart was hammering in her chest at what she might be about to hear.

As she approached the wharf, she could see a crowd of people, mostly women on a similar mission to her own. There would be many men from the Gorge somewhere on the river down towards Gloucester. Until boats started to arrive, there was no way to know whether they were safe. Although the rain had stopped, there would be plenty of water still to flow down the Gorge and no-one knew how long it was likely to be before the appearance of the sails of the first trow to make it home safely.

Elizabeth found Benjamin Blake in the crowd and immediately approached him to ask for news of the Oriel. He had none but said a messenger had been sent by horseback to Bridgnorth to see if they could gain news of any boats that had been in trouble in the flood. He assured her that he had a good and experienced crew on board the Oriel, which was a strong well-built boat, and he had every confidence that it would soon return safely. He persuaded Elizabeth to return home to the children and as soon as there was news, he would send a message to her.

Reluctantly, Elizabeth agreed, bade him farewell and started back along the riverbank towards the bridge. She had only gone about a hundred yards when a shout went up that a boat had been sighted and she turned and hurried back to the wharf. It was a long way off in the distance and there was much speculation as to what vessel it was. She found Owner Blake by the edge of the dock, peering in the direction of the on-coming sails. He knew the outline and colour of his own ship's sails and was disappointed to see that this wasn't his trow, and then the man standing next to him shouted out that it was in fact his boat, the Severn Lady.

Realising the crew may have news of other boats yet to appear, Elizabeth remained beside Benjamin on the wharf, awaiting the arrival of the Severn Lady. After about ten minutes the boat was tied up at the wharf and the crew, looking weary, began to disembark. The other owners crowded round them, asking what news they had of their boats.

'It's been bad,' one of the men told them, 'the level of the river rose faster than I've ever seen it. Boats that were tied up fared best, but the ones in the middle of the river had a hard time of it.'

The crowd were clamouring for answers. More than anything they wanted to know if any of the boats had been lost.

'Just one to my knowledge,' one of the men replied, 'but I'm sorry, I can't be sure which one. I didn't see it myself, just heard of it from another boat that tied up beside us at Bridgnorth.'

Elizabeth was now filled with dread. A boat had been lost! She knew only too well what that meant. The river in flood would have taken anyone unfortunate enough to fall into it.

There would be little chance of rescue for the crew of the stricken vessel. Owner Blake was obviously a very troubled man. Apart from the possible loss of life, the loss of another boat would have finished him. He was now pinning his hopes on the messenger returning from Bridgnorth being able to identify which boat had been lost, and said as much to Elizabeth, who was now determined to wait at the wharf until the man returned with news.

It was an hour later when they saw him riding along the riverbank from Buildwas Bridge. As he approached, he was surrounded by the crowd all shouting at once, desperately needing to know what the name of the lost boat was. Eventually, he was heard to call out the name Miranda. So, it was the Miranda, owned by Owner Reynolds, Elizabeth heard with relief. Her Arthur would be safe, thank God! Then she thought about the other women whose husbands wouldn't be coming home and tears of relief, mingled with tears of sadness for them, trickled slowly down her cheeks.

Owner Blake came over to her and said,

'I've just asked the messenger for news of the Oriel, and he tells me that she is tied up at Bridgnorth. Elizabeth, I'm so glad for you, well, for us all of course. Now, you go home to the children and I'm sure Arthur will be with you soon. If there is any other news before then, I will let you know.'

She thanked him, wrapped her shawl tightly around her and then set off once again for the bridge. Now that she was sure Arthur was safe, her thoughts turned to home and the children who she had left with Martha. Martha does her best, she thought to herself, but I wouldn't want to leave her alone with them for too long. She tends to lose concentration sometimes and doesn't spot dangers as well as she might.

She needn't have worried. When she arrived home the cottage was cosy and warm with a good fire in the hearth and Martha was giving the children their supper of bread and dripping. Elizabeth hugged them so fiercely that Jimmy asked what was wrong and where his father was. She reassured him that he would be home soon.

It was two hours later, just as night was falling, that the door opened, and Arthur stood in the doorway illuminated against the gathering gloom by the light from the fire. Elizabeth flew into his arms, almost knocking him off his feet.

'By, that's a welcome and a half!' he declared as he hugged her close.

'I've been that worried though!' she exclaimed. 'We heard a boat was lost but no one knew which one. I thought you might be gone Arthur.'

'Well, it was touch and go at one point. We were in the middle of the river when the flood struck but we weren't too far from the wharf at Bridgnorth and just managed to get her safely tied up before the worst of it.'

The children joined their parents and hugged their father, not completely understanding but sensing that some kind of disaster had been averted.

There was much sadness in the Gorge over the loss of the Miranda. Sadly, only one of the seven bodies were retrieved, and only because it had become snagged on an overhanging tree branch. The others had been carried in the flood downstream towards Gloucester, and maybe even on towards the ocean. Such was the price of working on the River Severn. Its power could be used, but it would never be tamed.

Up at the Hall everyone had heard the news about the flood and the loss of the Miranda. Margaret knew that Elizabeth would have been beside herself with worry about Arthur if he had been on the river when the flood struck. She was due a day off and decided to visit Banghams Wood the next Sunday to see how things were with them.

It was a cold but fine day as she made her way down the track to the Wood. She hadn't visited for quite a while because of the snows of winter and Elizabeth and Arthur gave her a warm welcome. With the pot of vegetables and bacon bubbling over the fire, they settled down to share their news.

They talked, of course, about the tragedy on the river. Elizabeth told her how she had been at the wharf that day as the first trow made it home, and how relieved she had been to hear that the Oriel had been tied up safely at Bridgnorth. It had left many widows in its wake, and Elizabeth said how grateful she was that she wasn't one of them.

Margaret had news of her own to tell them. Being the horseman at the Hall, Richard had the job of going regularly to Bridgnorth with the wagon to collect supplies for the stables, but for some months seemed to have been finding more and more excuses to make the ten-mile journey to the grain merchants. After his last trip he had sought Margaret out to tell her that he had proposed to Margaret Andrews of Bridgnorth.

When Margaret told them that Margaret Andrews was the daughter of the Grain Merchant, they both speculated that Richard had 'done alright for himself'. Elizabeth was of course, thrilled to hear that Richard was to be married, and by the sound of it, his status in the world was about to rise. Margaret said she thought he would probably be moving to Bridgnorth as Margaret Andrews had no brothers or sisters living and she expected that she and Richard would take over the business when her father could no longer manage it.

Although Elizabeth was sorry that she wouldn't be seeing much of Richard once he moved to Bridgnorth, she was pleased for him. In any case, since he'd moved into the stables at the Hall, he had seldom visited the Wood. Margaret told her the wedding was to be in June, but Elizabeth doubted whether they would be able to go if it was to be in Bridgnorth.

Dorothy was doing well at the Hall; Margaret told them as they ate their meal. She had learned her letters, and the mistress had quite taken to her. In fact, her duties were no longer those of a scullery maid, as more and more, the mistress entrusted her to look after the children, who were six and eight years old. Dorothy was very happy to do this, Margaret told her, not really considering it to be hard work at all. In fact, of late she had been allowed to sit in with the children's lessons, taught by John Smith, the young teacher who had been engaged to run the Charity School in Madeley Wood. As the Master was a patron of the school, Mr Smith gave two days each week to the education of the children at the Hall. Margaret suspected that Dorothy's interest extended beyond education, as John Smith was a handsome young man and it seemed that the attraction might be mutual. Margaret said she hoped their relationship might blossom. Dorothy could do worse than to marry a schoolteacher.

Margaret asked whether Elizabeth had seen anything of Joe over the winter, but she replied that sadly, she hadn't. Margaret told her she had met Liz and Abigail with their children a couple of weeks back in Madeley Wood on market day. She remarked that young Michael was growing fast now. She said that she hoped he would steer clear of the Hall, as he was the image of James Furlong, the under-butler and that would have left no one in any doubt that he was indeed his father. Quite apart from his features, his shock of bright red hair would definitely have given the game away. Little Elizabeth was a bonny child, Margaret told her, with golden curls like her mother, and looked the picture of health.

Talking of Furlong the under-butler, brought Will into their minds and they wondered where he was and what he was doing. It had been eight years since he had left the Wood on that fateful night, and nearly seven since they had received his note from Bristol, saying that he was about to cross the ocean to the Americas. Of course, there was no way they could have let him know that James had survived his attack, had not even remembered who had struck him, and no longer posed a threat to him. They just hoped that one day he would return. The family didn't feel complete without him.

As they were talking, Jimmy came in. He had been gathering kindling in the woods. He was fourteen now and growing fast. He had been apprenticed for some time to the coracle builder Bert Rogers down on the river. Coracles had been used on the Severn for generations for net fishing and eel catching, but with the increasing population it seemed that demand was growing faster than ever. Coracle building was a skilled craft and the Rogers' family had been making them for decades.

'How do you find working with Rogers, Jimmy?' Margaret asked him.

'I like it fine Aunt Margaret,' he replied, 'I'm learning how to build coracles and one day Bert says he'll let me try building one of my own.'

'That's wonderful Jimmy, better than working at the quarry or going down into the depths of the earth in a coal mine.'

'Aye,' Arthur agreed, 'but I do tell him not to get over-confident like. The river takes no prisoners, as we know.'

All this time, Martha hadn't spoken, and Margaret cast a worried look in her direction.

'You don't have much to say for yourself today, Martha. Are you not feeling well?'

Martha said that she was feeling alright, but she just wasn't her usual self. She usually made a fuss of Margaret whenever she visited, but today she had just sat quietly staring at the fire. Margaret looked questioningly towards Elizabeth, who just shook her head sadly without speaking. After they had eaten Margaret got up to leave and Elizabeth handed some scraps to Martha asking her to take them out to the hog pen, and while she was gone, she said.

'I am right worried about our Martha, Margaret. I don't know what's wrong with her, but she isn't eating like she used to and last week she lost some blood.'

'Is she in pain?' Margaret enquired.

'She doesn't complain of any, but I'm not so sure. She is very quiet like you've seen. All I can do is keep an eye on her.'

'Aye, that's about the size of it Liz,' Margaret replied, as Martha stepped back into the room.

Margaret said she needed to be getting back up to the Hall before the light went. Throwing her shawl over her head, wrapping it tightly round her chest and knotting it behind her back, she bade them all goodbye, and giving Martha an extra hug stepped out into the darkening afternoon.

Chapter 10

1727: Richard and Margaret Andrews had been married in the summer of 1725 as planned and he had thrown himself into learning the family business, which was doing well. He loved the work and although he missed his beloved horses at the Hall, he and Margaret were happy together. They had moved into Margaret's family home with her father and Richard's life was now financially secure with a good future ahead of him, as Mr Andrews had told him that one day, he would inherit the business as he was confident that he would do a good job and he knew it would be in safe hands.

Joe Bangham was well established at the Dale Company, as it had been called since Abraham Darby's death and the takeover by Thomas Goldney 11. Richard Ford, the manager of the company was greatly impressed with Joe. He had been made foreman of his shift the year before and had eagerly accepted the responsibility of dealing with the other men, planning the work, and ensuring that the job was done correctly.

As Joe was striding along the track back to the settlement that night, he pondered about the Bangham family and how things were changing. Liz and Abigail had seen Margaret at the market a couple of weeks previously and she had told them how well Richard was doing in the Andrew's business. Joe was pleased for him but understood that he wouldn't be seeing much of him in the future. It seemed that the family was drifting apart, with Will gone and Richard living in Bridgnorth. He wasn't able to get over to Banghams Wood to see Elizabeth and her family very often these days either. He had heard about the tragedy on the river of course and knew that Elizabeth would have been out of her mind with worry, but with things so busy at the works he'd been doing extra hours and hadn't had a day off for weeks.

As he strode into the cottage, young Elizabeth squealed with delight and ran up to him. He picked her up and swung her round as he always did. She was the image of her mother Liz, with her golden curls and ready smile and he doted on her. Abigail and Liz were sorting out the supper and Michael was busy drawing on a piece of slate with a lump of chalk. He was a bright boy and seemed particularly fond of drawing birds and animals. Abigail hoped that one day she would be able to send him down to the charity school which had opened at Buildwas. She was sure that, given some education, he would be able to make something of himself. As it was, he was a good lad and always willing to help his mother. He was particularly fond of going with her on market day, helping her to carry the provisions back over the hill from Madeley.

So it was that the following Wednesday, he, and Abigail set off up the track along the valley side to Madeley. Liz didn't go with them on this occasion as little Elizabeth didn't seem too well. It was a fine day, and they were happy in each other's company, chatting about the things they needed to get from the market. Abigail smiled fondly at her son. At eight years old he was a handsome little boy with striking features, and deep blue eyes. Of course, she knew that he had inherited his red hair from 'that man'. She still couldn't bring herself to speak his name and it hurt her greatly that whenever she looked at her beloved son, she was reminded of that fateful day when 'he' had forced himself on her. However, she pushed these thoughts from her mind as they began the descent towards Madeley and the market.

It was busy as always and they threaded their way through the crowd to the stall selling cheese. Abigail was holding tightly to Michael's hand, afraid to lose him in the crowd. She glanced down fondly at him and as she raised her eyes once more, she was shocked to the core, as standing in front of her, blocking her way, was James.

'Well, well,' he said, 'what have we here?'

'Get out of my way!' she declared angrily.

Ignoring her, he took hold of Michael's free hand and pulled him towards the edge of the crowd. Abigail had no choice but to follow unless she wanted Michael to be hurt. He was distressed by the way this man was pulling at his arm and shouted at him to let go. James didn't let go, but continued to pull them clear, leading them round the corner of the Inn wall.

'Get off him!' Abigail shouted, 'we want nothing to do with you!'

'But he's my son!' James shouted, 'I want to talk to my son!'

'What does he mean mother!?' Michael shouted, fighting back the tears.

'He's not your son!' Abigail screamed at him. 'He's my son and you have no rights where he's concerned.'

'Who are you kidding?' James sneered, 'You only have to look at him to know he's mine! He didn't get that hair from you, that's for sure!'

Abigail had no idea where this conversation might lead and the last thing she wanted was for Michael to hear anything about how he was conceived. She was desperate now to get away from him, but he was still holding on to Michael who was, by now in floods of tears. Just at that moment, Owner Blake and his wife appeared round the corner and recognised Abigail. They could see that a man was pulling at Michael's arm and Abigail's eyes were full of fear.

'Let the boy go,' Owner Blake said with conviction.

James weighed him up briefly and could see from his bearing and appearance that he wasn't a man to be trifled with. Basically a coward, he let go of Michael's arm, at the same time swearing to Abigail that this wouldn't be the end of the matter. With that, he strode off.

Abigail thanked Owner Blake for his help and Dorothea asked her if she was alright now. Looking at the boy and the man, it had been obvious to both of them that he was the father of the boy. They had known of course that Abigail had had to leave the Hall because she was pregnant, and now they understood how that had come about. Just another example of a man in authority taking advantage of a vulnerable young girl. They offered to help her buy what she needed and to set her on her way back to Dale Coppice, in case Furlong decided to look for her again. Michael clung to his mother but had now calmed down somewhat, and Abigail gladly accepted their offer of help. Half an hour later Abigail and Michael were making their way back along the track to Dale Coppice.

'Who was that man, mother?' Michael asked her suddenly. 'Why did he say I was his?'

'He's nobody!' Abigail replied sharply, having no idea how she would ever be able to explain it to Michael. He was inclined to ask her more questions, but something in her tone made him realise that he would be wise to say no more on the subject. He stored the incident away in his mind, and young as he was, was determined that one day, he would find out about the strange man with hair like his – he'd never seen anyone with hair that colour before, and somehow, he knew that meant something, but not exactly what.

Arthur had been away downriver for the best part of three weeks and Elizabeth knew he would be home any day now. It was always difficult to know precisely when he would return. It depended on how many other vessels would be lining up for trans-shipment of their cargoes in Gloucester. The river trade was growing by the day. Each time the Dale Works increased production, which seemed to be more or less constantly, more boats had to be commissioned to ship the goods out to the ports and to bring raw materials and other supplies back up-river.

Elizabeth was working on the vegetable plot, planting potatoes, and sewing carrots and turnips. It was back-breaking work and after she'd been at it for an hour or so, she stood up, placed her hands on her hips and arched her aching back. As she glanced towards the track, as she always did, just in case Arthur should appear, she gasped aloud as she saw him in the distance, coming round the corner of the lane. He had another man with him and at first, Elizabeth didn't recognise him.

She could see there was something familiar about the way he walked, throwing out one foot slightly with each step. Then suddenly, a light of recognition flashed in her mind. It was Will! He looked older and broader, and walked with a slight stoop as he climbed the track, but it was definitely him.

Elizabeth exclaimed his name and started to run down the track towards the two men.

'Will!' she shouted, 'Where have you sprung from?'

She embraced Arthur, saying how good it was to see him home at last, then turned to Will.

'You're a sight for sore eyes and no mistake, our Will!'

'It's good to see you Liz,' Will said quietly. 'There was a time I didn't think I would see any of you ever again.'

With that, he threw his arms around her and hugged her close. Elizabeth linked arms with both of them and the three of them trudged happily up the track towards the cottage. As they approached, Elizabeth called out to young Jane to come and meet her Uncle Will, and she skipped across the clearing.

As they entered the cottage, Martha was sitting by the fire and Will was shocked at her appearance. She had aged far more than the nine years that had passed since he'd left Banghams

Wood. Her ready smile was gone, and she just looked blankly at him as he entered the room, not seeming to recognise him. She seemed to have shrunk physically and her face was marked with the lines that told of pain she had endured.

Will looked round at Elizabeth, searching her face for answers, but she just shook her head sadly. He realised that once they were alone, he would be able to get his answers, but this was not the time.

'Let me get some food together Will, and then you can tell us where in the world you've been all these years.'

As she busied herself, Arthur and Will washed at the pump, teasing young Jane by splashing her with water as, stripped to the waist, they threw it over themselves. Elizabeth, hearing Jane's laughter, glanced out of the window to see what was going on. She smiled as she watched them, thinking that this Will who had returned seemed rather different than the man who had left on that fateful night. He seemed happier somehow, and more confident. She wondered whether he already knew that James hadn't died that night and in fact, had no idea who had punched him to the ground.

Finally the food was ready, and she called out to them to come inside. Arthur and Will put on their shirts, and they all sat down at the table to eat, all except Martha, who said she wasn't hungry.

As they ate their meal, Will was keen to find out about the rest of the family. He was surprised to hear that Joe was married now, to a girl from Dale Coppice and that they had a daughter, another Elizabeth! He of course asked after Abigail and was pleased that Joe was taking care of her and that she had a son, Michael who was growing into a fine boy despite his unfortunate beginnings. It appeared that Will had been given the news about James by Arthur, as they travelled back from Gloucester. Although he was relieved that he was no longer in danger of being arrested, he said that he was actually sorry that he hadn't finished him off that night.

'He damn well deserved it for what he did to our Abigail!' he declared.

He welcomed the news that Richard was now married to Margaret Andrews, daughter of the Bridgnorth grain merchant and had therefore risen in status. They chatted for a while about all the rest of the family and then Elizabeth's patience finally ran out, anxious as she was to find out where he had been all these years.

'Come on then Will, what happened after you left here?'

'Well, it's a long story,' he said, 'it's difficult to know where to start. Did you get the letter I sent you?'

'Aye, we did, although it didn't tell us much, did it? Except that you were bound for the Americas!'

'That's right, I set sail aboard the Matilda the day after I sent the letter off to you.

They all settled back to listen as Will began,

'When I left you, I managed to buy my passage to Gloucester on the Lucky Lady, then I travelled on a boat to Bristol and that's where I ended up for the next year or so. There was plenty of work on the docks, loading ships for the Africa trade and unloading the cotton and sugar from the Caribbean.

I heard many stories about the conditions on the ships travelling from Africa to the Caribbean loaded with human cargo, more dreadful than I care to share with you, Liz. I had thought that I might travel to America that way, but soon decided that I would have to find a different route as I couldn't stomach being a part of that nightmare world.

I still had a hankering for the New World as it appeared that, with a little luck, a man could make his fortune there. A better prospect seemed to be to join a ship bound for Williamsburg, Virginia, and make my way inland from there. Eventually, I had saved a little money, enough to pay my passage, steerage of course, and to have a bit left over to help me get settled in America. I took my chance when I heard the Matilda was preparing to set sail carrying goods for the colonies, along with people who were intent on making a new life in the New World.

'That's when I wrote you the letter Liz.'

They had all been listening intently, particularly Jimmy, who was eager to hear about the world outside the Gorge. Working down on the river, he had often wondered where the never-ending flow of water ended up. Arthur had of course, often talked to him about Gloucester Docks, but the world beyond that, had remained a mystery to them all.

'That was quite a shock to us all Will, to know you were already aboard the Matilda and on your way to the other side of the world. We feared we would never see you again!'

Will smiled.

'Well, here I am. I wish I could say that the journey across the ocean was a pleasant one, but I cannot.'

'It must have been exciting though!' Jimmy piped up, eyes shining.

'Well, we all started off with high expectations. It did seem like the start of a great adventure. We were going to a new world full of opportunity, where a man could thrive and build a good life for himself and his family. As we cast off from the Bristol docks, the deck was full of people waving goodbye to loved ones standing on the quayside, who they may never see again. There were smiles and tears aplenty, I can tell you.

'It didn't take long to realise however, that this was going to be no easy passage. Conditions below decks were dark and cramped, each person confined to a narrow bunk piled two high and with not enough length for a man to lay with his legs outstretched. What luggage we had, which wasn't much, had to share the space with us. Food was scarce, consisting largely of a kind of porridge made with oats and water, and a biscuit or two, or a lump of bread and a cup of gruel. Occasionally there was a piece of fruit to vary the diet a little. The privy was a platform of open planks at the prow of the ship, to be used with little privacy.

We knew the passage would take around six or seven weeks, depending on the weather. The captain told us the Atlantic storms could be terrifying, as we were soon to find out. Sailing largely into the prevailing winds, progress would sometimes be slow he told us, and our exact time of arrival in the New World was unpredictable.

We did our best to settle into the routine of life aboard ship. Many were seasick to begin with. It was difficult to sleep because of the noise, the feeling of being shut in, and the uncomfortable thought of the ocean many fathoms deep below us.

By the end of the first week, we were beginning to realise just what an epic journey we were on. We had left the land far behind us and there was none ahead of us, just rolling seas as far as the eye could see in every direction. The nights were the worst. At least during the day we could go up on deck for a period and see the horizon, which helped us cope with the sea-sickness. At night, however, below decks it was dark, with the smell of unwashed bodies and vomit constantly increasing.'

'It sounds horrible, Will,' Elizabeth said softly.

'It truly was,' Will replied, 'however, we had made our decision to come, and we knew we had no alternative other than to tolerate whatever the journey threw at us. It was about twenty-one days out that dysentery struck. Liz, Arthur, I can't tell you how horrendous it was. People unable to get themselves up on deck had to shit where they lay. If they had relatives with them, they had to clean them up and try to make them comfortable. Some had no relatives, like me, and I dreaded becoming ill, but I managed somehow to avoid the dysentery, thank God.

'The rats began to multiply, and lice were everywhere by then. People began to die, particularly the old and frail, and many a body was consigned to the deep. Children too succumbed, and that was piteous to witness. Parents were distraught, carrying their little ones up to the deck to be slid off the board into the icy waters of the Atlantic Ocean. Just as many died, some were born. Three little ones had come into the world on that ship by the time we reached America.

'We were about four weeks out when we encountered our first Atlantic storm. We know the Severn can be wild, but this was something completely different. Huge waves, sometimes as high as a house crashed around the ship, tossing it about like so much driftwood. Some of the crew had to scramble in the rigging to furl up the sails or they would have been ripped clean off by the force of the wind and water. The passengers were all ordered below decks in case they might be washed overboard. One member of the crew had been up in the rigging when the ship took a dive into the trough of a huge wave and the force of it tore his hands from the ropes and he plunged into the ocean, never to be seen again. Conditions below decks had by now become almost unbearable and we lay, petrified in our bunks, clinging on for dear life as the ship was thrown around. Some people had fallen out onto the floor as the ship plunged down into a trough, and stayed there, unable to drag themselves up long enough to crawl back into their bunks. All day the storm raged, but thankfully, by nightfall, had begun to subside. There were other storms as our journey progressed but none as vicious as that first one.

'After five weeks, we were all desperate to see land again. Of the fifty people who began the journey, ten of the passengers and one crewman had perished and the rest of us were weak from lack of decent food. Day after day we searched the horizon for some clue that land was near. Then, one morning we saw birds circling some way off and knew that our ordeal would soon end. The next day, some of us were on deck when a cry of 'Land Ahoy!' went up from the Crow's Nest. We slept better that night, knowing that the next day we would be arriving in the New World to begin our new life.'

Will realised that the room had become dark apart from the light from the fire. Elizabeth got up and lit the candles.

'My story is only half told but it's late and perhaps the telling of the rest of it will have to wait,' he said, smiling.

Jimmy protested, desperate to hear about the New World, but Elizabeth agreed with Will.

'You're right Will, even though we're all eager to hear it. But it's right good to have you home, and no mistake!' she declared.

With Jane's help she cleared away the remnants from the meal, handing the scraps to Martha to take out to the hog pen. After she left the room, Will asked Elizabeth what was wrong with her.

'We don't know Will, but she has a lot of pain and sometimes loses blood. She's not been her usual cheerful self for a while now, but we will just have to see what happens.'

Arthur brought a pail of water from the pump and after visiting the privy one by one, they splashed over their faces and prepared for bed. Elizabeth made up a bed for Will on the bench and then hugged him tightly, saying,

'It's so good to have you home safe and sound Will, I've missed you all these years.'

'I know Liz, I've missed you all too, more than you'll ever know.'

Chapter 11

The next day Will was determined to visit Dale Coppice to see Joe and Liz. Joe had been in his thoughts often over the last years. He knew he hadn't been fair to him, resenting the fact that he had wanted to leave Banghams Wood. Once he himself had made the break, he understood exactly why Joe had needed to get away. He could see now that the Darby Works represented change to Joe, and that is what he craved. He had been unable to accept that coppicing and burning charcoal was to be his life. Once he himself was forced to leave and travel into the world outside the Gorge, Will came to realise that his resentment towards Joe had been fuelled by his own desire to escape, but he had felt trapped in the Wood by responsibilities after Walter died. He was eager to see Joe and to show him that he no longer felt any animosity towards him. In fact, he had decided that he also would like to settle in Dale Coppice and maybe find work at the Coalbrookdale Company. He had had enough of travelling the world. He was home and this is where he intended to stay.

Assuring Elizabeth and the family that he would be back in a day or two, to finish his story, he set off with Jimmy the next morning, towards the river, intending to ask Bert Rogers to ferry him across. Jimmy was full of questions, of course, and as they walked Will told him about some of the more pleasant experiences he'd had in America. He told him about the vastness of the plains, the mountains and the wagon trains setting out loaded with settlers, full of dreams of a better life. Jimmy was enthralled and determined that one day he would take that trip down the river to find his own fortune.

The Severn was running strongly as Bert skilfully steered the coracle towards the northern bank. The wharf was busy, with several boats unloading or waiting to be reloaded with goods bound for Gloucester. Will could see that it had been extended since the day he'd left on the Lucky Lady all those years ago. He clambered out of the coracle, and up the bank to the Madeley road, then took the lane towards Coalbrookdale. As he strode up the valley, he began to realise the extent of the changes that had occurred since he had left the Gorge. The track itself was now a cobbled road. The further he went the louder was the sound of metal hammering on metal. The hiss of steam and the roar of the furnaces assaulted his ears. His lungs began to react to the acrid smoke from the piles of coal off to one side of the track, presumably being burned to produce the coke needed for the furnaces. The light of the sun was now dimmed by the smoke hanging in the air. There were horse-drawn wagons moving up the track from the wharf, carrying coal and ironstone, and every so often, one would be coming in the other direction carrying goods bound for the river. The overall impression was of a hive of industry, and Will had to admit that it was exciting.

It was mid-morning when he reached the settlement in Dale Coppice. As he strode into the hamlet, he saw a young woman with her back to him, filling a pail at the pump. A young boy was waiting to help her to carry it. As soon as Will saw the boy, with his bright red hair, he knew that this was Michael, and the young woman must be Abigail. He called out her name and she turned to face him.

'Will!' she declared, 'Is it really you?'

'Aye it is lass,' he answered, and running towards her now, he picked her up and spun her round, as he had used to do when she was a little girl. Michael was confused. Who was this man who picked up his mother and swung her round?

Abigail noticed the puzzled and rather frightened expression on his face and said,

'Michael, this is your uncle Will!'

'Hello Michael,' Will said.

'H. Hello,' he answered hesitantly.

At that moment, Liz, who was now heavily pregnant, appeared at the cottage door and linking Will's arm, Abigail led him over to her, with Michael trailing behind, struggling with the half-filled pail of water.

'Liz, this is our brother Will, the one that went to the Americas years ago.'

Liz greeted Will, saying she was pleased to meet him at last as she had heard so much about him. She invited him in and asked if he would like some ale, which he readily accepted. Abigail asked him whether he'd seen Elizabeth yet and he explained that he had come upriver with Arthur and been over at Banghams Wood the previous night.

Liz explained that of course, Joe was at the works, but would be home for supper. She was sure he would be happy to see Will as he had often spoken about him over the years and wondered whether he would ever return. Will said he was glad to be back and hoped to stay now. In fact, he said, he wondered whether he might find work at the Company.

'Well,' Liz told him, 'They do seem to be taking more men on every week, so it shouldn't be too difficult to find something.'

Will and Abigail chatted about life in the Gorge and within the Bangham family since Will had left. She briefly considered telling him about her meeting with Furlong but decided against it in case he should take it upon himself to confront him again. Will said he was amazed at the way the Works had grown. Given the huge increase in river traffic, it had been obvious that great changes were afoot. Abigail asked him about his adventures since he had left the Wood, but Will said he would wait until Joe got home before going into all that, rather than having to repeat everything. To Liz's delight, Will took great interest in little Elizabeth, playing 'pick up stones' in front of the fire with her while she herself got on with preparing the evening's meal.

Finally, there was a rattle on the latch, the door opened, and the two brothers set eyes on each other for the first time in nine years. Will had been a bit uneasy, wondering how Joe would react, as they hadn't parted on the best of terms. In the event, Joe shouted,

'Will! I had heard that you came upriver yesterday, but I could hardly believe it! By, it's good to see thee lad!' he exclaimed, striding over to Will, and throwing his arms around him. The two brothers embraced and slapped each other on the back in greeting, then stepped back to observe what changes the years apart had wrought.

Joe thought Will looked older and the lines on his face spoke of hardships endured but overcome. He looked as though he could do with some good food inside him, as though he hadn't eaten too well for some time. Later, as Will recounted his journey back across the ocean, which had been no less unpleasant than the one that had carried him to America, they understood why. In the meantime, Liz had served up the hearty stew and they sat down to enjoy the meal, Will tucking in with gusto as though he had indeed been starving for weeks.

After they had finished and Elizabeth was tucked up in bed, Joe wanted to know what had happened to Will since leaving the Wood. He quickly told them about the outward journey, but out of sensitivity to Abigail who he still thought protectively of as his little sister, he missed out some of the less pleasant details. Then he went on to recount some of his exploits in America, how he had worked for a while on the docks in Williamsburg, and then, when he had saved up a sum

of money, had heard of a wagon train of English settlers heading west through the Appalachian Mountains into a country
where a man could claim 300 acres of land and set up his own
farm. While in Williamsburg he had met and fallen in love with
a young woman, Sarah, and they were married before setting
out on the journey West.

Will looked sad and pensive when he spoke of Sarah, and
when Joe asked about her, his face darkened, and he fell silent
for a while. When he had recovered himself, he explained
that Sarah had been pregnant by the time they arrived in
the Shenandoah Valley after an arduous journey through the
mountains. He said it was hard to describe the conditions he
found there. He was given land, but nothing else. They had to
clear it of forest and build a log cabin to live in. The settlers
had helped each other to build their cabins, much as people
did in the Gorge, for which he was grateful. He said he could
never have done it alone.

In the meantime they had to live in the covered wagons,
which afforded little shelter against the weather. Finally, after
four months they had their cabin. By then, Sarah was almost
due to deliver their child. She went into labour in the middle
of the night and fought bravely to deliver the baby. It turned
out that the child was trying to come out feet first and Will
didn't know what to do to help. Neither could he leave her to
bring help. She battled for a full day before weakened by the
long and difficult journey and the conditions they had been
living in, she succumbed and she and the baby, a boy, were
buried the next day.

Telling them about this had been desperately hard for Will.
Although it had all happened four years ago, it was still raw.
He had loved Sarah dearly and they had dreamt of building a
life together. He knew he would never love anyone else the
way he had loved her. After Sarah and the baby had died, he
said he lost heart and couldn't face clearing the land to farm

it alone. He managed to sell it and the cabin to a settler in another wagon train which had just arrived, bought a wagon, and returned, defeated, to Williamsburg. There, he worked for a couple more years on the docks and then decided he'd had enough of the New World and would make his way back home. At that point he hadn't known what he would have to face regarding what he had done to Furlong, but his desire to come home had been greater than his fear, and he had boarded a ship loaded with tobacco three months ago, bound for Bristol.

By now the light had gone and they were all ready for bed. Michael had already fallen asleep on the straw mattress laid out for Will. They all expressed their sorrow at the loss of his wife and child, and Joe said he could stay with them as long as he wished. He would speak to Mr Ford the manager at the works in the morning, to see if he could get him work either at the furnaces or in the foundry.

Will thanked him and said he was glad to be home at last, and of course, relieved that there would be no repercussions about the reason for his departure. Out of respect for Abigail no one actually said what that was, although Joe and Abigail knew exactly what he meant.

The next day, Joe found Mr Ford and asked about a job for Will, explaining that he had just returned from America but now wanted to settle in the Gorge. Unfortunately Mr Ford, after some thought, said he wouldn't be able to find him something at the moment as he'd just promised work to a group of men from further up the valley. Joe was disappointed but understood and thanked him anyway. Just as Joe turned to leave, Mr Ford said he did need more men to work in a new mine he was planning to lease, and if Will was interested, he would be happy to give him a try.

When Joe returned home that evening, Will was still there, waiting for news and was of course disappointed that there was no job for him at the works. Joe told him about the new coalmine that was being opened up and Mr Ford had said there would be work there for him if he wanted it. Although Will had always sworn that he would never go into the mines, he knew he couldn't be too choosy right now and reluctantly decided to take up the offer. The next day he went back to Banghams Wood to give Elizabeth the news and to finish the story of his time in America. The following Sunday Margaret visited Banghams Wood, having heard the news that Will was back. They had a joyous reunion and Will had to tell his story all over again, much to Jimmy's delight.

After they had eaten their dinner, Will returned to Dale Coppice but before heading down to the river, insisted on walking Margaret back to the gate at the Hall. When they were alone and walking along the track, he asked her whether any-thing had ever been said about why he had disappeared after his attack on Furlong. Margaret assured him that as Furlong had eventually fully recovered, but apparently had no memory of who had attacked him, no one had ever connected him to the attack. As Abigail was living in Dale Coppice and rarely returned to the south of the river, she was sure no one would ever connect Abigail's child, and therefore the likely attacker to Will, so he needn't worry. Of course, Margaret was unaware that James Furlong had already met Abigail with her child who was so obviously his son, at Madeley Wood market. If she had been, perhaps she wouldn't have been so sure.

When Will arrived back at Dale Coppice he found an un-folding tragedy. It was a week before Liz's due date, but she had become worried during the day because she couldn't feel the child moving inside her. She knew the signs because of her first pregnancy, which had resulted in a premature still birth. This time she had believed it would be different because she was almost full term, and everything had seemed fine. She and Joe were now distraught, sure they had lost another child. When she finally went into labour at midnight two days later, it was with some terror that she told Joe to bring Mrs Spencer to help Abigail to attend to her. She was right to be worried, the baby, a boy, was already dead. Liz and Joe were heartbroken once again. Losing another child like this was devastating and they began to wonder whether they would ever have other children. The baby, born dead, couldn't be baptised, and therefore couldn't be buried in consecrated ground and consequently they buried him in the woods. Will's grief at the loss of his own wife and child, never far from his mind, resurfaced and the Bangham cottage in Dale Coppice was consumed by grief for many weeks.

Chapter 12

1728 had brought changes to the Darby Works. Abraham Darby's son, now seventeen years old, joined the firm, and managed the company along with Mr Ford. Joe was pleased to see another Darby involved in the Works. He had had a lot of respect for Abraham Darby, and Joe could see that the young man had many of his father's qualities. He was to see a lot of Abraham over the next few years, as he was often to be found working alongside the men, determined to learn all he could about the business of making and forging iron in preparation for one day taking over the running of the Works. Trade was good, the high-quality domestic goods they were producing were selling well, not only in England, but right across the oceans, as far as Africa and America.

Will had been taken on by Henry Cartwright, the gaffer at one of the mines leased by Mr Ford. He had of course been aware that mining was tough work, but he hadn't been prepared for the conditions underground. First of all, to get into the mine involved climbing into a cage suspended by a single hook attached to a gantry at the top of the shaft. Using a wheel and pulley arrangement, propelled by a horse, the cage was lowered the hundred or so feet to the bottom of the shaft. That was terrifying at first. Will had heard more than one story of cages breaking loose and plummeting down the shaft, taking men to certain death. After a while he got used to it, but the journey to the coalface, dragging a wagon behind him through the tunnel with only a candle to light the way, was always an ordeal. Once at the coalface itself, he had to toil with a pick, hacking away at the coal then loading it onto the wagon, which when it was full, had to be hauled back to the bottom of the shaft, where he transferred coal to the cage to be raised to the surface. He worked a twelve-hour shift from six in the morning until six at night. The work was hard and the wages poor, but Will was glad to be able to pay his way and was determined to stick at it until he could find something better.

Joe decided that he needed to expand his cottage now that Will was living with them, and together they added two more rooms. One was for Will and Michael to sleep in and the other provided a much improved scullery and wash house to cater for the needs of their increased family. Joe was glad to have Will around, to share the responsibilities of financing the household. For a while, everyone was happy with the arrangement. Joe and Liz gradually recovered from the loss of their little boy and began to hope that they would soon have another child.

Christmas that year was particularly special. With two wages coming in, the family were able to buy a few extras, and invited Arthur and Elizabeth and the children over for the Christmas Day feast. The weather, though cold, was dry, as thankfully the snows didn't arrive until well into January. It was good to be able to gather together, a rare occurrence these days. Elizabeth brought with her some news about Richard and Margaret. Margaret had told her that the horseman, Fred, had been over to Bridgnorth a few weeks ago and was given the news that they had been delivered of a little girl on the 3rd of October. They had called her Elizabeth, which pleased the child's aunt, of course. There was also much joyful reminiscing of years gone by, and as is usually the case on such occasions, the memories evoked were largely the happier ones. As Elizabeth and Arthur said their goodbyes, they all agreed that this was something they should do every year. It was just as well that they didn't know what 1729 would bring.

It was during the third week of February that Liz realised she was pregnant again. She was of course nervous about it and whether this time her baby would be brought successfully into the world. She told Joe she expected to give birth sometime during September. He was overjoyed, although also a little apprehensive.

The snows came and went without interfering too much with life in Dale Coppice. The Coalbrookdale Company was busier than ever, now casting parts for steam engines which were beginning to be installed in more and more pits in the area. They provided a more reliable method of pumping water from the mines, as well as lowering and raising the cages the miners used to get down to the coalface. This was a growing market and as usual the Company was at the forefront of the development of the technology. More workers were moving into the district every year and Dale Coppice was getting rather crowded. Some of the newcomers didn't fit in too well, many of them being heavy drinkers and best classified as rogues and vagabonds.

Liz and Abigail tried their best to keep their children away from them, but it wasn't easy. Michael in particular seemed drawn to the children of the rowdier inhabitants. At twelve, he was developing a mind and a personality of his own and Abigail struggled to control him at times. He seemed particularly attracted to Tom Williams who was a year older and full of bravado. He swaggered about the place with an air of entitlement that annoyed most folks but captivated Michael, who was never far from his side. He had suffered years of mockery and teasing because of his bright red hair, which had made him self-conscious and rather withdrawn. Spotting his vulnerability, Tom knew that he could use it to his advantage and soon 'groomed' him into becoming his constant and often useful companion.

One day in May, Tom told Michael he needed help with something and that they would need to be away after supper, but not to tell anyone about it. Michael was in a quandary. He wanted to tell his mother. but knew if he did, she would stop him from going. Loyalty to Tom won out in the end and he slipped out of the cottage when the sun was sinking in the sky, to meet him on the track on Lincoln Hill as arranged. When Michael asked Tom where they were going, he just smiled and said they were off to make some money, but when Michael asked how, he told him to wait and see. They strode off towards the river, but at the crossroads they came upon a couple of older men. They had a dog with them and were carrying sacks containing something heavy. Michael knew enough to realise that these were men who would probably not be up to much good. He hesitated and told Tom he wanted to go home, but Tom and the men broke out laughing, saying he was just a baby wanting to go home to his mother. Michael flushed bright pink then squared his shoulders and declared that he was no baby and he had only been joking. Of course he was going with them, he said.

The group set off, not as Michael had expected, towards the river, but parallel to it. They moved quickly over fields and through woods for two hours, Michael struggling to keep up with them. The light was virtually gone as they arrived at what was apparently their intended destination and sat down in the shelter of some trees to plan their next move. Michael was already worried when one of the men took out a tin of blacking, and handed it round to the others, who began to black up their faces. Now he understood what this was all about. These men were poachers, intent on stealing rabbits or hares or some such. He was horrified. He had heard men talking about what happened to poachers if they were caught.

After the passing of an Act of Parliament some years back, a man could be transported across the ocean or even hanged for taking a single hare for the pot from private land! Michael wanted nothing to do with this. He desperately wanted to go home but knew that he could never find his own way back in the dark. He tried to refuse to black his face, but the men insisted that he was one of them now and must get blacked up along with the rest of them. As he tried to resist, one of them grabbed hold of him and held his hands tight behind his back as the other ruffian smeared the blacking over his face.

Michael was terrified but knew there was no way out of it for him now. He was one of this gang of men intent on poaching and however much he wished he'd stayed at home and not listened to Tom; matters were now out of his hands. The men took heavy clubs out of the sacks. Michael and Tom were given the empty sacks and told to pick up the dead rabbits as they emerged from their burrows and were clubbed to death.

One of the men took the dog and went off in search of burrows. The dog was now straining at its leash, sensing blood. As it was let loose it yelped and scrabbled the ground at the entrance to a burrow on the far side of a small hillock, and after a few minutes rabbits began appearing at the exit, to be expertly clubbed by the other man. Of course, some got away but many were killed as they tried to escape. Tom and Michael collected the bodies, still warm, some of them not quite dead. They were told to finish them off by swinging them by their legs against the nearest tree. Michael was sickened. Of course he'd eaten rabbit many times, but never before had he been responsible for taking life.

A cry went up,

'Right men, that's enough, let's be off before the gamekeeper comes a lookin' what all the noise is about.'

At that moment there was a loud crack, and then another. This was unmistakeably gunshot. They all fell to the ground, peering into the darkness to find out where the shots had come from.

Then came a shout,

'Stay where you are! If anybody moves it'll be the end of 'im!'

One by one, men carrying guns appeared out of the blackness under the trees into the moonlight that was now flooding the clearing. Plainly this was not just one gamekeeper. It soon became apparent that the local militia had been summoned and now surrounded the gang, caught red-handed with sacks full of rabbits. The poacher holding the dog leash, let go, telling the dog to attack, but it hadn't got further than twenty yards before it was shot dead. Plainly, being unarmed, the gang was cornered and soon arrested. Michael began to cry, completely unable to comprehend what was happening to him. How had he got into this dreadful situation? He was a good lad, never in trouble before, and now he would go to prison – or worse!

Chapter 13

The Captain of the Militiamen waved his gun at the miscreants, telling them to sit on the ground with their backs to one another. One of the others stepped forward with ropes and bound their hands tightly. Michael was crying, his tears running down his cheeks in rivulets, streaking the blacking as they went. He was terrified, and then horrified as he felt the wetness seeping into his breeches as he lost control of his bladder.

They were held like that for what seemed like hours, until a wagon appeared through the gloom, and they were all loaded into it. Michael realised that they were being taken to a lock up somewhere, but not being exactly sure where he was, he had no idea where that would be. It could have been Shrewsbury, or Much Wenlock, or even Bridgnorth. One of the men asked the Bailiff where they were being taken but was told that they would know soon enough. Accompanied by four of the armed militiamen and the Bailiff, all on horseback, they set off along a path through the woods until they reached a rough trackway.

The moon was up now, and it was clear by the downward trajectory the track was taking that they were heading towards the river. For several minutes Michael was hoping that perhaps they were being taken to the Madeley lock up, but when they met the river, the party turned to the right and his heart sank as he realised that they must be heading out of the Gorge and over to Much Wenlock. The chances of his mother knowing where he had been taken lessened with every mile. They were still sitting back-to-back, so he couldn't see Tom, or either of the men, but he could smell their fear. They all knew that, caught red-handed with their spoils, they would be shown little mercy. For sure it would be hard labour, transportation or even worse, the gallows for them.

His assumption as to where they were going was correct and before long, they crossed the Buildwas bridge and headed south along the track towards Much Wenlock. An hour later they halted outside a two-storey black and white half-timbered building next to a church. In the half light, the building looked huge to Michael, who was only used to seeing rough built single storey cottages. They clambered out of the wagon and with the guns prodding their backs were herded through a heavy iron door at the base of the building into a dank, dark cell and the door clanged shut behind them. Through the iron grille in the door, the Bailiff told them they would soon be brought before the Magistrate but failed to say when that would be. One of the men asked for water but the Bailiff refused to bring any, saying that they would be given food and water in the morning.

It was cold as death in the cell, and there was only the flagstone floor to sit on, with a bucket in the corner where prisoners could relieve themselves. The stink of unwashed bodies and years of filth had soaked into the very stones, pervading the air. Each breath Michael took made him gag as he sat shivering in the corner, huddled up, trying to conserve what warmth his body still held. He was utterly without hope. How would his mother know where to find him? Who would help him now? He'd been caught red-handed and knew there would be no mercy shown. For once, Tom was quiet. Faced with the reality of what he'd done his habitual bravado seemed to have deserted him, and he sat, his legs drawn up and his bowed head resting on his arms clasped around his knees. The two men began quarrelling between themselves, each blaming the other for their predicament, until the gaoler shouted out to them to be quiet, or they would feel the force of his truncheon about their ears.

There was no sleep for any of them for what was left of the night. A few hours later the key turned in the lock and the gaoler opened the door. The light flooded in, and half blinded them after the semi darkness of the cell. He entered with some bread on a platter and a jug of water and placed them on the floor, another gaoler standing behind him to ensure the men didn't try to escape. Their hands were still tied together and with some difficulty they scrambled to get at the food, one of the ruffians pushing Michael out of the way to grab a handful of bread. The other man, who was older than the first and seemed to have a shred of humanity left, took some of the bread, tore a chunk off and gave it to Michael. They each took a swig of water which quenched their thirst for the moment but was not nearly enough to last the day.

Tom, who had regained some of his spirit, asked the gaoler when they would be going before the magistrate. He told them that it would be the following morning before he arrived, so they'd better make themselves comfortable, and with that, the door clanged shut once more, leaving them in semi darkness once again.

That day was the longest of Michael's life. Hour after hour passed with no respite from the fear that was eating away at his guts. They were given a little more bread and water later in the day, and a small piece of cheese each. The only light entering the cell was through the small grille in the door, no more than eight inches square. In the half light, a rat would occasionally make its leisurely way across the room, stopping only to collect the odd breadcrumb from the floor before strolling away and disappearing into the gloom again. Occasionally one of them would relieve themselves using the bucket but without any privacy. No one would tell them anything about what was to happen next. Michael slipped into a fitful sleep once or twice during the day and by the time night fell was so exhausted that mercifully he fell fast asleep and dreamed of home and his mother. When he awoke Michael realised once again that she would have no idea where he was. He was ashamed that his foolishness in following Tom Williams had led him to inflict this on his mother. How would she ever find him? He only hoped that she had heard news of the arrests. The disappearance of Tom as well as himself might prompt her to make the connection and realise that perhaps it was they who had been arrested and taken to one of the Courts in the area. He could do nothing now but hope that this was the case and that she would somehow find a way to help him.

His thoughts were interrupted by the sound of the key being turned in the lock. The heavy door swung open, letting in the early morning light and mercifully, a breath of fresh air. The magistrate would be arriving in a few hours they were told, and they would then be taken up to the courtroom above the cell. They were given a bowl of thin gruel each which they had to eat with their fingers, but they were all so hungry that it took them no time at all until they had cleared their bowls.

As the morning progressed, they could hear the sounds of people chatting and carriages rumbling along the street outside the door of the gaol and the occasional neighing of horses as men shouted instructions at them. There was a general bustle about the place and the sound of furniture being moved and footsteps treading the boards above the cell. They realised with some trepidation that the activity above their heads probably signified that the courtroom was being prepared for their appearance in front of the Magistrate. Eventually the door was opened once again, and a couple of gaolers armed with pistols instructed them to follow. They were led along to the other end of the building and up some stone steps to a door which was obviously leading into the courtroom.

At the door, Michael rocked on his heels, halting for a moment until he was prodded in the back with the pistol being held by one of the gaolers. He was conscious of his own appearance, his face still smeared with black, his breeches dirty and smelling of his own urine. What would everyone think of him? He surely didn't look out of place with these ruffians, but he knew he didn't belong here. If only he hadn't been so foolish!

The disgusted looks on the faces of the people in the public gallery as he walked down to the front of the courtroom, not to mention the way the Magistrate peered down at him with undisguised revulsion as he stood in the dock, convinced him that he was right. He could expect no mercy here. He was correct on that score but matters deteriorated further when they were told that because of the seriousness of the charges they faced, and the fact that they had been caught red-handed, the Magistrate had decided that they would be sent to Bridgnorth to appear at the next Quarter Sessions on Midsummer Day to be tried before a jury for poaching. They all knew that this meant the death penalty was to be considered, should they be found guilty.

Michael's legs threatened to give way. Bridgnorth! He knew that was another ten miles further away from his home in Dale Coppice and he was now convinced that his mother would never find him, and that he could be hanged without her knowing a thing about it. At that point, darkness took him, and he slipped silently to the floor.

Chapter 14

In Dale Coppice, two days earlier, Abigail was beside herself with worry. She hadn't seen Michael since supper. She hadn't even seen him leave the cottage as she'd been busy in the scullery, and so had no idea where he'd gone to. Night was falling fast and there was a full moon rising above the trees.

Joe and Will went around the clearing, knocking on cottage doors to ask if he was there. They knew he often hung around with Tom Williams and were not surprised to find, when they reached his home that he also was missing. As usual his father was drunk and completely unconcerned about the whereabouts of his son. His mother, however, was obviously upset and worried. She told them Tom had disappeared some time ago without saying where he was going.

Joe and Will searched the coppice and surrounding area until the small hours of the morning, of course, without success. Abigail feared the worst, either something had happened to him, or he'd got himself involved in something bad with Tom Williams, and, God forbid, had been caught. They all knew that there were poachers working the area, and each of them had the same thought. Where else would they have gone at dead of night without telling anyone? Still, though, the consequences were too awful to contemplate and each of them kept their thoughts to themselves.

After a sleepless night, Abigail watched the sun rise in the sky and wondered where on earth her son was. All that day she stood sentinel at the cottage door, waiting and praying for him to reappear. After another largely sleepless night she declared that she would go to find the Justice of the Peace in Much Wenlock, to see if he knew of any incidents in the area involving the boys. She knew it was at least an hour and a half's walk to Much Wenlock. Will and Joe were both working and wouldn't be able to go with her. They tried to delay her departure until the following Sunday when they would go themselves, but Abigail would have none of it. She had waited for news long enough and told them she would go by way of Banghams Wood, hoping that maybe young Jimmy or perhaps Arthur, if he wasn't away on the river, would go with her. She also knew she would have to pass by the Hall, which gave her some cause for concern. She had literally never set eyes on the place since the day she left it. She told herself she must take care not to be seen by anyone there. The last thing she wanted was for James Furlong to hear of her mission that day.

Fortunately, it was a fine day, and after she had eaten bread and dripping for breakfast and drunk a cup of water, Abigail threw her shawl around her shoulders and set off on her journey. Half an hour later she was knocking on Elizabeth's door in Banghams Wood. Pleased to see her, Elizabeth gave her a hug and asked her whatever was she doing here, and on her own too? Abigail recounted the events of the last few days and Elizabeth was obviously upset and worried at hearing that Michael was missing.

'I was wondering whether young Jimmy or Arthur, if he's here, might be able to come with me,' Abigail said, hopefully.

'I'm so sorry,' Elizabeth said, 'Arthur's away downriver and Jimmy's working on the coracles with Bert Rogers.'

Abigail was disappointed, but said she was determined to go anyway. Elizabeth said she would have gladly gone with her, but that she was currently nursing Martha, who was very ill, giving Abigail the distinct impression by sadly shaking her head, that it was only a matter of time. Abigail was obviously upset about Martha, but right now, her concern for her son over-rode all other emotions and she said,

'That's terrible Liz. Poor Martha. But then I must go alone. I need to find out what's happened to my son. I'll be alright. I'll go up past the Hall and take the track to Much Wenlock. I should be there before the sun's high in the sky.'

She went up to the bedroom to see Martha and was shocked by her appearance. She was very thin and pale and seemed to be struggling to breathe. Her face lightened when she saw Abigail, who bent down to kiss her forehead, saying,

'I hope you're soon feeling better, our Martha,' knowing full well that she never would.

Martha smiled wanly and nodded weakly. Abigail squeezed her hand and then quietly, sadly, turned and left the room. Elizabeth gave Abigail a drink of ale and some bread, and then waved her off as she disappeared along the track in the direction of the Hall.

As she passed by the gate into the Estate, she shivered, remembering the day Michael had been conceived. He had come to her room as she slept, and she had woken to feel his hands on her and his hot breath on her face. She'd tried to scream but he put his hand tight across her mouth until she could hardly breathe. Fear had made her give up the struggle. She had thought he would kill her if she resisted and so, she let him do what he had come to do. He had hurt her physically, of course, as she had never been with a man before, but the psychological harm he had inflicted on her would never go away. She could never quite rid herself of the feelings of guilt. She used to feel she must have brought it on herself by smiling at him one day as he entered the kitchen as she was cleaning the fireplace. Now that she was older, with more experience of the world, she knew that wasn't true. He had simply used her for his own gratification with no thought what effect that would have on her. Still, she felt that she should have resisted more strongly. And yet, she told herself, something good did come of it, and that was Michael, her pride and joy. And now, her mission was to find out what had happened to him.

She hurried along the track in the direction of Much Wenlock. After half an hour or so, she came to a farm, and asked the woman who was hanging washing outside the farmhouse, if she was on the right track to Much Wenlock. The woman told her that she was and should be there in half an hour. The terrain was rather rough, with many ups and downs in the stony road, and it was well over an hour before she found herself walking down the main street in Much Wenlock, towards the black and white timbered Guild Hall, where she assumed the Court and the Justice of the Peace would be.

She found the stone steps at the end of the building and climbed up to the door at the top. It was open and as she entered found herself in a long dark room with a long table at the far end behind which stood several large, ornate seats. She realised this must be the courtroom. To one side of the door, a clerk sat behind a raised desk. He glanced down at her with some disdain as he surveyed her appearance. She realised that he probably wouldn't be used to seeing someone of her station in life standing before him demanding his attention. He asked her what she wanted, and she stated that she had come to see the Justice of the Peace. He told her that the Justice of the Peace was a busy man and before he found out whether he would see her or not, he needed to know what her business was.

Nervously, she explained that she had come to find out what had happened to her son, who had gone missing, and she feared that something had happened to him. The clerk enquired what name this boy went by. Abigail explained that his name was Michael Bangham and that he went missing three days ago from Dale Coppice, Coalbrookdale.

At the sound of the name and address of the missing boy, a light of realisation illuminated the clerk's face, and he opened up the ledger before him. Running his finger down the page, he halted about halfway down and said,

'Yes, here we have it. I'm sorry to have to inform you that Michael Bangham is to be sent this very day to Bridgnorth Gaol to await trial at the Assize, for poaching and trespass, along with the rest of the miscreants he was taken with.'

Abigail's legs buckled and she grabbed the rail in front of the desk.

'I must see him,' she finally managed.

'Not possible I'm afraid,' replied the clerk in a dismissive fashion.

'But please, I must, I've walked from Dale Coppice today, but I won't be able to get to Bridgnorth. Please, just let me speak to him. He's my only child and I'm on my own. Please, I just need to see him before he's taken.'

Something in Abigail's tone touched the clerk and he told her to wait there while he found out whether there was anything he could do. After ten minutes or so he returned, instructing her to follow him. He led her down the stone steps and through the room beneath the courtroom. At the end were two huge iron doors with small grilles in them. Abigail realised with horror that her beloved son must be locked up in one of them. Between the two doors a huge, rough looking man was standing and it was obvious that he was the gaoler. The clerk spoke to him, explaining that the woman he brought had been given permission to speak briefly with her son, Michael Bangham. He nodded then stepped to one of the doors and called out,

'Bangham! You have a visitor!'

After a moment Michael's distraught face, still smeared with blacking, appeared at the grille.

Seeing Abigail standing there he called out.

'Mother! I'm so sorry Mother!'

At the sight of her son, Abigail burst into tears, then realising that this wouldn't be helping him, calmed herself and set about trying to understand how he came to be in this situation. Peering behind him through the gloom she could just make out Tom Williams, and immediately then, knew exactly how he'd got involved in all of this.

'I'm a 'feared Mother,' Michael said. 'They've told us what might become of us.'

'Try not to worry Michael,' Abigail forced herself to say. 'I'll find a way to come to Bridgnorth.'

A voice called out from behind Michael's back,

'Will you tell me ma missus? She'll be right worried.'

Abigail was too angry with Tom for getting Michael involved in all this, to make any reply.

'Right, that's it, missus,' said the gaoler, who had been standing beside her, 'time to go.'

Abigail put her fingers to the grille to touch Michael's in a desperate attempt to comfort him. Then the gaoler took her arm and dragged her away as she called out to him that she loved him. His voice quivered with emotion as he called after her,

'Mother, I'm so sorry!'

As Abigail left the Guildhall, she knew in her heart that Michael was in mortal peril. She understood as well as anyone what happened to convicted poachers. It was either the noose or transportation. Either way she knew it may well be a long time before she saw her son again, if ever.

Even though she felt sick, she knew she should eat something. She'd had nothing since leaving Elizabeth, and she had the long walk back to Dale Coppice before her. She had a few pence with her and bought some bread at the bakehouse. After she'd eaten it and drunk from the town pump, she set off wearily on her return journey. With her mind spinning, she barely noticed anything as she trudged along the track towards home. All she could think about was her beloved son in that horrible place, soon to be taken to an even worse one, with no certainty that he would ever escape it alive.

Bone weary, she decided that she must go straight back home rather than call in at Banghams Wood. The light was already fading as she made her way straight down to the river. There she found Jimmy by the coracle ferry and told him about Michael, asking him to tell Elizabeth. Then after she explained to Bert Rogers where she'd been, not being unsympathetic to poachers, he offered to take her over the river for free.

It was dusk as she walked up the track into the Coppice, almost stumbling with exhaustion. As soon as she entered the cottage she collapsed into the chair. Joe, who had just returned from the works, seeing what state she was in, asked,

'Abigail, whatever's the matter?'

The concern in his voice opened the floodgates and she began to rock back and forth, wailing and then crying, alerting them all to the fact that something dreadful must have happened. After five minutes or so, she had calmed down enough to tell them, through the sobs, that Michael was in Much Wenlock lockup and would soon be in gaol in Bridgnorth and on trial for poaching.

Everyone knew what that meant. and a shocked silence persisted for some seconds, until Joe finally stepped forward to put his arms round his sister, trying to reassure her that they would find a way to help her son. No one believed him.

When Abigail had calmed down, she remembered Tom Williams and asked Joe if he would go and tell his poor mother where her son was. As he stood outside their cottage door Joe could hear Williams shouting at his wife, obviously drunk as usual. Joe knocked on the door and after a minute or so, Tom's mother appeared. She had obviously suffered a blow to her face and Joe was tempted to go inside and sort the bully out once and for all. Of course, he knew better than to intervene between a man and his wife, and just quietly told her that Abigail had seen her son in the Much Wenlock Gaol. The poor woman reeled and grabbed the door jamb for support, thanked him for telling her and slowly closed the door, no doubt to suffer more abuse at the hands of her brute of a husband.

Chapter 15

1729: Troubles seldom come singly, and the following day, Joe received a message from one of the waggoners bringing materials up from the wharf. He had been asked by Jimmy to tell Joe that his sister Martha was very poorly, and anyone who wanted to see her again in this life, must go to her bedside as soon as possible.

It was Saturday and Joe decided the family would be able to visit her the next day. Abigail was horrified that with all the worry about Michael, she hadn't even told them about Martha. Of course, she couldn't have known just how ill she was, but still she should have prepared them for the bad news. As she had already seen her, Abigail offered to stay at home and look after little Elizabeth. She asked Joe to speak to Richard, if he was there, to ask him to find out when the Assize Court was to be held in Bridgnorth.

Will, Joe and Liz set off early, and were in Banghams Wood by mid-morning. As soon as they arrived, Elizabeth asked after Abigail. Jimmy had told them about Michael, and she knew Abigail would be distraught. Joe asked whether Richard would be coming to see Martha, and Elizabeth said she'd sent a message with Margaret who was asking Fred, the horseman at the Hall to pass it on to Richard when he next visited Andrews Grain Merchants. She was expecting him to come in the next day or two.

'Well, when he does come, Abigail said to ask him if he could find out when the Assize Court would be.' Joe said, 'I intend to go with her if I'm able.'

'I will, of course, and that's good, Joe, she's going to need plenty of support. But I'm right glad you've come, it doesn't look like our Martha's long for this world, as you'll see for yourselves.'

With that, Will and Joe went up to the bedroom and Liz, who felt she didn't know Martha very well and didn't want to intrude, stayed downstairs with Elizabeth, who offered her some herb tea. Joe and Will were shocked at Martha's appearance. She looked all skin and bone with her eyes closed and sunk into her head. Her breathing was very shallow, and it was obvious to them both that she wouldn't last long now. Joe sat down beside the bed and took her hand, stroking it gently. She opened her eyes and her lips curved into the special smile she reserved for her favourite brother, whispering,

'Joe, you came.'

'Of course I did lass,' he replied quietly.

'I'm weary Joe,' Martha whispered, then cried out in pain as whatever was attacking her body made itself sharply felt.

Will came to the other side of the bed and stroked her hair to comfort her, his own face contorted as he felt her pain. Elizabeth came in with a herbal infusion to ease her pain. Joe lifted Martha's head and helped her to drink, then she flopped thankfully back onto the pillow. After some minutes it was obvious the drink had done its job, and she was much calmer. Her eyes closed and her breathing, although shallow, was even now. She had fallen into a deep sleep. Her brothers kissed her gently on the forehead and then, full of sadness, joined Liz, Arthur, and Elizabeth downstairs in the living room.

'It's not good, is it?' Elizabeth asked, looking first at Will and then Joe, maybe hoping for some sign that she was wrong, but of course, she knew in her heart that their sister would not be with them much longer. After they had all eaten some bread and cheese and taken some ale, Joe, Will and Liz went up to Martha, who was still sleeping, one last time. Then sadly they said their goodbyes to Elizabeth and Arthur and left Banghams Wood to make their way back across the Gorge. No one spoke as they trudged wearily back home. They all knew they would never see Martha again in this life, and tragically, maybe the same could be said about young Michael.

In fact, it was three days later that the news was brought by Jimmy. Martha had passed peacefully away in the night and the funeral was to be held the next day. Will and Joe spoke to Mr Ford to ask if they might take an hour or two off work to attend their sister's funeral.

The next day dawned clear and bright and promised to be a warm one. As the Dale Coppice contingent strode along towards the Buildwas bridge, they were pleased to see Richard and Margaret just arriving in a horse-drawn trap from the direction of Bridgnorth. It was obvious to them all that Richard had definitely done well for himself. He and his wife were smartly dressed, and the trap was new and pulled by a handsome black and white pony.

Elizabeth, Arthur, and Jane, along with Margaret and Dorothy, walked down the lane to the church behind the coffin, which was carried by Mr Johnson on his cart. Thus the family gathered once more at the burial ground in Buildwas, this time to lay poor Martha to rest. It was indeed a solemn occasion. It seemed to them that Martha hadn't had much of a life, never having the pleasure of sharing her life with a loving partner, and never having the joy of children of her own. Still, they all felt that they had done their best for her and given her as happy a life as possible in the circumstances.

After the burial, Richard told Abigail he was sorry to hear about Michael, and that he had discovered that the Summer Assize would be held in Bridgnorth on Midsummer's Day. Joe,

Arthur, and Will joined them to discuss the situation and to see how they might help their sister. Richard told Abigail that he and Margaret would be happy for her to stay with them until matters had been resolved, one way or another. Margaret agreed that she would be most welcome. Arthur suggested that he could ask Owner Blake if he would mind if Abigail travelled down to Bridgnorth when the Oriel next set sail downriver, which should be in two weeks' time. Joe said he expected the furnaces to be blown out in the next couple of weeks, and he would be happy to accompany Abigail and see her safely to Richard's house. The kindness of her family overwhelmed Abigail, given the emotional state she was in, and she broke down in tears. Richard put his arms around her, and she buried her head in his shoulder, tears coursing down her cheeks. Eventually, she gathered herself and then asked if he might possibly visit Michael now that he had been taken to Bridgnorth, to make sure he was getting enough to eat and to tell him she would soon be there to visit him. Richard promised that he would of course do what he could for the lad.

Before the family parted, Dorothy had news of her own to give them. She and John Smith were to be married. He had finally proposed to her the week before and she had gladly accepted. This news brought some cheer to the family, and they all congratulated her warmly. She said the wedding was to be at the end of June, and the mistress had given them permission to be married in the private chapel at the Hall and she hoped that they would all be able to be there to share her wedding day. However, in view of what had just occurred and what was happening to Michael, no one could really say whether they would be able to attend or not, and Dorothy said that she understood, of course, that this wasn't the time to make firm arrangements.

Joe and Will were unable to return to Banghams Wood after the funeral as they had only been given a couple of hours off work. Consequently, after matters regarding Michael had been decided, the family parted company. Will walked ahead with Joe, Liz and Abigail following on behind. As they walked back along the north side of the river towards the wharf, Joe glanced at Will. He could tell by the expression on Will's face that he was angry about something. Knowing his brother as well as he did, he knew that his anger was better expressed than allowed to fester. To explore what might be troubling him, he said,

'Will, I can see you're angry. It's a bad do, isn't it?'

'If you mean Martha, yes, it is,' Will replied, 'she didn't have much of a life, did she?' Then after some moments, he looked back, making sure that Abigail was out of earshot, then went on, 'But what's really making me angry Joe, is the way people are treated in this country these days simply for taking food from the woods and fields. How can it be right for folks to be threatened with being strung up just for doing what they've been doing for centuries, catching rabbits for the cooking pot?'

'I know Will, it doesn't seem right. It doesn't seem enough for the rich to own the land, they think they have the right to own every living thing on it, including us, if we're honest! But the law is the law and I guess we have to abide by it, or change it, and as we don't have a say in who makes the laws, I don't see how we can.'

'I know you're right Joe, but we don't have to like it, do we? Maybe one day, we will get a say, and things might change. My God, I hope so. It's just not right that a youngster like Michael can be thrown into gaol and threatened with the noose just for getting mixed up with that bad lot. He's only a lad after all.'

They had reached the wharf and turned to say goodbye to Liz and Abigail, who turned up the pathway towards Lincoln Hill and home, as the men carried on along Dale Road, Joe towards the furnace, Will making for the mine.

The next two weeks were agony for Abigail. Michael was never out of her mind. He was still a boy, now forced into an adult world with all manner of ruffians. She feared for him, imagining all kinds of horrors which might befall him, being completely without protection in such company. She knew food would be scarce, certainly not adequate for a growing boy, and there would be no creature comforts such as a decent mattress to sleep on.

She did well to worry. Michael was given no special treatment in consideration of his tender years. He was thrown into the cells with the rest of the prisoners and when food did appear, he was lucky if he could manage to get his hands on a few scraps. If it hadn't been for the one individual who was kinder than the rest, who noticed that he hardly ever got anything to eat, felt sorry for him and shared a little of his food with the lad, he would have starved to death. As it was, he was rapidly becoming thin and weak.

Richard finally managed to visit him a few days after the funeral, and he was shocked to the core by his appearance. He immediately began to bring food for him, having bribed the gaoler to let his nephew out of the main cell to give him a chance to speak with him, and to make sure he could eat the food without the rest of the prisoners stealing it from him. After a couple of weeks, he began to look a little better. He was of course, in a state of permanent fear about what was going to happen to him. He told Richard that he'd had no idea what Tom Williams had planned when he'd gone with him that night, and if he had known, he would never have gone. He knew poaching was against the law and promised he would never do it again. Richard said he believed him and that he should try not to worry, saying that he would plead for him when the time came.

The Oriel was due to sail on the 6th of June and as luck would have it, the furnaces had been blown out the day before. Owner Blake had agreed to allow Joe and Abigail to travel down to Bridgnorth, saying he wouldn't think of charging them for the journey. At six o'clock in the morning of the 6th, Joe and Abigail set out for the wharf. Will had given Abigail a few shillings to take with her as she had no money of her own, in case she needed to buy anything for Michael, and Liz had packed some bread and cheese for their journey.

Arthur greeted them at the wharf, handing Abigail a bundle that Elizabeth had sent. Margaret had given her some old clothes, rejects from the Hall, and she had altered the coat, shirt, and breeches to fit Michael, so that he would be able to face the trial with a degree of self-respect. She had also washed and pressed a couple of dresses for Abigail herself, realising that as she was going to stay with Richard and Margaret, she would need something decent to wear. Abigail couldn't believe how kind everyone was being, and it gave her strength to know that both she and Michael were so loved.

They boarded the Oriel and settled down in a corner of the deck. Both Abigail and Joe were excited to be leaving the Gorge, in spite of the circumstances. Neither of them had ever been as far as Bridgnorth, even though, as Arthur told them, it was less than ten miles away. Abigail was pleased that at last she would be able to see Michael, as was Joe, but he had to confess he was also looking forward to visiting Richard and Margaret's home for the first time.

By mid-day they were tied up at the Bridgnorth wharfage. They thanked the master of the Oriel and said their farewells to Arthur, then disembarked. They were grateful to see that Richard was waiting for them. Having found out when the Oriel was due, he had brought the pony and trap to pick them up.

Ten minutes later they halted outside a house that neither Joe nor Abigail could believe was Richard's. After the squatter cottages they had lived in all their lives, this house looked huge. It had an impressive looking door in the middle with large windows either side, and above was a row of three more windows. It looked new, as though it had only just been built, which Richard confirmed was the case. His father-in-law, Mr Andrews, had insisted that he and Margaret needed a place of their own and had commissioned the building of this house for them. It wasn't as big as the Hall but was certainly comparable to the Rectory in Buildwas. They were very impressed, although it did make them feel rather like the poor relations, which of course, they were.

However, Margaret couldn't have been kinder and soon made them feel at home. She showed Abigail up to a small bedroom which she said was hers for as long as she needed it. There was a basin and jug of water on a stand, and she suggested that Abigail might like to wash after her journey, then told her to come downstairs when she was ready. Abigail was full of wonder at these surroundings. The windows had velvet drapes and there was a beautiful patchwork quilt thrown over the single bed. She briefly bounced up and down on it, truly amazed that such comfortable beds existed. She undid the bundle of clothes Elizabeth had sent and quickly washed her hands and face before putting on one of the dresses. On the dressing table was a brush and comb and she brushed her hair and looked at herself in the mirror. She couldn't believe the transformation!

She went downstairs and into the room on the left of the hallway which was apparently the dining room. The others were all there, and although obviously impressed with her changed appearance, no one embarrassed her by making comment. Margaret asked them all to sit down at the table and a meal of beef and vegetables was served by a young woman who apparently doubled as parlour maid and cook. Joe and Abigail were in awe. Neither of them had ever been served with anything by a servant. Of course Abigail had seen luxury from the other side, but never experienced it herself. It occurred to Joe, observing the easy way his brother dealt with the servant, that he had settled very well into this lifestyle.

When they had finished eating, Margaret suggested they go through into the sitting room. Once again Joe and Abigail surveyed the room with a degree of amazement, unable to believe that their brother owned all this. Joe in particular felt rather out of place in his old leather breeches and woollen frock coat, the only one he possessed. At least Abigail looked rather more suited to the surroundings in her new dress. However, Richard and Margaret soon put him at his ease, and he was glad he had come, not least because he could get to know his sister-in-law better. He'd had little chance to do so since her marriage to Richard. He liked what he saw. She had a pleasant face and thick brown hair piled high on her head and fastened with a comb. She was small in stature but carried herself well, obviously not having been subjected to hard labour. He could see why Richard had been attracted to her, and he was glad that they were well settled and apparently happy in each other's company.

They exchanged pleasantries for a little while until Abigail could contain herself no longer and asked Richard if he had seen Michael recently. He replied that of course, he had visited him several times since he had been brought to Bridgnorth. He did not, however, go into any detail about the state he had initially found him in. He explained that he had been taking him food and ensuring that he was given the chance to eat it. He told her he had explained to the gaoler that the lad's mother was arriving, and he had agreed to allow her to visit him tomorrow. Richard asked Joe if he would stay the night so that he might also see his nephew in the morning. Joe readily accepted the invitation. He told Richard that once he had seen the boy, he intended to hitch a ride on one of the trows returning upriver to the Gorge.

Richard asked Joe if he would like to take a look at the Andrews Grain Merchant business premises and perhaps to meet Mr Andrews. Joe readily agreed, eager to know all he could about his brother's life. Everyone back in the Gorge would want a full report. The men disappeared and Margaret and Abigail were left alone to get to know one another. Margaret said she was so pleased to spend some time with Abigail at last. She told her that Richard had always spoken fondly of her. Abigail felt she wanted to hide nothing about her past and Michael's origins, as she suspected that this woman was going to be important in their lives in future and she wanted to start their relationship as honestly as possible. She began to explain, but hadn't said more than a sentence or two before Margaret said,

'Please, Abigail, you don't need to explain. Richard has told me all about Michael and who his father was. You have had a difficult time and Richard and I want to be here for you, and for Michael. He is determined to speak for him at the trial and, if you are in agreement, to ask the Judges to release him into his care, as his apprentice, and assure them that he will nurture the boy and keep him on the right path, if they will give him another chance. Of course, there may be a fine to pay, but Richard is determined that he will pay it for you. He feels the lad is truly remorseful and was dragged into the affair by Tom Williams, who seems to be a thoroughly bad lot. Richard feels that if Michael is here in Bridgnorth, he will be away from his influence and free to grow into a fine young man. What do you say Abigail?'

Abigail sat in shocked silence for a moment or two, unable to comprehend that they would be prepared to be so generous to herself and to Michael. Obviously, it would mean Michael leaving home, and that would be hard for them both, but at least here, with Richard and Margaret he would be safe, and given the affluence of their lifestyle, he would definitely be increasing his life-chances by living here. Eventually she spoke, saying,

'Margaret, I don't know what to say. That is so generous of you. Although it would be hard to see him leave home so young, it would be a great relief to me to know that he would be in good hands, and with a better future ahead of him than I could ever give him.'

'That's settled then,' Margaret replied, 'When the time comes, Richard will plead for him, and he can be very persuasive you know,' she added with a warm smile.

Abigail was greatly comforted by this conversation, being able at last to see a better future for her boy.

When the men returned Joe was full of how impressed he had been with the Andrews' business, telling Abigail that it was a far bigger enterprise than he had ever imagined. Margaret told Richard that she had discussed their idea for helping Michael and was pleased to report that Abigail was in agreement. Richard said he was pleased and went on to explain it all to Joe, who was equally happy with the proposed arrangement for the boy.

'That's grand Richard, it'll be the making of him. He's not a bad lad, just needs to get away from Tom Williams and be given the discipline of decent employment.'

'Well, Joe, he'll get that alright. As you have seen, there's plenty of opportunity in the business for a hard-working lad.'

After a light supper they spent the rest of the evening talking about this and that, just catching up on family news. Eventually they all retired for the night. Joe was given a comfortable bed in one of the spare bedrooms and Abigail settled down to the best night's sleep she'd had in a while, feeling there was at last some hope that Michael might soon be free and setting out on a better life than she could ever have hoped he would have.

Chapter 16

Abigail woke early, washed, and dressed and went downstairs to find Richard and Joe in the dining room eating breakfast. Richard told Abigail he had arranged with the gaoler for her and Joe to visit Michael at around ten o'clock that morning. Abigail said again how grateful she was to everyone for being so kind. She couldn't eat much. She was too nervous about what she would find in Bridgnorth Gaol. Michael had been in custody for nearly two months. Goodness knows what state he'll be in, she thought to herself. Margaret had asked the servant to put some food and drink in a bag which she handed to Abigail who also put in the clothes that Elizabeth had given her for Michael, and they set off for the gaol.

The cells were situated beneath the building where the Assize Court was to be held, and when Joe had explained their business, the clerk on duty at the desk disappeared, and returned a few minutes later with a huge, rough looking man, whom they assumed was one of the gaolers. He looked as though he would be able to deal easily with any trouble the prisoners might possibly cause him, and Abigail's heart went out to Michael, thinking of him being in the care of such a person.

However, when Joe explained that they were here to see Michael Bangham, his attitude softened a little and he asked them to follow him down the stairs to the cells. It was a dingy, dark place that smelled of unwashed bodies and worse. Abigail heaved involuntarily. On each side of the passage were what could only be described as iron cages and in each one there were six or seven men, and in some of them, women also. They reached the cage at the end of the passage and in one corner was a boy. Abigail hardly recognised her son. He was dirty and unkempt and thinner than the day he had left home. Both she and Joe were shocked, not only by his appearance, but also at the conditions in which he was being held.

As they stood at the door of the cage, the gaoler called out, 'Bangham! You have visitors. Come forward now!'

Michael looked bewildered for a moment, then cried out, 'Mother, Uncle Joe! You came!'

The gaoler unlocked the door and Michael fell into his mother's arms.

The gaoler secured the cage and led them back along the passage to a small cell near the bottom of the stairs.

'You've got ten minutes,' he said gruffly.

After checking the bag Abigail was holding to ensure it didn't contain anything untoward, he left, slamming the door then turning the key in the lock, which sent a chill down Joe's back, giving him a hint of what it might be like to be locked up in this place. Joe's heart went out to his nephew who was crying now and saying over and over again that he was sorry, and that he was so scared. Abigail comforted her boy, trying to reassure him that she and his uncle Richard would do everything they could for him.

Even though Richard had been able to bring him some food, he was still thin, his face still bore the remnants of the blacking and his hair was matted. She had brought a damp cloth with her and gently cleaned his face and hands as best she could, then she brushed his hair and helped him to change into the clean clothes she had brought. Michael tucked into the food and drink as though he hadn't eaten for days. It was heart-breaking to watch.

'Time's up!' came the cry, and Michael clung to his mother as the gaoler opened the door and said, 'Come on Bangham, time to go.'

Abigail assured Michael she would be back to see him as often as she could before the trial, and told him to try not to worry, she was sure Uncle Richard, who had some standing in the community, would be able to help him.

Michael continued to hang on to Abigail, until finally the gaoler lost patience and dragged him away, and back to the cage at the end of the passage. To see him so roughly handled, his face full of fear, broke Abigail's heart. Once he was out of sight, Joe put his arm round Abigail's shoulders and led her back up the corridor and out of the gaol.

Once Joe had escorted Abigail back to Richard's house, assuring her he would try to get back for the trial on Midsummer's Day, he took his leave of them all to make his way down to the wharfage where he found Owner Onion's boat unloading some of its cargo and preparing to take the remainder upriver to the Gorge.

Abigail felt a little lost once Joe had gone. Although of course, as she was growing up, Richard had always been there in Banghams Wood, she had seen nothing of him in recent years, particularly since he had married Margaret and moved to Bridgnorth. She felt quite out of place for a while, particularly in these, what to her, were affluent surroundings. However, as the days passed, she began to feel more at home. Thanks to Richard's ongoing arrangement with the gaoler, she was able to visit Michael every few days, taking him food and drink. Margaret had kindly provided another change of clothes for him for the trial and on the 23rd of June, Abigail took them into the gaol for him to wear the next day. Time and again Michael had promised his mother that if he was freed, he would never get involved with poaching again. He had learnt his lesson, she was sure of it, and now it was up to Richard to convince their

Lordships that he meant it, and that he would make sure that the lad was as good as his word.

By the time Abigail returned to Richard's house, Joe had arrived, having once again travelled down on one of the trows heading for Gloucester. Abigail was pleased to see him, and with the support of her two brothers, she felt more able to face the coming ordeal of her son's trial. The day of the trial, 24th June, Midsummer's Day 1729, finally dawned. It was threatening rain from a black sky. Abigail, Joe, and Richard made their way to the Assize Court. It was with some trepidation that they entered the gallery of the courtroom, where people not connected with the trials themselves were allowed to stand to watch the proceedings. This trial of four prisoners who had been caught red-handed by the militia poaching on the estate of one of the county's notables, had attracted quite a crowd and the gallery was packed. Everyone knew that, following legislation enacted some six years previously, poaching could be punishable by transportation to America, or even by execution on the gallows. Speculation was rife. How could these felons escape severe punishment when they had actually been caught in the act with their ill-gotten gains still in their possession?

The courtroom was a dark and noisy place. Crowded as it was, it was hot and sticky, and the smell of unwashed bodies pervaded the place. The room fell silent however, as the seven judges entered the room from the left and took their places in their appointed seats on the raised platform at one end of the room. One of the judges, who all wore black robes and long white wigs, called out,

'Summon the jury!' and immediately a line of men, twelve in number, filed in to take up their places in the twelve seats ranged against the wall opposite the public gallery. Each one of them was solemnly sworn in, promising to exercise judgement without fear or favour. They then settled into their seats to await the beginning of the trial.

At the back of the courtroom, opposite the judges' platform was another raised area surrounded by a balustrade about four and a half foot high. Abigail perceived that this must be the dock, the place where she would soon see her own beloved son standing, to receive his fate. Her legs were shaking as the judge once again called out,

'Bring forth the prisoners!'

It appeared that all four of the poachers were to be tried together, presumably as what evidence was to be presented, applied equally to the role of each in the crime of which they stood accused. They emerged one by one from the top of a staircase behind the dock, presumably leading up from the cells below. They were a motley crew, dirty and malnourished after their months of confinement. Michael appeared at the end of the line and took up his place to the right-hand end of the dock. He stood out from the others, wearing the good, clean clothes Margaret had provided and with his hair tidy and his face clean. Abigail prayed that his appearance would convey to the judges that he was cut from different cloth than the ruffians whose company he had recently kept.

The Clerk of the Court asked each of them in turn, to state his name and the Parish from which he came. He then read out the charge for which each of them must answer, and one by one they were asked how they pleaded. They all, of course pleaded 'not guilty', as to plead guilty might result in an automatic death penalty.

However, there was plenty of evidence on which the jury would decide their innocence or guilt. The witness evidence was presented by the Bailiff of the Estate and substantiated by the Captain of the Militia. The Bailiff recounted that on the night in question, in the early hours of the morning he had been alerted to shouting of men and the barking of a dog in a wooded part of the estate.

Suspecting the noises were being made by poachers, he had sent for the local militia before approaching them. Within half an hour they had the poachers surrounded and declared their presence. One of the poachers, in an attempt to resist arrest, had set the dog upon the Bailiff but it had been shot dead by one of the Militia men before it reached him. Realising the game was up, the poachers had then given themselves up, been arrested and taken to Much Wenlock Guildhall, where they were officially charged with poaching and placed in the lock up before being sent to Bridgnorth to await trial. The Captain of the Militia was asked whether he agreed with the description of events which had been given by the Bailiff. He stated that he did and had nothing to add.

This was the case for the Prosecution, and to everyone in the room, most particularly the members of the jury, it seemed there could be little doubt that they were all guilty as charged. In fact, it took no more than two minutes for the jury to emerge from their huddle and agree the verdicts. The Clerk of the Court demanded the verdict on each of the defendants in turn. One after the other, the foreman answered 'Guilty.' As the Clerk asked for the verdict on Michael Bangham, Abigail gripped Joe's arm tightly, afraid she was going to faint.

'Guilty,' came the reply. Abigail involuntarily cried out 'No!' and looked at Michael who now looked terrified.

The presiding Judge asked each of the men in turn whether they had anything to say in mitigation of their actions. For the two men, there was little to be said, but when it came to Tom Williams, just thirteen years old, he did his best to convince the Judges that he was full of remorse and swore he would never do such a thing again, if he was given a second chance. The Judge, looking at his appearance and his arrogant manner, seemed rather unimpressed. Then it was Michael's turn. Richard stood up and catching the presiding Judge's attention, asked if he could plead Michael's case for him, explaining that he was a merchant of some standing and reputation in Bridg-north and that Michael was his nephew. Seeing that Michael did indeed seem out of place among the rest of the miscreants, and after conferring briefly with his colleagues on the bench, he agreed to allow Richard to speak for Michael.

Richard made his way down to the floor of the court and stood in front of the dock, facing the judges. The presiding judge asked him to state his name and business. He informed the court that he was Richard Bangham, a partner in Andrews Grain Merchants of Bridgnorth and uncle to the defendant Michael Bangham.

He explained that being the boy's uncle, he knew him very well, had indeed known him since birth. He told them the boy had been brought up well by his mother, but without the benefit of a father's guidance. Consequently, he had succumbed in recent months to the influence of malign forces, being cajoled into misdemeanours in the name of adventure, but on the night in question had had no idea where he was being led, nor to what purpose. The boy had no idea that the men were intent on poaching until it was too late. He had indeed tried to resist and run away back to his home in Dale Coppice, but was prevented from doing so by one of the men grabbing hold of him and while he held the boy down, the other had smeared his face with blacking as he declared,

'You're one of us now lad!'

Richard went on to say that Michael was full of remorse and understood that he had been led into doing wrong, but was determined, if he was given the chance to work hard and lead a good life, to make his poor mother proud. Finally, he said that if Michael was allowed to leave the court today, he would be taking him into his own home as his apprentice, and he truly believed that if he were to be kept away from Dale Coppice, taught to read, and write and the meaning of hard work, he could grow into a fine young man.

The judge looked directly at Michael and asked him,

'Is all this true boy?'

Michael stood as tall as he could, and in his strongest voice declared,

'It is, my Lord. I have sworn to my mother that I will never get involved with such matters again and will gladly live with my uncle, and do my best to make something of myself, if your Lordships will only give me the chance.'

There was a brief consultation among the judges before the presiding judge began to pass sentence on each of the felons in turn. To each of the men he declared that they would be transported to the Americas for a period of no less than seven years. The men rocked on their heels at this, but both knew it could have been worse. They could have been facing the death penalty. On Tom Williams he passed the sentence of three years hard labour.

Joe placed his arm around Abigail's shoulders in support, as the judge looked straight at Michael. He paused a moment before declaring that in view of his age and the fact that his uncle had pleaded for him so eloquently, the judges had decided to be merciful and then formally stated,

'Michael Bangham, you will pay a fine of £10 and be bound over to keep the peace for five years, providing that you remain in Bridgnorth and are apprenticed to Richard Bangham of Andrews Grain Merchants. On payment of the fine you will be free to go.'

Michael could hardly believe it. Abigail and Joe made their way down from the gallery and into the floor of the court, where Michael had now left the dock and was standing with Richard. He immediately flew into his mother's arms, who, with tears of relief tumbling down her cheeks, was thanking Richard for pleading so successfully for her son.

Michael turned to look at the other defendants who were now being led towards the stairs down to the cells. As he reached the top of the stairs Tom turned and looked at Michael with such a look of hatred in his eyes that Michael reeled under the force of it and couldn't help feeling that he had somehow betrayed his former friend.

Richard arranged with the Clerk of the Court that he would go immediately to get the money and the indenture papers and return forthwith to pay the fine to release his nephew. Consequently Joe, Abigail and Michael were obliged to wait in an anteroom until Richard returned. Within an hour he arrived back at court with the money and the indenture document which Abigail had already signed. The Clerk checked the document and recorded that it was all in order, then took the £10 from Richard and issued a receipt. He then declared that they were free to leave.

Within half an hour they arrived back at Richard's house, where Margaret had asked the servant to prepare a bath for Michael. Abigail spent the next hour tending to her son and when she brought him downstairs, he was barely recognisable. He looked quite the little gentleman, if a little under-nourished. Margaret, determined to begin the task of 'building him up' had asked Mary to prepare a meal for them all and it warmed all their hearts to watch the boy tucking into it.

Richard told Joe that if he would stay the night, he would get one of the men to take him and Abigail back to Dale Coppice in the trap in the morning. After the emotionally exhausting day they had all had and realising that Abigail would want to spend at least one night with her son before leaving, he readily agreed.

Richard explained the boy would be living with them. There was an attic room which they had prepared for him. He said he would let him rest for a week or so, to get used to his surroundings and to recover somewhat from his ordeal, but then he would be working at the business five days a week. On the sixth day he would be going to school in Bridgnorth where he must learn to read and write and do his numbers. If he was to progress in the business this would be essential, he declared, and asked Michael if he understood how important this was.

'I do Uncle,' he replied, and then went on, 'I won't let you down and thank you for all you did for me today.'

With that, Richard took Michael and Abigail up to the attic to see the room they had prepared for him. It was a low room with a small window in one side of the roof. Michael ran over to the window and standing on tiptoe, looked down on the street, and beyond, a hundred feet below he could see the Severn flowing swiftly by. This gave him some comfort as he knew this was the same water that had flowed along the Gorge only hours before. It was a link with home. After months of confinement with no view of the world outside, he was delighted he would now have his own window through which to look at the sky. Abigail was thrilled to see how pleased Michael was and once again thanked Richard for his kindness.

Michael was so happy with his room they struggled to get him to leave it and come down to join the others. In the event he was happy enough to spend the rest of the evening by Abigail's side. After the months of worry, the relief in the room was palpable and there was much merriment, sometimes bordering on the hysterical. Eventually it was time to retire for the night and Abigail went up to the attic with Michael, happy to be able to fuss over him and maybe for the last time, to kiss him goodnight and tuck him up in bed.

By ten o'clock the next day, Abigail and Joe were ready to leave Bridgnorth. Michael had spent a restless night, unused to the comfort of a bed, having slept on the floor of the gaol for months. Of course, he didn't want his mother to leave him and clung to her when the time came, but she gently withdrew her embrace, saying that she was sure he would be fine with his Uncle Richard and Aunt Margaret, and they would look after him. She said she would visit him as often as she could, and Richard said he would make sure the boy got to visit the Dale from time to time to see his mother. With that, Abigail and Joe climbed into the trap and set off on the journey back to the Gorge. Michael ran after the trap, waving wildly, until it had turned the corner at the end of the street and disappeared. Then he stopped, turned, and walked dejectedly back to Richard and Margaret who were waiting for him at the gate. So began Michael Bangham's new life in Bridgnorth.

When Abigail and Joe arrived back at Dale Coppice a couple of hours later, there was a strange atmosphere. For a start, it wasn't often that a pony and trap turned up in these parts, and it caused quite a stir. In addition, word had already reached the Gorge about the outcome of the trial. The poachers were local men, from Madeley Wood and Buildwas, and Tom Williams was himself from the Coppice. It was apparent that people thought they had got off lightly, fully expecting they would be given the death penalty.

Nevertheless, seven years transportation was still devastating for their families who would be left destitute and probably sent back to their home parishes for support, where they would no doubt end up in the local poorhouse. It was also highly likely that the men would never return, as in order to do so they would have to pay their own passage home.

Tom Williams hadn't come off much better, as three years hard labour for a boy of fourteen would be difficult to bear and there was some doubt as to whether he would survive it. His mother, Martha, was distraught. At the very least she wouldn't see her son for three years. Fred, his father was predictably angry that such a fate should befall his son and had already started telling anyone who would listen that Michael Bangham had lied to save his own skin.

Chapter 17

In spite of the general atmosphere around the Coppice, Joe and Abigail were certainly given a warm welcome in the Bangham cottage. Liz had prepared a meal for them, and little Elizabeth ran to her father for the special fuss he reserved for her. Abigail was glad to be home again after weeks away in Bridgnorth. She would have preferred to have brought her son home with her, but she knew he would have a good life with Richard and Margaret, and she would just have to bear the pain of separation. After worrying for months what fate would befall him, she decided it was a small price to pay for securing his future.

A week later, Dorothy and John Smith were married in the chapel at the Hall. Abigail said that for obvious reasons she would not set foot on the Estate and Will also declined, saying that he daren't risk coming face to face with Furlong, afraid he might try to finish the job he started all those years ago.

Joe and Liz left the children with them, and along with Arthur, Elizabeth and Margaret attended the wedding in the private chapel on the Estate. Dorothy looked beautiful, wearing a white dress given to her by the mistress and wearing a garland of wildflowers around her head. Joe was pleased to see that she and John were obviously very much in love. He seemed a decent sort and being the schoolmaster, had his own house in Madeley Wood. After the service, they were transported across the Gorge to their marital home in the pony and trap, loaned for the day by the Master. As her siblings waved them off, they were confident that Dorothy's future would be secure with her schoolteacher. Another Bangham was to go up in the world, and they were glad of it.

As Joe and Liz made their way up the lane towards the Coppice, Joe's joyful mood persisted. Six months pregnant, Liz was blooming and looked the picture of health. After the troubles he had recently witnessed in Bridgnorth, he was glad to be here having seen Dorothy now settled and, walking beside his wife, he felt secure in his own happiness. His little daughter was thriving, and she would soon have a brother or sister. Will had changed after his time in America, and he was altogether more pleasant to be around. As for Abigail, of course she was no doubt sad Michael was no longer to live with her, but he knew she was relieved he was safe from the malign influences he'd suffered in the Coppice, and now he'd been given the opportunity of having a good life ahead of him. Joe had been extremely impressed with Richard and Margaret, and the way they had been determined to rescue the boy. It had taken courage for Richard to stand up in Court like that to speak for the lad, and he had been proud of his younger brother.

For the next couple of months, life went on much as usual in Dale Coppice. Joe undertook some maintenance work on the furnaces along with some of his workmates and Will took some extra labouring shifts at the mine, so the family's finances held up pretty well. The weather around harvest time was poor though, and as a result, the cost of food rose steeply and many of the families in the area, not so fortunate as the Banghams as far as supplementing their incomes was concerned, suffered greatly.

The Williams for instance, already devastated by Tom's imprisonment and the loss of his wages from his work in the coalmine, had a hard time of it. Fred Williams of course, continued to drink and to blame everyone else for the decline in the family's fortunes, and his wife and the remaining children began to show signs of malnutrition. Things came to a head one day in late August, when his wife Martha, confronted him as he staggered into the cottage, having spent what little wages he'd earned in the previous week, in the ale house. Her desperation finally overcame her fear, and she could be heard all across the clearing, shouting at him, calling him cruel and a useless father and husband, as he could watch them all starve, rather than stop drinking. Suddenly, there was a roar of rage, followed by several screams and shrieks, and children shouting out to their mother. Then, suddenly, there was silence, except for the quiet sobbing of the infants. After a moment or two, Johnny, the eldest child came running out of the cottage and into the arms of Joe, who, along with Will, had been on his way to investigate.

'He's killed me ma!' he shouted, over and over.

Joe asked Will to take the lad and ask Liz to look after him, then went over to the Williams' cottage and cautiously entered. The scene that greeted him was one of utter carnage. Martha lay on the floor covered in blood which was oozing from several gaping wounds. One of the younger children, barely two years old, lay beside her mother, calling to her to wake up. Fred Williams was sitting on the floor, slumped against the wall, blood spatters across his face, still holding the filleting knife in his hand, and looking completely bewildered, obviously unable to comprehend what he had just done.

Joe told him to drop the knife, and when Fred looked at it, he seemed to see it for the first time, suddenly flinging it across the room as though it was on fire. Joe picked it up and took it outside to make sure it was well out of reach, placing it on top of the lintel over the doorway. Will was waiting beside the door and asked Joe what had happened.

'He's finally done it Will, he's killed Martha,' Joe said, with the conviction of someone who had just witnessed the carnage within.

'Go to Mr Ford's place Will and tell him what's happened. He'll be able to send a rider to fetch the Justice of the Peace from Much Wenlock, quicker than we could. I'll stay here and make sure he does no harm to anyone else.'

John Spencer and several of the other men had gathered outside the cottage and with their help, Joe was able to restrain Fred, binding his hands and feet where he sat, still slumped against the wall. He had made no move to stop the men as they took the four remaining little children, traumatised by what they had just witnessed, to Joe's cottage, where Abigail and Liz tried to comfort them as best they could. Martha's body had to be left where it was, until the Justice had been, so that he could record what he saw as evidence of what had occurred.

Everyone knew, of course, that Fred Williams was bound for the gallows, and the children, soon to be orphaned, would be sent to the poorhouse. All agreed that it was a complete tragedy, but one that wasn't entirely unexpected as they had all witnessed the family's decline and knew that Tom's imprisonment had hit Martha hard. He had been her main emotional support. The hunger of the past few weeks had proved the last straw and had given her the courage to stand up to her husband, which had unfortunately led to her losing her life.

The Justice appeared along with members of the militia within a couple of hours to survey the scene and to take Fred into custody. They placed him in an open cart and trundled him off to Much Wenlock gaol. As the family had no money, Martha was placed unceremoniously in a coarse white shroud and after a couple of days, taken away on a handcart to the burial ground. Only Joe and Will attended the funeral, which was brief and without ceremony. The five children had been placed in the care of Benthall Parish and were now in the poorhouse at Mine Spout, across the Gorge, destined for paupers' lives which would inevitably be short ones.

The whole incident had been distressing for everyone, and hit Liz, now seven months pregnant, particularly hard, and even Abigail, though it had been Martha's son who had led Michael astray, had had some sympathy for her, understanding how hard it must have been, to see Tom locked up for years. However, their own lives were hard enough, and instincts of self-preservation soon took over, the memories of those horrific events beginning to fade.

With Liz now in the later stages of pregnancy, by mid-September she could no longer make the journey to Madeley Wood market and so it fell to Abigail to bring the supplies they needed. She was always nervous about going to the market, forever fearful of running into Furlong, particularly when she had had Michael with her. Now that he was safely installed in Bridgnorth with Richard, she felt easier about taking the risk. So it was, that during the second week of September, Abigail set out for Madeley Wood market.

She was feeling quite settled about Michael now, glad that he was out of harm's way in Bridgnorth. She had already bought a few provisions, including some flour, but was astounded at the price of it. The poor harvest had resulted in the cost of flour and bread rocketing. She was just wondering how many more of the things they needed she would be able to afford to buy, when she heard someone call her name. Relieved it was a woman's voice, she spun round to see Dorothea Blake and her husband striding towards her.

First of all, they said how sorry they had been to hear about Michael, who had always seemed to them to be a good lad. Abigail thanked them and confirmed that he was now in Bridgnorth with Richard, and safe from the bad influences he had been subjected to. Dorothea said she was glad she had bumped into Abigail, as she had been hoping to see her. She was in need of a domestic servant to help with the general housework and also to help the cook with preparing and serving meals. She had wondered whether, now Abigail didn't have Michael to look after, she would like to come to Madeley Wood and take the position on offer. The pay would be four shillings a week and her keep.

Abigail didn't know what to say at first, thinking about Liz and wondering what help she may need until after the baby was born. Then it occurred to her that with her mother and sisters living next door in the Coppice, she would have as much support as she needed. Dorothea went on,

'Abigail, if you're not sure, perhaps you'd like to think about it?'

Now sure that Liz would be fine and although she had always thought she would never go back into service, she knew the Blakes were good people and she had been feeling for some time she couldn't stay indefinitely with Joe and Liz, now that their family was growing, and so she said,

'No. Thanks, I am sure. I would like to take up your offer. When would you like me to start?'

'Well, as soon as possible, shall we say Monday week?' Dorothea answered.

Abigail said that would be fine and asked where they lived. Owner Blake explained how she would find the place and they parted company, Abigail thanking them once again for their kind offer.

As she walked back to the Coppice, Abigail was excited that her life was about to change. Since Michael had gone, she had been feeling rather at a loss. She knew she ought to try to earn some money to help support the family if she was to stay with Joe but couldn't think what to do about it. She hadn't wanted to work at the mines or picking coal on the tips, but until now had been determined not to go back into service. This was different though, she told herself. Owner Blake was a decent man, and she would have nothing to fear from him, she was sure.

She was a little apprehensive about telling Liz and Joe, but in the end, they agreed that it was a good move. Joe had always liked Owner Blake and Elizabeth was still friendly with Dorothea, sometimes visiting her on market days, and would no doubt keep an eye on Abigail whenever she did. Furthermore, as they reminded her, it would be easier for Abigail to visit Michael in Bridgnorth as the Oriel usually called in there on its way to Gloucester, and they were sure Owner Blake would be only too happy for her to hitch a ride when convenient. So it was, that on the last Monday in September, Abigail packed her few belongings, said goodbye to Joe, Liz and Will, and made her way to the Blake's house.

The rain that had ruined much of the harvest had filled the reservoir early and allowed the furnaces to be blown in by the second week of September, and Joe was now back at work. Their second child, a son, was born on the 26th of October. He was a fine healthy lad who they named Nathaniel. They were ecstatic, Joe proud he now had a son who would carry on the family name. He loved his daughter Elizabeth dearly, of course, but she would marry eventually, and a son was different, it meant continuity, and also security for Liz when his own time came to leave this life.

Word got around that Fred Williams was to be tried at the Shrewsbury Assize for the murder of his wife. Everyone was interested, but he had never denied it and with the outcome certain, none could see the point in making the journey all the way to Shrewsbury to witness his demise. Joe had offered to be a witness, but the Justice said that as he hadn't actually witnessed the act and also that Fred Williams had confessed, that wouldn't be necessary. So it was, that Mr Ford gave them all the news one cold January morning as they arrived at the

Works, that Fred Williams was to go to the gallows that very day. Not one person shed a tear for him.

Chapter 18

The works was busier than ever during that winter of 1730, with several orders for steam engine cylinders on the books. There was talk of possibly building a boring mill so that the finishing of the cylinders could be carried out within the Company. Production of domestic items continued apace, with plenty of orders for cooking pots and other cast items for shipping to many markets in cities across the country. Shipments were still being sent across the oceans, through the port of Bristol. Iron wheels were also now being cast for use on the railway used for transporting goods down to the wharf, and raw materials in the other direction. Joe was as proud as ever to be working for the Coalbrookdale Company, taking great pride in the reputation for the quality of the iron their furnaces produced. Of course, he knew that all this progress was coming at a price.

This was very evident as soon as the furnaces were blown out and the smoke and fumes in the air dissipated. During the summer months the sun shone brighter, and the air smelled sweeter, but when autumn came and the furnaces were blown in once more, fumes hung in the air and the sunlight faded, partly blocked out by the tiny particles of soot that floated through the air, landing on the vegetation all around the Dale.

The winter that year was thankfully mild with little snow and frost, although there was plenty of mist and damp hanging around the Gorge, bringing with it the usual bouts of bronchitis among the inhabitants. Christmas was rather strange, with Abigail now away at the Blake's household and rather than coming back to Dale Coppice she went off to visit Michael at Richard's in Bridgnorth. Elizabeth and Arthur didn't visit because they were both suffering from the effects of the damp weather with heavy colds and coughs.

It was at the end of January that Liz noticed young Elizabeth looking rather flushed and she had a slight fever which as always, caused considerable anxiety. All manner of ills began with fever, from smallpox to measles, none of them pleasant and most of them dangerous. After a couple of days her condition worsened, the fever now raging through her body. The family were all distraught, Liz spending every hour she could beside her, sponging her down to assuage the fever and giving her herbal concoctions which she hoped would help her to fight whatever was causing it. The source of the trouble was unclear. No spots or lesions appeared on her skin, but the fever lasted for two more days before the crisis was reached. On the evening of the fifth day, Elizabeth became agitated, tossing her head about and flailing around in the bed. They feared they would lose their little girl, but then, around midnight she suddenly became still, and exhausted, fell into a deep sleep. The fever had broken, the danger had passed. All this time, Liz had been terrified that Nathaniel might catch the fever too, but thankfully he did not. Elizabeth was weakened by her ordeal, but Liz made sure she had plenty of rest and good food, and over the next few months her strength returned.

Will had been paying rather a lot of attention to a young widow, another Elizabeth, a cousin of Liz's, who had moved in with the Spencers after her husband had died in tragic circumstances. He had been working in one of the coalmines when the roof caved in, trapping him and two other men underground. They dug for two days to get the men out, but when they finally reached them, they were all dead, either from their injuries or suffocation. Elizabeth was left with a little boy, George, but with no means of support and was taken in by her uncle and aunt, John, and Susan Spencer.

Elizabeth was a pleasant looking young woman, not what you might call beautiful. She had a kindly nature but with a sadness and vulnerability about her that Will found attractive. Since his Sarah had died all those years ago, he had never looked at another woman, but now he began to feel that he could love this quiet, gentle woman. He knew he had much love to give, and Elizabeth certainly seemed as though she needed someone to care for her and her child.

It was early March when he told Joe how he felt, and that he intended to ask Elizabeth to marry him. She would of course, expect to move into the Bangham's cottage with Will, and both the brothers realised this wouldn't be ideal. Will said that perhaps it was time for him to build his own cottage in the coppice. Joe told him not to rush into anything as he had heard that the Darby's intended to build some new houses for the foremen and their families soon, and he was hoping to get one, in which case, Will and Elizabeth would be welcome to stay in his cottage. Now that had been settled, Will started courting Elizabeth, who was always referred to as Betty, in earnest, and was delighted to find that the attraction was mutual. They began to spend more and more time together to the delight of the Spencers and Liz of course, who was very fond of her cousin, and it was in early May that Will proposed and was accepted. The wedding was on the first Sunday in June at the Holy Trinity Church in Buildwas, followed by a wedding feast in the Spencer's cottage.

A couple of weeks later, Liz discovered that she was pregnant again. She and Joe were pleased but realised the cottage would become even more crowded with the arrival of another child. The baby would probably be born in March, Liz told him, and as the time approached, he decided to speak to Mr Ford about the possibility of having one of the new houses once they were built. Joe was a valued worker who had been with the Darby Company for seventeen years and Mr Ford had no hesitation in promising him one of the houses to be constructed on the other side of the valley. However, he said it would be several months yet before they were ready.

In the meantime, both families settled down well together. Liz and Betty, being first cousins and good friends, cheerfully shared the household chores and childminding. As her time approached, Liz was happy to have Betty around to help with the trips to market and the heavier duties around the home. She went into labour in the early hours of 19th March 1731 and by evening she and Joe had another son, whom they called Benjamin.

Elizabeth and Arthur visited the next weekend to see their new nephew, bringing Jane with them. She was thirteen now and growing up fast. Elizabeth told them that Margaret had secured her the position of scullery maid at the Hall, and she was to start the following week. Given Abigail's experience at the Hall, Elizabeth said she had some misgivings, but Margaret had assured her that she would look out for her. After all, Dorothy had worked there for many years, until her marriage to John, without any problems. As the families shared their meal, Joe glanced at Elizabeth and Arthur, noticing that they were both looking older. Of course, he reminded himself, Elizabeth was fifty years old now and Arthur well over fifty, so it wasn't surprising that the years were beginning to take their toll. He would have to keep an eye on them as time went on. They had their own cottage of course, which gave them some security, but if Arthur should become unable to work, they would need some help if they were to avoid Mine Spout poorhouse.

Matters came to a head sooner than Joe expected. It was about a month later that Jimmy turned up in the coppice to let them know that Arthur had suffered an accident while on a trip to Gloucester. It appeared that a heavy container of iron goods had broken loose from the ropes holding it in place as the Oriel had collided with another vessel in the docks and had caught Arthur a glancing blow on his right leg. Everyone agreed that it could have been worse, it could easily have killed him. As it was, his leg was twisted with a nasty broken bone. He was in great pain and the surgeon was sent for. As the other men held him fast, the surgeon had straightened his leg and as Arthur screamed out in agony, placed it in a splint. but at least his leg was saved. Jimmy told them that it looked as though his father would be unable to work for some weeks, and maybe longer, if his leg didn't heal properly.

Joe asked Jimmy to let Elizabeth know that he would come over to Banghams Wood on the following Sunday to see how things were, and to find out what he could do to help them. He fervently hoped that Margaret would be there too. He hadn't seen her for many months and was eager to catch up with her.

So it was, that the following Sunday Joe had gathered what provisions the family could spare and was crossing the Severn in Bert Rogers' coracle on his way to Banghams Wood. As he climbed the steps under Benthall Edge, he mused that it shouldn't really be called Banghams Wood any more as no Banghams now lived there. Elizabeth was a Green since marrying Arthur. Still, he supposed, perhaps it would always be known by the name, as often happened with place names which were frequently retained long after their origins were lost to living memory.

As Joe arrived in the clearing, he saw his sister was feeding the hog, a duty once performed by Martha, but the responsibility now falling to her. It struck him that Elizabeth must miss Martha very much. As she glanced up from tending to the hog, she noticed Joe striding towards her and let out a delighted shout,

'Eee! Our Joe, it's so good to see ye!'

'And you, Liz. I was so sorry to hear about Arthur's accident. How is he?'

'Come in and see for yerself,' she replied, emptying the rest of the hog's food into the trough, then leading Joe into the cottage.

Arthur was seated on the settle by the fire with his leg raised on a stool for comfort.

'Joe!' he declared, 'Thanks for coming over. This is a poor do and no mistake. Looks like it's going to be weeks before I'm fit for work again.'

'So I heard Arthur. Well, I've come over to see if there's anything I can do to help out.'

'Well, I won't deny that it will be a struggle Joe, but we still have Jimmy's wages and the rent from my cottage coming in.'

'And,' interjected Elizabeth, 'I do have a bit put by, so if it is only six weeks or so before Arthur can get back to work, we should be able to manage.'

'Well,' said Joe, 'Liz has sent a few things to help out right now, and I'll get over again in a couple of weeks with whatever we can spare.'

'Thanks Joe, we won't forget it,' Elizabeth said, then went on, 'Our Margaret should be here within the hour, and she may bring a few bits from the Hall, as she usually does.'

Joe said he was glad Margaret was coming, he hadn't seen her for months and was eager to hear her news. He was wondering whether she had heard anything about Michael. The horseman at the Hall may well have news of him as he would be regularly visiting Andrews Grain Merchants.

Elizabeth said she had seen Abigail when she last visited the Blake's and she seemed to have settled in well. She had been down to Bridgnorth for a couple of days after Christmas, and said she was pleased and proud that Michael, now fifteen, was growing into a fine young man. However, she had been rather worried that he seemed determined to find out about his father and had asked her again why the man with red hair had said he was his son.

'That's a tricky one,' said Joe, sitting down on a stool by the side of the fire.

'It is,' Elizabeth replied. 'Michael's no fool, and if she isn't honest with him about what happened, he won't rest until he finds out in some other way. God forbid, he may even approach Furlong directly. On the other hand, if she does tell him herself, goodness knows how he would take the news that his father had forced himself upon her. I'm glad it's not my decision to make.'

'Definitely! That's up to Abigail.'

'Anyway, here I am nattering away, and I haven't even offered you a drink of ale Joe.'

'Thanks Liz I don't mind if I do.'

At that moment the doorlatch rattled and Margaret walked in, flushed and a little breathless from the walk down from the Estate. Joe was shocked that she also was looking older. That's inevitable, he thought to himself, she's probably thinking the same about me. He stood up quickly and went to embrace her. When he hugged her, she felt a little thinner than he remembered, which rather alarmed him.

'Margaret, it's so good to see you. I was hoping you'd be here today.'

'It's good to see you too Joe. No doubt like you, having heard about Arthur I've come to see if there's anything I can do to help.' she replied, handing Elizabeth the basket of food which Cook had sent, it being surplus to requirements at the Hall.

'You're all so kind,' said Elizabeth, a little overcome by their assurances of help. Since they had brought Arthur home on the stretcher three days ago, she had been at her wit's end, worrying how they would manage. Of course, she hadn't said anything to Arthur, who felt badly enough about it already. With her two siblings being here promising their support, she began to feel that they would, after all, be able to survive without going to the Parish, which she dreaded having to do.

'So, our Margaret,' Joe began, 'how are things up at the Hall.'

'Much the same as ever Joe. Young Jane seems to have settled in, although I think she is a little homesick and I do my best to keep an eye on her Elizabeth.'

'I know you do, Margaret,' Elizabeth replied, 'and I'm grateful. I do worry about her.'

'Dorothy and John seem happy enough,' Margaret went on, 'He still visits the Hall once a week to instruct the children as the mistress doesn't want them mixing with the Charity School youngsters. Apparently when he is up at the Hall, Dorothy teaches reading and writing to the schoolchildren and he says she has made an excellent teacher, which is no surprise to any of us, I'm sure.'

'I'm so glad Margaret.' Joe asserted. 'Yes, we all knew she would go far. And what about Richard? Have you visited Bridgnorth yet? He's certainly gone up in the world. Who would have thought a Bangham would have become such a well-respected merchant? Still, I don't begrudge him any of it and he certainly made the most of his new-found status when he rescued Michael from gaol. You should have heard him in Court Margaret. It took some courage to stand up in front of the judges and successfully plead Michael's case.'

'I know, I wish I had been there Joe. I haven't been over to Bridgnorth yet, but I must make the effort. I could ride over there with Fred, the horseman, any time, I'm sure the mistress would give me a day off. You know, of course that they had a little boy, Richard, a year ago?'

'No, I didn't. To be honest Margaret, I don't get time to visit anyone these days, what with being so busy at the furnace. Still, it's good to know they're getting on with building their family. They'll be lucky children, that family will surely prosper and so will they.'

'Aye, that's true enough Joe,' Margaret agreed.

All this while Elizabeth had been busy preparing their meal and now served up the vegetable stew. It wasn't lost on Joe and Margaret that it contained no meat, reminding them that the Greens would certainly need some support over the next few weeks. The family continued to chat over their meal and then Joe asked if there were any jobs he could do, that Arthur would normally have dealt with.

Elizabeth assured him that Jimmy had been very good, stepping into his father's shoes when necessary. Just at that moment, right on cue, he walked in carrying an armful of kindling he had been gathering in the woods and placed them by the fire.

'Come on now lad,' Elizabeth said, ladling some stew onto a plate. 'Get this down you.'

'Thanks Ma,' he replied, 'I'm ready for it.'

Jimmy was now eighteen and a fine young man. He had served out his apprenticeship with Bert Rogers and was now building his own coracles, selling them from a hut he and Arthur had built by Bower's shipbuilding yard down by the Severn. He was beginning to make some money out of it, as with all the newcomers arriving in the Gorge over the last few years, there was plenty of demand. However, as yet he was quite slow at making them, wanting to gain a reputation for quality instilled in him by Bert, and wasn't making as much money as he might.

After an hour or so, Margaret noticed the light was fading and said she had better be getting back to the Hall. Joe offered to walk with her up to the Estate gate, and they bade farewell to Arthur, Elizabeth, and Jimmy, promising to come back as often as they could. Joe said Will would probably be over the following week and he would send them some money and food to help out. Elizabeth and Arthur both said how grateful they were.

As Joe was walking arm in arm along the lane with his sister, he asked,

'And what about you, our Margaret? How are you?'

'Oh, you know me our Joe, I'm fine. It's not such a bad life, you know. I sometimes just wish I could have married and had children of my own, but that wasn't to be.'

Joe had never heard her speak like this before, with that note of regret in her voice. He didn't know what to say. She looked so sad at that moment that Joe's heart went out to her and when they had reached the gate, he gave her an extra special hug to let her know how loved she was, even if she didn't have a family of her own.

Chapter 19

Over the next few weeks, Joe and the family were good as their word, making sure Elizabeth and Arthur were able to manage financially, one or other of them visiting regularly. It was in fact about eight weeks before Arthur was able to return to work. His leg was fully healed although still rather weak and painful, but he didn't allow himself the luxury of further convalescence, being determined to start bringing money into the home again as soon as possible, and he sent Jimmy over to the Blake's to say that he was fit for work. Owner Blake said he was glad, and that he could join the next trip downriver, which was due to leave the Gorge on the following Monday morning.

Whilst at the Blake's house, Jimmy saw Abigail, who told him that she also was going down to Bridgnorth on the Oriel. As she hadn't had any days off for several months, Dorothea had agreed for her to take a few days to visit her son, her intention being to then re-join the Oriel on its return trip from Gloucester. Abigail asked Jimmy to let Elizabeth know that she was going down to sort things out with Michael once and for all. When Jimmy gave her the message, Elizabeth knew exactly what it meant and she was pleased that Abigail was determined to explain things to Michael, but also rather fearful of what consequences might follow. He was apparently doing well in Bridgnorth, and she hoped the news wouldn't knock him off course.

When Monday morning came, Owner Blake told Abigail he was going down to the wharf in the pony and trap as he needed to speak to the crew of the Oriel before it set sail, and he would be happy to take her down with him. Abigail gladly accepted his kind offer. She had managed to amass a few things for Michael from the market and packed them along with a few clothes in the old leather bag that Dorothea had lent her. She now sat with it on her knee, beside Owner Blake as they made their way down the Gorge to the Wharf where the Oriel was tied up.

It was early autumn and the trees on the thickly wooded slopes of the Severn Gorge had turned to golden red. Abigail thought she had never seen them looking so beautiful. She was excited at taking the trip down the Severn, but even more excited, if a little apprehensive, at seeing her son again. She knew it was time to tell him about his father and how he had been conceived. He had to know. There was no way to deny the connection between him and Furlong, given their features and red hair and she knew that if she didn't tell him soon, Michael would take matters into his own hands and confront him directly. All these thoughts were running through her head as they arrived at the Wharf.

She saw Arthur standing beside the trow and raised her hand in greeting. She thanked Owner Blake for his kindness as he stepped down from the trap, handing the reins to one of his men from the Oriel. As Arthur stepped forward, he asked how he was feeling now. Arthur said he was fully recovered and thanked him for agreeing to his return to work. Owner Blake then turned away to speak to Tom Blythe, the captain of the Oriel, handing him some documents and giving him various instructions about the journey ahead regarding the cargo and how it was to be handled.

Arthur helped Abigail down from the trap, handing her a small bundle Elizabeth had sent, telling her it contained a jacket Margaret had passed on, from the Hall. It was too small for Jimmy but should fit Michael and it was, he said, a good one, far too good to go to waste. He took Abigail's bag and led her up the gangplank onto the Oriel, settling her down in one corner of the deck, for her journey down to Bridgnorth.

The loading of the Oriel was completed within the hour, and they were sailing South by mid-morning. By mid-day they were tied up in Bridgnorth and Abigail said farewell to Arthur as he helped her down the gangplank onto the wharf. She stood for some moments, a little unsure which way to go. She had never walked from the wharf to Richard's house, having only been carried there in the pony and trap before. As Richard didn't know she was coming, there was no one to meet her. She asked one of the men on the dock the way to Andrews Grain Merchants, as she expected that both Richard and Michael would in any case be at the business premises.

After about ten minutes, as she rounded the corner of the main street it came into view. Although Abigail couldn't read the sign, it was obviously a business selling sacks of feed and grain, and various farming and horse-related items were suspended from nails along the wall, above the window of the shop premises. Next to the shop there was a large open archway, wide enough to allow the passage of wagons, which led into an internal courtyard.

Abigail stepped inside the shop, causing the large bell above the door to spring into life. A smell of leather, mingled with the earthy smell of grain and animal feed, enveloped Abigail as she stood nervously by the counter, waiting for the arrival of someone answering the call of the shop bell. After a few moments a young woman appeared through the door behind the counter and, smiling, asked Abigail what she could do for her. Abigail enquired whether Mr Richard Bangham, or Michael Bangham were in the building. Looking Abigail up and down, the girl said in an offhand way, that they were both there, and if she would give her name, she would enquire whether they were able to see her. When Abigail told her that she was Abigail Bangham, sister to Mr Richard, the girl became rather more focussed and said if Abigail would care to take a seat on the bench under the window, she would find them at once.

The girl disappeared and after a few minutes, Abigail could hear the sound of footsteps quickly descending the stairs beyond the door, and Richard bounded into the shop. He was obviously delighted to see Abigail standing there and told her so as he embraced her. He said he was sorry she'd had to walk from the wharf, but obviously, he hadn't known she was coming.

Abigail said it was fine and she had found her way easily enough.

'Michael will be delighted to see you Abigail,' he said, 'come with me and we'll see where he's got to.'

Abigail followed him into the back of the shop and down a narrow corridor before eventually emerging into the court-yard, where they immediately saw Michael in the far corner, stacking sacks of grain. Richard called to him and as he looked up and spotted his mother, his face broke into a wide grin. He tossed the sack he was holding onto the pile in front of him. Each time she visited, Abigail was amazed at how much he had grown, and today was no exception. He was almost as tall as Richard and looked as strong as any of the men working in the yard. Abigail swelled with pride as she watched him striding towards her, his face beaming.

He embraced his mother, obviously delighted to see her, and Abigail held him close for a moment or two.

Eventually they parted, but Michael held on to her hand saying,

'Mother! I didn't know you were coming. Are you staying for long?'

'Well,' said Abigail, 'I can stay until the Oriel returns from Gloucester in four days' time if Uncle Richard and Aunt Margaret will allow me.'

'Of course you can Abigail,' Richard interjected, 'Margaret will be delighted to see you.'

Then Richard turned to Michael, smiled, and said,

'Take your mother up to the house Michael, and you can take the rest of the day off and spend it with her.'

'Are you sure Uncle?' Michael replied, 'There's still a lot of work to do here.'

'Don't worry,' his uncle asserted, grinning, 'You can make up the time later in the week if you really want to!'

With that, Michael picked up his mother's bag and she took his arm as they made their way along the street to the steps leading up towards the main part of the town, which had been built on a rocky outcrop some hundred feet or so above the River Severn. About ten minutes later they had arrived at the Bangham's house, Abigail being no less impressed with it than she had been that first day she had arrived to visit Michael in the gaol. She shivered at the recollection of that dreadful time, but when she thought about her current mission, she felt almost as much horror. What would this day bring, she wondered. She was determined to speak to Michael as soon as possible, to give him plenty of time to talk to her about matters before she would have to leave him again.

Margaret made a great fuss as she opened the front door in answer to the ring of the large cast iron doorbell as it responded to the pull of the chain that hung beneath it.

'Abigail!' she exclaimed. 'How lovely to see you!' adding 'I wish I had known you were coming. I would have met you at the wharf with the trap. I'm assuming you came down on the Oriel?'

'I did,' Abigail replied. 'I was wondering if I could stay with you for a few days, until the Oriel returns from Gloucester?'

'Of course, we'd be delighted to have you! Come on in, please!' Margaret declared.

'Uncle Richard told me I could take the rest of the day off to spend with mother,' Michael told Margaret.

'Of course, that's a splendid idea,' she replied, then asked him to take Abigail's things up to the spare bedroom on the first floor. Abigail followed him and after she had unpacked her bag, gave him the jacket that Elizabeth had sent, which he seemed pleased with, and went off to take it up to his room. Abigail washed her hands and face and brushed her hair, then returned to the drawing room where Margaret was waiting for her with her son Richard, sitting on her lap. Abigail made a fuss of the child, who had his father's looks but his mother's thick brown hair.

Margaret rang the bell pull beside the fireplace and a few moments later the parlour maid appeared. Margaret instructed her to bring the ginger wine and two glasses, and then to prepare some lunch for them all. Abigail was overwhelmed once more with the affluence of her brother's home, but at the same time, felt privileged to be there. It was a source of pride to her that her own brother should have risen so far in the world. She told Margaret that if she didn't mind, after lunch she would like to spend some time alone with Michael as she had something she needed to discuss with him. Margaret, having some idea what that may be about, suggested that perhaps they might go for a walk along the clifftop path which passed in front of the house.

When Michael returned Abigail was sipping the wine, conversing easily with Margaret, and looking very much at home in the comfortable drawing room. Young Richard immediately jumped down from his mother's knee and ran up to Michael who immediately picked him up and started to tickle him. Abigail was pleased to see that the child obviously thought the world of his cousin Michael. The parlour maid had now set out a light lunch for them all in the dining room and entered the room to inform her mistress that it was ready. They enjoyed a meal of broth and bread and then, after thanking Margaret, Abigail got up, saying to Michael that she would like him to join her on a walk along the clifftop, as she would like to admire the view of the River Severn far below. He readily agreed. It was his favourite walk, he told her.

Half an hour later they were sitting on a rock beside the clifftop path, looking down on the river, a view that Michael never tired of. It always reminded him of home as he watched the river flowing on its endless journey. Abigail was nervous. She knew she had to do this, to tell Michael about his father and what had happened to her all those years ago. She had to do it for Michael. In fact, she couldn't have done it for anyone else. She had never spoken to anyone about what had actually happened that night, but now she must. Michael mustn't be kept in ignorance about what kind of a man his father was. He must never be allowed to think he was a good man who he might feel he wanted to emulate. She couldn't risk him wanting to get to know him. She knew that James Furlong could easily have convinced the lad that what had happened was her fault, and she couldn't let that happen.

After five minutes Michael himself broke the silence.

'Mother,' he said, in a tone suggesting that something important was to follow. 'Mother,' he repeated. 'I have asked you this before, but...'

Abigail's palms suddenly grew damp, and her stomach churned as she realised what was coming.

'I need you to tell me the truth. Who was that man we saw at Madeley Wood market all those years ago? He said I was his son, and his hair was like mine. I have never seen anyone else with hair like mine, so you must tell me now, is he my father?'

Abigail sat for some moments, not speaking, but with her mind racing. She had practised this so many times over the years. She had always known the moment would come when she could no longer avoid telling him the truth, and she knew that moment had now arrived.

Finally, she managed, 'Michael, you are right, it is time you knew the truth.'

Michael sat forward, eager to hear what she had to say to him. Finally, after seven years, he hoped he was going to find out who his father was.

Abigail looked into his eyes and said,

'I'm going to tell you exactly what happened Michael, and it may not be what you want to hear, but I believe you are now old enough to understand, and I hope you will not judge me harshly.

'I was just fifteen years old, working at the Hall as the scullery maid. The man you saw at the market is James Furlong and he is the under-butler at the Hall. I knew nothing of the world, never having left Banghams Wood before the day I was sent up to the Hall. I was determined to do my best and worked hard. I had noticed James Furlong observing me sometimes and smiling at me, but I just thought he was being friendly and smiled back. You will never know how often I regretted ever smiling at him.

'Anyway, it was about six months after I entered service that one night as I was sleeping in my room in the attic, I was woken up with someone's hand across my mouth. I was very afraid as I didn't know who it was. I hope I don't need to go into detail about what followed in the next five minutes. I was terrified and thought he might harm me if I resisted and so I did not.'

Michael looked horrified.

'What are you saying mother. Did he force himself upon you?'

'Yes, Michael, he did. Afterwards he ignored me completely and I began to think it must have been my fault. I had smiled at him, and in my innocence, concluded that must have been why he did that to me. It was some weeks later that I realised that I was carrying you. I never told him because I didn't want him to have anything to do with you. I had to leave service to return to Banghams Wood, then when Uncle Joe built his house in Dale Coppice, we went to live with him there. I had hoped that you would never see him, and therefore never need to know the truth about how you were conceived.'

Michael was silent, obviously struggling to process the information she'd just given him. After some minutes, he stood up, and without a word, ran along the clifftop path, back the way they had come, leaving Abigail distraught. She realised he would need time and space to process what she had just told him, but as he hadn't indicated how he was feeling, she was terrified that he would be blaming her, thinking that maybe she had been too easy with her favours. She couldn't bear the thought of him thinking badly of her or losing respect for her. She sat for a full hour, completely unable to decide whether she should follow him back to the house and try to talk to him or leave him alone to ponder over what she had just told him.

Michael was in a state of utter confusion. He had waited so long to find out who his father was. It had recently become something of an obsession. As he was becoming a man, he needed to know what kind of a man had given him life. He needed to understand where he had come from. There had always been a void in his life where a father should have stood. His uncles had been kind and tried to be a father to him, in their different ways, but it wasn't the same. He had never felt a father's love, never been able to walk in his shoes. There were things he couldn't talk to his mother about, things only a father could understand, and he wasn't close enough to any of his uncles to confide in them in the same way.

Now he knew that his father, the man who should have been part of his life from the beginning, had never wanted him and he had only been conceived as an unwanted by-product of a selfish, evil act perpetrated on his mother. This was challenging his own view of himself. Was he like this man who had taken his pleasure from his mother against her will. From his position of power, he had violated an innocent, vulnerable girl, which was unforgiveable. He was his son, even looked like him, perhaps he was like him in other ways? He thought about the poaching affair. He had tried to forget about it as he was deeply ashamed of letting his mother down. Now it occurred to him that maybe he had a weakness in his character inherited from his father, a selfishness that had led him to ignore the hurt he may cause his mother, just to gratify his own selfish wish for excitement.

Then he thought of Miranda and was even more confused. She was the girl who worked in the shop, and he was finding it hard not to think about her. She was a pretty girl with plenty of spirit and every time he saw her, he had the urge to kiss her and hold her close. Such thoughts now seemed dangerous, even disgusting. Was this how his father had felt, and is that what led him to do what he did?

He had run into the house by the back door and past cook without speaking to her, going immediately up to his attic room. He needed to think. And yet, he didn't want to think. He wished his mother had never told him. He wished he could still imagine that his father was a good man. He would rather he had been a kind, dead man, than an evil one who was still living. At least then he would not have had to make the decision whether or not to meet him. He knew deep down that even though he was, in this respect, evil, he would still need to find out more about him if he was to understand more about himself. He also knew that this would hurt his mother deeply. She would not understand his need to know more about this man, and may see it as a betrayal, or worse, that he blamed her for what had happened, which of course, he did not.

His mother! As he lay on his bed, another, even more disturbing thought came into his head. When she looked at him, did she see his father? Each time she had looked at him, smiled at him, hugged him close, had she been reminded of that night? How could she love him, being the product of an act, which had brought her shame and ruin? A deep pain rose from the pit of his stomach, and a feeling of dread engulfed him. Could the love that had surrounded him all his life be an illusion? If each time she looked at him brought her pain, how could she also love him? Was this one reason why she had sent him to Bridgnorth, so that she need no longer be reminded of how he came into existence. Now the tears began to flow. He thumped his pillow in a mixture of fear and anger.

Meanwhile, Abigail was utterly distraught, but not altogether surprised, at Michael's reaction to her news. She was afraid she was about to lose her son. Would he understand? Would he blame her for what had happened? Could their close relationship survive this? She knew it would inevitably be changed. It could no longer be that of mother and child. To understand and accept her after this revelation, Michael would have to grow up somewhat and come to realise that his mother was, after all, just a human being with feelings of her own, and not some kind of superior being whose sole purpose in life was to love and cherish him. At the same time, he would have to deal with the knowledge that his father was a selfish, cruel man who took what he wanted without thought for his victims, and Abigail was sure she hadn't been the only one. All these thoughts were going through her mind as she made her way back along the clifftop path to the house.

As she arrived, Richard was also approaching the gate from the opposite direction, on his way home from the business. As soon as she saw him, the emotions she had kept in check throughout the afternoon, came tumbling out, and she fell into his arms, weeping and saying,

'Oh Richard, I know I had to tell him, but it was so hard and then he just ran off without a word. What shall I do if he wants nothing more to do with me?'

Richard knew immediately what she meant.

'You did the right thing Abigail. The lad needed to know the truth, however painful. Give him time. He's a bright lad and he'll work it out for himself. It's a lot for him to come to terms with. If you like, I'll have a word with him. He may need someone to help him to think it through. I won't force him to listen, just let him know I'm here if he needs to talk.'

'Thank you so much Richard,' Abigail managed through her tears, and began to calm down, reassured that Richard would be there for Michael as he wrestled with his feelings.

Michael didn't come down for supper that night. He couldn't face his mother yet. He couldn't bear to see the rejection in her eyes that he was now convinced would appear. She now knew that he was aware that she had been shamed and humiliated when he was conceived. There was, after all, no more possibility of sustaining the illusion. She must either love him for himself or hate him for being the object of her shame. He wasn't yet ready to find out which.

When the rest of the family had eaten, Margaret took some food and drink up to his room, knocking quietly on the door before entering. Her heart went out to him as she saw his tear-stained face and look of deep sadness in his eyes. She lit his candle and placed the tray of food beside the bed, before urging him to eat it, then quietly left without waiting for a reply. He couldn't face eating the food and eventually fell into a troubled sleep filled with disturbing images of a man with red hair but whose face was blank.

He woke early next morning and was out of the house before Abigail came down to breakfast, still not able to face her. He threw himself into his work, trying not to talk to anyone, his mind still full of doubts, about himself, his mother and yes, his father and how much of his own character he'd inherited from him. He avoided Miranda all day. Right now, he could do without those disturbing feelings.

For her part, Abigail had hardly slept, convinced her son must think less of her, even be ashamed of her, after what she had told him. She wouldn't blame him. She had been ashamed of herself for a long time after it happened, convinced that she must have led Furlong on. Of course, she had long realised that as the innocent child she had been, it wasn't her fault he had decided to satisfy his urges at her expense. Maybe Michael would come to realise that too, she thought.

Richard had observed Michael during the day, seeing that he was just getting on with his work and avoiding speaking to anyone. By mid-afternoon, he decided to try to speak to him about what he was going through and called to him to come up to his office above the shop. As Michael entered the passage to go up to the office, Miranda was coming the other way. Normally he would have smiled at her and said hello, but now he passed her with his head down and never even looked up, nor did he speak, even though she greeted him with her usual cheery 'Hello Michael!'.

He knocked on the office door and heard Richard tell him to enter. His uncle was sitting behind his desk, smiling at him.

'You wanted to see me, Uncle?' he enquired.

'Sit down, please, Michael.' Richard said, gesturing to the chair in front of the desk, then went on, 'I know your mother has given you some news that has upset you,' he began.

Before he could say anything else, Michael looked him in the eye and then asked,

'You mean, you know? Does everyone? Does the whole world know I came about in this way?'

'Michael, look, I understand how you must feel, but ...'

'Do you? How can you Uncle? My whole life has been a lie, my existence a source of pain and shame to those I love. It would have been better if I'd never been born!'

'Michael,' Richard said with an air of authority now. 'You must never say that or even think it. Your mother loves you, has always loved you since the moment she first held you in her arms. We all have and will always love you. How you came into existence will never change that.'

'How can she though Uncle? How can she look at me and not think about him and what he did to her?'

'Because, Michael,' Richard answered with his voice full of conviction, 'love is stronger than hate.'

At this, a glimmer of hope entered Michael's mind. Could this be true? Could a mother's love overcome hatred? He thought about that love. She had struggled to be father and mother to him, had sacrificed her own ambitions to the responsibilities of raising him, clothing, and feeding him, sometimes at the expense of satisfying her own needs. Even when he had let her down by getting involved in the poaching business, she had stood by him.

The few words his uncle had uttered – 'love is stronger than hate' had resonated with something within him and he knew he was right. By her every action throughout his life, his mother had shown him that she did love him, and suddenly he was ashamed he had ever doubted it.

Richard said nothing, just sitting quietly, wisely letting the lad work it out for himself. Eventually, Michael spoke,

'Do you think I could take the rest of the afternoon off uncle; I really need to speak with mother. I think I owe her an apology.'

Richard smiled and said, 'Of course lad, you get yourself away to your mother.'

With that, Michael quickly left and ran all the way up the steps and along the lane to the house, seeing Abigail sitting quietly by the window in the drawing room. She looked up as he approached, and he smiled at her. She smiled back with some relief. As he entered the drawing room she stood up and faced him. He went to her and embraced her, saying,

'Mother, I'm so sorry!'

'What on earth do you have to be sorry for?' she asked.

'For ever doubting that you love me. I couldn't believe that you could, after what happened.'

'My dear boy, that was never in doubt. You are my son, my son alone, no-one else's, and I love you more than life itself.'

With that, mother and son embraced, clinging to each other for some moments, each afraid to let the other go in case anything else should come between. Abigail spent another couple of days with Michael in Bridgnorth and as she was boarding the Oriel to leave, he assured her he wouldn't be seeking James Furlong out. He now had no desire to get to know the man. He couldn't help being a little curious about him, but his disgust at what he'd done had negated any residual desire he may have had to get to know him.

Abigail felt closer to her son than ever before. She knew now she had been right to tell him, ensuring the one threat to their relationship had been removed. Michael, for his part, felt more 'whole' than he had ever felt. The void that had been the place where a father should have been, wasn't exactly filled, but at least he knew he need no longer go on searching for answers, and that brought him some peace. He also understood his mother better and felt an overwhelming desire to care for her and to make sure that her life from now on would be easier. He waved to her as the Oriel drew away from the dock, swearing to himself that once he was earning enough to have a home of his own, he would insist that she give up her life in service and come to live with him. He would make sure she never wanted for anything, ever again.

Chapter 20

The next couple of years in Dale Coppice passed by without major incident. Will and Betty had remained lodging with Joe and Liz, an arrangement that suited them all well enough. However, with Will and Betty now expecting their first child together, and Liz pregnant again, the baby due in December 1733, the cottage certainly began to feel rather too small for them all, soon to be ten in number.

Abigail was still in service with the Blakes although she had told Joe and Will of Michael's plan to have her move over to Bridgnorth to live with him as soon as he could get his own place. In any case, Richard and Margaret were expecting their third child, and they would be needing the space for their own family, Michael told his mother. He was eighteen now and had completed his apprenticeship. Apparently, Richard wanted him to stay on at the firm as stock manager when he would be earning a decent wage. Consequently, she was hoping to be moving to Bridgnorth within the year. Joe and the others were pleased for her, they felt she deserved to be looked after for a change. Of course, with this news, Joe felt that his duty to look after Abigail was at an end and he was free to move his family out of Dale Coppice.

So, it was decided that Joe would enquire again about a company house. The building of a row that had been talked about a couple of years earlier hadn't materialised, but now he had heard that Mr Ford was about to lease a row of cottages near the new furnace at Dale End, known as Nailer's Row. Joe had now worked for the company for twenty years and he knew he was a valuable employee, with much skill and experience. Consequently, he believed he would stand a good chance of being given the tenancy of one of the two bedroomed houses. He spoke to Mr Ford as soon as the opportunity arose, who didn't hesitate in telling Joe that he would be pleased to let him lease one of the houses, for as long as he worked for the company. Joe thanked him and hurried home to give the others the good news.

June 1733 found the family preparing to move. Liz was happy to be getting one of the houses. A brick-built house with two sizeable bedrooms upstairs and a living room and a scullery on the ground floor, seemed like a 'step up' for the family. In addition, she was pleased to be moving her children away from the Coppice. Far too many rough sorts had continued to move in over the last few years. She was sorry to be moving away from her parents, as they weren't getting any younger. However, her sister was still living at home and Betty and Will would still be next door.

It was decided they would make the move as soon as the furnace was blown out, probably at the end of June. It was actually during the first week in July that the family's belongings were piled on a cart, borrowed from one of the waggoners who transported goods to and from the wharf. The Spencers were genuinely sorry to see them leave. Joe and John had become firm friends over the years, and of course, the Spencers would rather their daughter remained in the coppice. Liz reassured them that she would be only ten minutes' walk away down the hill and would still see them often.

Will and Betty, now heavily pregnant, were looking forward to having the place to themselves. They had agreed to rent the cottage from Joe at a nominal rent of a shilling a week. They thanked him for all his help, and Will offered to go with the family to help unload the wagon when they arrived at the cottage in Nailer's Row.

The wagon was piled high with their possessions, with Liz and the children perched on top. Will and Joe walked behind as they slowly made their way down the cobbled Dale Road towards the river. Nailer's Row was about two thirds of the way towards the Severn, standing to the right-hand side of the road. As always, there were other wagons coming and going to and from the river and the works. As they pulled up at the house, Liz reminded herself they would have to keep an eye on the children, as the houses had no front gardens and the doors opened straight onto the roadway. Furthermore, they were closer to one source of fumes and smoke as the new furnace was only a hundred yards or so further up the valley. With Joe's help, she clambered down off the wagon with Benjamin in her arms. Young Elizabeth climbed down behind her, helping Nathaniel to do the same.

When they entered the house, it seemed spacious. The living room was about twelve feet square with a cast iron fireplace with an oven beside the grate. Beyond the door at the back of the room was a narrow passage leading through to the scullery and washhouse. Beside the door to the washhouse, stairs ran up to the bedrooms. The front bedroom, being over the living room, had similar proportions and a small fireplace. The back bedroom was smaller, but Liz felt it was of ample size for the children. Looking out of the back bedroom window, onto the communal area she was disappointed to see only one privy to one end of the space. She had thought they would have their own private privy, but it was obvious that it was to be used by the residents of all five houses. Still, overall, she was pleased enough with the house, which seemed well built with higher ceilings and larger windows than she had been used to. She felt she would be able to make a good home here for the family, one they could be proud of.

Joe and Will soon had their possessions unloaded. They were pretty basic after all. They had left quite a few pieces for Will and Betty, Joe saying that he would soon be buying or making new furniture for their new home. They had brought their beds of course, and the old trunk, along with the settle and a couple of stools.

Over the next few weeks Joe and Liz worked hard to make their new home comfortable. They managed to pick up a few pieces of second-hand furniture and Liz made curtains for the windows. Life was rather different than it had been in Dale Coppice. As the vegetable plot Liz had been cultivating for years was left behind in the coppice, she had to start all over again with a new patch, which would take some time to establish. In the meantime, Joe brought some provisions from the plot in Dale Coppice whenever he could. There was no communal pump as there had been in the Coppice, and twice a day she had to carry water from the spring several minutes' walk away up the road towards the works. Also, as she had suspected, Liz had to pay rather more attention to the children now that they were living on the main road. No longer could she allow them to go outside alone, to explore the woods around the cottage or collect kindling for the fire. There was more or less constant noise as the wagons trundled up and down the cobbles and the hammering of the forges and noises from the foundry further up the valley resounded day and night. Still, Liz and Joe were pleased with the house itself and particularly with the privacy it gave them.

Betty went into labour on 20th August 1733. Her labour was quick and reasonably easy and by eleven o'clock that night she had given birth to a healthy little boy, who they named Walter. A week later Joe and his family visited the coppice to greet the new baby and Susan Spencer had prepared a meal for them all in their cottage. Liz was happy to visit her parents and to catch up with everyone's news. Will said he'd been over to Banghams Wood to see Elizabeth the week before. Arthur had been away downriver but as it happened, Margaret had also been visiting. He said Margaret had looked rather thin and drawn and he was worried about her, but apparently young Jane was doing well, and was now a kitchen maid.

Later, as the family were returning to Nailer's Row, Elizabeth and Nathaniel walked in front holding hands, Liz, and Joe, who was carrying Benjamin followed them down to Dale End. It was a lovely evening and the Dale looked particularly beautiful, with the late summer sun sinking in the West, throwing its golden light along the Gorge. He could see Banghams Wood in the distance and wondered how his sister and her family were faring.

Joe himself though, was content. He was proud of his little family, and the home he had now provided for them. Elizabeth, now nine years old was a bonny, bright girl with golden curls just like her mother, and she doted on four-year-old Nathaniel who was dark like his father. They were rarely apart, and he adored his big sister. Benjamin was two and a half and beginning to chatter in that delightful way two-year-olds do. Joe looked at Liz as they strolled down the lane and smiled. She glanced across and smiled back, saying.

'What? What's so funny?'

'Nothing,' Joe replied. 'Just that I love you, Liz.'

'I know.' she said. 'I love you too,' and right then, life was good for this Bangham family. Of course, life was not always predictable, and the following months were to bring even more change to the lives of Joe and his family.

The summer had been dry, and it wasn't until mid-September that the pools were full enough for the furnaces to be blown in, but Joe and a few of the men had been busy for a week or so beforehand, preparing to restart production. Mr Ford had told him they were going to try a new formula in the furnace, using coal from a new source. This coal he told Joe, should produce a better grade of iron, which might be more suitable for making wrought iron. Heaps of the new coal had been slow burning over the summer break and were now cooling, ready for the coke to be transported to the top of the furnace to be added to the limestone and iron ore. It took a couple of days to load up the platform with the raw materials that would be needed.

The furnace was lit and the sluice from the pool high above was opened, allowing the water to flow and turn the wheel to drive the bellows, and the furnace was charged using the proportions of material specified by Mr Ford. Within a few hours the furnace was roaring, and within a few more it was time to draw off the first of the iron by knocking out the clay plug at the base of the furnace. Joe was always a little nervous as the first iron of the season began to pour out of the orange mouth, sparks flying everywhere. He was particularly apprehensive because the proportions of ingredients had been changed. The intensity of the heat was always shocking and however many times he witnessed it, a certain level of fear gripped Joe. Ever since he had witnessed the accident when one of the men lost his arm, he had known what damage the molten metal could do to a human body.

On this particular day, Billy Owens, a young man who had been working for the company for several years, and was one of the most experienced workers, was on shift. Knowing that Billy was competent, Joe gave him the job of knocking out the clay plug at the base of the furnace to allow the molten metal to flow.

'Right oh, Joe,' Billy said, and picked up the sledgehammer, preparing to strike the plug. He swung the hammer and struck the plug, expecting that it would release a steady flow of molten iron into the trench below. However, whether it was because of the new formulation, or just a horrendous combination of circumstance, as the plug fell away, the metal didn't flow downwards, but shot outwards, hitting Billy full in the chest. As it bit into his flesh he screamed in agony. Joe quickly grabbed Billy, pulling him away from the metal, now pooling on the floor.

As soon as Joe was able to take a good look at Billy, he could see it was hopeless. The metal had cut across the middle of Billy's body, biting into his flesh, almost cutting him in two. The young man died almost instantly, and Joe realised it was a blessed relief that he did. The other men rushed over to where Billy lay. To their horror they could see that the lad was already dead. Mr Ford had arrived and told them to bring the handcart and in shocked silence the men loaded Billy's body onto it and took him home to his widowed mother, who was living in a cottage in Dale Coppice.

Joe was distraught. He blamed himself, as he had given Billy the job of unplugging the furnace. Maybe changing the formula had caused gas pressures to build up within the iron? He told himself he should have been aware that it might behave differently and maybe as foreman, he should have done the job himself. Logically, this was just an unforeseeable accident and Joe knew that, but it did nothing to assuage his feelings of guilt. He had gone with the men as they wheeled the body to Mrs Owens, and the sound of her wailing as she saw her son, continued to ring in his ears long after that terrible day. She was a widow; her husband having died in a mining accident some years before and Billy had been her only means of support. Joe knew she might now be destitute and could well end up in Mine Spout poorhouse. As it was, Mr Ford, being a good and honourable man and because Billy had died at work, paid for the funeral, and made provision for Mrs Owens so that she was able to live out her days in her home in the coppice.

The whole episode hit Joe hard. Although he continued to work at the furnace, the enjoyment had gone. The place now filled him with horror, and it took extraordinary effort for him to control his fear. He had a responsible job and he realised in a way that he hadn't previously, that the lives of his men were in his hands. Liz noticed the difference in him with sadness. He looked older and as though he was carrying a great burden. However often she told him he wasn't to blame for the lad's death, he couldn't forgive himself. Every day at the works he was reminded of Billy Owens, and how he would never know the joy of being a husband and father. In fact, over the years that followed, he took it upon himself to call on Billy's mother from time to time, to make sure that she was managing. It helped to lessen his feelings of guilt, but they never quite went away. After Billy's death, Joe was never quite the same. The memory of that dreadful day stayed with him, and not even the birth of their fourth and last child, Anne, in December of that year, could lift his mood.

The family continued to settle into Nailer's Row and to get to know their neighbours. There were a further four families living in the row. They seemed a decent enough lot to Liz and with a total of more than twenty children of various ages between them, the place was always full of the sounds of children playing in the backs. Initially, with thirty or more people all sharing one privy it wasn't ideal to say the least, but at Liz's instigation, Joe soon organised the building of two more initially, and they all determined to build a further two so that in the end each house would have its own. Water was more of an issue. With no pump serving the row, it all had to be carried from the brook up the valley. Joe and the rest of the men, who were all renting their homes from Mr Ford, determined to ask him to install a water pump. Within the year they had their pump and life became a little easier.

At the Works, the demand for steam engine cylinders was growing steadily. No less than ten had been produced in 1732 and Mr Ford, anticipating increasing demand in the years to come, had constructed a boring mill, which had recently begun work. Tipped off by Joe that there were jobs going, Will approached Mr Ford to ask him if he could move from the mine to the boring mill. As he had been a good worker, and out of respect for Joe, Mr Ford agreed to give him a trial. Will was delighted. Although the money wasn't much better than what he'd been earning in the mine, it was more regular and he felt the conditions, although still harsh, would be much preferable to crawling on his belly for what seemed like miles in the pitch black, to reach the coalface.

The young Abraham Darby 11 had now joined Mr Ford in managing the company, and the following year, rainfall had been particularly low in the Gorge, prompting them to install a horse driven pump so that the water flowing over the bellows wheel could be returned to the pools and re-used. Production could now continue the whole year round, which was a mixed blessing for the furnacemen. Although they now had continuous work and therefore wages, there was now no respite from the drudgery of twelve-hour days. In addition, a system of double shifts on Sundays was instigated in order to keep the furnaces working at maximum capacity, which meant working two full weeks before taking every other Sunday off.

Predictably, Will voiced his opinion that it just wasn't right to expect men to work nonstop for thirteen days or nights, urging Joe to object. Although he was unhappy about it, there was no way he could object without losing his job. There were plenty of men around the district who would have been only too glad to take his place, however long the hours might be.

The years continued to roll along, and Joe's work seemed to grow harder each year. With no break during the summer, and working two weeks at a stretch, the strain on Joe, who in 1737 was now forty years old grew steadily. The long hours and hard physical labour were beginning to take their toll. He could see that the progress being made in the business was coming at a price, particularly to the workforce, but also to the quality of life in Coalbrookdale. Billy Owens hadn't been the last workman to lose his life working for the Company. As activity increased and the size and quantity of their products grew, inevitably so did the dangers. At least half a dozen men had been maimed or killed in the years since Billy's demise, mostly it had to be said, in the mines, the forges and the foundry. As for the air quality, as the furnaces were now working all year round, there was no opportunity for the fumes to disperse, and a constant bluish haze hung over the narrow Coalbrookdale valley.

The children were growing fast. Nathaniel was now seven years old, the image of his father with his dark hair, and a bright lad with endless curiosity. Benjamin, five, was more like his mother and his older sister Elizabeth, with his curly blond hair and ready smile. Anne, being just two, already had a mind of her own and reminded Joe of his sister Dorothy when she was small. Liz remarked to Joe that the time was coming to think about finding a place for Elizabeth. She was thirteen next birthday and old enough to go into service. Joe wouldn't hear of it. He had no intention of allowing his eldest daughter to be a scullery maid, remembering what had happened to Abigail, and how her life had been ruined by 'that man'. He hadn't seen Abigail for a couple of years as she was living in Bridgnorth with Michael, and he wondered how life was treating her. He hadn't seen Richard and Margaret either for that matter. There never seemed time to visit people these days. Work dominated everything and he hadn't even had the chance to see Elizabeth and Arthur during the past year. He decided that on his next Sunday off, he would definitely make his way across the river to find out how they were faring.

He arrived at the clearing a couple of weeks later having been ferried across the river by Jimmy, who had given him some disturbing news. He said that Arthur hadn't been too well of late. He'd a bad cough that never seemed to get any better and he knew Elizabeth was very worried about him.

Joe had climbed the path from the river towards Banghams Wood, emerging from the trees behind the cottage, and found Elizabeth tending her vegetable patch. She hadn't seen him approach and he stood for a moment, just watching her. He could see immediately that she was looking older. She seemed bent over, and was moving more slowly than he remembered, pulling turnips.

He called her name, and she spun round to see him striding towards her. Her face lit up and she shouted his name, saying how pleased she was to see him there. Wiping her hands on her apron she held out her arms to embrace Joe warmly. She hadn't seen him for over a year, and it would be true to say that they both noticed that time was taking its toll on their sibling. Elizabeth had obviously lost some weight and looked rather tired. As for Joe, Elizabeth thought he looked older and a little more world weary, no longer the bright, eager young man who had stridden off to seek his fortune across the valley, all those years ago.

Arm in arm they entered the cottage. Joe was pleased to see that, as usual there was a pot bubbling over the fire. Some things never change, he thought to himself. Elizabeth explained that Arthur was in bed as he hadn't been too well of late. She didn't say what was wrong with him but the look of fear in her eyes told its own story. A few minutes later, Arthur, having heard Joe arrive, came slowly down the stairs. Joe was shocked. His eyes were red-rimmed, and his skin was deathly white.

'Sorry to hear you haven't been well Arthur,' he said.

'Just a bit of a chest,' Arthur replied, before being struck by a coughing fit, the sound of which was obviously terrifying Elizabeth, and told Joe that this was no bout of bronchitis. They had all heard the sound of that cough before and knew exactly what it was. Arthur had a fight on his hands. Consumption took no prisoners and Joe had never known anyone who had beaten it.

When the coughing subsided, Arthur slumped in the chair before the fire, his head in his hands. He looked utterly weary. Elizabeth gave him a drink of honey and warm water from the jug she had previously prepared and stood in the hearth to keep warm. He was calmer now and they were soon sitting in front of the fire, catching up on all the news. Elizabeth asked after Liz and the children of course, and Joe confided to her that he didn't know what to do about Elizabeth. The family was growing, and his wages weren't keeping pace with their demands. Elizabeth would soon be thirteen and must soon be contributing in some way to the family finances. However, he told his sister, the last thing he wanted was for her to go into service. Even though Jane, her own daughter had found work up at the Hall, she understood Joe's reluctance. What had happened to Abigail had hit him particularly hard.

A thought occurred to Elizabeth. Last time Margaret had visited the cottage, she had mentioned that Dorothy had visited the Hall with John the week before, when he came to teach the children. She had told Margaret how well the Charity School was doing now and that soon they would have to get some help to deal with the smaller children, who really just needed someone to supervise them and to play some simple games with them, to get them ready for more serious learning that would follow. Elizabeth wondered whether Dorothy and John might be prepared to take Elizabeth in, to teach her to read and write and do sums, while at the same time she could help out with the little ones. That way, she would be getting some education and her keep, but not of course, be paid enough to send money home. Joe said that would be a small price to pay for her to learn to read and write.

Elizabeth suggested she could mention it to Margaret when she next visited. Perhaps she could ask her friend, the lady's maid, to write a note to Dorothy asking her if she could possibly call on Joe when it was convenient. Joe wondered whether that might not be asking too much of his sister, without telling her what he wanted to speak to her about. Elizabeth, however, thought it would be better to speak with Dottie face to face and if he wasn't able to get the time to go to Madeley Wood, she was sure that Dottie would be glad to spare the time to visit him if she was able. So it was decided, and Elizabeth said she would speak to Margaret on her next visit.

Joe spent another couple of hours with Elizabeth and Arthur and by the time he left he knew that poor Arthur would not be long for this world. As he walked down the steps to the river, he was wondering how Elizabeth would possibly manage when Arthur's time came. She would still have Jimmy of course, and the rent from Arthur's cottage, but it would be difficult for her. He would of course do what he could, but that wouldn't be much. They were hardly managing themselves and there just wasn't enough money coming in to take on responsibility for Elizabeth as well. As he arrived at the river, he put the matter to one side and gave his attention to clambering into Jimmy's coracle to be ferried across to the far bank.

'What did you think of father?' Jimmy asked, his voice full of concern.

'Well, to be honest Jimmy lad, I don't think it looks too good for him,' Joe replied.

'I know you're right Uncle Joe.' Jimmy went on, 'I'm right worried as to how Ma and me will manage, but I guess this isn't the time to be thinking about that, although I have been wondering whether I ought to ask Owner Blake if I could take father's place on the trow. The money would be better than what I'm making with the coracles.'

'Well, don't do anything rash Jimmy,' Joe told him, 'Let's just see how things work out first.'

'You're probably right Uncle,' Jimmy said, and with that, they parted company and Jimmy cast off the coracle to return to the other side of the Severn.

Chapter 21

When Joe arrived at Nailer's Row, he was eager to tell Liz about his plan for Elizabeth. She wasn't entirely supportive of his idea. She didn't really want to see her eldest daughter, who was now very helpful with the little ones, leave home just yet. At the same time, she knew the family finances were struggling to keep them all, and one less mouth to feed would certainly help the situation, and she would certainly be happy to see her daughter learning to read and write. Living with the schoolmaster and mistress would inevitably offer her opportunities of meeting people of higher social standing, greatly increasing the chances of her eventually marrying well and rising in society. Therefore she put aside her own misgivings at losing her daughter and told Joe she would certainly support his plan if Dottie could find herself able to take Elizabeth on at the school.

One Sunday afternoon, a month later, a pony and trap pulled up outside Nailer's Row. This was a rare event. In fact, no-one could remember such an occurrence. As Joe looked out of the window, he was delighted to see his sister sitting on the trap beside her husband who was holding the reins of a brown and white pony. Joe rushed outside to greet them. He assumed that Margaret must have succeeded in sending the note as planned, but he was utterly astonished that Dottie and John had made the effort to visit them.

He suggested that John tie up the pony at the post at the end of the row, and then helped his sister to climb down. He was unsure whether to embrace her. She looked so fine, clean, and tidy in a neat jacket and skirt, and he was conscious of his own grubby appearance. He needn't have worried. This was Dottie, and she hadn't changed a bit. She threw herself at him and gave him a huge hug.

'Joe!' she cried, 'It's so good to see you!'

Liz, who had also been hanging back, a little unsure of herself, not really having had much to do with Dottie over the years, finally stepped forward. Dottie extricated herself from Joe's embrace and stepped towards Liz, arms outstretched.

'Liz, it's lovely to see you, it's been too long!' Then, seeing the children standing behind her, exclaimed, 'Gracious! I can't believe how they've grown!'

'Please, come inside,' Liz offered, with as much grace as she could muster, although she was a little daunted at meeting this young woman who, though family, seemed so confident and far above them in status.

By then John had tied up the pony and joined them.

'This is nice Joe,' Dottie declared as she surveyed the cosy room with its roaring fire with a colourful rag rug in front of the hearth. Liz had just completed the rug and was particularly proud of it. Everywhere there were signs that every attempt had been made to make it comfortable, presumably Liz's doing, Dottie thought. From the heavy curtains to the white lace cover on the trunk, and the little ornaments here and there, the whole gave an appearance of being a well-cared for home, albeit not an affluent one.

'Please,' said Liz, 'do sit down. Joe, pull up the settle nearer to the fire, and can you fetch the stool from the scullery?' The children sat on the trunk under the window, except young Anne, who climbed on her mother's knee.

Eventually they all settled down in front of the fire and the conversation turned to the reason for their visit. Liz was glad she had already mentioned to Elizabeth the possibility that she might be going to live with her Aunt Dorothy and her Uncle John at the schoolhouse. She hadn't been too keen on the idea, but when it was explained to her that she would be able to learn to read and write and would avoid going into service, which would have been the other alternative, she had begun to accept the idea.

'Dottie, John,' Joe began, 'I'm so glad you could see your way to visiting us. Can I assume that you received a note from Margaret?'

'We did Joe,' John replied, 'and we have been wondering why you asked us to call.'

'Well,' Joe went on, pausing rather awkwardly, then continued, all in a rush, 'as you know, our Elizabeth is going on thirteen now and we have been wondering, frankly, what is to be done with her. We don't want her to work at the pit heaps, or to go into service with strangers,' then, after another brief pause he said, 'Look, I'll come straight to the point if you don't mind, we were wondering whether you might be in need of some help around the house Dorothy, or even with the younger children at the school. She is wonderful with the little ones, and I'm sure she could be of real help to you.'

There was a short silence, when Joe and Liz were beginning to think they had been too presumptuous in even asking. Then Dorothy said,

'Well, as it happens, this may be the answer we are ourselves looking for, isn't that right John?' she said, smiling at her husband.

'It is,' he replied, smiling back at her. 'You see, Dorothy is with child, and will certainly be needing more help around the house and with caring for the child when it is a little older, as when I am away, she would like to go on teaching at the school.'

Joe and Liz declared how happy they were to hear their news.

Dorothy went on,

'Thank you so much, both of you. Actually, you are the first to know. As for Elizabeth,' at this, she turned towards her, asking, 'Elizabeth, would you like to come and stay with Uncle John and I? I would be happy to teach you to read and write, and you would be able to help me around the house and with the children?'

Dutifully, Elizabeth replied.

'Yes, thank you Aunt Dorothy.'

'Are you sure Dottie? I wouldn't be able to give you anything for her keep,' Joe said, rather shamefacedly.

'Don't worry about that Joe,' John interjected, 'Elizabeth will earn her keep, I'm sure.'

'When is your baby due Dorothy?' Liz asked.

'Dottie, please Liz, everyone calls me Dottie! The baby should be born in about six months, round about Christmas time.

'In that case Dottie,' Liz asked, 'when would you like her to join you?'

'Well, the sooner the better Liz,' Dottie answered quickly, leaving no one in any doubt that she welcomed the idea of having some assistance.

'Dottie, John, that's wonderful,' Joe declared, 'That's a great weight off my mind, I can tell you.'

'That's settled then,' Dottie said, 'you can bring Elizabeth over as soon as you like. Do you know where our house is, Joe?'

'I'm sorry, I don't Dottie,' he replied.

John proceeded to explain exactly where the school and the schoolhouse were, and it was agreed that Elizabeth would be brought over to them in two weeks' time when Joe next had his day off.

The main business of the day settled, Liz insisted on offering them oatcakes and ale, and they spent the rest of the afternoon chatting about family news. John was happy to talk about the school and how the numbers of children were growing, as the employers in the district began to see the benefit of educating their workforce, at least in the basics of reading and writing. The number of the benefactors to the school was growing by the year, John informed them, which could only be a good thing for the children of the district. As the light began to fade, Dorothy and John took their leave, saying they were looking forward to seeing Joe and Elizabeth in two weeks' time.

So it was, that two weeks later, Joe and his daughter made their way along the road to Madeley Wood, then climbed up the hill to find the school and, next door to that, the schoolmaster's house. It was a two-storey house, and it looked rather grand, and a little daunting to Elizabeth. Most of her life had been spent in a squatter's cottage, and this house was definitely a step up even from Nailer's Row, never mind from a cottage in the woods. Elizabeth had been reluctant to leave her mother when the time came, and Liz was sad to see them go, but she knew it would be for the best. Her daughter was being given a chance to change the direction of her life. If she stayed with them, she may never learn to read and write, and most certainly would never meet anyone of a higher social status who could offer her a good life.

Now, as they stood on the doorstep of the schoolmaster's house, they both felt a little nervous. Joe had never seen where Dotty lived before and from the outside it looked pretty grand. Not as grand as Richard's but certainly a step up from Nailer's Row. Understandably Elizabeth was full of trepidation at the prospect of living here, away from her family, and until the door opened, couldn't imagine what it would be like, never having stepped inside such a grand house before. Joe pulled the chain hanging beside the door. The brass bell rang loudly and within a minute or so John opened the door. He smiled warmly, saying,

'Joe, Elizabeth, how good to see you! Please, do come in, Dottie's in the parlour.'

Parlour! thought Joe. My, my sister has definitely gone up in the world! He followed John into the room on the left of the hallway which was, indeed, it would seem, the parlour. There was a cheerful fire in the hearth and Dottie, who had been busy with a crochet needle, stood up as they entered.

'Oh do come in you two and warm yourselves at the fire. I'll make us some warm milk and then I'll show you your room Elizabeth.'

Dottie disappeared into the room at the back which Joe assumed must be the kitchen. John asked them to sit down and picking up the small bag of Elizabeth's belongings they had brought with them, placed it on a chair by the parlour door.

Joe surveyed the room with a mixture of pride and envy. He was proud that his little sister had done so well for herself, but then he had always known she would. The envy came from realising that he could never aspire to such a home for his family. Although wages at the works were higher than agricultural workers' pay, it would never be enough to be able to afford a place like this, with the accompanying lifestyle. However, he reflected, at least his daughter would be able to enjoy it.

Finally, Dottie returned with a tray carrying cups of warm milk, and oatcakes. When they had finished, Dottie offered to show Elizabeth her room. Elizabeth was thrilled to hear that she was to have a room of her own and happily followed her aunt into the hall and up the stairs to a room off the landing at the back of the house. It was a small room with a narrow bed and dressing table with a mirror and a brush and comb placed neatly upon it. A chair stood under the window with a cheerful cushion placed on the seat. Elizabeth was entranced. She had never imagined she would ever have a room like this, and it was to be hers alone! She had been sad to leave her family but having this room to herself certainly began to make up for that. She smiled broadly at her aunt, saying.

'Thank you so much aunt, it's lovely!'

'Well, I'm glad you like it, and I hope you'll be very happy here with us.'

'Can father come to see it?' Elizabeth asked eagerly.

'Of course, come on, let's go down and get him.'

Elizabeth followed Dottie back down to the parlour, where she eagerly asked Joe to come up and see her room.

Joe could see why Elizabeth was so pleased with it. It was a neat little space that she would be able to call her own. She'd never had that luxury, always having to share her space with her brothers and sister. In fact, she was so happy with it that she didn't want to go back down to the parlour and insisted on testing the bed, then climbing on the chair to look out of the window at the yard outside. There were no factories here, just the woodland as far as she could see, and in the yard below, the brown and white pony that had brought her aunt and uncle to Nailer's Row, was peering out of his stable. Oh yes, she thought, she would be happy here!

Finally Joe persuaded her to come down to the parlour, while he took his leave. He could see that his daughter would be well cared for here, and he was glad she would certainly now have more opportunities in life than he could give her. He thanked Dottie and John profusely and said that either Liz or himself would visit their daughter as often as they were able, although with the long hours he was having to work, and Liz having the little ones to care for, he couldn't say how often that would be. John said he understood of course, but told him not to worry about Elizabeth, he was sure she would settle in well with them and she would certainly be kept too busy to fret too much about being away from home. Once she had settled in, Dottie would start by teaching her to read and write, in preparation for her to help out with the little ones as soon as possible.

With that, Joe embraced his daughter, telling her to work hard learning her letters, and to obey her aunt and uncle at all times.

'Of course I will father,' she declared, then clung fiercely on to him, not wanting him to leave.

He gently extricated himself, then, shaking hands with John and kissing his sister on the cheek, left quickly so as to avoid his daughter becoming upset at his departure. He knew it was to be several weeks before he saw her again, and as he strode away, he felt the emotion well up in his throat. She had always been the apple of his eye, and he would miss her greatly. Mentally shaking himself he took a grip on his emotions, telling himself once again that she would have a better life here, now and in the future, than he could provide for her. Squaring his shoulders, he quickened his pace and strode quickly down the track towards the river and home.

Chapter 22

Michael had been Stock Manager at Andrews Grain Merchants for a couple of years now. in 1738 he had managed to rent a small house near the business and finally realised his long-cherished ambition of bringing his mother to live with him. No longer would she have to be in service to someone else. She could run her own home, which she took to with much enthusiasm.

It stood at the end of a small terrace of houses which had been built a century before. However, it had been well maintained and was of ample size for the two of them, having two bedrooms, a sitting room, and a scullery at the back. Abigail had lost no time turning it into a comfortable home for herself and her son. She was thrilled to be living with him again after being apart for so long, and she was proud of the young man he had become. She knew she had been right to agree to him staying with Richard and Margaret. It had been the making of him. She was happy to be living in Bridgnorth, which was a bustling market town, quite unlike Coalbrookdale, or even Madeley Wood for that matter. Their house was in the lower town, near the river and although it was quite a climb up to the high town to visit Richard and Margaret, she did see them quite often. Richard sometimes called in when he was down at the business, which was literally only a few strides away.

For their part, Richard and Margaret were busy not only growing the business, but also their own family. Margaret was kept busy with their four children, Elizabeth who was nine years old, Richard was seven, Walter four, and the youngest was Joseph who was now two. They were well known in society in Bridgnorth with many influential friends in the district. Of course Margaret's family had been well established in the town for over fifty years, since her grandfather had set up the business in the 1680's. Richard, a quick learner, had taken well to the running of it and was proving to be a good businessman. They were prospering, and as the business grew, so did Michael's prospects.

He was now working in the office full time, and after some instruction from Richard, was keeping the company accounts as well as dealing with the stocks. Through his hard work and diligence, he had made himself indispensable to his Uncle Richard. It was an arrangement that suited them both. Mr Andrews, Richard's father-in-law had now retired and was in poor health, leaving Richard to run the company single handed. This meant that Richard needed to get out to visit potential clients more often and had less time to spend in the office, and he was glad to have someone he could trust dealing with the day to day running of the business.

Michael was happy to have his mother under his protection, and she in turn was more content than she had ever been. She had no need to worry over money and it felt good to be cared for. Michael loved to treat her from time to time, and she would often visit the market in High Town, when she would buy a little something for herself or to decorate the house. Christmas was approaching and it occurred to Abigail that it would be nice to look for a little something for Michael. So it was, that the next Wednesday morning she set out to climb the hill to High Town.

She had just closed the door and turned to walk towards the steps when she stopped dead. Passing by the door was a wagon, with two men sitting at the front. As she looked at them, her heart stopped. She hadn't seen him for years, but there was no mistaking the bright red hair, undimmed by age. He was the one person on earth she never wanted to set eyes on again. James Furlong. Her legs almost buckled, and she shrunk back into the doorway to avoid his gaze.

She was panicking now. It was obvious that this was the wagon from the Hall, making its monthly visit to the grain merchants. Perhaps Furlong needed to visit Bridgnorth and decided to make the journey on the wagon with the horseman. Or, she realised with horror, he had heard that Michael was working here and was determined to confront him. What should she do? Peering round the door jamb she saw the wagon turning to go under the archway into Andrews' yard. She must warn Michael. The last thing she wanted was for him to be confronted by Furlong without warning. She wasn't sure whether Furlong knew Michael was there or not, but either way she knew there would be trouble if they met. She hurried along to the shop, and without waiting went straight through to the stairs and up to Michael's office, where she knew he would be at this time of day.

'Michael, he's here! He's just gone into the yard right now!'

'Mother!' Michael declared, 'Whatever is the matter? Who's here? What are you talking about?'

'It's him Michael. Furlong.'

'You mean, from the Hall? Dear God, what does he want here?'

'I imagine he wants to see you!' Abigail exclaimed.

'Well then, I'd best go and see him, but I hope he isn't expecting this to be a joyous occasion!'

'Michael! No!' Abigail exclaimed, but Michael, retorted,

'Mother, this has gone on long enough. He can't hurt us anymore, and he needs to know that it's useless to try. I want nothing to do with the man.'

With that, he jumped up from behind his desk, a thunderous look on his face that terrified Abigail. She was afraid of what he might do when confronted by Furlong. He ran out of the room, down the stairs and out into the yard, followed by Abigail.

When Abigail emerged from the passageway the two men were already confronting one another. She had always known Michael bore a strong resemblance to Furlong, but until she saw them standing face to face, she hadn't realised just how strong. There could be no doubt, if ever there was. They were father and son. The sight of this man who looked so much like him, had stopped Michael in his tracks and for a moment he was lost for words.

Furlong spoke first,

'Do you remember me?' he asked.

Dear God thought Michael, he even sounds like me!

'Why should I?' Michael asked.

'Because I saw you once at Madeley Market, and I wanted to see more of you, but your mother wouldn't allow it.'

'What makes you think I would want to see you?'

'Because I'm your father.'

'No!' Michael declared, 'You are no father of mine. I know exactly what you did to my mother, and I could never accept you as my father, so you'd better leave now, and don't ever come here again. I want nothing to do with you.'

Predictably, Furlong's mood changed instantly, and he spat out the words,

'What I did to your mother? Good grief, what did she tell you?'

Abigail knew exactly what was coming and stepped forward in desperation, intending to stand between the two men.

'It's alright mother,' Michael said gently, and with some authority, asked her to step aside.

Seeing Michael's obvious affection for his mother, which he had never experienced himself, from anyone, Furlong felt an uncontrollable urge to hurt them both.

The words Abigail was dreading to hear, spewed out of his mouth.

'I suppose she told you that I forced myself on her! Not a bit of it!'

Abigail glanced in horror around the yard, to see the horseman from the hall and the workmen all standing there, listening intently, and watching the scene unfold.

After pausing to let that sink in, Furlong went on,

'She wanted it, but then she was always very free with her favours!'

At this, a terrible anger welled up in Michael's chest and he lunged at Furlong. Being younger and stronger, one blow from Michael's fist sent Furlong sprawling on the ground. Abigail cried out to her son to stop, afraid of what he might do. This man had already caused her to lose her brother for nine years and she didn't want to lose her son as well. Michael, however, would have gone on punching him if two of the other men hadn't run over to restrain him. Furlong was bleeding from his nose and had apparently banged his head on the ground as he fell.

'Get out!' Michael shouted at him, 'Get out of my sight and never come back. If I ever see you here again, I'll kill you!'

Being the coward he was, Furlong stumbled to his feet and staggered towards the archway, but not before glaring at Abigail with such evil intent that her blood ran cold. Then, as he stumbled away, he called out to Michael,

'Just you wait, you'll regret this, you'll see!'

Michael went over to his mother, who was crying now. He put his arms around her saying,

'Come on mother, don't worry about him, he can't hurt you anymore.'

But Abigail wasn't so sure, she looked around again at the men, who had heard everything, and felt she would never be able to hold her head up in Bridgnorth again. Furlong had once again blighted her life. Would she never be rid of him?

Fred, the horseman, was only too eager to share the story of the events in Bridgnorth with the rest of the servants at the Hall. Everyone had agreed that Furlong deserved to be taken down a peg or two. The following Sunday was Margaret's day off. It was a bright late Autumn morning as she made her way down the steep path on Benthall Edge towards Banghams Wood, enjoying the red and gold of the autumn leaves. They were just at the point when a strong wind would have blown them down, but right now, they reminded Margaret that autumn really was her favourite season. When she arrived at the cottage, she lost no time in giving Arthur and Elizabeth the news about Michael and Furlong.

'Poor Abigail!' Elizabeth declared, 'Will she never be free of that man?'

'Well, from the state of Furlong's face, Michael certainly did his best to make sure he wouldn't trouble them again. He's such an evil man though, I fear he'll not give up that easily, now he knows exactly where Michael is.'

'I fear you're right,' Elizabeth agreed. 'Anyhow, tell me, how's our Jane getting on? I was hoping she'd be visiting last week, but she didn't come. Is she alright?'

'Yes, she's fine Liz,' Margaret reassured her. 'It was just that the Hall was full of houseguests last weekend, come for the shoot, so none of the servants were given time off. She asked me to tell you she'll definitely be down next Sunday.'

'That's good, I was beginning to get worried, and in any case, I think she should come and visit her father. He's not getting any better Margaret. I'm right worried about him to be honest.'

At that moment, Arthur, having heard them talking, appeared at the bottom of the stairs.

'Now now Liz, don't you be worrying about me, I'll be right as rain when I get rid of this chest. Good to see you Margaret,' he said, before another coughing fit took hold.

Margaret cast a worried look at Elizabeth, and they both knew that sadly Arthur would never be rid of 'this chest' as he called it. His eyes were red-rimmed, his face pale and drawn. They knew the signs all too well.

'I told you to stay in bed today, Arthur, you need to rest,' Elizabeth told him as the coughing subsided.

'We'll all get more rest than we want one day,' he retorted, stepping up to the fire and sinking wearily down in the arm-chair.

Elizabeth served some broth from the pot over the fire. Arthur said he wasn't hungry, but the sisters enjoyed their dinner and then chatted for an hour or so, about this and that, just catching up on family news. As they did so, they both noticed that the years were taking their toll on their sister and after Margaret had left, Elizabeth wondered what would become of her when she was too old to go on working at the Hall. She would have no home of her own to go to when the time came.

For her part, as she trudged back up the steep winding path to the top of Benthall Edge, Margaret was wondering how Elizabeth would manage if she was left on her own. How different, she thought, for the gentry. They need never worry what would become of them when they grew old. As for herself, she couldn't help feeling rather bitter that after years of service, the day would eventually come when she could no longer fetch and carry for them, and would be discarded, asked to leave to make room for someone younger and fitter. Without a home and family of her own, she may well end up in Mine Spout poorhouse.

Ten minutes later Margaret knocked on the back door at the Hall, and it was opened almost immediately by Jane. She was twenty-one now and had grown into a bonny young woman. She had Elizabeth's eyes but Arthur's light hair. She was now one of the kitchen maids, helping the cook, Mrs Bramble, to prepare the copious amounts of food to feed the family and the host of servants living in the Hall. Jane was a willing worker, and popular among the other servants. In spite of the hard work demanded of her, she always seemed to have a ready smile and brightened up any room she entered.

'Aunt Margaret!' she declared. 'How were Ma and Pa?'

'Well,' Margaret replied sadly, 'I'm afraid your father isn't well at all Jane, and your mother is hoping you'll be able to visit him soon.'

'Yes, of course I will. Cook has said I can definitely take next Sunday off to visit them.'

'That's good Jane, they will both be pleased to see you. But if you've finished your chores, why don't you come and sit by the fire, and we can have a chat before bed?'

'Well, that would be nice, and I have just finished my work. I'll just ask Cook if she needs me to do anything else.'

The door to the kitchen was open and Mrs Bramble, who had heard the exchange, called out,

'Go on girl, go and catch up on Margaret's family news!'

'Thanks Mrs Bramble!' Jane replied, grinning at her aunt.

Margaret took off her coat and hung it up in the passage-way and as they walked along towards the servant's hall, who should step out of the open door at that very moment but James Furlong. His face was still bruised from the encounter with Michael's fist, and from the look of hatred on his face, that wasn't the only thing that was bruised. His ego had obviously also taken a battering.

'Two for the price of one! What a treat!' he sneered as he planted himself firmly in front of them.

Margaret would have loved to punch him in the face herself, or at the very least and in no uncertain terms, tell him to get out of their way. Of course, as Under Butler, he was her senior in the hierarchy of the household, and she knew it was more than her job was worth to challenge him. She simply said,

'Please let us pass.'

He pushed his leering face up close to Jane's as he sidled past them, making sure that his body brushed against hers, and Margaret's blood ran cold as she understood the message he was sending. In his twisted mind, Jane was now fair game. Jane was visibly shaken.

As he disappeared into the kitchen, and they had stepped inside the servant's hall, closing the door behind them, Margaret asked,

'Are you alright Jane? Has he tried anything on with you before?'

'Not really,' she replied, 'only he never misses a chance to leer at me.'

'Well for God's sake be careful, and make sure you lock your door at night.'

'I will Aunt, of course.'

That night Jane made sure that her bedroom door was locked and to make doubly sure she placed the chair up against the doorknob.

Chapter 23

Furlong continued to seethe with indignation at his humiliation by Michael in Bridgnorth, and a plot began to form in his mind as to how he might make the Banghams pay. As he had stood inside the door of the servant's hall, he had heard Jane tell her aunt that she would visit her parents on the following Sunday. Well he thought, maybe it was time to show this family that they couldn't get away with humiliating a Furlong.

Sunday morning saw Furlong quickly making his way along the path across the meadow, towards the kissing gate leading to Benthall Edge. He knew the girl would be leaving the Hall after she'd finished her morning duties in the kitchen, and he would wait for her on the path leading down to Banghams Wood. When he reached the gate, he looked around to make sure no one was watching, then went through and hid himself in the bushes a few yards along the path.

About half an hour later he could hear Jane singing to herself as she strode towards the gate. He peered through the branches and could see her manoeuvring her way through it, carrying a basket, no doubt full of things for her mother and father, given to her by the soft-hearted cook. Amazing how generous she can be with other people's food, he thought to himself. Jane was deep in thought as she passed through the kissing gate, then after walking a few yards along the path she looked up and was startled to see James Furlong step out in front of her.

'Well, well, what have we here,' he said menacingly, 'and all alone!'

Jane was terrified, but as her mother had told her many times, the only way to deal with bullies was to stand up to them. She stood tall and declared,

'You don't frighten me, Furlong! You're just a bully who likes to take advantage of women.'

Incensed that she should have the temerity to stand up to him, he took a step towards her. She realised she had a choice. Knowing what he'd done to her aunt all those years ago, she knew she could either accept her fate, or attack. Fatefully, she chose the latter.

'I know exactly what you did to my aunt all those years ago, so don't think you got away with it. Everyone knows what you are.'

'And I know what you Banghams are,' he sneered. 'You think you're so good, don't you? But you're no better than the rest of us. I know it was that no good Uncle of yours that attacked me and left me for dead, and then scurried off like the coward he was.'

Jane was taken aback at this. The family had always assumed he didn't know who had attacked him.

'And you talk of that aunt of yours! She likes to tell herself that what happened was my fault, but let me tell you, she enjoyed it, and I don't suppose I was the first!'

Anger rose in Jane's chest, and she let rip,

'You liar! You're just scum Furlong, no woman's safe where you are and never was! Now get out of my way and let me pass!'

Furlong stood firm, showing no sign of moving, then Jane strode forward and tried to push past him. Angered by her determination to resist him, as she reached him, he lifted his hand, bringing it crashing down on the side of her head, and she fell to the ground. She tried to get up, but he struck her again and this time she lost her footing and fell sideways, tumbling down the steep sided valley. She screamed as she fell, knowing that the land here fell away steeply. Benthall Edge was at least a couple of hundred feet high. Her scream stopped abruptly as she hit a tree trunk and her neck snapped.

Furlong, realising that she could never survive such a fall, looked round to make sure there had been no witnesses, then turned and walked back to the Hall as though nothing had happened. Unfortunately for Furlong, there was a witness, and a reliable one at that. The gamekeeper from the Hall, Mr Sykes, had been out in the woods, setting traps, and he had heard the kerfuffle on the path above him. Looking up, he could plainly see Furlong and Jane. He could hear raised voices but couldn't distinguish what was being said, although the tones were clearly angry. Then he saw Furlong raise his hand and strike Jane and when she tried to get up, he saw him hit her again and she tumbled off the path.

The girl had screamed, and he had watched in horror as she came crashing down Benthall Edge, passing the spot where he was standing and then, with a sickening thud that silenced her scream, she crashed against a tree stump some hundred feet below. Sykes clambered across to the path and made his way quickly down to where it passed beneath the spot he judged the girl to be. He scrambled up through the brambles until he found her, lying akimbo against the tree. Her head was at an odd angle and her eyes were staring up at the canopy of leaves above her. It was obvious that she was dead. Poor lass, he said quietly to himself, gently closing her eyelids.

He knew he wouldn't be able to move her himself, and he also knew he now had pressing business at the Hall. He had a murderer to apprehend.

Sykes had no choice but to leave Jane where she lay until he could bring some men to carry her home to her mother and father. He respectfully covered her face with the kerchief from around his neck and arranged her skirts to give her some dignity. When he had finished, he made his way back down to the path and then up towards the kissing gate and across the meadow to the Hall.

When he arrived, he went straight to the master's study and knocked on the door.

The Master called out 'Come!' and he entered, saying,

'Sir, I'm sorry to trouble you, but there is a matter of great urgency that we need to deal with.'

'What is this matter that demands my immediate attention Sykes?'

Sykes proceeded to explain he had just witnessed the death of one of the servants. Jane, the kitchen maid had just been murdered by James Furlong, and he had seen the whole thing from beginning to end, and he described exactly what had happened.

'Are you sure the girl is dead?' the Master asked.

'I am sir. I went down to where she lay and there is no doubt of it. Her neck is broken.'

'Well, this is a bad business Sykes. Is the girl still lying where she fell?'

'She is sir. I could not move her on my own. In any case I thought that maybe as Justice of the Peace you might like to view the body before it was moved.'

'Good thinking Sykes.' the Master replied. 'I will certainly need to record what I see. First, we must deal with Furlong. Is he in the Hall?'

'I don't know sir. I don't think he knew I had seen every-thing, so I imagine he returned here afterwards, thinking he'd got away with it.'

'Come then Sykes, we must apprehend him and see what he's got to say for himself. I see you still have your gun. We may yet need it.'

With that, they left the study and went down the back stairs to the servant's hall. They found Furlong sitting in front of the fire enjoying a drink of ale and looking as though he hadn't a care in the world, until he looked up and saw the Master standing there with Sykes behind him. Still he didn't realise the significance of this most unusual occurrence. The Master never usually came down to the servant's hall. Yet here he was. He knew this would not be a social visit but didn't yet connect it with the events that had occurred earlier. The Master stood for a moment looking at him and then announced,

'Furlong, I have to place you under arrest for the murder of Jane Green, the kitchen maid.'

'What? No! I know nothing of this!'

'Sadly for you Furlong, I have a reliable witness who saw the whole thing.'

Sykes now stepped forward, glaring at Furlong, saying,

'I was in the woods this morning and I saw what you did, and what happened to the girl. You didn't even have the decency to see if there was anything you could do for her.'

The colour had drained from Furlong's face now. He knew that the game was up, although he still tried to plead his innocence, now changing his story somewhat, trying to assert that it was just a terrible accident. Sykes however, said he was willing to swear under oath that he saw him deliberately strike the girl twice, the second time causing her to fall from the path down the sheer drop of Benthall Edge, and as a consequence to break her neck as she struck a tree trunk.

Furlong visibly shrunk. He knew his fate was sealed. They tied his hands and locked him in a room in the cellar until he could be taken to the gaol at Much Wenlock.

The Master then instructed Sykes to find four men to accompany them to where the girl lay, and to bring the handcart. Sykes first went to find Margaret, knowing that Jane was her niece, to let her know what had happened. She was distraught. Elizabeth and Arthur would be destroyed by the news that their daughter was gone. She must go to them and be with them as they were given the news. She followed the men across the meadow and through the gate. She saw them stop just a few yards along the path where the Master had noticed the basket Jane had been carrying snagged on a branch a few yards down the slope. He remarked to Sykes that he could see many broken branches where the girl must have fallen. Margaret's legs almost gave way as she thought of her dear niece tumbling down that sheer drop, no doubt fully aware there was nothing to stop her plunging to her death. She must have been terrified.

The Master led the way down the path as it curved round to a spot where Sykes told him that Jane was lying just above them beyond the brambles. They found her as Sykes had left her and the Master surveyed the scene. It was obvious from the angle of her neck that she must have died the instant she struck the tree. He looked up the steep slope of Benthall Edge and could see the trail of broken branches marking out the path she had taken as she fell, and it led directly to the top, where he could just discern her basket, snagged on the branch. There was no doubt in his mind that the description of events given by Sykes was correct. He even noted a bruise to the side of her head where Furlong must have landed the first blow. The evidence was clear, Furlong was a murderer and he, as the Justice of the Peace would not rest until he got his just desserts and this girl, and her family had justice.

As the Master turned away and returned to the path, he instructed the men to lay the girl on the handcart and bring her up to the Hall, where she could be attended to with dignity. Margaret stepped forward and said,

'Begging your pardon Sir, but I think her mother, my sister, would dearly want her daughter to be taken home. It's just in the wood at the bottom of the path. Would it be possible for the men to take her their instead?'

'Well Margaret,' he replied, 'now that I have seen her body, I can see no reason why she shouldn't be taken to her mother and father.'

Then he turned to Judd, one of the men who had come with them, and told him to take her down to her mother's home. The Master then strode back up the path with Sykes, to go back to the Hall to deal with Furlong.

While the men were retrieving Jane's body, Margaret hurried ahead to break the news to Elizabeth and Arthur. When she arrived at the cottage she found Elizabeth alone, sitting by the fire. She had been worrying rather, wondering what had happened to her daughter whom she had been expecting to arrive. When she heard the latch, she was relieved, thinking that it was her daughter at last. When the door opened and she saw Margaret standing there, she immediately knew something was wrong.

'Margaret!' she exclaimed, 'What's to do? Where's Jane? I've been expecting her since noon.'

Unsure where to begin, Margaret hesitated for a moment.

'Margaret, tell me! What's happened to her?'

'Oh Liz,' Margaret began, the tears already beginning to trickle down her cheeks. 'She's gone Liz.'

'What do you mean, gone?' Elizabeth said, with rising panic welling up in her chest.

'Liz, something terrible has happened,' Margaret began, 'She was making her way down the path to see you, when Furlong confronted her.'

'Nooo!' Elizabeth now knew what was coming and the colour drained from her face. She gripped the arm of the chair beside her, waiting to hear the worst news she would ever hear, but at the same time, not wanting to listen to the words.

'I'm so sorry Liz, apparently Furlong struck her, and she overbalanced and fell down Benthall Edge.'

Elizabeth let out a heart-rending wail and collapsed to the floor. A second later, Arthur appeared at the doorway to the stairs. He had heard everything and stood for a moment in complete shock and disbelief.

'Margaret,' he managed, 'this can't be true! Not our precious daughter!' Of course, immediately the nightmare of losing his little Eliza all those years ago flooded back. His legs now gave way, and he flopped down on the bottom step of the stairs.

'Arthur, I'm so sorry!' Margaret said through her tears.

She stepped forward and helped Elizabeth into the chair, then she had no choice but to tell them that their daughter was, right this minute, being brought home to them by men from the Hall.

Elizabeth looked at her in disbelief.

'But look,' she said, 'I've got a stew bubbling for her supper!'

'Oh Liz. Come on, we must prepare.'

At that moment, there was the knock on the door that Margaret dreaded, and when she opened it, the men were standing there with the handcart carrying Jane's body.

As they picked her up and carried her into the cottage, a coughing fit took hold of Arthur, and he put his kerchief to his mouth. As he took it away it was covered in blood. Everyone knew what that meant, but for the moment their attention had to remain with Elizabeth, who had collapsed again at the sight of her beloved daughter being carried home with her face covered. Margaret once again helped her back into the chair by the fire.

The men placed Jane gently on the table in the living room and Margaret thanked them as they left, then turned her attention to dealing with Elizabeth and Arthur. She found a sheet and placed it over Jane, then tried to get Arthur back up the stairs to his bed. He was weak and it took some time for her to manage it. He was in complete shock and his eyes were full of despair. She gave him a drink of the herb tea that was beside the bed, then went back downstairs to attend to Elizabeth.

She found her standing over her daughter, having pulled the sheet back and removed the kerchief. Her face was contorted with pain as she bent down to kiss Jane gently on her forehead before looking up at Margaret with a look of utter despair and anguish.

Meanwhile, the Master and Sykes had reached the Hall, and as Justice of the Peace, the Master formerly charged Furlong. He still tried to protest his innocence, swearing it was all just a dreadful mistake. He hadn't meant to hurt her, and it was just an accident.

Ignoring his pleas, with his hands and feet bound, Fred, the horseman and two other men loaded him onto the cart and with the Master and Sykes riding beside the wagon, he was taken to Much Wenlock gaol and was thrown into the same cell his son had occupied years ago, to await his fate. No one doubted what that would be.

Chapter 24

Margaret was desperately trying to decide what to do next. She knew she would have to return to the Hall soon, but she couldn't leave Elizabeth and Arthur with their daughter lying dead on the table. She would have to send for Jimmy who would be working down on the river, but how could she get a message to him without leaving the cottage?

She went upstairs to Arthur and found him in a dreadful state. The blood soaked rag he was holding to his mouth told the story. He was in the last stages of the disease and wouldn't last long. What a desperate situation, thought Margaret. His daughter lying dead downstairs and him not long for this world either! She helped him to take a sip of the herb tea on the table beside the bed, but he coughed and spluttered, bringing up more blood. His eyes were full of pain and despair, unable to comprehend what had just occurred. Settling him down as best she could, Margaret went back down the stairs to see what she could do to help Elizabeth. Poor Jane would have to be washed and laid out as soon as possible but she wasn't sure Elizabeth would be capable of doing it.

As she entered the room there was a knock on the door. When she opened it, she was relieved to find Rose Bottoms and Ella Forester standing there. They had heard the news and had come to see if they could help.

'Well, we could really do with some, thanks,' Margaret told them, and opened the door wide for them to enter. They both gasped in horror as they saw young Jane lying on the table, the sheet pulled up to her chin, and Elizabeth standing over her, gazing at her with tears streaming down her face, just silently mourning her loss.

'What can we do?' Rose asked Margaret.

Margaret replied softly, hopefully out of earshot of Elizabeth.

'Well, we do need to wash her and lay her out properly, but I don't think Elizabeth is up to it.'

However, Margaret obviously hadn't spoken quietly enough, as Elizabeth immediately said, with some passion,

'No! Thank you all the same, but if anyone's going to wash my daughter, it will be me!'

'Of course,' ventured Ella, 'but we can help you Liz, it's the least we can do.'

They had just finished and covered her with the sheet when Jimmy burst in. He was breathless, as though he had been running, which of course he had. Hearing the news from one of the grooms from the Hall who had been on an errand to Madeley Wood, he had hurried home immediately.

'Oh Ma!' he declared when he saw Jane's body laid out on the table, covered with a sheet. He went straight to Elizabeth and took her in his arms. With the tears flowing once again she stood with her head on his broad shoulder, as he tried to comfort her. Eventually she calmed down a little, then Margaret said,

'Jimmy, it was that monster Furlong, you know. That man has been a curse to this family, but this time he'll get what's coming to him. The gamekeeper, Mr Sykes saw everything.'

'Where's father?' Jimmy asked, knowing that all this would devastate him, and could well overwhelm him given the state of his health.

Margaret told him that he was upstairs, and the look on her face and slight shake of her head told Jimmy that he needed to go to him immediately. He gently extricated himself from

Elizabeth, helping her into the chair, then ran up the stairs, taking them two by two, to see how his father was faring. When he saw him, his worst fears were realised. His face was deathly white and his eyes staring. The blood stained cloth he had been holding to his mouth had fallen from his hand which was lifelessly dangling over the side of the bed.

Jimmy stood for a second, unable to comprehend that his father too, was gone.

'No! Aunt Maggie, come quick!' he called out loudly and bounded across to where his father lay, finally at peace.

He lifted Arthur's arm and placed it under the sheet, which he drew up to his chin, then gently closed his eyes on the world as Margaret entered the room.

'Oh my God!' she exclaimed. 'This will be the end of Liz!'

'I know Aunt Margaret. How will she ever cope with losing both of them? How will any on us, for that matter?'

His face was grim as he fought to control his own emotions. Realising he was now the man of the family, he squared his shoulders and leaving Margaret to straighten Arthur's body and cover his face with the sheet, he slowly went downstairs to give his stepmother the news.

Ella and Rose were thankfully still there. As soon as they saw Jimmy's face they exchanged worried glances, sensing that things were bad, and both instinctively moved to stand behind Elizabeth, to support her as she was given the news that was surely coming. Elizabeth, who had been standing beside her daughter's covered body, looked up and saw Jimmy standing there with such an expression of pain on his face, she mistakenly assumed that he had just realised that his father wasn't long for this world.

'I'm sorry lad,' she murmured, 'he's bad, isn't he?'

'Oh Ma!' Jimmy exclaimed, quickly stepping towards her, and once again taking her in his arms. As he held her close, he knew he had to tell her.

'Ma, I'm so sorry, but Da's gone!'

He felt her go rigid in his arms and she quickly pushed him away.

'What do you mean, gone? He's upstairs in his bed. You've just seen him!'

'No, Ma, he's gone. This was too much for him!'

Saying nothing, but with a look of disbelief still on her face, Elizabeth hurried up the stairs and into the bedroom. At the sight of Arthur's body covered with the sheet, an unearthly wail issued from somewhere deep within her and she collapsed to her knees beside the bed with her head on her husband's lifeless chest. Margaret knelt beside her and threw her arm around her sister to give her some support as her body shuddered with the deep sobs that engulfed her.

Downstairs, Jimmy pushed his own emotions to one side. He must take charge of the situation. He thanked Rose and Ella for helping with Jane. He said he would help his aunt and mother to deal with his father, but he wondered whether Alf or Tom might take a message to Johnson, the undertaker in Buildwas, to ask him to call as soon as possible. Ella and Rose both reassured him that a message would be taken down to Buildwas without delay.

Margaret knew she would not be going back to the Hall that night. She would have to help Jimmy to lay Arthur out, because looking at the state of her sister, she wouldn't be able to do much. Her sobs had subsided, but she still knelt beside her husband, as she raised her head to look at Margaret, and her eyes looked as though all the life had left them also. Her beloved daughter was gone and now the only man she had ever loved was gone too. At that moment, she didn't want to live either.

Margaret gently helped her up and led her to the chair in the corner of the room.

'You sit there Liz, Jimmy and I will do what's necessary,' Margaret assured her. My God, thought Margaret, I'm not sure she will be able to take this. It's more than anyone should have to bear.

Jimmy understood what had to be done and brought up a bowl of hot water, and he and Margaret washed Arthur and laid him out, covering him with a sheet. As Jimmy went to cover his face, Elizabeth, who had been watching them, let out another wail and getting up with some effort, made her way to the bedside, kissing her husband for the last time, before the sheet was drawn across his face.

They had just finished when there was a knock on the door. Jimmy hurried down to open it, finding Tom on the doorstep.

'Jimmy lad!' Tom declared, 'We're all that sorry to hear the news about Jane and Arthur.'

'Thanks,' Jimmy answered quietly, unable to say anything else as he struggled to contain his emotions.

'I've come to give you a hand if you need it, and Alf's off down to Buildwas to take your message to Johnson.

'Thanks Tom, maybe you could help me get Jane upstairs. She can lie beside me Da until Johnson gets here.' As he said these words, the emotion finally broke through, his face contorted with pain. Tom quickly stepped forward, placing a hand on Jimmy's shuddering shoulders. Tom had no words that could make any of this better, so he just stood quietly, sharing the moment with Jimmy.

Eventually, Jimmy recovered some composure, and they went upstairs to arrange Arthur's body so that Jane could be placed beside him. Elizabeth, once again seated on the chair, with Margaret comforting her as best she could, watched quietly now as Tom and Jimmy moved her husband's body to one side of the bed. Minutes later, they carried Jane into the room and laid her gently beside her father.

The full horror of Elizabeth's situation was now laid bare. She felt her life was over. The two people she loved most in the world were gone and she knew she would never be happy again. Margaret stayed with her that night, making sure that both she and Jimmy had something to eat and drink, although neither of them really wanted anything at all. Margaret slept with Elizabeth and Jimmy slept in the chair by the fire downstairs. At first light there was a knock on the door and Jimmy was roused from his fitful sleep, shocked once more as he remembered the events of the previous day. It was Johnson, the undertaker, come to measure up and make arrangements.

He expressed his sorrow at the tragic turn of events that had befallen the family. Jimmy thanked him then led him up to the bedroom where Arthur and Jane lay side by side. He did what he had to do, ensuring the bodies were properly laid out, then told Jimmy he could arrange the funerals for three days' time at the Buildwas burial ground at noon if that was convenient. Johnson said he would return with the woollen shrouds and coffins early on the day of the funerals.

Elizabeth had fallen into an exhausted if fitful sleep but had woken to the sound of Johnson and Jimmy talking in the next room, and she and Margaret had thrown their shawls around their shoulders and had just now appeared, in time to see Johnson leaving the room. Jimmy was shocked at the sight of Elizabeth. She looked old and vulnerable in her grief. He vowed to himself that he would look after her, just as his father would have wished. He went across to her and put his arms around her shoulders, gently guiding her down the stairs into the living room. Margaret followed them and began to busy herself preparing some breakfast for them all. Elizabeth still seemed in complete shock, still unable to process what had happened.

Eventually, when they had eaten, Margaret declared she would have to return to the Hall, asking Jimmy if he would be alright. She said she would somehow get word across to Dale Coppice, Nailer's Row, to Dottie in Madeley Wood, and also up to Abigail and Richard in Bridgnorth.

Word of the tragedy in Bangham's wood, spread quickly through the Gorge. Margaret had given the message to John, asking whether he or Dorothy would be able to let Joe and Will know about the double tragedy that had befallen the family. Indeed, news of Jane's death had reached them even before Dorothy arrived in the trap the next day. Joe was at the works, but Liz explained they had already been given the dreadful news about Jane. When Dorothy told her about Arthur, she was shocked to the core, declaring,

'Poor Elizabeth! How will she ever get over this?'

She said that Will of course had taken the news about Jane particularly badly, wishing more than ever he'd finished Furlong off all those years ago. Refusing refreshment, Dorothy said she was sorry, but she had to get back up to the school as she was teaching the little ones that afternoon. Liz promised to tell Joe about Arthur as soon as he came home, and meantime, she would make her way up to Dale Coppice to let Betty know.

At about the same time as Dorothy was arriving at Dale End, the news had broken in Bridgnorth. Elizabeth had spoken to the Mistress about trying to get word to Abigail and Richard. The whole household at the Hall was in shock over what had happened, and she said she would do what she could to help. In fact, she had suggested that Margaret ask her lady's maid to write a note to Richard, and then instructed the Butler to tell the stable boy to ride over to Bridgnorth to take it to Andrew's Grain Merchant. Richard and Michael were both in the office when the boy arrived with the note. Richard quickly opened it but as he read the contents the colour drained from his face.

'Oh my God!' he declared.

'What is it Uncle?' Michael quickly asked him, 'What's happened?'

'I hardly know where to start.' Richard replied. 'Poor Elizabeth.'

Unable to find the words to tell Michael this terrible news, Richard collapsed into the chair behind his desk and handed him the note.

As Michael read it, he too turned white as a sheet. It was too much to take in. His cousin Jane was dead, and at the hands of that monster Furlong! And Arthur gone too! His Aunt Elizabeth would never cope with this double tragedy, and then his thoughts immediately turned to his mother. How would she take the news?

With mounting horror, Richard declared 'Your mother must be told! Would you like me to do it?'

Michael hesitated, and then said 'If you don't mind Uncle, I think I should be the one to ...'

'Yes, of course,' Richard replied. 'As for myself, I intend to ride over to your Aunt Elizabeth's this afternoon to see if there is anything I can do to help.'

With that, Richard went down into the yard and asked one of the men to saddle up his horse. Then he wrote a note to Margaret, explaining what had happened and that he would be home in the evening, telling Jed the young apprentice, to take it up to the house. Minutes later he was riding along the road towards the Gorge. Meanwhile, Michael had arrived home, finding his mother busy sewing in front of the fire. She looked up as he came into the room.

'By, you're home early lad!' she said, smiling, 'I haven't even christened our supper yet.'

The smile disappeared from her face when she saw Michael's expression.

'What is it? What's the matter?' she demanded.

'Oh mother, I don't know how to tell you.'

'Good grief lad, tell me, what on earth's happened.'

He still had the note in his hand, and he wished he could have just handed it to her, but of course, she had never learnt to read. He had to find the words.

'Mother, I'm so sorry, there is no other way to tell you this. Cousin Jane and Uncle Arthur are both dead.'

'Cousin Jane! How can that be, she's only a lass! I know Arthur's been ill for a while and not expected to get better, but Jane as well. Our Liz will be distraught! What on earth happened?'

Will paused and took a deep breath before answering, knowing he would soon have to answer his mother's next question.

'Oh mother, the poor girl was murdered!'

'Oh Mother of God! Murdered! How? Do they know who did it?'

So now the moment had come. He had to tell her that it was Furlong, his own father and the cause of her own ruin who had now murdered her niece. He knew she would blame herself in some way, as indeed he was beginning to blame himself for striking and humiliating Furlong. Had that fuelled his anger and prompted him to take out his revenge on poor Jane?

In the end, he simply said,

'They are saying it was Furlong mother.'

'Furlong! Oh no! But how? When? For goodness's sake Michael, just tell me what happened!'

'I don't know the details. All we know is what is in this note sent by Aunt Margaret. Apparently, he met Jane in the woods on Benthall Edge and some sort of argument occurred. We can guess what that was about. Anyway, he struck her, and she stumbled off the path and down Benthall Edge, falling almost to the bottom before striking a tree stump which killed her instantly. As it happened the gamekeeper saw the whole thing, so Furlong's been arrested for her murder and taken to Much Wenlock.'

Abigail was stunned. So, he had attacked Jane as he had herself. Of course, Jane was older than she had been and rather more worldly wise, and so had no doubt resisted, which is why that monster had struck her. As Michael predicted, Abigail had already begun blaming herself.

'If only I'd told the Mistress or Master what he did to me. Maybe he could have been given his just desserts at the time and Jane may still be alive.'

'Mother you mustn't think like that. In any case, it would only have been your word against his, and to put it bluntly, they wouldn't have taken the word of a scullery maid over that of the Under Butler, now, would they?'

'Well, with the gamekeeper as a witness, he's not going to get away with this is he?'

'No, he certainly isn't. He'll hang for certain.'

'Oh Michael, how do you feel about that. He is your father after all, regardless of the circumstances of how you came to be.'

'Mother,' Michael pronounced with some force, 'I do not consider that monster to be my father, so don't worry on my account. In fact, I intend to go to the court to witness the trial, and the punishment for that matter. I want to be able to tell you that he is no more, and you need never worry about seeing him ever again.'

'And what about poor Arthur? I'm guessing the shock of Jane's death will have proved too much for his weakened body?'

'It would seem so Mother. Uncle Richard has ridden over there and when he gets back, we should know more. I expect the funerals will be in the next day or two.'

'What a tragic affair that will be, and no mistake,' said Abigail, 'I can't imagine what Liz is going through. I don't think she'll ever get over this.'

'I fear you're right mother, it's too much for anyone to bear, particularly given the manner of poor Jane's death.'

When Richard arrived at Bangham's Wood, he knocked on the cottage door with some trepidation. Jimmy opened it and was obviously pleased and somewhat relieved to see Richard standing there. He motioned for him to come in, thanking him for coming over and telling him that Elizabeth was upstairs. He quickly climbed the stairs and found her in the bedroom, seated beside the bodies of her husband and child. The room was cold as it must be until the day of the funeral, and Richard realised that he must get his sister downstairs, or she would catch her death. He was utterly shocked at her appearance. She looked up as he entered the room, but her eyes showed no hint of recognition. She was very obviously still in shock. Jimmy had followed him up and whispered,

'Uncle Richard, I can't get her to leave them. She should come down and get warm, and eat something, but has refused all food since yesterday.'

Richard knelt down beside his sister, putting his arm gently round her shoulder.

'Liz,' he said quietly, 'It's Richard. I'm come to see how you are. Will you come downstairs now, and warm yourself by the fire?'

She looked up again, and the sound of his voice, and the familiar lines of his face broke through her despair, and the light of recognition flickered in her eyes. She whispered his name and with a slight tilt of head indicated that she would go with him. With some effort, as she had been sitting for so long, she rose from the chair and gazing down at her beloved Jane and Arthur lying under the sheets, she turned sadly away. Placing his hand under her elbow, Richard guided her to the stairs and down into the living room where he led her to the chair in front of the fire.

Ella Forester had brought some broth round earlier and Jimmy tried to persuade Elizabeth to eat something. At first, she waved it away with her hand. Eventually however, Richard managed to persuade her to take a little, telling her that she needed to keep her strength up for the days ahead. He didn't spell it out, but she knew he was thinking about the ordeal of the funerals which would soon have to be endured.

Not wishing to cause Elizabeth any more grief than was necessary, Richard motioned to Jimmy that he wanted to speak to him alone, and they went into the scullery. Assuming that his uncle wanted to know exactly what had happened, Jimmy, who was just about holding on to his emotions, said,

'I'm sorry Uncle Richard, I probably don't know much more than you do. We only know that Furlong met Jane on the path near the kissing gate and then struck her, and she fell off the path and down Benthall Edge until she hit a tree stump and her neck was broke.'

At this, Jimmy's voice faltered with emotion.

Richard placed a reassuring hand on his arm, then, when he had recovered somewhat, Jimmy went on to say they had brought Jane's body to the cottage. He hadn't been there, but Margaret had earlier come to warn them, thank goodness. Apparently when his father left his sick bed to find out what was going on, the sight of his daughter laid out on the table had been too much and he had collapsed into a terrible coughing fit. His lungs must have finally given out and although Aunt Margaret had managed to get him back upstairs into bed, when he arrived home an hour later, he found his father dead.

His emotion now took over and Jimmy's face contorted, his shoulders shook, and the tears fell. Richard threw his arms round the young man to console him as best he could but wondered to himself how anyone could deal with such a horrific double tragedy. When Jimmy had regained his composure, they returned to sit awhile with Elizabeth. Richard felt there were no words to express his feelings and decided that he would just sit quietly with her for a while.

Eventually he spoke to Jimmy to ask him if there was anything he could do. Jimmy thought for a moment before saying,

'Well, I was wondering how I would let Joe and Will know about the funeral. I don't feel I can leave Ma here on her own with – you know...'

'No problem,' Richard said immediately, 'I'll ride over there before I leave for Bridgnorth.'

'Oh Uncle Richard, that would be a weight off my mind.'

At that, Richard picked up his coat before taking a sovereign out of his waistcoat pocket and pressing it into Jimmy's hand. Jimmy tried to refuse it, but Richard insisted that it was the least he could do to help his sister at this terrible time. At least it would pay for the funeral, he said.

Jimmy would have rather refused it, but he had to admit that there hadn't been much money around since his father had taken to his bed, and he had been worrying how he was going to pay for the funeral. He thanked Richard for his generosity, saying he wouldn't forget it.

'I know that lad, and if there's anything else, don't hesitate to ask me.'

Jimmy told him that the funerals were to be two days hence on the following Thursday at noon in Buildwas, and he hoped he and Aunt Margaret would come, and perhaps they would bring Aunt Abigail and Michael. Richard said that of course, they would all be there, and would meet them at the bridge. Jimmy told him that Ella and Rose had kindly offered to prepare the funeral meal. Richard said that he was sure that Margaret would insist on bringing something with them to help out with it in any case.

With that, Richard knelt down beside his sister, kissing her gently on the cheek and telling her that he would see her again in a couple of days, then he said his goodbyes to Jimmy, who thanked him again for coming. With one last smile at his sister, Richard took his leave. After riding the couple of miles over Buildwas bridge and along to Dale End to give the message about the funerals to Liz at Nailer's Row, Richard returned to the bridge to take the Bridgnorth road. He arrived just as dusk began to fall, going straight to Michael's house to tell his sister exactly what had happened. He knew she would be taking this badly, given her history with Furlong.

Chapter 25

James Furlong was slumped on the floor in the corner of the very cell beneath Much Wenlock courtroom his son had occupied over ten years earlier. He wasn't the only occupant. Apart from the rats he was sharing it with a ruffian who looked as if he was no stranger to such a place. Furlong, of course, felt he should not be here at all. He truly believed he was innocent of any crime. It had been an accident. The stupid girl only had herself to blame. If she had taken more care, she wouldn't have slipped off the edge of the path. Curse that damn gamekeeper Sykes, he thought. If he hadn't been around, no one would ever have suspected he had anything to do with it.

Furlong seethed with indignation that he should have been thrown in here with such a person as this criminal, who was so obviously far beneath his station in life. How could he endure a whole week of this until the Assize hearing? He was sure he would be acquitted. He would convince the jury it was an accident. The girl wasn't around to say anything different, and in the end, it was only his word against Sykes's. He was an Under Butler, the jury were bound to take his word over that of a mere gamekeeper!

As he had been charged with murder, he was to be tried at the Assize. As it happened, the next one was due to be held in Much Wenlock in eight days' time, on the Monday of the following week, before a jury in the courtroom above. In the meantime, he determined to keep his head down and have nothing to do with his fellow prisoner. In such a confined space this proved harder to do than he had imagined. The ruffian amused himself by intimidating Furlong. Food was scarce and he always ended up sharing the scraps with the rats. There was nowhere to wash, and the privy was a bucket in one corner of the cell. With each passing day he felt more humiliated and even his natural arrogance began to desert him.

In Banghams Wood, the day of the funeral had been set for Thursday. It was early morning when Johnson turned up with the coffins. He had brought two apprentices with him and between them they wrapped the bodies in plain woollen shrouds as the law dictated and placed them in their coffins. Elizabeth still could not believe that Arthur and Jane were gone. She sat staring into the fire as the coffins were brought down the stairs and carried out to the waiting cart. Margaret had arrived an hour before and had made sure that Jimmy and Elizabeth had warm drinks and some food inside them, to sustain them through the difficult hours ahead. When all was ready Jimmy gently took his stepmother's elbow and said,

'It's time Ma.'

Elizabeth looked up at him with a pitiful, disbelieving expression on her face, hesitating for a moment before struggling wearily to her feet Margaret threw her shawl around her shoulders and guided her out to the waiting cart. Now she couldn't avoid seeing the coffins and her legs buckled. Jimmy put his arms under hers to support her. Johnson suggested that she and Margaret ride up on the front of the cart, while everyone else could walk behind. Margaret helped her up onto the cart then climbed up beside her. Elizabeth sat next to Johnson, steadfastly keeping her eyes to the front. As they were leaving Ella and Rose arrived to speak to Jimmy to reassure him that they would be setting out the funeral meal for when the family returned. He thanked them and said how he could never have managed all this without their help.

The weather that day was perfectly appropriate to the desperately sad occasion. One of those mists that seem more like low cloud had settled across the Gorge, shutting out the sun and making it feel as though a cold, damp blanket had been thrown across the world. The procession slowly made its way down the track and as they approached the bridge, Margaret could see Richard and Margaret waiting for them in their carriage, with Michael and Abigail seated behind. They all greeted each other solemnly then Richard manoeuvred the carriage in behind the cart and followed it over the bridge, turning to the left and heading towards Buildwas. Joe, Liz, Will and Betty were already there when they reached the church and Dorothy and John arrived with young Elizabeth shortly afterwards.

So it was, that the Bangham family once more gathered around an open grave in the Buildwas burial ground at Holy Trinity Church. As Joe surveyed the scene, he was thinking that it was sad that the only time he saw his siblings these days was at a funeral, and this one was of course desperately sad. Jane was too young to die, and in such a violent fashion, which in turn, had hastened the death of her father. As he looked around the family, he reflected how everyone was ageing, particularly, and understandably, Elizabeth. She looked weighed down with the burden of her grief. At that moment, Joe knew she would never get over the loss of the two people she loved the most.

After the coffins had been lowered into the grave, Arthur first, and then Jane, the vicar recited the usual words and they each in turn, starting with Elizabeth, threw handfuls of soil into the grave, and then turned slowly away and began to make their way back up to Banghams Wood. Now Elizabeth and Margaret rode with Richard and Margaret in their carriage, with the rest of the family walking behind. As they walked some way behind the rest, Michael spoke to Jimmy, saying how sorry he was for his loss. He also brought up the subject of Furlong's trial, saying that he intended to go. Jimmy said that for his father's sake, he also was determined to go to see justice done, for not only did he blame Furlong for his sister's death, but also indirectly for his father's. Michael said he had heard that the trial was to be before a jury on the following Monday and the two men agreed to meet and go to the Courtroom together.

When the funeral party arrived at the cottage, Ella and Rose had laid the table with refreshments and Margaret brought in a basketful of bread, cakes, and ham to add to the rest of the food. None of them knew it, but this was to be the last time they would all be together in their family home. The siblings had all been born in this cottage, built by their grandfather with his bare hands. Their roots were here, but as with any family, their chosen pathways were diverging and the bonds that had held them together were loosening. No-one felt this more keenly than Elizabeth, who now felt utterly rudderless, and without the love of Arthur to tether her to reality, and Jane to give her life meaning, she was lost.

Of course, everyone was very attentive of Elizabeth and tried to bring her into the conversations about times gone by when they were young and their mother and father were around, but she felt completely detached and unable to relate to anything they were saying. It all seemed so meaningless. When the time came for them to leave her, one by one they assured her that they would be there if ever she needed anything. She allowed herself to be embraced by them in turn, managing a half smile and a nod in acknowledgement, but her heart was numb, the coldness of grief stifling all feeling.

Will and Betty had decided to go down the steps to the river and across in Bert Rogers' coracle, as it was a shorter way to Dale Coppice than taking the track towards Buildwas. As Joe and Liz made their way back down to the bridge and home, they reflected on the day. They agreed it had been good to spend a little time with their daughter, Elizabeth. They saw precious little of her these days. Liz remarked how grown up she looked. Quite the little lady! Dorothy and John were doing a good job of educating her, and not only in reading and writing. Joe commented that she had a certain confidence about her, and her speech had become more cultivated.

Joe remarked that Michael in particular had looked troubled. He was very attentive to his mother and was obviously concerned at how all this had affected her. He supposed that Abigail might well blame herself for what happened to Jane, as Furlong had never been brought to book for raping her and had been allowed to go on abusing women all these years, eventually leading to the murder of Jane. Michael had told him that he intended to see Furlong tried, and hopefully finished off once and for all. However, Furlong was still his father, and Joe wondered how he would deal with maybe seeing him hang. Liz agreed it was a lot for Michael to deal with, but she felt sure that Richard would continue to support him as he had all along. Joe agreed, saying that his brother was a good man and had chosen his wife well. Margaret was as kind and generous as her husband. He suspected that Richard had helped Jimmy out with the cost of the funeral, always ready to share his good fortune with his family. Michael had also told him that Jimmy intended to meet him in Much Wenlock for the trial. He of course, also needed to see justice done and Furlong punished for the deaths of his sister, and also his father's sudden demise. Joe did wonder whether he and possibly Will, ought also to go to the trial, but on balance, he felt that those most directly involved, Michael and Jimmy, should be the ones to represent the family.

Joe's deepest concern however was reserved for Elizabeth. He told Liz that he was afraid she would not get over this. Margaret had said she would visit as often as she could, but everyone knew that would be no more than once a month as long as she was still working at the Hall. Of course, Margaret herself was looking much older and Joe wondered how much longer she would be able to carry on, but then where would she go? The thought struck him that maybe she would be able to go to live with Elizabeth and Jimmy in the family cottage, but of course, that would be up to Jimmy, who was now head of the household.

As they turned into Dale Road, Liz said she would call at Lorna Bailey's house to pick up the children while Joe went on home to light the fire. Lorna had kindly offered to have them while she and Joe attended the funeral. Joe had barely got the fire going when Nathaniel and Benjamin burst in. They were excited and seemed to have had a good day, playing in the brook with the Bailey children, and wanted to tell Joe all about it. To calm them down he told Nathaniel to go out to the store to bring some coal for the fire. Liz came in carrying Anne in her arms. She was a pretty, if serious little girl with eyes that looked as though they had seen this world before. Nathaniel strode back in with the coal bucket. He would be ten years old next birthday and growing fast and Joe was thinking it would soon be time to find him an apprenticeship. He determined to speak to Mr Ford about it soon.

Richard and Margaret had just arrived home, having dropped Abigail and Michael off on the way. Elizabeth, Richard, and Walter, who were all in their nightclothes came running as their parents entered the hallway. Nanny had allowed them to stay up until their parents arrived home, but young Joseph had already been put to bed. After the sad day they had spent in the Gorge, Richard and Margaret were glad to see them, and to make a fuss of them before Nanny eventually put her foot down and ushered them all upstairs to bed.

Abigail was worried. She felt this tragic train of events may yet claim another victim if, as she suspected, Elizabeth was unable to deal with her loss. She had seemed somehow detached from everything and everyone. And then there was Michael.

He seemed determined to go to Furlong's trial on the following Monday in Much Wenlock. She fervently wished he wouldn't go. She couldn't imagine how he was going to deal with seeing Furlong tried and possibly hung for Jane's murder. He was still his father and however much Michael assured her that he meant nothing to him, Abigail wasn't so sure that when it came down to it, he would be able to remain so detached.

Michael woke early on Monday morning and was riding towards Much Wenlock before eight o'clock. He found Jimmy outside the Guildhall. Michael cast a glance towards the cells beneath the Courtroom. He knew that place all too well and the memory of that dreadful night flooded back. He knew that was where Furlong would have spent the days since his arrest, and he knew how desolate he would be feeling right now. With a supreme effort of will he pushed the thoughts out of his mind, knowing he would have enough to deal with this day without re-living the past, let alone feeling sorry for Furlong. He followed Jimmy up the stone steps outside the building and into the Courtroom itself.

There was quite a hubbub as the twelve men of the jury took their seats to the right of the judges' bench. There were five judges, looking impressive in their gowns and wigs, the one in the centre seated a little higher than the rest. The jury was now sworn in one by one. Opposite the judges was a low balustrade behind which the public were permitted to stand to observe the proceedings. Having arrived early, Michael had met Jimmy outside the Guildhall and they had now secured a spot at the front of the crowd. They stood side by side, nervously waiting for the trial to begin. Of course for Michael, this was evoking memories of the day he himself had been brought into this courtroom, before being sent to Bridgnorth to be tried at the Assize. He knew that Furlong would be at that moment, climbing the stairs outside the rear door of the courtroom, to await the judge's instruction. All eyes were on the judges. Finally it came,

'Bring forth the prisoner, James Furlong.'

A hush now fell over the courtroom. Michael clenched his fists in anticipation. His stomach churned and he turned to watch Furlong being brought into the room. He was shocked at the sight of him. He had spent over a week in that ghastly rat-infested cell and had probably had little sleep, or food for that matter. He was hardly recognisable. To his surprise, and in spite of himself, for a fleeting moment Michael felt a little sorry for him, until he reminded himself that here was the man who had ruined his mother's life and murdered his cousin.

Furlong's feet were shackled, and his hands cuffed. He was led down the side of the courtroom, past the assembled spectators, to the dock where accused prisoners were required to stand, facing the jury, to the left of the judges' bench. Furlong stood with his head bent, looking at the floor. Not so arrogant now, thought Michael, but just at that moment, Furlong raised his head and as he did so, saw Michael standing at the front of the crowd. Their eyes met and once again Michael was struck by a feeling of recognition, as though he was looking at an older version of himself, and he sensed some of the fear Furlong was feeling. He dragged his eyes away and looked towards the jury. They were staring at the accused with some animosity. The story of how Furlong had cold-heartedly murdered an innocent young woman had obviously already reached their ears, and it looked as though they would take some convincing that he was innocent. Michael felt Jimmy tense beside him as he looked at the monster who had taken his lovely sister and loving father away from him and he looked as though he would gladly have jumped over the balustrade and throttled him there and then, if he hadn't believed the law would soon do it for him.

The judge spoke directly to Furlong, saying,

'James Furlong, you have been accused of the murder of Jane Green on Sunday, the twenty first day of September. How do you plead. Guilty or not guilty.'

Furlong did his best to stand tall, then declared in the loudest voice he could manage,

'Not guilty, Your Worship.'

The judge then asked that the witnesses, if there were any, be brought forward to give evidence.

In the event, there were only two witnesses, the main one being the gamekeeper Mr Sykes who now entered the courtroom and stood before the judges. He related the story in a way that left little doubt as to its veracity. As he told the court about the callous way the defendant had struck Jane so hard that she had tumbled off the path and fallen to her death, there were several shouts of 'string him up' until the judge rapped the desk with a gavel and called for silence in the court. However, as Mr Sykes went on to say that the defendant had callously walked away from the scene of the crime without even going to check whether poor Jane was still alive, further shouts rose up. Jimmy looked across at Furlong and could see him diminish before his eyes. His shoulders sagged as he listened to the damning testimony and heard the calls for him to be hung.

When Mr Sykes had finished his evidence, the Master from the Hall who was the Justice of the Peace was called forward and he corroborated the version of events which had just been described. He confirmed that he had arrived at the scene shortly afterwards and found the deceased lying dead with her neck broken, exactly as Mr Sykes had said, and had seen evidence that she had fallen from the path at the top of Benthall Edge before plunging to her death. At this there was more murmuring amongst the crowd, with more pleas for the murderer to be hung.

The judge once again demanded silence and then turned to the jury. As there were no more witnesses to be called, he instructed them to come to a decision as to whether the defendant was guilty or not guilty of the crime of murder. The jury had no need to retire. After forming a huddle and conversing for no more than two minutes, Michael observed them nodding to each other, and the foreman of the jury stood up.

The judge asked whether they had reached a verdict upon which they were all agreed. The foreman replied that they had. The judge looked across at Furlong who had turned a deathly white, then turned back to the foreman of the jury and asked the question,

'Do you find the defendant, James Furlong, guilty or not guilty of murder?'

The court was completely silent as everyone held their breath, waiting for the answer. When it came, it was loud and clear,

'Guilty, your Honour.'

Furlong hung on to the front of the dock to stop himself from sliding to the floor. Michael was surprised to find himself suddenly wanting to vomit. He now knew that before this day was out, he would have to witness his own father being hung on the gallows which he had walked past as he had arrived that morning. Jimmy just hissed 'Yess!' through clenched teeth.

The judge turned to Furlong saying,

'You have been found guilty of a most heinous crime, the coldblooded murder of an innocent young woman. Do you have anything you wish to say to the court before I pass sentence?'

Furlong could produce no words in his own defence. In fact, he could utter no words at all, and simply shook his head at the judge.

'Very well then,' said the judge, who then turned to the judges to each side of him in turn, obviously seeking their opinions as to what the sentence should be, although there was in fact, little doubt. Finally, and slowly, he took the square of black cloth handed to him by the clerk and placed it on his head, before stating loudly,

'James Furlong, you have been found guilty by a jury of your peers of the crime of murder and there is only one punishment to fit such a crime.'

He paused for a moment and Furlong looked terrified, shaking his head. The judge finally went on,

'You will be taken from here to the place of execution and there you will be hung by the neck until you are dead.'

A cheer went up in the room. Michael felt numb and Jimmy was relieved. Jane and his father would have their justice. Furlong himself looked horrified and clung to the front of the dock as the two court officers gripped him by his arms and then dragged him down the side of the courtroom to the door at the back. As they left the courtroom, everyone, including the jury, followed them out. They all knew that the punishment would be delivered immediately. The gallows had been prepared in readiness, as Furlong knew only too well, as he had heard them being built the day before. They were just behind the Guildhall, beside the church. A crowd had already gathered to watch the spectacle and now it was swollen by the people who had been in the courtroom, including Michael and Jimmy.

Furlong had to be dragged towards the steps of the gallows. He resisted at every step. He knew it was hopeless, but his mind could not accept that within minutes he would be no more, and his body wanted to live, his legs refusing to carry him towards his end. The officers now removed the shackles round his ankles and the handcuffs, then tied his hands behind his back. Finally, they managed to get him up the steps to stand on a low stool in front of the trapdoor. He looked round wildly in a last vain attempt to find a saviour, and his eyes landed upon Michael, pleading for him to do something to save him. Michael could stand it no longer and looked away. Jimmy, however, did not. He was determined to witness to the last moment, the end of this monster.

A hessian sack full of sand had been placed on the trapdoor. The noose, attached to it by a long rope thrown over the beam above, was placed round Furlong's neck. His eyes were wild, and he was trembling. The final humiliation came as his bladder let its contents dribble down his trousers as he took his last desperate breaths. At a signal from the presiding judge, the hangman pulled the lever and the sandbag dropped through the trapdoor, yanking Furlong off his feet. The noose tightened around his neck, and to the cheers of the crowd, Furlong was swinging about wildly and kicking his legs for a full ten seconds before the life left him and he hung, still and silent. The crowd continued to cheer for some moments, but they too eventually fell silent and began to drift away. The spectacle was over, justice had been dispensed.

Michael felt empty but also relieved that this ordeal was over. He had come for his mother's sake, and now at last he could tell her that Furlong was no more and would never trouble her again. As for his own feelings, not surprisingly, he was somewhat confused. Whatever this man had done, he had still been responsible for his own existence. He knew he must consciously dismiss such thoughts from his mind. They could serve no purpose now. He must concentrate on his mother's feelings.

Jimmy on the other hand, was elated. He had felt nothing but hatred for this evil man and he was happy that he had gone forever. His duty done; he could now return to his stepmother to tell her that her grief had been avenged.

It took just a few hours before news of the hanging reached the Gorge and everyone was glad of it, especially Joe, Dorothy and Will, who was glad that finally the hangman had finished the job he started all those years ago. Of course, they had all felt Elizabeth's losses particularly keenly and hoped that Furlong's death may help her to find some closure.

Over the next few months they all, whenever they were able, visited Elizabeth to see how she was coping, but it was obvious that, as they had all suspected, she would never get over the events of that terrible day when Jane had been carried home and laid out on the table, and within minutes, her beloved Arthur had gone too. It was obvious to everyone that her health was declining. She wasn't eating properly and hadn't had a good night's sleep since. In fact, Elizabeth survived less than twelve months. It was in early May 1739 that she was struck down by a particularly bad cold, which her weakened body could not fight. It turned to pneumonia and within a week she was dead.

Chapter 26

After Elizabeth died, the Bangham family's roots in Banghams Wood withered away. The old family home had now passed to Jimmy Green and his descendants. Margaret no longer visited the cottage on her days off, partly because the steep pathway down to the wood was now too much for her. Indeed, it was only two years later that she accepted she would have to leave service, as she could barely even manage the stairs up to the attic where she slept. The Master was very fair and gave her a small annuity in view of her decades of service. However, it was not enough for her to live independently. She had resigned herself to going to Mine Spout until one day, Michael arrived at the Hall. He had heard from Fred that Margaret was to retire, and after he and his mother had discussed it, they decided to ask her to come to live with them. The business was doing well, and Richard, appreciating Michael's contribution to its success, had rewarded him with generous wage increases over the years. He could afford to rent a larger house, and he had already begun to look around for something suitable. Margaret was relieved and delighted, and in the Spring of 1742, left the Hall for the last time to live out the rest of her days peacefully in Bridgnorth with her sister.

Will and Betty had no more children. Although they would have loved a little girl, it never happened. They continued to live in Dale Coppice. George was apprenticed to a carpenter in Madeley Wood, and eventually Walter joined Will, in the

Boring Mill. The family's finances became a little easier and life was tolerable, although Will could never quite rid himself of the feeling of injustice that his life should be one of constant struggle just in order for his family to survive. In America, even though the tragedy he'd suffered had led him to return to the Gorge, he had nevertheless glimpsed that a different life could have been possible, if circumstances had been different. He realised that he might have created a better, freer life there, and more than once as the years passed, he wondered if he had given up on the New World a little too easily. As the Bangham boys grew, he often talked to them about the land of opportunity across the ocean, and he could see that Joe's Benjamin, in particular, always sat enthralled, looking at him with eyes shining, whenever he did. Usually, Liz would intervene to change the subject at this point, unwilling to allow young Ben's imagination to be fired with thoughts of leaving the Gorge to seek his fortune on the other side of the world.

Nathaniel had been apprenticed to the Coalbrookdale Company as a mould maker in the moulding shop near the upper furnace pool. Now thirteen, he was a bright young man and had settled in well to the world of work. Joe was proud of him. As for Joe himself, he had to admit that as the years went on, the system of working thirteen twelve hour days without a break was beginning to take its toll on his body. Fortunately, the furnace was just a short way up the valley from Nailer's Row and at least he was able to go home for half an hour or so, during breaks. There were worse jobs in the Gorge and worse men to work for than Mr Ford, and Joe knew it.

With the children growing up and off her hands, Liz was now earning some money, taking in washing from middle class households, round and about. While they could afford to pay a washerwoman, they weren't rich enough to afford live-in servants, and as the works expanded, so did the demand for this service and Liz had no shortage of customers. Joe wasn't too happy about this. He felt that his wife shouldn't have to wash other people's dirty clothes, but Liz was adamant. She enjoyed the feeling of independence being able to contribute to the household budget gave her,

A small half-day school had recently been set up by Mr Ford, to offer some limited education to the children of his workers, and Nathaniel and Benjamin were now learning to read and write. Joe was delighted. Maybe his children would, after all, have an easier life than he had had.

Although the hours were long and the work hard, Joe was still proud of working for the Coalbrookdale Company. However, somewhere in the back of his mind, a feeling had begun to form. He hadn't quite managed to put a name to it, until, one day he had occasion to visit the Clerk's office, which was opposite The Grange, where the Ford family lived. Next door was Dale House where Mr Darby and his daughter Hannah had lived since his wife's death two years earlier. As he was leaving, he stood for a minute or two, looking up at the grandeur of the two buildings. As he watched, a carriage pulled up, drawn by two fine black horses, and Mr Darby climbed out, followed by Hannah. Although their clothes were simple, they were of good quality, Hannah looking particularly fine in her long grey dress with white lace collar with a black velvet cloak around her shoulders.

At that moment, something clicked in Joe's mind. He couldn't help comparing this young woman's appearance to his own daughter, Anne's, in her simple brown shift. He thought back to the early days of his time with the Darbys. When he joined, there were less than a dozen men employed by the company. Although old Mr Darby was the owner and manager of the business, he had never acted as though he was above his workmen. Rather, he seemed to like to be considered as one of them. As Joe observed old Mr Darby's son Abraham and Hannah alighting from the carriage and entering the front door of their fine home, he realised just how much had changed in those twenty nine years. While he had a roof over his head and a family, in spite of working hard, his station in life had, if anything, become lower. He still barely earned enough to sustain the family, so much so that, to his eternal shame, his wife now had to take in washing to make ends meet. His sons, instead of being properly educated as young Abraham had been, must be content with half a day a week of learning, which he suspected was provided to offer more benefit to the Company, than to the children of their workers. He was forty five now, and he was beginning to realise that, however hard he worked, he would be unable to improve his standard of living.

He turned away, and as he walked back down the valley, with the roar of the furnaces and the sound of metal on metal ringing in his ears, the contrast between the vision of gentility he had just witnessed, and the sight of the mean cottages with grubby little children standing beside their mothers as they hung out their washing, or tended their vegetable plots, was stark. So this is the truth of my life then, for all my hard work, I have risen no further than any of these poor souls, he thought. He now realised the feeling that had been forming in his mind was crystalising. It was resentment. For the first time, he acknowledged to himself that the life he had imagined when he made that journey across the Gorge all those years ago, to find employment with the Coalbrookdale Company, had not entirely lived up to the promise he had imagined. How could a man who had worked as hard as he had, for almost thirty years, now be so much worse off than the man who had employed him. While the Darbys had prospered, he had not. His life had become harder and there was no prospect of it becoming any easier. He would have to work until the day he died, or became too ill and weak to work, and had to go to the poorhouse.

As he now approached the new furnace once more, he realised he must put aside these thoughts and concentrate on the job in hand. The furnace was no place to be distracted. Men's lives depended on his attentiveness. However, when he returned home at the end of his shift, Liz noticed that there was a change in her husband. After twenty years of marriage she knew his every mood and couldn't rest until she had found out what was troubling him. Liz realised that such thoughts may well bring danger to the family and said so. She told him that they had to be content with what they had, a home, money coming in and four healthy children, and that he must dismiss these notions. Joe knew she was right. Harbouring discontent was no help to anyone if nothing could be done about it, and he determined to put it out of his mind, for the time being, at any rate.

That night however, as he lay beside Liz, waiting for sleep to come, his mind drifted back to a Christmas Day long ago in Banghams wood, when all the neighbours joined them in the cottage, his father at the head of the table and Elizabeth at the other end, with a roaring fire in the hearth, as much food as they could eat, and drink more than they could take, and for a while, he indulged in the memory. Life had seemed simpler then. They hadn't had much money, but then they didn't need much. They had their squatters' cottage with rights to remain there as long as they wished. They had the means to grow their own food, chickens in the yard and a hog fattening in its pen. They were able to make enough to live on using the resources around them, coppicing the woodland and building their clamps, and in the summer-months could earn more, helping out at the farm up at the Hall. They made their own choices about what work they would do each day, and if they wanted a day off, they took it. How different, he mused, from his life now. Instead of being ruled by the seasons and the weather, it was ruled by the clock and the incessant demands of the furnace. Had he known what his life here would be like, would he still have made the same decision to leave the Wood, to be part of the changes that were surely coming? Maybe he would have taken the same decision sooner or later. The world was changing and whether he liked it or not, he was part of that world. Confounded by this inescapable logic, he turned over and drifted off to sleep.

After that, although he continued to work for the Coalbrookdale Company, it was never again to be with the same level of belief and commitment. All around now, his eyes were to be opened to the injustices, and not only within the ironworks. In many ways, the Darbys were one of the better employers in the area. In some of the coalmines he observed little children no older than six years old now being sent underground, to work long hours in the blackness with only a single candle to bring comfort. He saw the young women, forced to pick coal off the spoil heaps to sell to their betters or to bring warmth to their families in times of deprivation. He saw men and women, maimed or worse, leaving their families destitute and to be returned to their parishes, or sent to Mine Spout poorhouse to live out their miserable lives. He did tell himself that actually, his family was better off than most, working as he did, for the well-respected Coalbrookdale Partners, but from time to time, the resentment resurfaced, as he observed the mine owners and ironmasters growing rich, while he and his family remained forever trapped in a life of drudgery.

PART TWO

RIDING THE TIDES

1748

Chapter 27

Benjamin Bangham almost stumbled along the road running down the Coalbrookdale valley, totally exhausted. He had been labouring non-stop for Mr Darby and the furnacemen at the old furnace for days. Ben had been apprenticed to the company for the last couple of years. He was only seventeen but tall for his age and working at the furnace had already toughened him up. He was strong and fit, but the last week had taken its toll and he was utterly weary.

Mr Darby, understanding that because of the shortage of charcoal, the Company would only achieve its full potential when he could successfully use coke to produce iron suitable not only for casting, but also for forging, had been experimenting with different ingredients in order to perfect such a product. So far, this had proved impossible. The iron they had been smelting was too brittle to be hammered into shape and was only good for casting in moulds. He had been so determined to find the solution, that he had remained at the furnace top for six days and nights, experimenting with differing proportions of raw materials until finally he was satisfied with the results. He had collapsed with exhaustion and Ben and his workmates had to carry him home to Dale House. The men were not much better off. None of them had had much sleep for a week.

As Ben entered the cottage in Nailer's Row, his mother Liz was in the scullery preparing supper along with his sister Anne.

'You look done in Ben,' his mother pronounced. 'Supper's almost ready so why don't you get those boots off and set yourself down in front of the fire, you'll feel better.'

'I will Ma, but Mr Darby's worse than the rest of us. He collapsed at the furnace, and we had to carry him home. But we did it, Ma!'

'Did what?' Anne piped up.

'You wouldn't understand, our Anne. It's just that Mr Darby's been determined to improve the iron we make, and he's been trying all sorts for days, and today we did it!'

At that moment the doorlatch rattled and Joe and his son Nathaniel strode in.

Ben was full of his news.

'Da, Nat, we finally did it today! Mr Darby reckons we can now make good iron fer t'forges an' word is, this'll mean more work than ever afore. There's already talk of them settin' up more furnaces if they can find t' land.'

Joe looked decidedly unimpressed, thinking there was already more than enough work to be had. At over fifty years old his body was feeling the strain of the hard toil he'd endured for the past thirty-odd years working for the Darbys.

Nathaniel received the news with more enthusiasm.

'Well I 'ave to say, yer've got to admire 'is determination, and 'is success will be our success too. I just hope we'll see more of the rewards on it.'

'Come on now,' said Liz, ladling the stew onto their plates, 'enough company talk. Set yourselves down and get this inside you.'

When they had eaten, Ben said he needed to get some sleep and after a splash over in the scullery and a visit to the privy, he wearily climbed the stairs and fell into his bed. Nathaniel sat in front of the fire opposite his father while Liz and Anne cleared the table and washed the bowls.

''Ave you seen anything of Cousin Walter?' Joe asked him. 'They say they've been busy at the Borin' Mill with an order of cannon bound for the Navy.'

'I 'aven't,' Nat replied, 'I 'ad 'eard about the cannon though and I do think it strange that the Darbys have got so involved in working on cannons, them being Quakers an' all.'

'Well it's all about money as usual I suppose,' Joe replied cynically.

'How is Uncle Will? Ave you 'eard anything?'

'Nay I 'aven't, so I suppose no news is good news. He was lucky to escape with 'is life though when that drive shaft broke in t'Borin' Mill. As it is, it doesn't look likely he'll ever get back to where he was.'

'Well, I'll mek mi way up to Dale Coppice on Sunday an' see how things are,' Nat declared.

'Aye that's a good idea,' Joe agreed, taking hold of the coal tongs, and stretching down to pick up a red hot coal to hold above his pipe bowl, then sucking hard to draw the heat into the tobacco.

With that, father and son sat in companiable silence, gazing at the fire until Liz and Anne joined them, and the conversation turned to the rest of the family's affairs.

The following Sunday was Nat's day off and as he'd promised his father, after breakfast he left the cottage to make his way up the steep slope towards Dale Coppice. He had always been fond of Uncle Will, who was never short of stories to tell his nephews about his travels to the New World, describing in full colour, a world the boys would probably never see.

Will had recently suffered a horrendous accident at the mill, when a drive shaft had broken, sending shards of metal flying through the air in every direction. He'd been lucky to survive, but as it was, a large piece of iron had embedded itself in his chest. Fortunately it turned out to be largely a flesh wound, and the metal had been easily extracted by the surgeon. However, he had lost a lot of blood and was weakened by the ordeal.

The day was fine, and as always, as he climbed the steep path, Nat found time to survey the views across the valley. In the distance, he could see Bangham's Wood, where his great grandfather had first built his squatter's cottage over seventy years before. His father, Joe, had been born and raised there before crossing the valley to join the Darby works over thirty years ago. No Banghams were left there now, he mused, all either dead or moved away, some here to Coalbrookdale or Madeley, and others downriver to Bridgnorth, although the wood still bore the family name.

He always enjoyed visiting Dale Coppice. He had been born there, the family moving down to Nailer's Row when he was five years old. Although he could remember little about living in the coppice, he had visited his Uncle Will and Aunty Betty often. They still lived in the squatter's cottage his father had built when he'd first begun to work for Darby, even though subsequently it had been extended to provide a comfortable enough home for the family. Uncle Will had two sons, George, and Walter who had been named after Nat's grandfather. Nat had always got on well with his cousins and was looking forward to hearing their news.

He approached the hamlet in the woods with a little trepidation. He had realised from his father's attitude, that he was very worried about Will. He knew that even though the metal had been safely removed from his chest, he wouldn't be out of danger yet. If an infection set in, everyone knew the outcome could very well be fatal. As he stepped into the clearing, the sound of wood chopping emerged from behind the cottage, and there he found Walter cutting up logs for the wood store.

'Work's never done is it, Walter?!' Nat exclaimed.

Walter stopped and turned to see who had arrived.

'Nay Nat, it never is. Good to see you!'

'And you Walter. I came over to see how your Da's doin'.'

'Well, 'e doesn't complain. In fact 'e doesn't say much at all these days. I think this business has taken more out of 'im than 'e cares to admit. Anyway, come away in, I'm sure Ma'll have something on the go. She usually 'as!'

As they entered the cottage, Will was sitting in the armchair near the fire that was burning brightly in the hearth. He was smoking his pipe and staring into the fire. He didn't even look round when Walter and Nat came in, presumably thinking it was just Walter returning, having finished replenishing their store of wood.

'Look who's 'ere Da!' Walter exclaimed.

At that, Will turned, and Nat was shocked to see his face etched with pain. Nevertheless, his uncle smiled enthusiastically at the sight of his nephew. He had a soft spot for Nat, who had always been a good lad, ready to help anyone, and with good grace, whenever help was needed.

'Hello Uncle,' Nat said, 'how are you feeling now? I was right sorry to 'ear about your accident.'

'Oh thanks lad, I'm not too bad. It's still a bit painful but the surgeon did a good job and thinks the worst is over. I just need to tek it a bit easy like. Give the old body time to mend.'

Betty emerged from the scullery, a jolly looking woman of ample proportions with a ready smile. She opened her arms to give Nat a hug.

'By, it's good to see thee lad!' she exclaimed with obvious joy. 'Come and sit thisen down,' she went on, ''ere on the settle, and tell us what news you bring us.'

'Well Aunt Betty,' Nat began, 'all's well in Nailer's Row just now, but they've all been wonderin' how Uncle Will was, so I said I'd come up to find out.'

''Well that's good of you lad. As you can see, 'e's better than 'e was, but it's a slow job. E's not so young as he was and can't spring back like 'e used to.'

'I'm still 'ere, tha knows!' Will piped up.

Betty bustled over to him and, kissing him lightly on the top of his head, said,

'I know love, but we've all been that worried about you. Anyhow, it's good to see yer getting back some of yer old spirit,' she added, smiling, and sending Nat a wink.

Slung above the fire Nat was pleased to see a cooking pot steaming away as usual, and Betty pronounced cheerfully,

'Now, young Nat! You'll be eating with us,' in a way which brooked no argument, not that he was inclined to give any.

Within minutes a hearty ham and vegetable stew was served up with a chunk of Betty's acclaimed freshly cooked bread. As he ate, Nat wondered at how homely and peaceful this little room always felt. He understood this was no accident. The family had never had much money, although things must have improved since George and Walter had been earning. But no, it was due to Betty's relentless cheerfulness and the loving care she had always taken over everything she did, even when times had been hard. She was a good soul, and Will had been lucky to find her, particularly after the grief and sadness he'd had to bear after losing his first wife and child, during his time in the New World.

After they had finished eating, Nat turned to Walter,

'Are they still involved in borin' cannon at t'mill Walter?'

'Aye, we just finished another load, but there's talk of it coming to an end soon. Mr Darby's non too keen on the company being involved in the arms business.'

'Well, I've alus wondered how 'e could carry it on, him being such a keen Quaker an' all.'

'Well, I 'ope he knows what 'e's doin' and can find other work for us, or we'll all be out of a job.'

'I don't think you need worry Walter. Ben was only telling us last week how Darby's been working on smelting iron for the forges and seems to have made some sort of a breakthrough. It seems they intend building a new furnace as soon as they can find t'land, so there'll be plenty of work in t'forges, whatever 'appens.'

'Aye, I 'ad 'eard somethin' about that,' Walter replied. 'In any case it seems like there'll probably be plenty o' work to do borin' cylinders for them new-fangled steam engines.'

'And what about you George, how're things?' Nat enquired of his cousin, who had been sitting quietly staring at the fire. He was the only one of the Bangham family who wasn't employed by the Darbys. He had been apprenticed to Tom Hunter, the carpenter in Madeley, and had little interest in the goings on in the iron trade itself although it was certainly of benefit to him.

'Well enough, Nat. We're al'us busy, there's plenty of work for the company owners hereabouts. They're never short of money to buy new furniture for their grand houses. Of course, there's alus plenty of burying boxes to be made, never something I relish doing, but it has to be done.'

Never happy to dwell on such grim topics, as she began to clear away the bowls, Betty interjected,

'By the way Nat lad, I met your Aunt Dorothy at Madeley market last week. By, she's looking older to be sure, but she insisted she's well.'

'Ah, did she have any news of Elizabeth, Aunt Betty?'

'Aye, she certainly had! She's courtin' a young chap from Madeley Wood, and it seems serious, too!'

'Well Ma and Da'll be glad to hear that! I wonder when she'll be bringing him to see us — that's if she's not ashamed to now that she's a teacher and gone up in the world. Did Aunt Dorothy say what this chap does?'

'She didn't, but she did seem to think he'd be a good match for Elizabeth.'

'Well, at any rate, I'm pleased for her.'

'Aunt Dorothy did have news from Bridgnorth though. It seems that cousin Michael is to be married in the spring, but that your Aunt Abi 'asn't been well for some time and they're all worried that she won't even see t'spring.'

'Oh, poor Aunt Abi, she didn't have much of a life to begin with, I hear, although I believe Michael's always looked after her since she moved to Bridgnorth. Da will be sad to know she's so ill, but whether he'll be able to go downriver to see her I don't know. What about you Uncle Will?' he added, 'Do you think you'll be able to visit them?'

'I doubt it lad,' Will said sadly. 'Even if I was well enough, I couldn't take the time off work. If I can work, I must work – you know how it is,' he went on with that note of defeatism Nat heard so often among his older relatives.

After an hour or so, he noticed the light was fading and announced he must be getting down the track while he could still see his way. Betty had wrapped up a still warm loaf of bread and handed it to him saying,

'Here, take this for your Ma, lad, and tell her I'll get down to see her in a few days, it's time we had a natter.'

'I will Aunt Betty, and thanks for dinner, it was grand, as always.'

After shaking hands with Will and his cousins, Nat was enveloped in Betty's ample embrace once more and told to 'Come back soon!', to which he asserted he would, gladly, whenever he could manage it.

Chapter 28

As Nat arrived back at Nailer's Row, the family were eager to hear the news from Dale Coppice. Liz was pleased to hear that Elizabeth was courting a young man from Madeley, but a little put out that she hadn't come to tell them herself. Nat said he was sure she would bring him down to meet them all soon.

'How was Betty?' Liz enquired, keen to hear news of her favourite cousin.

'You know Aunt Betty Ma, always one way. You're always sure of a welcome there. She sent you this by the way,' he added, handing over the bread to his mother. She said to tell you she'll be down soon so you can have a good natter.'

Liz smiled, 'That's good, I haven't seen her in weeks.'

Joe was sad to hear about Abi, and wondered when or how he might get over to Bridgnorth to see his sister.

'You really should try to get down there soon Joe,' Liz declared. 'When it's your next Sunday off couldn't you at least take the Saturday as well? You could go down river and back in two days, couldn't you?'

'I suppose so, although it would mean losing a day's pay.'

'Money's not everything love, and Abi will be desperate to see you if she's as ill as they say.'

'Aye, well, I'll have a word with Mr Darby when I get a chance.'

Two weeks later, Joe did speak to Mr Darby, explaining that he needed to take a day off the following Saturday to visit his sister in Bridgnorth.

'Well, Joe,' Mr Darby said, 'Of course, you must visit your sister so as long as you can arrange for someone to take over your shift for the day, I have no objection.'

'Well, thank you sir. John Walters can manage it fine,' Joe assured him, 'he's been working with me for the past year or so and I know he'll do a good job.'

So it was that the following Saturday morning found Joe aboard the Severn Lady sailing down to Bridgnorth. It was some years since he'd ventured outside the Gorge, and he hadn't seen his sisters Abi and Margaret, or his brother Richard for that matter, for at least five years. He hadn't been able to tell them he was coming, so he knew they would be surprised to see him. He was apprehensive as to what he was going to find when he arrived. None of us are getting any younger, he mused, as he stood on the deck, watching the steep sides of the Gorge slip by to give way to fields and hedgerows.

He was remembering the last time he'd made this journey by boat. He'd been going to the Bridgnorth Assize to see his nephew Michael being tried for poaching. It seemed like a lifetime ago that he'd watched his brother Richard pleading in front of the judges for him to be released into his care. That day had changed Michael's life forever, as Richard had taken him on as his apprentice and he had never looked back. The last Joe had heard, Michael was more or less running Richard's Corn Merchant's business day to day. As soon as he was able, he had taken his mother Abi, and later his aunt, Joe's sister Margaret, after her life of service at the Hall, to Bridgnorth to live with them.

Joe had to admit that the Banghams of Bridgnorth had prospered, while the Coalbrookdale Banghams had just about managed to scratch a modest living. Not for the first time he wondered if he'd made the right move when he crossed the valley to join the Darbys all those years ago. He had been so full of hope then, sure that a bright and prosperous future awaited him. His brother Richard had moved in an entirely different direction, marrying the only daughter of a well-respected Bridgnorth corn merchant, and had risen in society. This just reinforced the Joe's belief that it wasn't how hard a man worked in this world that determined where he would end up. Far more important were the connections he made, and the strokes of luck he might have along the way.

However, he was determined not to let any envious thoughts spoil this visit to his family. He knew Richard wasn't one to 'lord it' over anyone. He was a good man who had never missed an opportunity to share his good fortune. Joe was excited to be seeing his sisters.

The river was busy with traffic going to and fro, carrying iron ore and coal upstream to Coalbrookdale and returning with finished goods, including the huge cauldrons, or cooking pots, many of which were bound for the Americas, downriver towards Bristol and the sea. Joe had heard many were destined for use in the sugar plantations of the Caribbean and had also heard that there was much exploitation of African labour there.

Will, who had travelled to the New World when he was younger, had learned much about how Africans had been shipped across the ocean in appalling conditions for centuries, to be used to grow and harvest the canes and turn them into sugar using the Coalbrookdale cauldrons. Will could have chosen to work on the ships that travelled from Bristol to Africa, where they picked up human cargo, and then to the Caribbean to deposit them to work the plantations. However, to his credit, he would not do it, choosing instead to sail directly to America on a ship carrying settlers. He had travelled inland to the Appalachians intending to build a life there, until the death of his wife and child persuaded him to return home to Shropshire.

Often, Joe had thought about all this as he saw the cauldrons being taken on the waggons past Nailer's Row to the wharf, and had regretted that he played a part, however small, in the exploitation of those fellow human beings. This trip was no exception, and the Severn Lady was fully loaded, not only with cauldrons but also firebacks, cast fireplaces and cooking utensils of all kinds. Joe dragged his thoughts away from the pots and their possible dreadful uses, back to the day ahead and looked forward once again to seeing his siblings, even in these rather sad circumstances.

After another half hour or so, as the boat rounded a bend in the river, the sheer rock face with the upper town of Bridgnorth perched on top came into view. At its base he could see the wharfage, busy with several boats, their crews loading and unloading their cargoes. As soon as the Severn Lady was tied up alongside, Joe bade farewell to the crew and strode down the gangplank.

Joe made his way to the Andrews Grain and Corn Merchant premises and was amazed to see that they had been somewhat expanded since his last visit, reinforcing his notion that the Bridgnorth Banghams had very definitely left their relations in Coalbrookdale far behind in terms of wealth and status. Nevertheless, he was eager to see them all and stepped into the now rather grand shop which had been extended to take in the passage behind. A young man of about fifteen was behind the counter, and from his appearance Joe was convinced this must be one of Richard's children. The family resemblance was unmistakeable. He reasoned this must be Richard, his eldest son.

Joe introduced himself as his uncle, from Coalbrookdale, and the lad smiled, saying.

'I'm sorry, I didn't recognise you Uncle Joe!'

'No reason why you should lad,' Joe responded, 'I haven't been over here for nigh on five years. You must be Richard, I'm thinking.'

'I am sir,' Richard confirmed. 'Would you like to see Cousin Michael? He's just upstairs in the office.'

'I would, thank you Richard.'

With that, the lad opened a door leading to steep stairs and Joe followed him up to the office above the shop. Michael was sitting behind the desk, working on the ledgers in front of him, and he glanced up as the door opened, no doubt expecting to see Richard standing there. When he saw Joe, he jumped up from his chair and strode across the room towards him, declaring,

'Uncle Joe! I'm so glad to see you. Did you come by the river? We could have sent the trap for you if we'd known you intended to visit.'

'Nay lad, we heard from Aunt Dorothy who had it from the mistress at the Hall, that your mother's been ill, and I had to come to see how she is. I managed to get today off, so here I am.'

With that, uncle and nephew embraced, then Michael said,

'Mother will be so pleased to see you Uncle Joe. You're right, she is very poorly. The surgeon thinks it's her heart. We're all very worried about her. Aunt Margaret has been wonderful, looking after her when I'm out at the business. She'll also be delighted to see you, and so will Uncle Richard and Aunt Margaret.'

'Well, I'll be glad to see them all too,' Joe replied. 'But I'm amazed at what you and Richard have done with this business Michael. It's certainly expanded since I was last here!'

Joe was thinking that this young man in front of him had truly made the best of the opportunities his Uncle Richard had given him. Who could imagine, looking at him now, that the first time he'd arrived in Bridgnorth he had been a child of twelve in the back of a cart transporting him to the assize for his trial! He had been a piteous sight standing in the dock with the rest of the poaching gang that day, while Richard pleaded for him in front of the judges. In the end, they had agreed to release him into the care of his uncle, who was already a well-respected merchant in Bridgnorth. That had been eighteen years ago, and Michael had obviously justified the faith Richard had placed in him. He was sure Abigail must be very proud of her son.

After talking a little about the changes the years had brought to the business, Michael declared,

'Look, Uncle, I'm just about finished here, so why don't we go up to the house to see mother. You will be staying the night, I take it?'

'Well, yes, if you can put me up, I'll hitch a ride back to the Gorge on one of the trows tomorrow.'

'No Uncle, I'm sure Uncle Richard will insist on Jed driving you home in the trap. It will be much quicker, and he won't expect you to go back on the river.'

Instructing Richard to make sure he locked up promptly at five o'clock, Michael led Joe through the yard behind the shop as he checked up on the men to make sure that all was in order before they strode through the archway and into the street.

Joe wasn't surprised to find that Michael no longer lived in the lower town, but high on the clifftop, in the same area as Richard's grand home, although it was a little less imposing. It was at the end of a terrace of houses, with large windows and a fine front door. It was two storeys but with a basement below the level of the pavement, and glancing through the window, Joe could see a large kitchen.

They climbed the four steps up to the front door and entered the wide hallway which had an impressive stairway leading up to the first floor. At the far end was a closed door and on the left was a second, which Michael opened, leading

Joe into the room where a fire was blazing in the hearth. It was a lovely room, luxuriously furnished, or so it looked to Joe. No cheap furniture here, he noted.

As they entered, an elderly lady seated in front of the fire turned to see who had arrived, and Joe was astonished that it was his eldest sister, looking very different than the last time he'd seen her.

'Joe!' Margaret declared. 'You're the last person I expected to see! Come here!'

With that she struggled to her feet and Joe strode across the room, taking her in his arms, saying,

'Our Maggie! It's grand to see you. It's been too long!'

Joe couldn't believe the change in his sister. She was obviously having trouble moving around, and the lines in her face had deepened. He had to remind himself that he hadn't seen her for five years, so it wasn't surprising that she looked older. She was no doubt thinking the same about him, he mused.

'It has that, lad,' Margaret replied.

'I've come to see our Abi, Maggie. How is she now?' he enquired, with some trepidation, fearing the answer.

'Not good, is she Michael?' Margaret replied, glancing at her nephew.

'No, she isn't Aunt Margaret,' then turning to Joe, offered to take him upstairs to see his sister.

'Of course Michael,' Joe agreed, 'I need to see for myself how she is.'

When they entered the bedroom and Joe's gaze rested on Abigail, he was shocked to see that she was looking somewhat older than Margaret, even though she was more than a decade younger. Her face was drawn and grey. She tried to sit up, although it was beyond her strength to do so.

'Joe! I thought I'd never see you again,' she murmured in a weak voice.

He immediately dropped down by her side and took hold of her hand, saying,

'Eee, our Abi, I'm sorry you haven't been well. I had to come over to see you, everyone in the Dale is wanting to know how you are.'

'Oh Joe,' she replied weakly, 'as you can see, I'm not good. Can't seem to get my breath somehow.'

Joe glanced up questioningly at Michael, who was standing at the other side of the bed, and he sadly shook his head, telling Joe all he needed to know. Michael rang the bell pull beside the fireplace and a minute later a young woman appeared.

'Sally, please prepare some soup and bread for lunch. There'll be three of us today, but bring some for Miss Abi first, and we'll try to help her to eat something.'

'Yes sir,' she replied, before bobbing in a short curtsey and leaving the room.

Joe was impressed with the confidence with which Michael dealt with his servant, as he had been with the obvious respect for him that he'd seen displayed by the men earlier. He couldn't help thinking about his own sons, destined to toil in the furnaces and foundries of the Darbys, with little chance of gaining a status in life remotely approaching their cousin's.

Forcing himself to dismiss such envious thoughts, he turned his attention back to his sister. It was good to see her again, even in such sad circumstances. Maggie had made her way up to the bedroom and now asked about Liz and the children, and whether Joe had seen anything of Elizabeth. He told her that apparently, she was courting a young man, Rod Sheldon, but that they hadn't met him as yet.

'But Michael has some news of his own, isn't that right?' she said, glancing at her nephew, who smiled as he replied,

'I have indeed! I am to be married Uncle Joe, in four weeks' time.'

On hearing this, Abi said quietly,

'I won't live to see it, son.'

Michael now dropped down beside his mother saying,

'Nonsense, Mother, of course you will!'

'Nay lad, I won't, but Sarah's a good lass and will make you happy, I'm sure.' There were tears in her eyes as she spoke these words.

They spent some time with Abi, and when the maid brought the soup, Maggie helped her to take a few sips, but the effort left her breathless and exhausted, after which she drifted off to sleep.

After lunch, Michael suggested that Joe call in on Richard and Margaret. He had sent them a message to tell them Joe had arrived, and they had replied that they would be in that afternoon and would of course, be pleased to see him. They lived about a hundred yards or so along the clifftop path and it took Joe only minutes to arrive at the house, which seemed even more imposing than the last time he had seen it. Once again, the contrast between his life and that of the Bridgnorth Banghams, as he thought of them was stark, and as he stood before the door in his old leather breeches and woollen frock coat, he felt ashamed of his own appearance. Nevertheless, he told himself as it seemed he'd had to do all his life, he was as good as anybody, and squared his shoulders as he pulled the bell chain.

A young woman, obviously the parlour maid, opened the door and looked him up and down with an expression that re-inforced the thoughts he'd just been entertaining.

'Can I help you?' she asked, disdainfully.

Joe stated his business as plainly as he could, saying, 'I'm here to see Mr Richard if he's at home.'

'Who shall I say is calling?' the girl asked.

'Mr Joseph Bangham, his brother,' Joe replied in his strong-est voice.

The girl's attitude immediately changed, her tone softening as she invited him into the hallway. She asked him to wait while she told the master he was here, then knocked respectfully on the door on the left.

Master! Joe thought. My brother has certainly gone up in the world!

An instant later Richard appeared in the doorway, exclaiming,

'Joe! How good it is to see you. How are you, how are things at home?'

'Well, thanks Richard,' Joe replied, 'but I wish I could say the same of our Abi. It's not good, is it?'

'I'm afraid not Joe. She's gone downhill rapidly these past few days. I was going to send you word, but you obviously already heard, I'm guessing from the Hall and our Dottie.'

'Yea, Betty saw her at the market two weeks ago and this is the first chance I've had to get away.'

'Well, come on in and warm yourself,' Richard said, showing him into the parlour, where his wife Margaret was sitting by the fire working on a tapestry on the stand in front of her. As Joe entered the room she immediately stood up and crossed the room to welcome him with a hug and a peck on the cheek.

'It's so good to see you, Joe. It seems so long since we met.'

'It is Margaret, too long,' he replied.

'You will be staying the night.' Margaret asked, more as a statement than a question.

'Michael's kindly invited me to, but I'll need to get back tomorrow. I intend to hitch a ride on one of the trows heading back upstream.'

'Nonsense,' Richard interjected, 'you must go back in the trap, I'll ask Jed to take you whenever you're ready to leave.'

'That's good of you Richard, but really, there's no need, I'm happy to go back on the river. In fact, I'm looking forward to it.'

'Well, if you're sure Joe,' Richard replied, rather crestfallen at Joe's refusal to accept his help.

'I am, but thanks anyway Richard,' then changing the subject, Joe went on, 'Now, I hear Michael is to be married soon. Is she a local lass?'

Margaret spoke up enthusiastically,

'She is Joe, and a lovely young woman. Her father's in trade but he has a thriving carpentry business and she's a good match for Michael. Of course the most important thing is that they are in love!' she added with conviction.

'Well, I'm happy for him. I must say Richard, you have been the making of that lad. He's a credit to all you've done for him over the years, both of you.'

'Well, whatever we've done for him would have been wasted if he hadn't had it in him in the first place,' Richard replied.

They chatted on about the goings on in the family, and not having seen each other for five years, there was a lot to catch up on. Afternoon tea was served by the maid at four o'clock on the dot, comprising of tea and scones, and Joe made the most of the luxury of the surroundings until he felt it was time to get back to Michael's. He wanted to spend more time with Abi and Maggie, and finally took his leave, promising to come over more often in the future, and hoping they may indeed find themselves able to visit Coalbrookdale, as time allowed.

After dinner, Joe spent the evening sitting with Abi and Maggie. As he chatted with Maggie about her life in Bridgnorth and his at Dale End, Abi listened quietly, nodding, and smiling at his news from time to time. He knew this would be the last time he would sit with his sisters like this, and Joe savoured every precious moment. Finally Abi had fallen deeply asleep. Joe kissed her lightly on the forehead and he and Maggie went downstairs to join Michael in the sitting room, where he found he had been joined by a striking young woman whom Joe assumed to be Sarah. They indicated that she had called round meet Michael's Uncle Joe, who was flattered that anyone would take the trouble to come along especially to meet him. Of course, he realised the attraction of spending the evening with her betrothed was rather more powerful than that of meeting an elderly uncle to be!

Joe judged she was about twenty five years old and had obviously come from an affluent family. Her clothes were finely made and tasteful and once more Joe felt ashamed of his own appearance. However, she put him at his ease by her warm smile and polite interest in what he had to say. She was pretty without being showy, intelligent in a modest sort of way and Joe thought she would indeed be a good match for his nephew.

After an hour or so Maggie offered to show Joe up to the spare room, and after bidding Sarah and Michael goodnight, they made their way up the stairs. Joe called in once more on Abi, who was still sleeping peacefully, although her breathing was rather laboured. Kissing her once more on her forehead he whispered 'goodnight' and made his way to his bed. Maggie insisted that she would sit with Abi a little while before going to bed herself.

Chapter 29

Joe was woken up as the clock downstairs in the hall was chiming six. He could hear that there was a bustle about the place and then the unmistakeable sound of weeping. He immediately knew what that meant and jumped out of bed, and dressing quickly, went immediately to Abi's room. There he found Maggie sitting beside the bed weeping softly now. One glance at his sister Abigail told Joe that she had already left this world, and by the colour of her face, sometime during the night.

Maggie looked up as he entered, declaring,

'Oh Joe! She's gone! I decided to sit up with her because I could tell by her breathing she wouldn't last much longer, but I must have fallen asleep around three o'clock. When I woke, I could see she'd already gone! I should have stayed awake!'

'Maggie, you mustn't think like that. Abi was tired and ready to go. I could see that last night. Where's Michael now?'

'He's downstairs, preparing to send a message to Richard and Margaret. He's taken it hard, of course. Abi's always been there for her him and it wasn't always easy, on her own.'

Joe had knelt down beside the bed now and taken hold of Abi's hand which felt like ice. She must indeed have been dead for hours, he thought to himself. His face contorted in grief, he silently smoothed away a lock of hair that had fallen across her face and kissed her lightly on her forehead before rising and saying,

'I'll go down and see if I can do anything for Michael.'

'Aye, right,' his sister answered. 'I'll be finding her best nightgown. Perhaps Margaret will help me to wash her and lay her out.'

At this, the enormity of what had happened seemed to hit her forcefully and she broke down in tears once more.

'Joe! Whatever will I do without her? I should have been the one to go first!'

'Well we can't choose can we Maggie? We all just have to be grateful for what time we have and live each day as if it's our last.'

'Aye, I know you're right Joe, but she's always been my little sister, more like the daughter I never had, if I'm honest!'

'I know lass. Come here now,' he said gently as he put his arms around her.

After a few moments he gently withdrew from their embrace and left the room to find Michael. He found him in the dining room, leaning against the mantle, his head on his forearm, his shoulders shuddering slightly, testament to the struggle he was having to control his emotions. As Joe entered the room, his heart went out to the young man and he strode over to him, placing a hand on his back.

'I'm that sorry, son,' he said softly.

Michael raised his head and Joe could see that his eyes were brimming with tears.

'I can't believe she's gone Uncle.'

'I know lad, it's so damnably final, and it never gets any easier when it comes, whether sudden or not,' Joe said softly, then went on, 'have you sent word to Richard yet?'

'No, I haven't. Will you go and tell them Uncle, I don't think I...'

'O' course I will lad. I'll go straightaway.'

Richard and Margaret were shocked to hear that Abi was gone. It had been expected, of course, and everyone knew it, but in the end, it had come too suddenly for any of them to prepare themselves. They hurried over to Michael's to see what they could do. Decisions would have to be made about the funeral arrangements. Richard's practical mind was already wondering whether Michael would have her buried in Bridgnorth or would he rather she was laid to rest with her father and mother at Buildwas, in the Gorge. It would of course, be Michael's decision, and he was determined to support him, whatever he decided.

When they arrived at Michael's, they found him upstairs now, sitting quietly beside his mother, looking utterly lost. At the sight of his sister lying there, deathly white, her lips tinged with blue, Richard was struck with grief and rocked back on his heels. His wife placed an arm round his shoulders to steady him and give him some support. After a moment, he gathered himself enough to utter,

'I'm so sorry Michael, I didn't expect this so soon.'

Michael looked up now, his eyes dull with grief,

'I know Uncle, I can't believe she's left us.'

The family stayed quietly in the room for some time before finally Richard suggested the men should go downstairs and leave the ladies to carry out the necessary task of washing and dressing his sister. Richard and Joe led Michael, who still seemed in a daze, down to the sitting room. Richard rang the bell and shortly afterwards the maid, eyes red-rimmed, arrived. He asked her to take hot water up to the bedroom. He had no need to explain why it was needed. It was obvious the girl had already heard the news of her mistress's death. She bobbed a curtsy and quickly left to perform the task he'd given her.

Richard and Joe realised they would have to talk to Michael about the funeral arrangements.

Joe began, 'I expect you'll be burying your mother here in Bridgnorth?'

Michael, who had been gazing at the fire in the hearth, looked up sharply, answering with some force,

'No! She'll be going home Uncle Joe, to the valley.'

'Are you sure lad?' Richard queried. 'Wouldn't you rather she was here, near to you?'

'No Uncle, she wanted to go home. In fact, she made me promise only last week, that she would be laid alongside her mother and father, at Buildwas, so that's where she'll be going.'

So it was decided, there was to be another Bangham funeral at the Buildwas burying ground.

After spending a few more hours with his siblings, Joe declared that he must get back to Dale End, and as, because of the day's events, he hadn't had time to organise his journey back on a trow, he asked Richard if he could, after all, be taken home in the trap.

Richard readily agreed, sending a message to Jed at the yard to bring the trap up to the house within the hour. After they all had a bite to eat, even though no-one actually felt hungry, Joe went back upstairs to say a final farewell to his sister. Maggie and Margaret had placed her in a white lace nightdress, brushed her hair and added a little rouge to her cheeks. The distress lines that had formed over her months of struggle had disappeared and she looked entirely at rest, which gave Joe much comfort. Once more, he kissed her gently on her forehead, whispering,

'Sleep well, our Abi,' before sadly turning away, going downstairs and taking his leave.

It was mid-afternoon when Joe arrived back at Dale End. The family was shocked at the sad news he brought. Even though they hadn't seen much of Abi in the last few years, they all knew her story and felt that life hadn't dealt kindly with her, particularly in her younger years, and they were sad for it. They also knew how fond Joe had always been of his sister, and they grieved for his loss as much as their own. It was too late in the day to visit Dale Coppice, but Liz offered to make her way up there the following morning. They assumed Richard would let Dorothy know through his contacts with the Hall, they being regular customers of Andrew's Grain Merchants.

It was two days later that they received news from Owner Blake, brought by one of his crew members, that he'd been asked to deliver a message to the Banghams in the Dale. Abigail's funeral was to be held on the coming Friday, at Buildwas, at noon. Joe, Nat, and Ben all managed to get a couple of hours off to attend, as did Will and his sons. It was decided however, that the women would not go, as none of them had really known Abi well, particularly in recent years, but Joe was thrilled to see his daughter Elizabeth arrive with Dorothy.

It was a sad affair, made even more so as the Bangham siblings realised that occasions when they could all meet were becoming fewer, now being restricted mainly to funerals. After Abi was laid to rest, this was made all the more obvious as the Bridgnorth contingent left to hold the wake at Richard's house. None of the Dale men were free to join them as they all had to return to their work.

However, before leaving, Joe did manage to have a brief conversation with Elizabeth,

'Nat tells me there's someone you might like us to meet, Elizabeth?' he asked with a smile.

Elizabeth blushed slightly,

'There is Da, and I will bring him down to Dale End soon.'

At that, Joe hugged his daughter, saying they were all looking forward to meeting this young chap of hers.

Chapter 30

A sadness settled over Nailer's Row as Joe continued to grieve over his sister's untimely death. However, a couple of weeks later, there was much excitement as a pony and trap turned up outside the window. Quickly opening the door, Nat exclaimed,

'By, it's good to see you, our Liz!'

'Elizabeth, if you don't mind, Nathaniel!' she replied with a smile.

As Joe heard the name he jumped up from his chair in front of the fire and strode over to the window to see if he'd heard right. He called out to Liz who was in the scullery preparing food,

'Our Elizabeth's here Liz, and she's brought yon chap of hers with her!'

Liz, and Anne, who had been helping her, rushed out of the scullery hoping to get a look at him before he came into the house. Peering through the window they observed a tall young man with dark hair jump blithely down from the trap before turning to take Elizabeth's hand to help her to the ground. Nat took the reins of the pony and tied it to the post at the end of Nailer's row while Elizabeth and her 'chap' made their way into the cottage.

Elizabeth went straight to her father, giving him a hug and kissing him lightly on his cheek. Joe was all smiles for his favourite daughter. When he had first taken her up to Madeley all those years ago, it had broken his heart to lose his eldest daughter, but he knew that living and working in the school-house would offer her a better life than he could ever give her. Now he could see that his sacrifice had been worth it. She looked magnificent, dressed in a green jacket and grey skirt, her auburn hair was shining and piled high beneath the green felt hat perched jauntily on her head.

Elizabeth turned to her mother and stepped forward to embrace her tightly.

'Mother, it's so lovely to see you,' she said in her rather educated tones. 'How have you been?'

'I'm fine love,' Liz assured her, returning her daughter's ready smile. She noted with satisfaction, the slight aroma of lavender which enveloped Elizabeth. Quite the lady, she thought with pride.

'And who is this?' she went on, turning towards the young gentleman who was standing back a little, observing the family reunions, and politely waiting to be introduced.

'This is Rod, mother, my dear friend Roderick Sheldon.'

Joe had now stepped forward and offered his hand to the young man, who eagerly took it and shook it firmly saying,

'Pleased to meet you at last, sir.'

This impressed Joe. He wasn't used to being called 'Sir'. Rod then turned to Liz, who dried her hands which had been covered in flour, on her apron, before grasping his outstretched hand in both of hers, shaking it eagerly.

'Well, you must have some tea with us,' Liz declared. 'Sit yourselves down and I'll go and get things sorted.'

With that, the family made themselves comfortable in front of the fire, Elizabeth and Rod on the settle, Joe in his chair and Nat on the stool next to his father. Anne disappeared with her mother to help prepare the refreshments.

'Where's our Ben, father?' Elizabeth enquired.

'He's at his work today, it's his weekend on. They still expect us to work thirteen days in a row you know.'

'Of course, yes, I'd rather forgotten that Father,' and a brief silence fell on the room. Then Joe suddenly spoke,

'What's your line of work Mr Sheldon?'

'Please, call me Rod, sir, everyone does.'

'So, Rod, what exactly do you do to earn your living?'

'I work in the company office at Wilkinson's, Sir'.

'I wish you wouldn't keep calling me 'Sir', lad, I'm not used to it. Anyhow,' he went on, 'that sounds like a good position. 'Ave you been there long?'

'I have, I was apprenticed to Mr Wilkinson when I was twelve and I've been there ever since.'

'Well, it's good to meet you at last, lad,' Joe went on.

Rod glanced at Elizabeth who gave him an encouraging nod.

'I wonder if I could speak with you in private Sir,' he said quietly.

Joe had picked up his pipe and was just bending down to pick a coal out of the fire, but stopped abruptly, glancing up at his daughter and then at Rod, who was looking embarrassed.

Of course Joe had a good idea what was coming. Putting his pipe down in the hearth he replied,

'Aye lad, come into t'back room.'

As they entered the kitchen, Joe spoke quickly to Liz and Anne, who had been busy preparing some food.

'Rod wants a word, mother,' he said, with a wink seen only by Liz, who smiled and gestured to Anne to follow her. As they entered the room Liz grinned at Elizabeth, the slightest of nods passing between them confirming that this was an important moment.

Joe sat down at the table, inviting Rod to join him.

'Right lad, what did you want to say to me?' Joe began.

'I came to ask you for your daughter's hand, Mr Bangham,' he announced firmly, pausing for a moment before continuing,

'I have a small house and regular employment. I love her dearly and know I could make her happy.'

Joe asked him a few questions about his family and circumstances, but knew it was just a formality. He had already decided that he liked the look of Rod Sheldon. For sure, he seemed like a polite, respectful sort of chap, and Elizabeth was obviously besotted with him.

'Well lad, I'm happy to agree. Just make sure you look after her. I 'ope you'll be as 'appy as me and her ma have been.'

They both stood up and Joe took his future son-in-law's hand, shaking it firmly.

When they returned to the front room they were confronted with a sea of expectant faces, all eager to know what had just happened.

Joe put them all out of their misery by announcing,

'I'm right glad to say that our Elizabeth and Rod are to be wed.'

Liz jumped up and went over to her daughter, hugging her tightly, saying,

'Eee lass, I'm that pleased for you!'

'Thanks Mother,' Elizabeth replied with tears of happiness appearing in her eyes.

The atmosphere in the room was joyful that afternoon and there was much discussion about the wedding, where the young couple would live, and their hopes and dreams for their future life together.

It was two months later that they were married in St Michael's Church, Madeley and. It was a proud day for Joe and Liz, to see their eldest daughter married to someone with 'prospects' in life, which actually meant someone who wasn't toiling in an ironworks or down a coalmine for his living. Rod's parents offered everyone a meal after the service as they lived just a few hundred yards from the church, and the two families spent the afternoon getting to know one another. The newlyweds then settled down in Rod's cottage in Madeley to begin their life together.

Chapter 31

Over the next few years, it became apparent to everyone that Mr Darby was convinced that using coke instead of charcoal in the production of iron such that it was suitable for forging, would mean the company would be able to keep up with the growing demand for wrought iron. He knew that that production would need to be expanded which meant increasing furnace capacity. Early in 1754, there was finally talk that Mr Darby had bought some land at Horsehay Farm, a few miles north of Coalbrookdale and intended to build a furnace specifically for producing iron for forging using coke.

Although there was already a pool on the site, it was to be extended to supply water to power the wheel which was to blow air into the furnace. Ben, along with many other Coalbrookdale men, and other workers from further afield were brought in to do the work, numbering around sixty in all. The old pool was drained, and work began to strengthen the dam wall to hold back the increased volume of water that would be needed. After the plugging of leaks in the old dam wall with coke and charcoal dust, and raising the level for its new purpose, work was almost complete. The men knew that this was a precarious state for the dam to be in. A period of prolonged rain could fill the reservoir and put pressure on the partially completed new earthworks before they could be lined with stone slabs thereby ensuring their stability.

Then, at the beginning of December, disaster struck. There was a period of several days of torrential rain, and the men watched in horror as the reservoir began to fill. By the seventh day, they could see that the dam wall, still not fully compacted, might easily begin to crumble. Seeing what could be about to happen, several of the men were standing on top of the dam, desperately trying to compact the surface to stop the water from soaking into it, thereby destabilising it. From where he was standing, off to one side, Ben could see that water was now beginning to flow down the front of the dam from a point some two feet below the top. Realising the dam wall could be breached at any moment, he shouted to the men on the top,

'Get off there! It's going to go!!'

The men turned to look in Ben's direction, to see him waving his arms about wildly, indicating that they needed to get off the dam wall. Looking down at the outside wall of the dam now, they saw the water gushing out from the earth below their feet. Now they all understood what Ben had been trying to tell them and turned on their heels, heading for the far side of the dam. All but one of them made it in time. The fourth, Archie White, a lad of sixteen, did not. Ben watched in horror as he saw the boy disappear in the torrent now sweeping along the valley floor.

Ben ran along the top of the hill, following the course of the water that continued to pour down the narrow valley, trying to keep sight of Archie. The water was flowing too swiftly for him to keep up however, and it was carrying the lad far out of his reach.

It was two hours later that they found him. His body had finally been jammed up against a dry stone wall to one side of the valley. He'd never stood a chance. It hit Ben particularly hard as he'd witnessed the whole thing, even tried to avert it, but he'd failed, and in some way felt responsible. If only he'd realised a few seconds sooner, maybe the lad would still be alive, he told himself.

It was early the next day when they placed Archie on a cart and took him home to his family in Madeley Wood. Ben would never forget the sounds of anguish issuing from the depth of his mother's soul as she collapsed on the ground at the sight of her youngest son, lifeless, on the cart.

Of course, the dam was soon rebuilt, and this time completed. Nothing was allowed to stand in the way of progress after all. Ben was kept on at Horsehay, working with the other men on the construction of the new furnace which was finally blown in on the 5th of May 1756. As he was one of the original Coalbrookdale men, he had been given a place to lodge in a room in the tenement at Horsehay Farm along with four others. It wasn't much of a life, working sometimes twelve hours a day when the weather held, and all sleeping in one cramped room. However, he could see that some of the migrant workers who had been employed by the Darbys were living in even worse conditions. Many were virtually camping out in the woods until they were able to build their squatter cottages. There were now several hundred men, many of them with wives and children, barely surviving in the woods around Horsehay.

Life at Dale End continued much as before. Nat was working at the Old Furnace as a mould maker, quite a skilled job, and he was making good money, relatively speaking. Joe was still a foreman at the New Furnace. He was finding life hard. The forty years of exposure to smoke and fumes were beginning to take their toll on his health. He was susceptible to bouts of bronchitis, particularly during the winter months when the weather could be cold and wet for weeks on end. Of course, he could rarely take the time off work to get well, as that would mean losing pay, and he continued to struggle on each winter until spring arrived and his symptoms eased. Nat worried about him, often telling him to ask Mr Darby for an easier job with less hours, but Joe wouldn't listen. He was still the man of the house and as such, he felt it was his place to be the main provider for his family.

'Anyway,' he would say, 'none on us knows when you might be moving out to a home of thine own, and this house is only ours while I'm working fer Darby, as you well know.'

Joe knew that the roof over his family's head depended on him working for the Company. No job, no home. That was just the way things were, and so he struggled on, the fight becoming harder with each passing winter.

Of course, every man knew that the welfare of himself and his family depended on Abraham Darby in one way or another. Indeed everyone was shocked and apprehensive when, in early August, news reached the valley that Mr Darby had been thrown from his horse on a trip to Bridgnorth. No one knew how badly he'd been hurt but it was said that Mrs Darby was on her way downriver to her husband to see how things were with him and hopefully to bring him home. For several days the uncertainty continued. Uncertainty about Mr Darby's health meant the same for his workers. However, to everyone's relief, news finally reached them that he had suffered no more than a broken arm, and the next day, he was seen riding up Dale Road in the carriage with his wife, his arm in a sling, but otherwise looking unharmed. The valley breathed again.

By Christmas the Horsehay furnace was in full production. A new railway had been built to carry raw materials to the new furnace and finished iron pigs back down to the forges in the Dale. The Coalbrookdale men were given a day off to visit their families and were allowed travel down on the new railway. When he arrived at Nailer's Row, Ben was given a huge welcome by the rest of the family, who hadn't seen him for months. They enjoyed a pleasant Christmas that year. For once, they all, even Joe, were feeling well and there was plenty to eat and drink. Joe and Liz felt happy that they had raised all four of their children to adulthood and all, in their own way, were finding their place in the world. Although Liz had suffered several miscarriages and a still birth in the early years, their surviving children had thrived. It would be true to say they felt a little smug about that.

However, life has a way of biting back, and the next couple of years were to prove rather more challenging for the Coalbrookdale Bangham family.

Chapter 32

In contrast to Christmas in Nailer's Row, the atmosphere in Dale Coppice was far from festive. Since Will's accident in the Boring Mill, he had struggled to continue working. The accident had caused muscle damage and he was unable to regain his former strength. In the end, operating the boring machinery had become too much for him and he was forced to ask Mr Darby for a labouring job. As he had been a good worker, his request was granted, but of course, his wages were reduced accordingly, which angered him greatly. He began to resent more and more that he had to trudge down the valley to the mill, to be paid what he considered a pittance while he toiled away at everyone else's behest.

Walter understood how Will felt, and why, but that did nothing to ease their relationship. Walter was now the main wage-earner. His brother George had married Sally, a girl from Madeley Wood, a couple of years after Will's accident, and was living in a house of his own. Will's tendency to feel resentment, which had been evident in his youth, and often directed at his elder brother Joe, now resurfaced. He was consumed with self-pity, feeling he didn't deserve to be humiliated by the fact that his own son was now providing more for the family than he could. Even Betty's habitual cheeriness began to fade in the face of her husband's constant, and worsening, angry moods. The Bangham household in Dale Coppice was no longer a happy one.

For Walter however, in spite of the looming problems at home, that Christmas proved to be momentous. He had known Susan Bly for as long as he could remember. They had played together as little children, along with her brothers and sisters. Walter's brother George was older, and seldom joined in with their games, and so the Bly children had been Walter's constant companions, chasing around the woods, foraging mushrooms, wild garlic, and onions, and climbing trees.

Walter had always thought of Susan Bly as the sister he'd never had and he was very fond of her, and she of him. However, Susan had been sent away into service at the age of fourteen and since then he had seen little of her. It was the day after Christmas Day that he saw her now, striding into the clearing carrying a basket. He recognised her immediately by the colour of her auburn hair but otherwise, he was shocked at the transformation. She was no longer the little girl he'd known all his life, but was now a beautiful young woman, moving with a graceful swinging of her hips as she walked towards him. He stared open-mouthed as she smiled broadly on seeing him standing at the cottage door.

'Walter! It's good so to see ye!' she exclaimed, walking quickly towards him. Setting her basket on the ground she stepped up to embrace him. Walter felt as though a thunderbolt had struck him and rather awkwardly responded to her as she hugged him warmly, but then quickly drew away as his body responded to the closeness of her. His heart was pounding in his chest. He was confused. How could Susan Bly, someone who had always seemed so like a sister, engender such feelings in him?

Seeing his face flush, Susan sensed his embarrassment and quickly said,

'Well, I must get on home, mother'll be waiting. I've brought some things from the big house. Food and such, left over from yesterday. I'm staying over tonight, maybe I'll see you tomorrow?'

Walter could barely speak but managed to mutter,

'Yes, course, that would be good. I'm off work tomorrow as it's Sunday.

'Right then,' Susan replied with a broad smile, which caused Walter's heart to perform another somersault, then picking up her basket she turned and walked over to her family's cottage across the clearing.

Walter stood at the door, watching her striding away with her easy grace until she reached the door to the cottage, and turned back to look at him smiling once more. He smiled back now and raised his hand in greeting, then she opened the door and was gone. He stood for a moment, savouring the feelings raging around his body, then finally turned and entered the cottage, to see Betty standing with her back to the fire, looking at him with a knowing smile on her face.

'I see Susan's home then. She's made a nice young woman don't you think Walter?'

Walter turned to hang his coat on the hook behind the door, lingering slightly, trying to control his feelings, then mumbled,

'I hadn't notice Ma.'

'Right then,' Betty replied, grinning broadly, 'well, p'raps you could go and chop some wood, we're getting a bit low in the wood store.'

Glad of a chance to escape her gaze he readily agreed. Taking his coat off the hook again he quickly walked round to the rear of the cottage and threw himself into chopping wood to relieve the tension that had built up in him since setting eyes on Susan Bly. He spent a restless night, finding it hard to get the feeling of her body close to his out of his mind. The next morning, he plucked up the courage to call at the Bly cottage and was immediately invited in by Susan's mother Grace.

'Come in lad!' she exclaimed, 'Set thisen down by the fire there. What can we do for thee?'

'Thank you, Mrs Bly. I was wondering whether Susan might like to take a walk this mornin'?'

Hearing his voice, Susan had appeared at the door to the bedroom, and once again treated him to one of those smiles, which set his heart racing.

'Mornin' Walter,' she said. Just two words, but the sound of her voice was like music to him.

'I wondered if you'd fancy a bit of a walk like?' he asked her.

Susan and her mother exchanged glances, Grace indicating with a slight inclination of her head that she was happy about that, and Susan readily agreed, putting on her coat and, throwing her shawl around her shoulders for extra warmth, replied that she'd like to take a walk with him.

In spite of the winter chill, they spent most of that day together walking and chatting easily now, as they remembered some of the escapades they'd had while scampering around the woods together. The bonds they had formed in those far off days rekindled now, and with each passing hour they both realised that this was a relationship they wanted to nurture. As the sun passed its zenith, Susan declared that reluctantly, she would have to return home. She was expected back at the big house before teatime. As they turned for home, Walter could resist no longer and gently grasped her arm, turning her to face him. Then slowly, he placed a hand under her chin and lifted her face towards him. Their faces grew closer until he gently placed his lips on hers. She didn't resist, but mirrored his gentleness and for a wonderful, lingering moment they were both in ecstasy. Both knew that this was something special and even though they had only had this one day, and not knowing how long it would be before they could be together again, they declared their love there and then.

They walked back to the cottage arm in arm, something not missed by either of their mothers, peering through the cottage windows, watching for their return. Their fathers, were of course, oblivious to all of this.

When Susan and Walter reached the Bly's cottage door, they lingered for a while, unwilling to part, but eventually, Betty, who had been quietly watching them, saw Walter stoop to gently kiss Susan on the lips, and then he opened the door for her, and she was gone.

Watching her son striding back across the clearing with a spring in his step she knew that before too long they could well be celebrating a wedding in the Coppice. Of course, she said nothing to Walter as he came into the cottage, but in her heart, she knew this was something special.

January brought storms and heavy snows, making life harder, particularly for Will and Walter as they had to negotiate a way through the drifts down the side of the valley to the mill, and to clamber wearily back up the steep hillside at the end of their twelve-hour shifts.

Still working as the foreman at the New Furnace, a little way up the valley from Nailer's Row, Joe had no such trouble getting to his work, although he was still suffering from bronchitis, and altogether feeling every one of his sixty years. Liz too, was looking her age. As they sat in front of the fire one evening Joe glanced up at her and couldn't help noticing that her hair was almost white now and the lines in her face considerably deeper. She was still 'his Liz' though. Their marriage had been a good one, he mused, even though there had been struggles along the way.

By the end of February the snows had almost gone. The mood in the valley lifted with the prospect of spring around the corner. The trees and hedgerows had begun to show signs of burgeoning life at the tips of their branches. Passing along the top of the bank of New Pool one morning, Joe noticed something in the water. Clambering down to take a closer look, to his horror he saw a face peering up from beneath the surface, the dead eyes searching the sky above Joe's head. It was a face he recognised. A face he'd seen only yesterday.

He called out to a group of workmen making their way to the furnace, to come and help him to drag the body of Darby Ford, Mr Darby's nephew, out of the water. This was not an easy task, as the body had already stiffened. Joe knew enough about death to know that this meant that he had been dead in the water for many hours. He remembered seeing him as he left the works the previous evening around six o'clock, and Joe reasoned that he must have died shortly afterwards. Whether he had stumbled in the dark and fallen in, or whether there had been foul play here, would be determined soon enough. It was undoubtedly a tragedy. The young man was about the same age as Anne, Joe's youngest, and his heart went out to his family. It had seemed as though Mr Darby may have been grooming him to join the business, as he had been spending time at the various forges and furnaces in the valley. Joe sent one of the men to fetch the horse and cart and they laid his body on it, closing the staring eyes to give the lad some dignity and covering him with a blanket. Someone had sent a message to Mr Darby who now arrived on horseback to confirm that it was indeed the body of his nephew. He was, of course, devastated to see him lying dead under a blanket, but unwilling to show his feelings in front of his men, he simply asked one of them to bring the cart up to the house immediately.

Four days later, the funeral procession passed by Nailer's Row on its way to the river and thence to cross the river to the Quaker burial ground at Broseley. People along the route stood in silence as it passed, the men respectfully removing their hats. The death was of course investigated by the authorities, but how he ended up in the pool was never determined. In the end it was put down to just another tragic accident.

Change was now coming rapidly to the Gorge. The Company was building other furnaces to satisfy the growing demand for iron for forging to be used in the production of all manner of wrought iron goods, or iron for the casting of rails and machine parts for steam engines, as well as military hardware. Of course, the latter was against Quaker principles and often the 'raw' iron would be supplied to other manufacturers for turning into cannon and other machines of war.

Of course, every new venture needed more men to work it and the woods and fields around were now full of squatter cottages. If a man could raise a house and give it a roof overnight, he could claim it as his own. One might think that the landowners thereabouts would have put a stop to this practice but in fact, it mostly suited them because it encouraged the new industrialists such as Mr Darby to lease even more land from them on which to build their furnaces and factories.

The Coalbrookdale valley was constantly shrouded in fumes from the furnaces and heaps of coal being turned into coke by slow burning for days on end. Some days were worse than others, depending which way the wind was blowing. On still days it settled in the floor of the valley in a yellowish fog that stung the eyes and burnt the back of the throat, leaving lungs struggling to take in enough breath. On such days, mothers tried to keep their little ones indoors for fear of them succumbing to the dreaded coughing fits, when they struggled to catch breath. Indeed, it was said the Darby children didn't escape it, even though the family had long since moved to Sunnyside, high on the western slopes of the valley. Apparently, they had been particularly ill with bronchitis recently. Joe himself still struggled with his breathing every winter, as did Anne. In fact, since she was a small child, she had often been struck down by it.

Susan Bly was allowed to visit her family on the first weekend of every month and Walter made sure that he was always around, at least on the Sunday. Their love blossomed with each day they spent together. Walter now knew he wanted to spend the rest of his life with Susan, but he also knew that if and when they married, she would be asked to leave service. With his father only on labouring pay he wasn't sure that he would be able to support them all. He would need to find a way of boosting his income before he proposed to her. He wondered if he could move on to the night shift at the mill, which paid better, but he felt it wouldn't be ideal to start his married life spending the nights away from his new wife. He was in something of a quandary, and decided to see if he could find another way of making some extra money, before declaring himself.

Eventually, spring arrived. April showers washed the air clean for a while, allowing the sun to break through the gloom. The dull brown of the woods shrouding the steep sides of the valley turned into a riot of colour, which after the grey, cold days of winter, lifted everyone's spirits.

One morning Mr Darby called at the furnace with a young man who he introduced as his son-in-law, Mr Richard Reynolds. He had recently married Mr Darby's daughter Mary and was now joining the firm as a company secretary.

'Glad to meet you sir,' Joe mumbled, removing his cap.

'This is Joe Bangham, Richard,' Mr Darby announced, 'he's been with us for, how long is it now Joe?'

'Nigh on forty-year sir.'

'Goodness, that long?'

'Good to meet you Joe,' Richard acknowledged, then they continued on their tour of the works.

As they walked away, Joe was thinking that the young man seemed pleasant enough, and that after the death of his nephew, Mr Darby would be glad of his son-in-law's involvement in the business.

Chapter 33

Spring turned to summer in the Dale, and life rolled along without incident for the Bangham family for a while, though the same couldn't be said for Mr Darby. After the tragedy of losing his nephew in early June, word reached the workmen that his brother Edmund had suffered a tragic accident. On a visit to Abingdon he had apparently fallen from his horse, suffering a fractured skull. After lingering for a few days, he had unfortunately passed away. They brought him home to the Dale and a few days later another solemn funeral passed by Nailer's Row.

Watching the procession, Nat's thoughts turned to his own brother, Ben. He was still working up at the Horsehay works and they saw little of him. He wondered how he was faring. Nat knew Joe's health was beginning to fade and he wondered how much longer he'd be able to work at the furnace. He also knew that as the eldest son, he would be the one to support his parents and his sister Anne, when the time came for his father to give up his job. As he was also employed by Darby, Nat hoped that even when Joe left the works, the family would still be allowed to stay in Nailer's Row, although that was by no means certain.

His cousin Walter was also thinking about his own father. Will wasn't getting any stronger, and battling his way to work through the winter snows hadn't helped. Walter was beginning to wonder how much longer he would be able to keep going. Another hard winter might mean the end of work for Will. He thought of Susan. With the uncertainty surrounding Will's health, he felt unable to ask her to marry him. Without Will's wage the family would struggle to manage as it was and all it would take would be for Walter himself to suffer an accident, or unexpected illness to push them over the edge into destitution. Even though most people were living with such insecurities, he didn't feel able to ask Susan to leave her secure position right now and contented himself with seeing her once a month until matters improved.

June was wet, July was wetter, and it was becoming obvious to all that the harvest that year was not going to be a good one. Everyone knew what that meant, of course. The price of food was bound to rise. By the end of July, the price of corn had already doubled, and people were beginning to struggle to buy corn to bake bread. Of course, the poorest fared the worst and the soonest, but by the middle of August even households with two or more wages coming in began to suffer.

In the furnaces, foundries, and mines, wherever men gathered in fact, the first whisperings of unrest were to be heard. Many of them had large families with plenty of mouths to feed. Some of the luckier ones had a strip of land where they could grow a few vegetables, and they might have a chicken or two, but all of them knew that before long, without bread, or the corn to make it, the little ones would begin to starve. Some accepted the situation as an inevitability of their station in life. Others did not and talk of forcing the farmers to reduce the price of their corn was rife up and down the Gorge and the Dale.

By the end of August, it could no longer be ignored. The farmers and landowners grew nervous, as did the mine owners and iron masters. There was a general air of foreboding; a feeling that something momentous was about to happen.

Susan brought what she could from the big house when she visited, and Betty and the other women could at least grow vegetables, but without bread everyone was beginning to feel constantly hungry. The chickens gave them eggs, and the men caught what they could in the woods, but it was never enough. The children suffered worst, their growing bodies unable to get enough nourishment, and they started to show signs of malnutrition.

'There's only one way this is going to get any better, tha knows!' Will declared one evening as he shared a meagre meal with Betty and Walter.

'You're right Da, and everyone knows it. The greedy farmers must stop profiting out of other's empty bellies and reduce the price of their corn.'

'Oh, yes? And just how do you think they can be made to do it, lad?

'Well,' Walter went on after glancing briefly at his mother, 'there's talk of takin' action to mek 'em do it.'

At this, Betty looked fearful, saying,

'Eee lad! You be careful what you get mixed up in! No good ever comes from fighting them as 'ave t' money!'

At this, Will suddenly jumped up, declaring,

'Well, someone 'as to.' His eyes were shining with anger now and he seemed to have grown several inches taller.

'Word is,' interjected Walter, 'the Broseley miners have already gone on strike and formed something they're calling 't' Levellers'. They reckon to be marching to Wenlock market next market day to 'persuade' 't farmers to reduce the price o' their corn.'

'Well, if you ask me,' Will added, 'they're going to need a deal more than 'persuasion'!'

'And what about t' Dale miners? 'Ave you 'eard owt about them, lad?' Will asked Walter.

'Not so far Da,' he replied, 'but I expect we will, afore too long. People can't stand much more o' this.'

Betty was looking extremely anxious now, worried that her menfolk, both of whom she knew could be hot-headed, might take it upon themselves to join the mob if it should make its way up the Coalbrookdale valley.

'For goodness' sake you two, leave it alone! You never know where it might end once you get involved in such things!'

Will glared at her, saying,

'Woman! Mind your tongue, this is men's business. If we want food on t' table and a bit of dignity as well, we'll need to fight for it if them wi t'money aren't prepared to share in times of 'ardship.'

At that, Betty fell silent, afraid of causing Will to get even more angry, thereby making matters worse.

When Susan came home on the following Saturday, Walter told her about the conversation he'd had with Will, wanting to hear what she thought. Cushioned from hunger as she was, living at the big house, perhaps she didn't quite understand the desperation the people of the Coppice were feeling. She urged Walter not to get involved, fearing for his safety, and also for his job. She knew that if he went against his employers he could be dismissed, and she was also secretly dreaming of the day they could be married.

As they parted the next day, she once again pleaded with him not to get involved, but in all conscience, he felt unable to promise that he wouldn't. He was beginning to wonder how anything was going to change if nothing was done to bring it about, and they parted in a rather strained mood.

A few days later Walter came home from his shift full of news. Will was already at home, sitting in front of the fire smoking his pipe. He glanced up when Walter entered.

'Any news lad?' he said as Walter took off his coat and cap. He hung it behind the door then turned to face his father.

'There surely is Da!' he confirmed and went on to give him the news he'd heard from one of the bargemen at the wharf.

The Levellers had had some success at Wenlock market. A large company of them had turned up blowing horns to announce their arrival and to indicate they meant business. Immediately confronting the farmers, they gave them two hours to reduce the cost of their corn to five shillings a bushel saying any who refused would have their corn taken. Some did reduce the price, but others refused, and the mob took their corn anyway.

Walter had Will's full attention now, and he spoke with feeling,

'By, there's some brave men among them miners, I'll say that.'

'That's not all Da,' Walter went on. 'It turns out t'next day they went on to Shifnal and did t'same there. They even took old Justice Jordan with 'em. Some of 'em actually broke into houses and barns; to take not only food though.'

Betty looked as though she wanted to speak but knew better than to get involved in this particular conversation, given Will's mood.

'Well,' said Will, 'I'm not sayin' that's altogether right, but such things 'appen when men are hungry! So what next, do they say son?'

'Next on their list seems to be Madeley Wood, tomorrow,' Walter replied.

'Well, lad, it's time we stood up to be counted, we should go.'

Walter glanced from his father to his mother, and he could see that she was terrified of what Will would do. He knew his father as well as she did. If Will got directly involved, in his current frame of mind Walter knew he wouldn't know where to stop and might well end up going too far.

'Nay father, you need to stay here to look after Ma. I'll go. At first light I'll head off to Madeley Wood market to find out what's afoot.'

In spite of his readiness for a fight, Will had to admit to himself, given the current state of his health, he wasn't fit to go marching over hill and dale, even in pursuit of natural justice. He reluctantly realised he would have to leave that to the younger generation.

Chapter 34

As dawn was breaking Walter strode out of the coppice, heading over the hill towards Madeley Wood. As he neared the top of Lincoln Hill, he was joined by three other men walking up from the Dale. He knew two of them vaguely. Richard Corbett and Bill Cadman were both employed at the works in the valley below. The third man was a stranger to him, but obviously all three men knew one another.

'You'll be joining us then?' Richard asked, without explaining what Walter might be joining them for, presumably until he was sure of him.

'If you mean, am I joining you at Madeley Wood, I certainly am, if yer'll 'ave me.'

The three men nodded their assent and they fell in behind one another along the narrow path. The mist was beginning to rise up out of the Gorge and the sun was breaking through as they strode along. Walter couldn't help feeling excited. It was good to be taking charge of his life for once. He'd been used to being at the Company's beck and call most of his life. Now he was tasting freedom for the first time since he'd been a child running free in the woods, and he realised he had forgotten just how wonderful that felt.

As the path began to descend towards Madeley Wood village, they could hear a distant blowing of horns, as if a hunt was in full gallop somewhere in the distance.

'Sounds like it's begun!' Richard called back over his shoulder, 'We must hurry if we don't want to miss it!'

They quickened their pace now, virtually running down the track, and the further they went the louder was the sound of the horns. They began to hear the shouts of men, lots of men, and they sounded angry.

Walter's pulse began to race and not only with the exertion of running. He was beginning to wonder what he'd got himself into. It was too late now, he told himself, and was determined to throw himself into whatever might be demanded of him. He had to remember why he was here. His family, his friends and neighbours would starve if something wasn't done about the supply of food.

Below them, down towards the river, he could see a huge mass of men. Many of them were waving sticks in the air and the whole crowd was moving now, away from the river, and from the direction they were taking, they were heading for the market.

Walter and his fellow Dalemen fell in behind the mob, for that is what it now was, and several minutes later they were striding up the road towards Madeley Wood market. As they neared the carpenters' workshop, Walter came face to face with his brother George, who looked utterly shocked to see him in the midst of this noisy and threatening mob. After a moment, George deliberately averted his gaze, obviously wanting nothing to do with this business. Walter was disappointed in his brother. I suppose he's got plenty to eat, as his business depends on ironmasters and landowners buying his fine furniture, but he should still be thinking about his Ma and Da back in Dale Coppice, he thought angrily.

They were approaching the market now and Walter's mind was suddenly taken off brooding about his brother as several shouts went up at the front of the mob. They had obviously reached the farmers' stalls. The leader of the men, Charlie Fox, a collier from Broseley, demanded that they sell him corn at five shillings a bushel, to be distributed among the men to feed their families. At first, the farmers resisted; then things threatened to become rather ugly.

One man at the front stepped forward with his stick raised threateningly over the head of the nearest farmer. Emboldened, several others stepped forward taking up similarly aggressive stances. For several minutes it seemed as though this would end in violence. Then Charlie Fox called out to the farmers, who were looking very apprehensive.

'Look here!' he shouted, 'ye can see how t'is! These men will not take 'no' for an answer. If you won't sell your corn to us at a price we can afford, I'm sorry to say they'll tek it anyway. They have many a hungry mouth at home, and that outweighs anything else right now. I would advise you to sell it to us as I have said or lose it.'

For a full minute no-one moved. The farmers stared at the men and the men glared back. The farmers had heard what had happened at Shifnal and were reluctant to provoke the mob further. When it became obvious that they must acquiesce or lose everything, they formed a huddle behind the stalls, then one of them stepped forward,

'We can see that right now you leave us with no choice. We will sell you corn at five shillings, but make no mistake, we view this as daylight robbery and will be speaking to the Justices about it. You won't get away with it!'

So it was that several sacks of corn were handed over to the ringleaders of the protestors in exchange for what money they had brought with them, and the crowd of men turned on their heels, moving back towards the river. The corn was distributed among them, and no-one went home empty handed that day.

As Walter and the others were about to leave, Fox came over to them and introduced himself. Knowing that they came from Coalbrookdale, he wanted to inform them to be prepared, because the Darby home, now at Sunniside, and their farms round about, would be next in line for their attention. He knew they had plenty of grain stored away and there were many children going hungry for the want of it, he told them. Walter had to admit he was shocked to think that this mass of angry men was soon to invade the Dale.

As he strode back over Lincoln Hill, Walter was conflicted. His livelihood depended on the Darby works. The last thing he wanted was to see it destroyed by an angry mob, should Mr Darby refuse to meet their demands. So far, he believed they hadn't resorted to destroying houses or businesses, but he had seen for himself, the anger, bordering on hate, in the faces of the men as they demanded corn from the farmers. He knew that such anger could easily escalate into violence, against men and property. It was in this state of confusion that he arrived back at Dale Coppice. His mother was relieved to see him and immediately threw her arms around him.-

'By, lad, I've been that worried!' she exclaimed.

'No need Ma, the farmers agreed to sell their corn to us and there was no violence. This is our share Ma,' said, taking the corn he'd been given out of his pocket, wrapped in his kerchief.

For fear of upsetting her, Walter said nothing about his fears for the following day, but later, when he arrived home from work, while Betty was busy in the scullery, he decided to speak to Will about it.

Will was, of course, eager to hear what had happened over at Madeley Wood and was pleased to hear that the farmers had been forced to back down.

'Well it was a bit of a success I suppose.' Walter replied, 'at least we got some corn, although not even enough to bak a loaf of bread! But Da, I don't know what to do,' Walter went on.

'Why son, what's up?'

'They say they're coming to the Dale soon, and I'm afeared after seeing t'anger on the faces of some on 'em, if the Darby's stand their ground, p'raps they'll attack the works, or worse still, the men guarding it! Should I be giving 'em a warning?'

'Nay lad, you should not! For a start, I don't think the Darbys will refuse to let 'em have some corn or other food. They've got more sense than to do that. They'll work out some compromise, I'm sure on it.'

'But Da, it could be that Uncle Joe, or Nat or Ben might be called upon to defend the works. What then?'

'Well, if that brother of mine is daft enough to side wi't Darbys, on 'is own 'ead be it.'

At that moment, Betty appeared from the scullery.

'On 'oose 'ead be that then?' she queried anxiously.

'I've told thee afore woman, this is men's business,' Will admonished her.

With that, the conversation turned to other matters, leaving Walter still uncertain about what to do. Tomorrow would just have to take care of itself, he thought. As he lay in bed that night his thoughts turned to Susan. What would she think about his involvement with the day's events in Madeley Wood. She would be home in a few days, so he would soon find out, he thought uneasily.

Chapter 35

Nat had been striding down Dale Road after leaving work that evening, when he'd met Richard Corbett, who lived further up the valley. Richard had put him in the picture about the day's events in Madeley Wood and said he'd been pleased to see his cousin Walter join them. Nat immediately knew what was coming, and as he expected, Richard demanded to know whether he would do the same, because soon they would be coming to the Dale, and every man would have a choice to make. Would he be on the side of the masters or his fellow workers and their families?

Now Nat was truly in a dilemma. He made no commitment to Richard but tried to glean as much information from him as possible. He needed to discuss this with his father, although he suspected he knew which way he would jump. Unlike his brother Uncle Will, Joe wasn't one for taking risks. Knowing that his livelihood and even the roof over his family's head depended on keeping his job at the Darby works would more than likely dissuade him from risking everything by falling in with the mob.

As for his own view, Nat knew just how desperate some of the Dale families were for food. Already he'd noticed the little ones outside their squatter cottages clinging to their mother's skirts, growing thinner by the day, quite apart from the tell-tale swollen bellies. Something must be done, he thought, and simply demanding more money or cheaper corn hadn't seemed to work so far. As he approached Nailer's Row, his sense of apprehension grew. He realised that one way or another, there was going to be conflict in the family, as well as between neighbours and fellow workers and employers up and down the Dale.

Nat said nothing until their evening meal was over, then sitting by the fire with Joe, he finally broached the subject, relaying what Richard Corbett had told him, about how the mob had forced the farmers to sell their corn cheaply by threatening violence, and how they were modelling themselves on the Levellers, who had plotted a peasant uprising over a hundred years before.

'Well, I've been expecting it. Things are getting bad, particularly among families with little 'uns to feed.'

'That's not all Da,' Nat went on, 'Richard told me that our Walter went with them today.'

'Oh no! What about that hot-headed brother of mine?'

'Well, he never mentioned Uncle Will.'

'You can bet he'll be behind Walter joining in though,' Joe insisted. 'Nothing good will come of this if it results in violence, you mark my words!'

Nat pondered whether to tell Joe what Richard had said about Sunniside soon being targeted. He knew that to do so would place his father in an impossible position, and depending on what he did next, may well put the two of them at serious odds. He felt that he couldn't stand by and watch little children starve without doing something about it, but he wasn't yet sure what that would be, he just knew he had to act, somehow.

After a considerable pause, he finally said,

'There's more, Da.'

'Oh yes, what's that then?' Joe replied.

'They say they intend to come over to Coalbrookdale next on't way to Wellington, an' they'll be headin' up to Sunniside to demand corn from their barns, an' anything else worth tekkin'.'

'Good God! We have to warn 'em Nat!'

'Warn 'em, Da?! Surely, they're right? If there is corn in their barns the Darbys should share it among their workers, or at the very least, sell it to 'em cheaply.'

'Life in't that simple Nat.'

'Look Da,' Nat continued, 'I canna stand by and do nothin' while little 'uns are starvin'!'

Liz, who had been sitting, quietly listening to the exchange, now spoke up,

'Nat, you're Da's right. We should have nothin' to do wi' it. No good can come of violence.'

'But Ma, it may not come to that. The Darbys are sensible folk and largely kind people. Mebbe they'll come up with a solution to avoid violence.'

'Mebbe they will and mebbe they won't,' Liz went on, 'but when all this is over, which it must be one day, they won't forget whose side this family was on.'

'Ma's right,' Joe interjected. 'Who are these Levellers any-way? Most of 'em aren't from round 'ere. From what you say most of 'em are miners. They may well have grievances. Some of them mine owners don't give a fig for their workers. But that doesn't give 'em the right to come into our Dale, stirrin' up trouble.'

At this, Nat reacted angrily,

'But Da, there are children going just as hungry here as any-where else, and what have the Darbys done about it so far. Precious little I'd say!'

At that Joe got quickly to his feet, retaliating just as loudly with,

'Enough! This has to stop, right 'ere Nat! I won't 'ear any more of these Levellers, as they call theirselves. Not in this 'ouse!'

Nat fell silent, unwilling to challenge Joe's authority, particularly in front of his mother, but he was thinking plenty. He was wondering if he would be able to accept this edict from his father. Surely, he had a right, as a man now, to be true to his own beliefs, not just blindly accepting his father's.

An awkward silence fell on the room and after half an hour or so, Nat announced that he was off to his bed. Liz and Joe glanced at one another, understanding that Nat's silence on the subject of the mob did not mean acquiescence on his part. They both feared for the unity of their family, which had never been in question before.

Joe for his part had no doubts. He was sure this was no way to go. It would only make matters worse, he told himself, and the very next day he had a word with Tom Owen, manager of the New Furnace site, naming no names, but telling him there had been rumours that the Levellers, as they called themselves were planning on coming to the Dale. Mr Owen thanked him, saying that he had also heard the rumours and he would be passing it on to Mr Darby.

In fact, conversations on the same topic were already going on up at Sunniside, the Darby residence. Word had reached them about the unrest around the district. They had been given detailed accounts of what had gone on in Broseley and Shifnal, where the Riot Act had even been read, and the rioters response had been to shout a loud 'Huzza!' saying that they 'valued neither them nor it'. The Darbys also knew that they had descended on Madeley Wood last market day, which was altogether too near to home, and they feared it would be the turn of Coalbrookdale next. As there was no market for the 'Levellers' as they called themselves, to focus on, they were unclear as to just how they themselves would be confronted.

Mrs Darby had much sympathy for their workers and their families. She knew as well as anyone just how hard life was for them at the moment. Partly out of empathy for their plight, and partly out of her instinct for self-preservation, she decided to act before an ugly situation developed. She instructed her staff to go out and buy as much flour as they could find, even if it meant travelling further afield. The kitchen in Sunniside was turned over to producing little else than bread for the next few days, which she intended should be distributed among the poor in the valley in exchange for the Levellers leaving the Darby home and enterprises alone.

Mr Darby, for his part, after consulting with his partners, took a different approach. He reasoned that money would be just as effective in warding off trouble and made sure he had plenty of guineas available, to hand over to the ringleaders for distribution as they felt fit, in exchange for them moving on without attacking either his works or his home.

***

After the Madeley Wood experience, Walter had been in a quandary, trying to decide whether or not he should join them when they finally arrived in the Dale. His mother spoke quietly to him whenever his father was out of earshot. She was clear that no good could come of it, particularly if things turned violent. Will on the other hand, was full of how important it was to fight for what's right and what could be a more deserving cause than feeding children, he wanted to know.

However, on the Friday, two days after Madeley Wood, something happened which made Walter's mind up for him. Tragedy hit the Bly family. Susan's uncle Fred worked in one of the coalmines in the Gorge. Her aunt, Mary Bly, already mother of four, two of them barely able to walk because vitamin deficiency had caused them to have rickets which had bent their little legs, went into labour for the fifth time. Undernourished and weak, she never made it. The baby was a tiny scrap of a thing and didn't live more than a day longer than its poor mother. Fred Bly was left with four children to bring up on his own, and more than likely they would be joining their father underground in the mine before long.

Susan arrived at the clearing the next day and discovered what had happened. Her Aunt Mary and Uncle Fred had lived in the neighbouring cottage all their married life and Susan was particularly close to Mary. Fred was Susan's father's youngest brother and Mary wasn't many years older than Susan, even though she had already had four children. To Susan, she was more like an older sister, and she was distraught. More than that, she was angry. She knew as well as anyone that hunger and poverty had caused this tragedy. Now she understood why Walter had been moved to take part in the protests and when he told her about what had happened in Madeley Wood, she told him as much when they were taking their usual walk through the woods, the only place they could find any privacy.

Their emotions were running high, Susan with the grief of losing her aunt, both of them angry at the events that had brought her death about, and Walter with his burning need to do something about it. His opportunity would present itself the next day, but he was full of trepidation at what might result from his decision to join the protestors.

Susan was due back at the big house by suppertime and both knew their time together was limited. She would need to return to the cottage soon. In their need to comfort each other they clung together under a huge oak tree, sheltering from the light drizzle that had begun to fall. Their embrace became more passionate and the need to assuage it too urgent to resist. As Walter pressed his body closer to her, Susan could feel his hardness and her own body responded. Inevitably their love was consummated there and then, beneath the oak tree. Afterwards they were consumed by the wonder of it. How could two human beings become one in such a wonderful way. They both swore their love to each other forever, and Walter asked Susan if she would become his wife, to which she readily agreed.

First, he told her, he must do what he could to fight for the food people desperately needed. He must join the coming protest in Coalbrookdale. Although Susan was fearful of what might happen, she said she understood why he had to go, but, she said,

'For goodness' sake, be careful! It's a dangerous business to get into, but you must do what you feel is right.'

Susan's blessing was all Walter needed and he now knew what he had to do. He would fight for justice, for these people, for his own family, for his own kind. He was ready to join the Levellers and do whatever it took to change the lives of the ordinary people around him. With that, they made their way arm in arm back to the Bly home, parting with a lingering kiss at the cottage door.

Finally, when Walter went to work on the Monday, he was told by Bill Cadman at the Boring Mill, that the Levellers were planning to advance up the valley from the river the next morning, and he must be prepared to join them. As he was on the day shift that week, he assured Bill that he would be ready and waiting when they arrived.

***

In Nailer's Row, Nat had also been in a similar dilemma. Should he follow his own instincts and join the Levellers when they arrived in the Dale, or should he obey his father and have nothing to do with them? He wished he could speak to his brother Ben to see what he felt about it all. However, he was still working up at the Horsehay furnace and hadn't been home to Nailer's Row for several weeks. Nat remained in this state of indecision, telling himself he would know what to do when something finally occurred.

So, the stage was set for the confrontation that was to come and as the sun came up on the Tuesday morning, the sound of horns, dreaded and welcomed in equal measure, echoed along the Coalbrookdale valley.

Chapter 36

A crowd of men had gathered down at the river, just by the wharfage. Some had come along the river from Broseley, others along the tracks from Madeley, Buildwas, and many smaller hamlets and settlements throughout the Gorge. Charlie Fox was once again the obvious leader and he jumped up on the wall by the wharf, to exhort the men to be ready to stand their ground, shouting,

'We go this day to the Darby place to demand food and drink. It's time these maisters started to share some on what they 'ave!' Our childer have been goin' 'ungry long enough. What do you say, men?!'

At this, a loud cheer went up and the signal was given to begin blowing the horns. By now they numbered around fifty men. Many had brought sticks or clubs with them, most of them with no intention of using them. Rather, they wanted to intimidate the farmers, mine owners and ironmasters, to convince them that they must meet their demands, or else suffer the consequences.

Working in the Boring Mill, Walter heard the call of the horns. In fact, no one could have missed it reverberating as it was around the steep-sided Coalbrookdale Valley. Even high on the western slopes, the inhabitants of Sunniside were wakened from their slumbers by the haunting sound.

Finally, with a loud 'huzza' the men began their progress up the road towards the Darby works. Bill Cadman signalled to

Walter and a couple of other men who had said they would join them, that it was time to go, and they made for the door. However, the foreman Ted Crowther reached the doorway before them, telling them to get back to their work.

'Let us pass Crowther!' Bill growled.

Ted Crowther called out loudly, so that anyone in the mill would be able to hear him,

'Any man who joins that lot out there, will never set foot in this place ever again. The choice is yours!'

'So be it. Let us pass man!' Bill repeated in a tone that brooked no argument.

The foreman stepped aside then, seeing they were determined to go, whatever the consequences. The crowd had almost reached the Boring Mill and they certainly looked a rough and intimidating lot. Walter could see that at the front of the crowd was Charlie Fox, who had led them at Madeley Wood, along with a couple of others who were constantly blowing their horns. The rest of the men were shouting and brandishing sticks or pieces of iron in the air. There were colliers, the coal dust ingrained in the lines of their faces, quarrymen whose clothes were grey with stone dust, and ironworkers with arms like tree trunks. These weren't men to be messed with. At the sight of all this aggression, Walter faltered slightly, wondering again what on earth he'd got himself into.

Seeing Walter hesitating, Bill shouted,

'Come on Bangham!' and grabbed his arm, pulling him in behind the mob.

As they approached Nailer's Row, the inhabitants came to their doors to see what was going on, including Liz. She was shocked to recognise her nephew in the midst of the mob, and shaking her head in disbelief, called out to him,

'Walter! No!'

Even though he couldn't hear what she'd said amidst the uproar of the crowd, he guessed what it was, and shaking his head, he strode on up the road. He'd made his choice and there was no going back now.

Liz was full of fear. She had known since the conversation she and Joe had had with Nat, that he had been struggling to decide what to do if the 'Levellers' did arrive in the Dale, but she had no idea what conclusion he'd reached. She hoped to goodness he would make the right decision. If this does end in violence, goodness only knows where that will lead, she thought to herself.

Nat was working at the old furnace he heard the sound of the horns in the distance and realised that the mob were on their way up the valley. There was much consternation among his workmates. Like Nat, most of them were conflicted. Should they join the fight for food for their families, or fight to safeguard the Darbys' interests, which of course, were also their own.

The mob carried on up the road, passing the new furnace where Joe was working. In the midst of knocking the plug out of the furnace mouth, he was unable to leave to see what was happening but could hear the commotion, even above the roar of the fire and knew what it meant. Like Liz, he was now afraid for Nat. He had no idea which way he would go, but just hoped to God he made the right decision. He was aware of course, that Walter had already joined the rioters. Two or three of his workmates took the wrong decision in his view, and in spite of his pleading, also fell in with them.

Walter was feeling angry but at the same time excited. Buoyed by the feeling of being part of something bigger than himself and seeing the pitiful sight of undernourished children clinging to their mother's skirts outside the cottages lining the road, he was now sure he was doing the right thing. How could anyone who called himself a man, stand by and do nothing as people starved? He felt the same as he had the week before, striding down the hill to Madeley Wood. Once again, he felt strong and free and in control, and it was a heady feeling.

At the old furnace, the sound of the horns was growing ever louder, and Nat was still no closer to making his decision. Then, at the last minute, from the direction of Sunniside they saw a waggon trundling down the road towards them. As it drew nearer, they could see it was stacked with loaves of bread and a couple of barrels of ale. Thank God, thought Nat, the Darbys have acted at last. It arrived at the furnace at the exact moment they saw the noisy crowd rounding the corner, approaching the site.

At Fox's signal the crowd halted, and he stepped forward towards the steps of the furnace, at which point the clerk, Frank Hughes, who was standing at the top of the steps called down to them,

'Mr Darby has provided enough bread here for you to take home to your families, and ale for you to drink. Now, take it, and go!'

The bread was distributed among the men, and they were all given a drink of ale, which seemed to take the heat out of the situation for the moment. However, no sooner had the bread and ale been distributed, than Charlie Fox approached Frank Hughes, saying they had a message for Mr Darby, if he would be good enough to carry it to him.

'Tomorrow is Wellington market day,' he said, 'and that is where we will be bound. Tell Darby that if he won't allow his men to join us, we will destroy his works. Tell him we will not stop until every man woman and child in this district has a full belly!'

To emphasize the point, many of the men shouted out loud,

'Aye, tell 'im that!!' or similar words.

With that, they began to turn around and march back the way they had come, muttering that they would be back, make no mistake!

Nat had been watching the proceedings, pleased that it seemed as though disaster had been averted, until that is, he had overheard Charlie Fox telling Frank Hughes of their intention to return the next day. He had seen his cousin Walter near the back of the crowd and had felt guilty he hadn't had the courage to join him. At the same time, he felt relieved. However, he understood he would have another decision to make tomorrow.

The valley was buzzing with talk of insurrection, of the power of people to change things if they worked together. They would make the masters listen. If they wanted to keep their businesses, they would have to take notice. Without the men to dig their coal, make their iron, or harvest their grain they would have no businesses.

Of course, not everyone took this view. Many, mainly the older inhabitants, were profoundly apprehensive. Over the years, they had seen efforts to improve the lives of the poor come to nothing, and often with terrible consequences for anyone who had the courage, or foolishness, depending on your point of view, to lead such a movement. The law as it stood showed no mercy to anyone who challenged the system. They knew only too well that their sons and grandsons who marched against the bosses and landowners would be in mortal peril, and they did their best to dissuade them from such a course of action.

Joe was no exception, and that evening he and Nat talked long into the night as he tried to persuade his son of the folly and uselessness of joining the mob the next day. In the end, Nat was persuaded to at least give the Darbys the chance to act further. The fact that they had already provided the waggon load of bread for the rioters to take home to their families gave him hope that they would do still more for them. As he lay in bed that night, he made up his mind not to follow the mob to Wellington, but to stand and defend the works if necessary.

Before he left for work next day, he told Liz of his decision. She was of course hugely relieved but at the same time, now worried for Ben. If the mob intended to go on to Wellington, they may well pass by Horsehay, and she had no idea what frame of mind Ben was in. If anything, he was more hot-headed than Nat, more like his Uncle Will in fact, and she feared he could easily be persuaded to join them.

Chapter 37

As Nat arrived at the furnace the next morning, he found
Frank Hughes addressing the workmen. Many of them, like
Nat, had heard Fox informing him they would be back to invite
them to march on to Wellington market that very day. Hughes
reassured them that Mr Darby understood their plight and was
determined to help where he could. He pleaded with them to
resist the invitation to join the mob, but to stay and defend
the works, which was, after all, their only source of income.

Looking around at the men it was obvious to Nat that his
words had provoked a mixed reception, some of them nodding
in agreement, others staring at the floor with a determined
expression on their faces. This can go either way, Nat thought,
but he was still clear in his own mind what his course of action
would be. He would stand and defend the works.

The sound of horns in the distance told everyone that the
mob was once again assembled and making its way up the
valley. The ominous sound grew louder, mingled now with the
shouts of angry men. Once again Walter had joined the crowd,
this time no longer with any reluctance on his part. When
he had returned to the mill the previous day, Crowther had
refused him entry, saying,

'Nay man, your time 'ere's finished. You made your choice
today, now be on your way and don't come back!'

Anger had bubbled up inside Walter. Anger at the injustice
of it. Could a man not stand up for what's right in this country

he asked himself, as he made his way back up to Dale Coppice. His thoughts inevitably turned to Susan – he had been hoping to marry her soon but now, until he found other work, he could not. His father of course, was proud of him. Proud that he had stood up to 'the bosses', demanding justice for the poor and hungry. At that moment, the fact that they had just lost their main source of income had done nothing to lessen his pride. Walter told Will of the plans for the next day. Now he had nothing to lose he said and would be joining them at the wharf at dawn.

Far from being proud of Walter, Betty on the other hand, was fearful, and because of that, she was angry. Angry that these two men in her life sometimes seemed completely lacking in common sense. How on earth did they think they would be able to survive on Will's meagre pay? She knew of course that they were securely housed in the coppice as Joe owned the cottage and would never evict them, but they still had to eat, for goodness' sake, she thought. She also thought of Susan. She had been hoping Walter would ask her to marry him, unaware that he had in fact already proposed to her, but now that he had lost his job, she knew he couldn't until he found other work.

So it was that Walter was striding along with the mob as it approached the old furnace. They were all in high spirits. The sun was piercing the gloom and the day was warm. But Nat was watching with foreboding as they rounded the corner, expecting a confrontation there and then. However, as they neared the entrance he saw them veer off to the right, Fox apparently leading them along the road towards Sunniside. It was obvious they were making their way up to the Darby house for a direct confrontation with Mr Darby.

They marched on up the hillside until they reached a pair of large iron gates, the entrance to the Darby estate. As they approached, several men appeared on the other side of the gate. One of them more imposing than the rest and obviously a man of some authority, probably the bailiff, Fox thought, immediately spoke up,

'What is your business here?!' he called out in a loud voice.

Fox stepped forward and replied,

'We come for Darby's answer! Either he tells his men to come with us to Wellington to demand that the farmers sell us their corn at seven shillings a bushel, or we'll be attacking his works!'

A loud cheer went up, the mob waving their sticks and iron bars in the air in a most threatening manner, and the men on either side of Fox blew their horns once more, loud, and long. The men beyond the gate, shocked at the sight and sound of these angry men who were obviously set upon destruction, took a step backwards, apart from the bailiff, who stood his ground.

'Well? What answer does he give?' Fox went on.

For a moment or two there was silence as everyone, on both sides of the gate, wondered what would happen next. Then in a loud voice, the bailiff spoke up,

'Mr Darby, sympathetic to your cause, has instructed me to hand you twenty guineas to be distributed among your number, in exchange for you going about your business, leaving the works alone.'

He took out a purse which obviously contained coins of some sort, saying,

'Well, what is your answer?'

Fox was disconcerted. He had not expected this. For a moment he was unsure what to do but then turned to the men,

'What say you men, will we accept this money to leave the Darbys alone?'

There were mutterings among the crowd, then someone called out,

'Well, the Darbys aren't bad maisters and they did give us bread yesterday!'

'And ale!' someone else shouted. 'Tell him if he brings us ale and more bread, we'll accept the money and leave 'em in peace!'

Fox turned back to the bailiff.

'You 'eared what they say? Tell Darby if he sends more bread and ale for us now, we'll take his money and be on our way. What say you?'

The bailiff said he would go up to the house to speak to Mr Darby and if they would wait there until he returned, he would see what he could do. He departed for the house, leaving the other men to guard the gate, though to be truthful there wasn't much they could have done if the mob had decided to charge them. Fox told his men to relax and await the return of the bailiff.

Half an hour later, he appeared once more, sitting on top of a waggon-load of bread and ale, and instructed the Darby men to open the gate to allow it through. The protestors swarmed around the waggon as Fox distributed the contents, and there was enough for each man to eat and drink. When it was all gone, good as his word, Fox called to the men to get ready to march once more, and the bailiff handed him the leather purse from his greatcoat pocket. After checking its contents and satisfying himself that it did contain the promised twenty guineas, he shouted out,

'Right men! Time to go! And it's to Wellington we go this day!'

Satisfied they had achieved enough, they strode off back down the road, the sound of their feet, the horns, and the shouts fading with every minute that passed. Walter strode along beside Richard and Bill, somewhat relieved that they had had some success without needing to use any violence. The bailiff and his men returned to Sunniside to inform Mr Darby that, for now at least, his works was saved.

The company of protestors made its way back down the hill. They had to pass by the old furnace to reach the track that led to Horsehay and then on to Wellington. The men still working at the site watched with considerable fear as the mob made its way down the slope towards them. Were they intent on attacking the works, or had Mr Darby managed to avert that disaster in some way? The men at the works had armed themselves with anything they could lay their hands on, so as to be ready for the attack, should it come. Nat, now convinced which side of this particular issue he was on, was standing on the steps of the furnace as they approached and from his vantage point could see his cousin Walter in the midst of the crowd. For a moment, Walter looked straight at him, then quickly diverted his gaze. Nat understood what that meant. Walter was obviously, and understandably disappointed that he had chosen not to join their cause.

Frank Hughes, the company clerk, also stood on the steps of the furnace. To reach the track going north, the protestors had to pass through the courtyard beside the furnace build-ing and as they approached, the tension mounted. Charlie Fox finally arrived at the bottom of the steps and halted. Hughes called down to him, in a loud, authoritative voice.

'If you intend to attack this works, let me warn you, we are ready for the fight!'

Charlie called up to him,

'Look, we are hungry men with hungry families at home. All we ask is that we can buy food at a price we can afford. How can that be unlawful? We are not here to attack anyone or destroy anything. We simply want to walk to Wellington market to demand corn at a fair price.'

Nat was relieved that for now, he wouldn't have to fight these men, many of whom were after all, his friends, and neighbours, not to mention his cousin Walter.

Looking down at the mass of angry men below him, who vastly outnumbered the workers at the furnace, Hughes had to admit he also was pleased to hear the conciliatory tone Fox had adopted. In fact, he secretly felt some sympathy for their cause. Looking directly at Fox, he pronounced,

'In that case, be on your way, but don't think of trying this again on your way back, whatever happens, because we'll be ready for you, make no mistake!'

With that, Fox gave the signal and the horns blasted out again as the company of men which, as it had gathered more volunteers in its progress up the valley, had swollen to around a hundred, filed past the works and out onto the track towards Horsehay.

Word of the unrest in the district and the events which had taken place at the various markets had of course reached Horsehay. Little else had been spoken of in the works and houses of the settlement. Of course, here they were experiencing the same food deprivation as everyone in the rest of the area. The surrounding woods were full of squatters' cottages, most of them with many mouths to feed, and everyone could see with their own eyes what effect their meagre diet was having, particularly on the children. The breadwinner in each poor home had to be given the lion's share of anything that was available. Without food they could not work and without work, all would starve.

Ben's anger had been growing as he'd watched what was happening to his neighbours and workmates and their families. He had heard that the protestors had already visited Shifnal market, to the northeast of Horsehay, and the word was that Wellington was to be next.

At about mid-day, a waggon-load of ironstone arrived at the Horsehay works, drawn up from Coalbrookdale along the new tramway by a team of six horses. The waggon driver brought worrying news. He told them of the confrontation with Mr Darby and how he had avoided catastrophe by persuading the protestors to go on their way without attacking the works. However, he told them, the mob was now on its way to Wellington market and would soon be arriving at Horsehay.

Asked by the foreman how many were there, the waggon driver, as people will often do when re-telling a tale, exaggerated rather, reporting there were several hundred angry men, all brandishing metal bars and wooden clubs, and all intent on making mischief along the way. So it was with some apprehension that the management at Horsehay awaited the arrival of the mob. Many of the men, including Ben, had been expecting it. They had heard of the confrontations at Madeley Wood and Shifnal, and also that there had been an exchange at the Coalbrookdale works the day before. They had therefore had plenty of time to consider where they would stand should the unrest reach Horsehay.

Ben, like everyone else, had observed the plight of many of the families living in the area, who had already been living on the poverty line before the price of food had shot up. As a single man, Ben himself had fared better, but that didn't stop him feeling angry on behalf of the little children he saw begging for food by the side of the road. Of course, like his workmates, he understood that to stand with the men who were approaching might put his own livelihood at risk, and so just as his brother Nat had been, he was conflicted.

At about mid-day they heard the horns in the distance. The call to arms was powerful, it sounded like a cry from the souls of the poor and hungry. Ben was stirred by it and in spite of all the thoughts of caution that had gone before, he was drawn to their cause. As the mob approached, they began to shout out to the men at the works to come and join them. One by one, men began to peel away from the group that had gathered outside the works to observe what was happening. Ben saw Walter in their midst. Their eyes met, and Walter called out to him,

'Ben! Come on man!'

Ben hesitated, but only for a moment, then he was striding towards Walter. His decision was made, for better or worse. Walter was delighted that his cousin had joined the cause, and the men clapped each other on the shoulder, now brothers in arms, as they saw it.

Intent on reaching Wellington as soon as possible the mob did not halt at Horsehay. Charlie Fox and the horn blowers led them along the track heading north. Many of the Horsehay men had joined them and their number had now swollen to well over a hundred. The sun had now disappeared, and dark clouds were gathering on the northern horizon. After they had been walking for about half an hour, a wind began blowing into their faces and twisting the leaves on the trees, telling them it was blowing for rain. Minutes later, the rain finally arrived, tumbling down in sheets, the wind driving it into their faces. and turning the track to mud.

Chapter 38

While the unrest had been escalating, the landed gentry and farmers of the district had not stood idly by. They had been busy organising a sizeable force of men, many of whom were their employees, dependent on them for food and shelter thereby ensuring their loyalty. By mid morning they had amassed several hundred men down at the wharf, far outnumbering the protestors.

In Nailer's Row Liz and Anne stood at the window and watched in horror as they passed by. Two men, obviously gentry, were riding at their head. Most of the men carried clubs or sticks but quite a few, to Liz's dismay, carried guns. She was sure Nat wouldn't have got involved with the rioters, from what he had told them that morning, but she had no idea what her younger son, Benjamin would do if the company of rioters were to pass by the Horsehay works. Joe had told her of his fear that if they were on their way to Wellington as everyone thought, they would more than likely do just that. Of course, she already knew that her nephew, her cousin's boy, Walter was already involved, and she feared that once Ben saw him in the crowd, he might be inclined to join him. She was totally unaware that her worst fears were at that moment being realised.

It was about an hour after the last of the mob had left Coalbrookdale that the magistrates Edward Cludde and Edward Pemberton arrived at the old furnace, riding at the head of their followers. Using the recently created tramway from the Dale to Horsehay, they travelled swiftly northward. They had managed to keep their mission secret from Fox and the mob who, slowed by the rain and mud were making fairly slow progress heading to the north of Horsehay planning to rest briefly at Ketley before going on to Wellington market.

At around two o'clock the mob had arrived at Ketley and was resting by the village green. Some of the villagers, sympathetic to their cause, brought them water to drink and what little food they could spare. They were wet and tired. However, they were buoyed up with the belief that this day they would be returning with food enough for themselves and their families too. They were all, including Walter and Ben, oblivious as to the fate that was about to befall them.

Having sent a couple of scouts ahead to see how the land lay, Cludde was informed that they were at that moment resting on the green at Ketley. He decided to use his men to surround the mob before closing in on them, sending a company of men around the village to enter from the Wellington direction. The trap was set and at his signal, his men began to move forward. However, at the last moment, Fox heard a commotion. After all, a company of several hundred men could not be completely silent. He strode along the street, back the way they had just travelled and was horrified as he rounded the bend, to see hundreds of men approaching, with the magistrates Cludde and Pemberton leading them. He Immediately realised the danger they were all in.

He ran back to the men shouting,

'The magistrates are here, but this is a peaceful assembly! Stand with me!'

The men were fearful but, listening to their leader, with some trepidation, they did stand firm as Cludde, and his men rounded the corner. Cludde halted his horse and immediately proceeded to read the riot act. He called out,

'Our sovereign Lord the King chargeth and commandeth all persons, being assembled, immediately to disperse themselves, and peaceably to depart to their habitations, or to their lawful business, upon the pains contained in the act made in the first year of King George, for preventing tumults and riotous assemblies. God save the King.'

Then, addressing Fox directly he told him that he would give them one hour to disperse, or they must suffer the consequences. Everyone knew what that meant. Anyone taken by the magistrates and charged with riotous assembly, could suffer transportation to America, or even death. Immediately now, some of the men began to peel away, disappearing into the woods around the settlement. To Ben's dismay, Walter was standing at the front with Richard and Bill, beside Fox, apparently all determined to see this thing through. Ben himself though, never having had the level of conviction of his cousin, decided to leave, but remained in the woods within sight of the protestors to observe what would happen next. He must be able to tell his family what had befallen Walter, should the worst happen.

By the time the hour had almost passed most of the men had departed, but a small group of about thirty stalwarts remained, including Fox and the other ringleaders who were determined to defy the order to disperse. Finally, the hour was up and Cludde once more called out to the protestors that they must now disperse immediately. Still they did not move, Fox protesting loudly that this was a lawful assembly of free men who only wanted food for their starving families.

At that point, Cludde, who had finally run out of patience, gave the order to fire in the air and several shots rang out. At this, some of the remaining rioters turned and ran, many of them making it to the shelter of the narrow passageways between the surrounding houses, then escaping off into the woods. Ben was glad to see Walter among them. However,

Cludde's men were now pursuing the men attempting to escape. To Ben's horror he saw Walter stumble in the rush to get away and was immediately pounced upon and held firm by a burly farmhand. In the end, more than a dozen of the rioters, including Fox and the horn-blowers were captured. Ben watched in despair as Walter was bundled back onto the village green where the others were being closely guarded by the armed men. It was to be two days before he found out for certain what had subsequently happened to him. Now that he knew there was nothing that he could do to save his cousin, he turned and ran as fast as he could back to Horsehay, taking the less well-trodden tracks to avoid the remnants of Cludde's force as they made their way south.

Walter heard Cludde call off the chase, presumably satisfied that he had the ringleaders in his hands, then he ordered that they be taken to Wellington lockup without delay. The captured men were roped together and led off towards the Wrekin. As they trudged along, no one spoke, all deep in their own thoughts. Walter was, of course, now terrified. He knew as well as anyone what fate might befall him. They were to spend some time in the lockup, but he was sure that from there they would be taken to the next assizes, which might be in Shrewsbury or Bridgnorth. He fervently hoped it would be Bridgnorth, as the most likely route would take them through Coalbrookdale. If that was the case, there was a chance he may just be able to see Susan somewhere along the way. It could be years before he saw her again, if ever. He knew as well as anyone that riotous assembly or demanding money with menaces were serious charges and if found guilty, he could suffer transportation to the Americas, or worse, could even be hanged. His blood ran cold at that thought and he quickly pushed it out of his mind.

He thought about Susan. Would she wait for him if he was transported? Indeed, would he ever be able to return? He knew of many who had been transported there and they had never seen home again. On the other hand, his own father Will, although he had gone of his own free will, had managed to return from the Americas some nine years later, and with Susan waiting here for him, he swore to himself that he would find a way.

He thought of his father and mother. How would they manage without him? Will couldn't go on working for long now, and they would be destitute without his wages. He fervently hoped that his brother George would step in to help them, or maybe Uncle Joe could help. He knew Joe owned the cottage in Dale Coppice and was sure that at least he wouldn't evict them.

As for himself, the fact he hadn't actually been the one demanding money or goods would be no defence and he knew it. Just being part of the mob was enough to convict him. He now realised what a momentous decision he'd taken two weeks ago when he'd made his way to Madeley Wood to join the protestors. How he wished he could go back to that time and take a different path. Now his life was changed forever. Not only his life either, but that of his mother and father and of course, his beloved Susan.

Thankfully the rain had now stopped and after walking for about an hour they stopped in front of what was obviously a lockup. It was a small building without windows, just having a twelve inch square grille in the door to allow light to enter the bare room. The men were detached from the ropes and herded inside. The only furnishings were a couple of benches along the walls. On the floor at the base of the wall opposite the door stood a bucket, presumably for the purpose of allowing the prisoners to relieve themselves as necessary. The stench was already overwhelming and could only get worse with twelve men closely confined for hours on end. The men quickly claimed their places along the benches and prepared to spend an uncomfortable, sleepless night.

The sound of the heavy door being slammed shut behind them and metal bolts being shot, struck terror into Walter's heart. So this, or indeed, worse, was to be his life from now on and he wondered whether he would be able to survive it.

Chapter 39

The foreman at Horsehay, to the relief of Ben and the others when they arrived back at the works, knowing that Mr Darby had shown some compassion for their plight, didn't dismiss them, simply telling them they would lose a day's pay for walking off the job. Ben was now desperate to find a way to get down to the Dale. He needed to let his uncle Will know what had happened to his son. There was a waggon leaving later that day and at the end of his shift he managed to hitch a ride down the valley. Short of time, as he would need to return to Horsehay that evening, he went straight to Nailer's Row to give the news to his own family. They were of course shocked to hear that Walter had been taken.

Joe was angry; angry at his brother for encouraging Walter to get mixed up in it all. He was also angry at Ben for doing the same, although he at least had had the good sense to run when he got the chance. He said he would go up to Dale Coppice to tell them what had happened, but Nat glanced at his mother and from the look on her face knew she thought the same as he did. For Joe to visit his brother in this frame of mind would probably result in an angry confrontation that wouldn't help anyone, least of all, Betty.

'Let me go Da,' he offered.

'Yes Joe, let Nat go,' Liz added, 'It's pouring down again now.'

As Joe's chest had been playing him up in the last few days, he had to admit to himself that it made more sense for Nat to climb up to the Coppice tonight, particularly as the rain had started up again, so he reluctantly agreed.

Liz, of course, had insisted on Ben eating supper with them and would have loved him to stay the night, but he insisted he had to get back to Horsehay. He had been in enough trouble for going off with the protestors and knew he must be ready to start work at six the next morning, or he wouldn't have a job to return to.

Nat walked with him a little way along the road before turning off along the track leading up the hill to Dale Coppice. When he arrived, Will was standing at the door, gazing anxiously towards the track where it emerged from the woods, obviously hoping to see his son step into the clearing at any moment. When he saw Nat, he realised this wasn't just a social call. Will had expected Walter back hours ago and was now very concerned as to what had happened to him. Betty had already risked his wrath by declaring,

'I knew you shouldn't have encouraged the lad to get involved Will! God knows what's happened to him!'

Will had uncharacteristically remained silent at this onslaught, fearing that she may well be right. He had simply planted himself in the doorway, praying that his son would appear at any moment which was just as Nat now found him.

Nat strode towards him saying,

'Uncle Will, I have some news of Walter, but not some you'll be glad to hear, I'm afraid.'

'I thought as much lad,' Will replied, 'Ye'd better come in.'

He stepped aside and motioned to Nat to enter. Betty was on her feet, having heard Nat's voice and hoping that at this time of a working day he must be bringing news. As Nat came in, she took one look at his face and knew she must prepare herself for the news to be bad.

'Nat! What is it lad? What's happened? Is it our Walter?'

'I think you'd best sit down Aunt Betty,' Nat replied, 'it's not good news I'm afraid.'

Betty remained standing, Will now standing beside her, both waiting for Nat to explain. He hesitated, and then began,

'Our Ben arrived about an hour ago with the news, but he's had to get back to Horsehay, so I said I'd come up to put you in the picture.'

'Well, for God's sake Nat, get on with it then!' Will exclaimed.

'Well,' Nat began, 'Walter did get involved with the protestors. They called at Darby's place and then went on up to Horsehay intending to go to Wellington market. Our Ben joined them at Horsehay and walked up with Walter as far as Ketley where they all rested a-while. Some of the locals gave them food and water. After about half an hour Cludde and Pemberton turned up with a few hundred men and the local militia, to try to persuade the protestors to leave and go home. Cludde read them the riot act and gave them an hour to disperse. Most of them did, including Ben, but about thirty or so remained.'

Unable to contain herself any longer, Betty cried out,

'No! What about our Walter? Did he leave then?'

'No Aunt Betty, I'm afraid he didn't.'

At this point, as Nat paused, Betty dropped down onto the settle, beginning to understand where this was going.

'Anyway, at this point Cludde apparently gave the order to fire in the air.'

'Good God, no!!' Betty interjected.

Will was grim faced and silent.

'At that point,' Nat continued, 'Walter ran towards the woods.'

'Thank the Lord!' Betty exclaimed.

'But unfortunately, Aunt Betty, he stumbled and one of Cludde's men grabbed him and held him firm.'

Betty wailed now, knowing precisely what this meant. Her beloved son was in the hands of the courts for rioting and one of two things would happen to him now. Either he'd be transported to America or, God forbid, hanged.

Will now sat down heavily in the chair before the fire.

'Where've they taken 'im Nat.'

'Well Ben didn't know. He saw them being led away in the direction of Wellington then more than likely, the next Assizes that could be at Shrewsbury or Bridgnorth.'

Betty's tears now began to flow. She could hold them back no longer, but Will had no patience for tears, he was too full of anger, predictably directed at the gentry.

'Those bastards!' he shouted out. 'Things'll never change in this country. Them as 'as, just get more and t'rest on us mun starve!'

Betty was still sobbing loudly.

'I'm that sorry Aunty Betty,' Nat said, sitting down beside her and putting his arm around her shoulders to offer her some comfort.

'What'll become of him Nat?' she asked tearfully, all the while knowing the answer. She knew she may never see her son again.

'How will you let George know, Uncle Will?'

'I don't know lad, but I must find a way. P'raps he'll be able to find out where they've taken him. The Justice of the Peace in Madeley might know.'

Betty was beginning to regain control and after a minute or so she said,

'What about Fred Bly, Will? He'll be needing a coffin from the carpenters for Mary and the child. They say they're being buried in Madeley. Maybe he'll be bringing it up, or whoever does, could take him a message?'

'Do you want me to go over and ask, Uncle Will?'

'Aye lad, p'raps you'd better. George might well be bringin' it up to 'em.'

At that, Nat went off to speak to Fred. He knocked quietly on the cottage door, not wanting to wake any of the little ones that might be sleeping. When Fred opened the door Nat was shocked at the sight of him. His eyes were red rimmed but circled in white where he had obviously wiped the tears away. He looked confused and wild, as though he still hadn't grasped what had happened to his family. Of course, Nat knew that not only had he lost his wife and baby, but that it was likely he may lose the other children also. They may be taken to the poorhouse if he couldn't look after them.

'Fred, I was so sorry to hear about Mary and the little 'un,' Nat began haltingly.

'Aye, well, thanks,' he mumbled, then, 'what can I do for ye?'

'Well, Uncle Will was wondering whether George would be bringing – you know – the...'

He was completely unable to finish the sentence. It seemed just too cruel to utter the word 'coffin'.

'Tha means will I be seein' t'undertaker? Ye might as well say it Nat, nought's goin' to change by ignorin' it.'

'Well, yes. Anyway we need to get a message to our George. Our Walter was taken by the militia today, but we don't know where they've taken him. Uncle Will thinks George could find out from the Justice in Madeley Wood.'

'Good God! Is there no end to the misery round 'ere! Aye, I'll tell 'im lad. They're bringing t'coffin tomorrow. In fact, it might be George who comes, but if not, I'll pass on thy message.'

'And could you let Susan's mother and father know as well, Fred, I believe her and Walter'd been doin' a bit of courtin'.'

'Good God, yes, I'd almost forgotten! The lass'll be devastated! O' course I will, I'll pop over later.'

Nat thanked him then returned to the Bangham cottage. He told Will and Betty that he must be getting back down the hill before the light went completely, and promised to let them know if he heard anything about what was happening to Walter and the others.

With that, he gave Betty a particularly affectionate hug, shook hands with Will, and took his leave.

Chapter 40

As Betty had suspected, George turned up the next day to attend to Mary Bly and her child. He arrived driving the waggon carrying the plain wooden casket, all that Fred could afford. He first went to the Bly cottage and with the help of John, the young apprentice he had brought with him, carried the coffin upstairs to the bedroom where Mary and the baby lay covered with a sheet. The women of the settlement, including Betty, had already washed them, and now he wrapped them in their woollen shrouds. Fred had followed them up the stairs and now stood beside the bed with tears streaming down his face. He gently pulled back the edge of the shroud to gaze for the last time on his wife's face. The infant, it had been a boy, was tucked into his mother's arms and Fred could just see a mop of dark brown hair peeping out. The sight of that tiny lifeless head was more than Fred could bear and he groaned and started to sob now. George stepped up to him and placed a comforting arm across his shoulders.

'What in God's name am I to do now George?' Fred muttered in a low voice devoid of any hope.

The thought of his little ones alone downstairs penetrated his grief for a moment, and he kissed his wife on the forehead for the last time, then turned and left George and John to their business. Once Fred had left the room, they carefully placed the bodies in the coffin, securing the lid. As Fred, who was downstairs now, comforting his children, heard the nails being hammered in, he all but collapsed, grabbing hold of the table for support.

After a few minutes George and John appeared at the foot of the stairs.

'All is done Fred. The funeral is arranged for the day after tomorrow. Would you like us to take her now and we'll meet you at the burying ground at noon.'

Fred looked into George's eyes with desperation and confusion in his. He was obviously having trouble taking all this in, and took a few moments before replying,

'Aye lad, ye may as well. She's gone from me now. Nothing more to be done except to lay her and the little 'un to rest.'

'Right Fred, we'll bring her down now.'

As they carried the coffin out of the cottage door to place it on the cart, Fred remembered about Walter, and told George that his Ma and Da needed to see him about his brother. However, Betty and Will were already, like the rest of the residents of their little community, standing at their cottage door to see one of their own depart on her final journey.

Once the coffin was secured on the waggon, George stepped over to his parents. He had already heard from one of the Madeley men who had been on the protests that his brother had been taken. He had also made enquiries of the Justice before leaving Madeley that morning, as to what was to become of the captives.

He would have had plenty to say to his parents about what he thought of Walter's actions in taking part in such foolishness, but out of respect for their feelings and because there were other neighbours standing around paying their respects, he kept such thoughts to himself. He simply said quietly,

'I heard about Walter Da. It looks like they'll be taken to the next Assize, which will be in Bridgnorth in two weeks' time.'

'God, no!' Betty exclaimed and George stepped forward to comfort her.

'Try not to worry Ma,' he said, putting his arms around her. To Walter he said,

'I'll see what I can find out Da, and I'll try to get back with news in a day or two.'

Will's face was ashen and for once he had little to say. Since he'd heard about his son being taken, the reality of what he had encouraged him to do had finally sunk in and had hit him hard. Once again, he was forced to see that his actions had consequences. Had he learned nothing? Once before his rashness had changed the course of his life, and now it had done the same for his son's. Will knew that without his influence Walter would never have embarked on this foolishness. Betty knew that too and had barely spoken to him since Nat had told them what had happened. All he could manage was,

'Aye, thanks lad. If they tek 'em to Bridgnorth, maybe they'll be passing through 't Dale to get theer, let us know.'

'I will Da, you can be sure o' that.'

With that, he and John climbed aboard the cart and with a nod to Fred who was standing forlornly at his cottage door, they drove slowly off down the track.

The next morning found Joe making his way up to Dale Coppice to see Betty and Will. In spite of his anger at Will for probably encouraging Walter to take part in the protests, he was concerned for them both. He knew his brother well enough to know that now he would be bitterly regretting his part in it. He would know that it was more than likely that his son would be transported, if that is, he avoided the gallows. From what he had told them on his return from his self-imposed exile, his journey and subsequent struggles were horrendous, and it was possible that Walter's, as a prisoner, would be even worse.

Joe found them both in a desolate state as he had expected. When he entered the cottage, they were sitting either side of the fireplace, heads downcast, and as they looked up at him, he could see that Betty's eyes were red-rimmed. Will looked years older, a look of despair in his eyes.

'Joe!' Betty exclaimed as he stepped inside, 'You know about our Walter?'

'Aye, I do lass,' Joe replied, 'and I'm right sorry for it. E's a good lad an' it's a pity 'e got involved in all this.'

'Aye, it is!' Betty exclaimed with a scowl at her husband sitting in the chair opposite her.

Will flinched under her gaze then spoke to his brother,

'I can't believe it Joe, there were 'undreds of men there, so they're saying, so why did our Walter 'ave to be one as was took?'

'Aye, I know, it's 'ard to reason why these things 'appen Will.' Joe knew that to try to apportion blame to Will right now would help no-one, and so he kept his own counsel on the matter.

'George was just 'ere, picking Mary Bly and the little 'un up, an' he tells us that they're tekkin 'em to Bridgnorth Assize.'

'So I believe, Will. Our Nat 'eard the same. Will tha go?'

'I dunno know Joe. George intends to.'

'I thought as much.'

'What I can't get out o' my 'ead Joe, is what lies ahead of our lad.'

Betty's need to show her brother in law her usual hospitality prompted her to get up, offering to share their meal with him. It was at that moment bubbling in the pot over the fire.

'That'll be grand Betty,' Joe agreed.

The brothers sat silently for a few moments until Betty had disappeared into the scullery to prepare to serve the meal, and while she was out of earshot, Will went on quietly so that she couldn't hear him,

'I've seen what 'appens to prisoners what are transported Joe. They're treated worse than Africans on them slave ships because they're worth less. If they survive the crossing they're lined up and sold to the highest bidder to be used as slaves by the settlers. I'm afeared 'e won't survive it.'

''Ave faith Will. 'E's made of sterner stuff than you think, and I believe 'e has a sweetheart waiting back here for him?'

'You mean Susan Bly? Aye he has if she's prepared to wait for him.'

At that moment, Betty reappeared, and their conversation was cut short.

Unable to do anything for Walter at the moment, Joe turned his attention to his brother and sister-in-law. He would need to find a way to help them survive. He knew that without Walter bringing a wage in, they would never manage on Will's labouring pay, even assuming he would be able to carry on doing it. From the look of him at that moment, that may not be long. Joe assumed that in any event George would help them out. As for the cottage, even though it would leave his own family a bit short, he said,

'Look Will, don't worry about t' rent on this place. It's thine, rent free for as long as tha needs it.'

Will squirmed in his seat, knowing that Joe was aware he would be unable to pay his rent even if he wanted to, and he was ashamed for it, mumbling,

'Don't worry, I'll pay thee when I can.'

Walter had, as he expected, spent a sleepless night sitting on the bench in the lockup, sandwiched between two burly miners. As daylight began to percolate through the grille in the door, he was able to survey his fellow captives. He knew Richard Corbett of course, and Charlie Fox, who had been the main ringleader. As such, Walter knew he would be shown no mercy and was bound for the gallows. One of the horn-blowers, Henry Crowther, a miner from Broseley was also there, and given his role in rallying the mob, Walter thought that he was probably destined for the same fate. By their appearance, Walter could see that most of the other men were miners or quarrymen. That much was obvious from their dress and the fact that he could see they were all used to hard manual work, evidenced by the huge muscles on their arms and legs, with one exception. He was a youngster who couldn't have been more than fourteen years old.

The lad was in considerable distress. This day had not turned out as any of them had planned, but with the rashness of youth, the lad had obviously been swept up in the adventure. He had probably never even given a thought to the possible consequences and was now in shock and terrified at what his future may hold. He was staring at the floor and although his face was hidden Walter could see his shoulders were shaking with emotion and his heart went out to the lad. In spite of concerns of his own he determined to do what he could to support him through the trials ahead.

Of course, they were all downcast, none of them doubting the fate that now awaited them. Like Walter, as well as fearing what their own future held, their thoughts were of their families back home and wondering how long, if ever, it would be before they saw them again. They all knew that without them, their loved ones would be destitute and destined for the Poor House either in the Dale or back in their home parishes, unless other family members could step in to support them.

Suddenly, the silence was shattered as the door bolts were shot and the door swung open revealing a couple of militiamen holding a jug of water and a few of loaves of bread. They simply placed them on the floor and then stepped back, slamming the door behind them. The men, having eaten and drunk nothing for nearly twenty four hours fell on the bread, tearing chunks off until Fox shouted to them,

'For God's sake, share it! We have no idea how long we're going to be here. All must share in whatever they give us.'

At this, the men stepped back and sat down on the benches again. Fox stood up and proceeded to share out the bread among those who hadn't yet had any, including Walter who had noticed that the youngster hadn't moved either, no doubt afraid to tangle with his burly cellmates. Walter tore off a piece from his portion of bread and offered it to the lad saying,

'Here you are son,' then went on to ask him his name.

The boy looked up, his eyes still full of fear, his face streaked from the tears he had been unable to suppress.

'Freddie Furlong,' he mumbled, eagerly taking the bread from Walter.

'Well Freddie,' Walter replied, 'Stick with me lad, we'll get through this together.'

Freddie gave Walter a weak smile then tucked into his piece of dry bread with gusto.

An hour or so later the door opened again, and the Captain of the Militia stepped inside.

'You are soon to be taken to Bridgnorth, and there will await the Assizes in two weeks' time. Be under no illusion, insurrection is a serious business, and you may expect little mercy.'

Having delivered this message, clearly aimed at removing all hope of reprieve from their minds, he stepped back outside, the door was slammed, and the men were left in the semi darkness, each with their own thoughts once more.

Freddie once more froze in terror, but Walter managed to catch his eye and give him a reassuring nod, and the boy seemed to relax a little.

Chapter 41

As George drove the cart bearing Mary Bly back to Madeley, his thoughts were all for the plight of his younger brother. George had never really been close to his stepfather Will. His own father had been killed in a mining accident when he was just a child and his mother had later married Will, so Walter was his half-brother.

Over the years George had become aware his stepfather had a bit of a reputation as a 'hothead'. As a young man he had left the Gorge under a cloud. In a fit of anger, he had almost killed a man and was forced to flee rather than be arrested and certainly hanged. For nine years he lived in voluntary exile in America until finally returning to face whatever fate would befall him. As it happened the man hadn't died and couldn't even remember the event, and Will was able to resume his former life in peace.

George had always been protective of his younger brother who had been a kind and generous child, if a little too much under the influence of his father, whom he adored. George knew his brother's nature well. He was no rebel, but he had a caring nature and would have found it hard to see starvation creeping into the Gorge, without being driven to do something to help relieve the suffering. He would have found an eager confidante in his father, Will, who would, George was certain, have been encouraging him to join the protests as he himself was unfit now to do so. If only he'd known what was going on, perhaps he could have persuaded Walter against it. He had been shocked to see him with the mob in Madeley the week before, but had realised in that moment, that it was too late. Walter was involved and not in the mood to listen to reason.

Having left home to marry Sally some years ago, George had seen little of the family. He'd been busy building up his carpentry business in Madeley. Demand was high for furniture among the rising ironmasters and mine owners in their fine new houses. He felt a little guilty about neglecting his family. If he'd been more in touch with developments, maybe he could have given Walter wiser counsel than that which he'd received from Will. But it was too late now, and he swore to himself he would do everything in his power to help Walter. One thing he could do for him immediately was to tell his sweetheart, Susan Bly, what had happened. Maybe he could help her to visit Walter. He knew the Justice fairly well as he had made many items of furniture for him. He may be willing to help arrange a visit once the prisoners had been transferred to Bridgnorth. But first, George needed to break the news to her, if she hadn't already heard.

They had now arrived at his workshop in Madeley and unloaded the coffin, carefully placing it on a trestle in the back store-room ready for the burial the following day. He realised of course, that Susan would most likely be attending her aunt's funeral in any case but felt that it would be tragic if that was where she discovered that her sweetheart was languishing in a lockup somewhere, awaiting trial for riotous assembly, with all the consequences that could bring. He decided to visit Harden House that evening, where he knew she was working as a chamber maid.

George and Sally lived in a cottage adjoining the workshop with their two children, John, and Alice. Sally was a good manager and with George's business thriving, she had no need to go out to work, spending her days looking after the children and making a comfortable home for her growing family. She was now expecting their third child, being due to deliver the baby in a couple of months' time. When George came in for his supper, she greeted him with her usual cheery 'hello', telling the children to welcome their father with a hug after his hard day's work. The family ate their supper of vegetable stew and bread with relish. George surveyed his little family, the children looking well and happy. He was thinking how lucky they were that he was able to earn enough money to meet the rising cost of food, unlike many of his neighbours, who were on fixed wages, many of them living in tied cottages and unwilling to demand more from their employers for fear of losing their livelihoods and consequently their homes. When supper was over, he explained to Sally he intended to visit Harden House to speak to Susan Bly about what had happened to Walter.

'She may already know, George, but I don't envy you having to break it to her if she doesn't,' his wife asserted.

'Aye, I know,' George replied, 'but I don't want to risk her having to find out at the funeral tomorrow. The day's going to be hard enough for them all as it is.'

At this, his wife stepped forward and kissed him on the cheek saying,

'George Bangham, you're a good man, but then I knew that when I married you!'

George smiled at her, slipping an arm around her waist, and giving her a brief hug before taking his coat from behind the door and stepping out into the misty twilight of the autumn evening. He made his way up the hill to Harden House, known to one and all as 'the big house'. As he knocked on the back door, he was wondering how on earth he could break the news to Susan. After a moment or two the door was opened by one of the maids, the kitchen maid, by her appearance.

'I'm calling to have a word with Susan Bly miss, is she around.'

'Wait 'ere sir, I'll go an' ask fer ye,' the girl muttered, then turned and disappeared inside, closing the door, and leaving George standing on the doorstep. After a few minutes the door opened and there stood Susan Bly. As soon as she saw that the visitor was George, her lover's brother, she knew that something was wrong.

'What is it, George? Is it Ma and Da, or Walter? What's happened.'

'Oh Susan, I'm afraid it's Walter.'

'What? Is he ill?!' she almost shouted.

'No, he's not ill, but he is in some trouble.'

'Oh my God!' Susan declared, 'I've been so afraid this might happen. I had heard,' she went on, 'that there was trouble up at Ketley, with shots fired and many arrests!'

'You're right Susan, the protestors were met by the militia at Ketley and I'm afraid Walter was taken.'

Susan stood stock still for a moment trying to comprehend what George had just said.

'No!' she declared, 'There must be some mistake! Please God, not my Walter!'

'I'm so sorry Susan, but it's true. I got it from the Justice, who told me they're being held in the lockup in Wellington at the moment but will be taken to Bridgnorth in a day or two to face trial at the Assize in two weeks.'

The full force of these revelations now hit Susan. She knew as well as anyone that being convicted of riotous assembly could at worse result in a death penalty, or at best, in transportation to the New World, for either seven or fourteen years. She rocked back on her heels, grabbing the door jamb for support. Tears flowed as George stood, helplessly, waiting for them to subside. Eventually she recovered her composure enough to say,

'Oh George, what's to be done? Is there no way to help him? He'll be terrified.'

'Well, I intend to find out exactly when the trial is to be and to travel down to Bridgnorth to see if I can at least visit him, and maybe try to find a way to help him.'

'I wish I could come with you George. I have to try to see him.'

'I'll see what I can do Susan, I'm not even sure whether visiting will be allowed.'

'I am due a couple of days off as it happens, I'll ask the mistress in the morning. Of course I'm already taking time off for Aunt Mary's funeral tomorrow, but I'll let you know what she says when I see you in the morning.'

'Very well Susan, I'll try to find out the exact date of the Assize.'

'Well, I'll see you tomorrow then George, and maybe we can make arrangements then.'

With that, George bade her goodnight and made his way back down the hill towards the river, and home.

In Nailer's Row, the conversation that evening was all about Walter, wondering what fate would befall him. Nat had heard that the Assize was to be held in Bridgnorth in two weeks' time and it seemed logical that this is where the prisoners would be taken, rather than hold them a further three months until the next one In Shrewsbury.

Nat and Will did consider perhaps going to the trial but decided that Walter's brother George would probably be undertaking that duty. However, Joe did insist that he would visit his brother Will on the coming Sunday, to see how they were coping, and to make sure that someone at least, and probably George, would be going to Bridgnorth, if indeed that was where it was to be held.

Chapter 42

The next morning George visited the Justice to enquire more precisely when the trial of his brother and other prisoners was to be held. It appeared that they were definitely soon to be moved to Bridgnorth and held there until the next Assize, in just over two weeks' time.

The funeral of Mary Bly was to be at noon and George and John loaded the coffin onto the waggon. Fred arrived with his brother John, Susan's father. Her mother had remained at the Coppice to look after her nieces and nephews. Now they walked slowly behind the coffin and as they rounded the corner, Susan joined them. She was of course, deeply upset at losing her aunt Mary, but also couldn't escape the thought that her demise had in some way prompted Walter to get involved in the riot and had also been the reason why she had more or less encouraged him to go.

She herself felt an overwhelming sadness at the position the poor found themselves in, while the rich seemed to want for nothing and had no trouble fulfilling their dreams. Day after day she saw it at the big house. Food was never a problem, and the mistress's every demand was satisfied without question. The house was full of beautiful things, furniture, china ornaments, and more books than anyone could read in a lifetime.

These thoughts drifted through her mind as they walked towards the churchyard, and she realised that in spite of what had happened to Walter, she was proud of him for standing up to them and doing what he felt was right. She knew that if convicted, and she supposed there was little doubt of that, he may well be transported to the New World for seven years; she dared not contemplate the alternative. She also knew that she would wait, for a lifetime, if necessary, for her man to return.

As the coffin was lowered into the freshly dug grave, Fred gave a loud moan, and his shoulders began to shake as he tried to suppress the sobs that were now wracking his body. John was standing beside his brother and threw an arm around his shoulder to offer some comfort. The injustice of this whole situation hit Susan afresh as she observed her uncle Fred, consumed by his grief. Poverty had caused this. She was in no doubt about that, and anger welled up inside her, almost overpowering the grief. How could she, she wondered, go on working at the big house, observing their privileged life, while all around the poor were starving.

Of course, in reality she knew she had little choice. Marrying Walter had now become a distant dream. It would be eight or nine years at least before he returned to claim her as his bride, and until that time, she would have to remain in service, or live in poverty like the rest.

After the funeral was over, she said goodbye to her father and uncle, then sought out George to discuss his plans for visiting Bridgnorth. He told her that the Assizes were to be held on the 27th of September and he intended to attend the trial. If she wanted to go with him, he would take the horse and cart and would be leaving early in the day. If the court was to convene at around ten o'clock, they would need to leave Madeley at around seven in the morning.

'Do you think we'll be able to speak to Walter, George?' Susan asked hopefully.

'Difficult to say Susan. It may be possible, but there's no guarantee of it.'

Susan's face darkened at his answer. Maybe at the very least she would be able to slip him a note somehow. She desperately needed to let him know she would wait for him, no matter how long it took. She would have to give him some hope if he was to endure the privations that he was surely about to suffer.

'I'll be ready George. I'll come to the house at daybreak on the 27th then.'

***

At that moment, Walter and his fellow prisoners were being loaded onto a waggon for their journey to Bridgnorth. They had been roped together once more in case they harboured any thoughts of escape. Walter had no way of knowing whether his mother and father, or for that matter, Susan had heard what had happened to him or where he was being taken. He was counting on Ben, who had been at Ketley with him, and who must have seen what had happened to him, passing the information on to them. Was it too much to hope, he wondered, that his father and mother might be watching out for him as the waggon passed through Coalbrookdale, as it surely must if heading to Bridgnorth? He desperately hoped he would be able to give them, or someone else, maybe Aunt Liz, a message for Susan. He needed to let her know that however long It took, he would one day return to fulfil his promise to her.

The prisoners were told to sit on the floor of the waggon, there being no seating of any kind to offer a little comfort. As the waggon rolled along the rough track, the men felt every jolt of the wheels as it trundled over the rocky surface. It was going to be a long and painful journey, Walter realised, although probably more comfortable than other discomforts he may well be facing before too long. He had heard his father's stories about his passage to the New World and it had sounded terrifying, what with the conditions on board ship, the disease, and the Atlantic storms they had inevitably met along the way. However, in spite of all this, there was just a tiny portion of him that was excited. He had often dreamt of leaving the valley to see more of the world. Well, now he would, although he fervently wished it could have been in other circumstances and that he was to be travelling with Susan by his side, as his wife. Of course, he could not even begin to imagine just how dreadful the years to come would be, as what he would need to endure was completely outside his personal experience.

After an hour or so, the Horsehay Furnace loomed up on the horizon. Walter wondered whether he would see Ben. At first, he was nowhere to be seen. Probably at work inside the furnace building, Walter thought. But as they approached several men were gathering outside the door of the furnace building.

Ben had heard one of the men shout that it looked as though they were bringing the prisoners past the works. He assumed correctly that they must be taking them down to Bridgnorth Assize and he hurried out to watch them pass. He saw Walter slumped against one side of the waggon, and Ben called out to him. As soon as Walter saw him, he shouted out,

'Tell Susan and me Ma and Da!'

'Aye lad, it's done!' Ben called back to him as the waggon trundled past. Walter managed a weary smile before it passed out of sight round the bend in the track, to continue on its way south to Coalbrookdale.

Ben was full of remorse because he hadn't helped his cousin to escape. If only Walter had run before the shooting started, they could have got clean away. He supposed he hadn't run then because he was standing beside Fox and the other leaders and didn't want to appear cowardly. By the time the first shots were fired in the air, it was almost too late. Even so, he might have managed it if he hadn't stumbled as he ran. Once Cludde's man had his hands on him, Walter was finished and there was nothing Ben could have done to save him, but that fact didn't make him feel any less guilty.

As the track began to descend Walter peered over the side of the waggon. He knew they must be descending to the Coalbrookdale valley, and sure enough, ahead of them he could see the furnace roaring its heat and throwing sparks into the smoky air. As they approached, the sounds of industry grew louder; metal on metal, materials being tipped into the mouth of the furnace, the creak of the water wheel and the heartbeat of the bellows blowing air into the fire.

Walter had hoped to see Nat, but he wasn't among the small group of men who had gathered to see them as they passed the Old Furnace building. Word quickly spread that the prisoners were being brought down the valley, and all along the roadside, little groups formed to watch them pass, some shouting encouragement, others remaining silent for fear of repercussions if they showed support for the unfortunate men.

Freddie began to cry now and strained against the ropes to raise himself up to see over the sides of the waggon. It was obvious to everyone that Freddie's home must be looming. Suddenly, from the right hand side of the roadway a woman ran forward calling his name.

'Ma!' Freddie cried out. 'Ma, I'm sorry! I got took!'

She ran to the side of the waggon and stretched up, trying to catch hold of her son's hand as he reached down towards her. She held it briefly before one of the militiamen dragged her away from the cart. Freddie cried out then,

'Ma, Ma!' before collapsing back into the bottom of the waggon, his face contorted with grief and fear.

Walter was also scouring the faces, hoping that he might see his Susan or his father or mother, but to no avail. Then as they approached Nailer's Row, he spotted Aunt Liz standing at her doorway. He called out to her, and she bravely stepped forward, calling out his name,

'Walter!'

'No talking to the prisoners!' shouted one of the militiamen who were accompanying the waggon.

Walter knew he had one chance to send his message to Susan and called out loudly,

'Tell Susan I'll be back Aunt Liz!'

That's all he managed to utter before the militiaman struck him with the butt of his gun and he fell back into the bottom of the waggon. Liz had heard his words and immediately knew exactly what they meant.

'I will Walter!' she called out, hoping that he would have heard her.

She realised that Walter needed to let his sweetheart know that he would come back one day, and to wait for him, and Liz swore to herself that she would personally deliver his message.

Walter, although dazed from the blow to his head, was nevertheless relieved to hear her voice in the distance. He knew Aunt Liz would pass on his message and Susan would know that his thoughts were all for her, in spite of the awful situation in which he found himself.

The waggon rumbled over the cobbles towards the river, then turned right and Walter knew they would shortly be crossing the Buildwas bridge. As they did so, he glanced down at the swirling waters of the Severn. The river! The thought suddenly struck him that it would be this very river that may soon carry him to his fate. If he was to be transported, he would be placed on a barge and taken down the Severn to the port of Bristol, there to be thrown into the hold of a ship that would take him across the ocean to the Americas, away from his home and everything and everyone he had ever known, including his beloved Susan. He glanced round at his fellow prisoners and wondered whether they were thinking the same. His glance landed on Freddie and the thought struck him that he would probably have little idea of what was to come, and Walter hoped he had the resilience and strength to face it.

A couple of hours later the waggon pulled up outside a half-timbered building which the men rightly assumed was their destination; the gaol where they were to be imprisoned until their trial. They were taken to a door at the rear of the building, to stone steps that obviously led to the cells. Still roped together, they stumbled their way down and through a heavy door at the bottom, which clanged shut behind the last man to enter. Walter peered into the gloom as the daylight was extinguished. What could only be described as rows of cages ran down either side of a narrow passage. In each cage, Walter could just make out groups of rough looking, dirty and unkempt figures, who looked up sullenly at the new arrivals in their midst.

He was horrified. The smell was dreadful, unwashed bodies, stale urine and worse. He didn't belong here. How had his life come to this? A hopelessness descended upon him as, one by one, their ropes were removed and they were herded into a cage that was already occupied by several prisoners, who made it obvious they weren't taking too kindly to be having to share their accommodation with these newcomers.

Walter knew he would have to spend at least two weeks in this dreadful place until the Assize hearing, and at that moment he had no idea how he would endure it. However, the human spirit is indomitable, and somehow the days passed, but not without taking their toll on him. Unable to wash, relieving himself in a bucket without privacy, and with every waking hour dreading what would happen next, he was slowly ground down. He began to feel like a criminal and he was filled with shame. He tried to help Freddie Furlong as much as he was able in the circumstances which distracted him slightly from his own misery. But in fact, all that kept him going was the thought of Susan, and he clung to that like a dying man would cling to life.

Chapter 43

Liz had been as good as her word and had made her way to Madeley the next day to seek out Susan Bly. She called on George and Sally first, to ask where she might find her. After taking some refreshment with them, she climbed the hill to Harden House. Making her way round to the back door, and although a little intimidated, being unused to approaching such a grand building, she knocked quietly on the door. After what seemed ages, a young girl opened it. She was obviously a kitchen maid, judging by her appearance. However, seeing this lowly person standing there, she raised herself up to her full height and enquired,

'Yes, Modom! What d'yer want?' in a rather superior tone which didn't quite work.

Liz understood that being a servant in such a big house would have convinced this girl she was a cut above ordinary folk. She responded by summoning up her most assertive voice, and requested to speak with Susan Bly, the chamber maid, stressing the 'chamber' to make sure the girl knew that she had 'connections'. The girl said nothing but disappeared, closing the door behind her, and leaving Liz standing there.

Several minutes had passed and Liz was about to knock again when the door opened, and Susan stood looking down at her. At first, she didn't recognise her as she had only seen her a couple of times, when visiting Betty and Will in Dale Coppice.

However, when Liz explained who she was, Susan immediately understood that perhaps she had news of Walter.

'I have, Susan. I saw him yesterday as they were taking them down to Bridgnorth and he gave me a message which I promised to bring you. It was only short, but I'm sure you'll understand it. He said,

'Tell Susan I'll be back!'

Immediately tears sprang in Susan's eyes as she said,

'Oh my God, how will he ever stand it Liz? From what George has told me, transportation for seven years is the best he can expect. We all know that few ever return.'

'Aye, it's a dreadful business Susan. But at the risk of making matters worse for himself 'e was determined to get this message to ye, in fact 'e got the butt of a gun across his head for doing so.'

'Oh Walter!' Susan exclaimed then stepped down off the doorstep, closing the door behind her, and broke into heaving sobs.

Although Liz didn't know her too well, her heart went out to this young woman whose love had been so cruelly snatched away, and she put her arms around her to comfort her. They stood like that for some moments until Susan's sobs had subsided. Liz knew no words of hers could bring relief from the grief she was suffering. Susan spoke first, with conviction,

'Well Liz, I'm determined to go to the trial, and hope he can tell me himself, if George can arrange for me to visit him.'

'I hope you can Susan, it would mean the world to him, I'm sure.'

'Thank you so much for coming Liz. It is a comfort to me to know that even in the awful situation he's in, he is still thinking of me.'

'It was the least I could do Susan, Walter's always been a good lad. My favourite nephew if I should say such a thing!

Well, I'd best be on my way, I have shopping to do at the market, if I can find anything worth buying.'

Susan now kissed her lightly on the cheek and thanked her once again, then watched her make her way through the garden gate, before opening the door and disappearing inside.

Liz now made her way to the school, hoping to have a word with Elizabeth. She hadn't seen her or Rod for several weeks and was hoping to ask them to come down one Sunday. She knew Joe missed his daughter. They had been close before she left home at fourteen to join her Aunt Dorothy and Uncle John at the schoolhouse.

She had grown into a lovely young woman and Liz and Joe were proud of her. As she approached the school, she could see that the children were outside in the schoolyard, taking a break from their studies. She saw her daughter standing by the gate, obviously keeping watch over her charges. Elizabeth's face lit up when she saw her mother, and she stepped outside the gate, coming forward to give her a hug.

'Mother! I never expected to see you here today! What brings you over to Madeley Wood?'

'Hello love,' Liz replied, 'by, it's right good to see ye, and looking so well too!'

'I am well mother. In fact I have some news for you. We were going to come over at the weekend, but as you're here you may as well know now.'

'News? I 'ope it's good news, we could all do with some of that right now, you've heard about Walter?!'

'I have mother, it's a dreadful business. Poor Aunt Betty and Uncle Will must be devastated.'

'They are, and I came to give his sweetheart Susan a message from him. But what is this news o' yours love?'

'Well, you're going to have a grandchild mother!' Elizabeth told her, smiling broadly.

'Oh! That's wonderful Lizzie!' she declared, using her diminutive name reserved for special occasions. 'Your father'll be thrilled an' no mistake! But when can we expect this little one to arrive?'

'Early spring, we think, if all goes well. It's early days yet, as you can see,' she said, patting her flat stomach.

'Well, you look after thisen lass. That's a precious bundle you're carryin'.'

At that moment the school bell rang out telling the children it was time to return to their studies.

'I have to go mother,' Elizabeth said quickly, before hugging her once more and telling her they would visit soon, maybe in a couple of weeks' time.

Liz had a spring in her step as she made her way over to Coalbrookdale after picking up a few bits from the market. So, she was to be a grandmother! The next generation was about to make an appearance and she was happy for it.

***

That evening, sitting by the fire opposite Joe, watching him contentedly smoking his pipe, Liz reflected on her conversation with Susan earlier. Life could be so cruel sometimes. All Walter had done was to try to stand up for the poor folk who were starving, and now his life and that of his sweetheart had changed forever. Then of course, she thought about Elizabeth's news. She hadn't told Joe yet. She'd been saving it until they could sit quietly after supper. Now she smiled as she thought how lucky she'd been to spend her life with the man she loved, had always loved, since the day they met, when he'd turned up in Dale Coppice to build his cottage. At that moment Joe looked up,

'What's amused thee lass?' he said quietly.

'Oh, nothin', I was just thinkin' how lucky we've bin Joe.'

'Aye, I suppose we 'ave. Four children raised up.'

'And now, a grandchild on the way,' Liz added with a broad smile.

Joe looked confused for a moment, then his brow cleared as he realised what she must mean.

'Elizabeth?' he simply asked.

'Yes Joe, she told me this morning. Due early spring, she thinks.'

'By, that's good news and no mistake lass. Who'd have thought it, a grandchild at last!'

'Well, I was beginning to think it wouldn't happen for them either, but I'm right glad it has! I wish I could say the same for Walter and Susan Bly. I called to see her today, to give her Walter's message and the poor lass is distraught. I 'ave a feeling there would have been a wedding there before long but that's not going to 'appen now, is it? Not for a long time anyway, if ever.'

'Aye, that's true. In truth, that brother o' mine has a lot to answer fer, encouraging Walter like that. Still, I know it's not turned out as he meant, and he's devastated 'isself. I told him I'll do what I can to 'elp 'em now they've lost Walter's wage. At least they'll still 'ave a roof over their 'eads.'

'That's good love, families 'ave to stick together in times of trouble.'

She got up and kissed him lightly on the head before saying, 'Well, I'm off to my bed. You comin' up?'

'I'll be there in a bit, when I've locked up and seen to t'fire.' he replied, but when she'd gone, he decided to finish his pipe, indulging himself in happy thoughts of his grandchild for a few minutes, before damping down the fire, locking the front door, and climbing the stairs.

Chapter 44

As the days dragged by in Bridgnorth, Walter sank deeper into despair. He still had no idea whether he would see anyone before the trial. He was horrified at the thought that he may be sent down to Bristol for transportation, or God forbid, even hanged, without seeing his family or his beloved Susan one last time.

The conditions were appalling. As the trial day approached, he was conscious of his appearance. He had hardly slept and there had been no opportunity to wash or change his clothes. He was aware that he must be hardly recognisable from the man who had been brought to the gaol two weeks earlier. He only had to look around at his fellow prisoners to realise that he must now look every inch the criminal the judges would assume he was. He expected no mercy and told himself the best he could hope for was seven years in exile, so he must prepare his mind for it.

Then one morning a loud hammering was heard outside the small grille that passed as a window, and with mounting horror, one by one they realised they were building the gallows. They all knew that if any of their number were sentenced to death, execution would follow immediately. Walter glanced at Charlie Fox, knowing that he was almost certain to be one of them, and could see that he was visibly shaken, flinching at the sound of each nail being driven into wood. So the day of the trial would most probably be the next day, and tonight may be the last on earth for some of his fellow prisoners. Walter prayed it wouldn't be his.

***

George had ridden up to Dale Coppice earlier in the week to let Will and Betty know he intended to take Susan to the trial and to ask them if they wanted to go with him. However, when he saw Will, it was obvious that all was not well with him. He looked grey and short of breath, unable to walk more than a few yards without resting, and seemed to be having difficulty using his left arm and leg.

Betty was obviously very worried and said as much when Will stepped outside to visit the privy. She told him that Will had suffered some kind of attack two days ago. She said he had been in a deep depression since Walter had been taken, seemingly quite unable to come to terms with it, and was angry with himself because he had encouraged his son to join the mob. Then, two days ago, when he woke up, something had obviously happened to him during the night. She didn't know what was wrong with him, exactly, but he certainly wasn't fit to be travelling to Bridgnorth, and reluctantly she said that if he couldn't go, she would have to remain here with him, in case his condition worsened.

When Will returned, George could see just how much he was struggling to walk as he crossed the room to sit down heavily in the chair by the fire once more. Of course Will knew that there was something seriously wrong with him. He was having trouble keeping his balance because of the weakness that had developed in his left leg, and his left arm looked weak. After sitting quietly for some moments gazing at the fire, he looked up and spoke to George,

'Looks like I'm not fit for visitin' Walter, George. Will ye explain to 'im why?'

'I'm sorry to hear that Da, but yes, o' course, I'll explain.'

George looked at Betty who now had tears in her eyes as she thought of Walter and how hurt he was going to be that they weren't in court.

He stepped across to her and put his arm round her shoulders, saying,

'I'll be back to let you know what 'appens, as soon as I can Ma.'

'Will you 'ave time to see any o' the Bridgnorth Banghams George?' Will asked. 'No doubt they'll 'ave heard that one of ours is in court again. Our Richard once saved Abi's lad from God knows what, but I don't think he'd be doing the same for our Walter, grown man that he is, even if ye asked 'im.'

'No Da, I'm sure you're right. Walter went into this with his eyes open and if he hadn't considered what the consequences might be, he wasn't thinking straight.'

George glanced at Betty who was scowling accusingly at Will, but he just stared at the floor and said nothing.

'Anyways Da, we're only there for the day and we'll have to get back after the trial, so there won't be time for visiting relatives, and to be honest, I don't even think they'd know who we were, we've not seen any of them for years.'

Will nodded sadly, wondering how Margaret was. She was his big sister and would be well in her sixties now, but he hadn't set eyes on her since Abi's funeral. His brother Richard and nephew Michael had been there that day too of course, both looking older. Now, Will realised he may never see any of them again.

George stood up and said he'd have to be getting back over to Madeley while the light held. He kissed Betty on the cheek, and placing a hand on Will's shoulder, told him not to stand up, then he left the sad little house and mounted his horse to make his way home.

***

It was one of those crisp autumn mornings, a little frosty and with a mist lingering in the valley, and Susan pulled her shawl around her more tightly as she walked down the hill to meet George. She was excited at the prospect of travelling to Bridgnorth to see Walter, and at the same time, terrified of what the day may bring. She hoped George had managed to arrange for them to visit Walter, but in any event, he would know that just by her being there, she was giving him the answer to his message. She would wait for him, however long it took. That is what her presence there would tell him.

So, it was to be just George and Susan who would be at the trial to support Walter. George was already harnessing the horse to the waggon when Susan arrived at the workshop.

After greeting her he said,

'I have some good news, Susan. I spoke to the Justice about Walter, and he has given me a note authorising the gaolers to allow us ten minutes with him before the trial begins.'

'Oh George, that's wonderful, thank you!' she declared, stepping forward to kiss him lightly on the cheek.

It took them a couple of hours to reach Bridgnorth, where they enquired from one of the stall holders at the market in the town square where the Assize hearings were to be held. In the event they needn't have asked anyone because as they rounded a corner in the street, there before them was a half-timbered official looking building and at the side of it they noted with horror that a scaffold was waiting threateningly for the outcome of the day's business.

Susan visibly paled at the sight and gripped George's arm. Covering her hand reassuringly he said,

'Not for our Walter, lass, I'm sure of it.'

The place was very busy. Market day and Assize hearings had brought people in from far and wide to view the anticipated spectacle, and they had some difficulty finding somewhere to leave the waggon and horse. Eventually, they found a space at the back of one of the inns, then made their way back towards the court building.

Entering the main door, they looked around for someone in authority to speak to about visiting Walter, hopefully before the trial began. There was a clerk sitting behind a raised desk to one side of the door and George took out the note he'd been given by the Justice and approached the desk.

Handing the note to the clerk, George enquired whether it was possible for himself and the young lady with him to see Walter Bangham. The clerk peered down at him over his glasses, then carefully opened the note and read its contents. George didn't know exactly what it said as his reading skills were poor, but whatever it was, it seemed to have had the desired effect as the clerk gestured to a burly looking chap, probably one of the gaolers, George thought, to approach him. Then he told him to take them down to the cells to visit Walter Bangham.

'Ten minutes only,' the clerk told George, who thanked him and taking Susan's arm, proceeded to guide her towards the door at the far end of the room as he followed the gaoler. He led them down the stone steps into the depths of the building. Susan was shaking now, emotional at the prospect of seeing the man she loved but afraid of what she was about to find. How was Walter holding up in this awful situation, she wondered.

The gaoler led them into a side room and told them to wait while he fetched the prisoner. He clanged the door shut behind him and in the half-light George and Susan exchanged fearful glances at the sound, realising how terrible it must be to be confined in a place like this.

A few moments later, the door opened, and the gaoler pushed a figure inside, saying,

'Ten minutes only, Bangham,' then banged the door shut again, and the sound of the heavy bolt being shot rang out.

The figure before them was almost unrecognisable. He was dirty and unkempt. His beard and his hair were matted, and he had lost weight, even in the two short weeks he'd been there.

'Susan!' Walter declared, 'you shouldn't have come!'

Susan was shocked. This was the last thing she'd expected. She had imagined he would be happy to see her, and would have immediately taken her into his arms, even with his brother standing there.

'I had to come Walter. I had to see you again, before ...' her voice trailed off as she was unable to complete the sentence.

Walter was staring down at his feet, utterly ashamed of his appearance, and thinking that she must find him revolting. He was in no doubt that after weeks of not washing and living in filth in this rat-infested place, he must be disgusting to her eyes.

Looking at him Susan understood how he must be feeling, and conquering the revulsion that was indeed welling up in her as her stomach heaved at the stench, she stepped forward and took his hand that was hanging limply by his side.

'Walter, I came to tell you that I love you, and will always love you, whatever happens today. If you are sent away, I'll be here when you return and we will be wed, just as we planned.'

Walter raised his head now and looked into her eyes with tears in his.

'I'm sorry lass!' he said. 'You deserved better than this. I have no right to ask you to wait for me.'

Susan now raised her hand and placed it on his mouth to silence him.

'I will wait for you Walter Bangham, so no more of this. You just remember, whatever happens, I'll be here waiting, so make sure you come back to me.'

Walter pressed his cracked and dirty lips to her hand, saying,

'God bless you. I love you, Susan Bly.'

George had stepped back into the shadows to allow them to have a moment or two to themselves, but as time was short, he now stepped forward and spoke for the first time,

'Walter, I'm so sorry you're in this situation.'

'George! I know, but I'm guessing you think I brought it on myself!'

'Well, I know you Walter, and how much it would have hurt you to see starvation stalking the Dale. I'm sure you only did what you felt was right, and for that I'm proud of you little brother.'

'Are Ma and Da here?' Walter asked with dread in his voice.

'I'm sorry, they aren't. Da's not been too well, and Ma thought it might be too much for him. They said to tell you they were sorry not to come.'

'Well, I'm not George. I wouldn't want Ma to see me like this. Tell them I love them, and I'll be back.'

Glancing at Susan, he went on, 'I've got a lot to come back for!'

At that moment, the door bolt was shot back, and the loud, gruff voice of the gaoler rang out,

'Time's up Bangham.'

Susan clung desperately to his hand before the gaoler dragged them apart and Walter, terror mingled with love in his eyes, disappeared and the door was shut behind him.

Susan could no longer hold back the tears and George stepped up to her putting his arms round her and allowing her to rest her head on his shoulder until her sobbing ceased.

The gaoler now returned and led them both back up the stairs and out of the courthouse.

Chapter 45

The trial was due to begin at noon, so George and Susan had a couple of hours to spare and returned to the inn to take some refreshment. It was packed with people and talk of the day's trials was loud, with much speculation on the probable outcome, the consensus being that at least one of the ringleaders of the recent riots would be hanged. After several minutes of this Susan could stand it no longer and said she felt faint and needed some air.

They left the chatter behind and took a walk down to the river. The wharf was crowded with trows, some loading goods to be transported down to Gloucester or Bristol, and just as many goods being unloaded from ships that had come upriver bearing goods and raw materials to be trans-shipped to up-river trows bound for the industry of the Gorge and beyond. Susan thought she had never imagined there were so many ships in the world, never mind on the Severn. Would this be where her beloved Walter would be brought, she wondered, to be taken down to Bristol and the great ocean beyond and carried to the other side of the world? The thought made her shiver, and she pulled her shawl tightly around her shoulders.

George checked his pocket watch and seeing it was now eleven o'clock, said,

'We'd better get back up to the court, Susan, if we are to gain entry 'afore noon.'

Ten minutes later they joined the queue waiting to enter the courtroom. They thought they had left it too late and wouldn't get in, but just managed to squeeze in before the courtroom official declared that the room was full and slammed the door shut, leaving several dozen people unable to enter, much to their annoyance.

George and Susan were ushered into an area to one side of the room, obviously reserved for onlookers to the proceedings, people not directly involved in the trials. Neither of them had ever been inside a courtroom before, and what they saw didn't exactly fill them with confidence in the justice system. The room was dark and noisy, with an atmosphere of menace about it. It was hot and airless, and the smell of unwashed bodies was overpowering. It was obvious to George and Susan that most of the people in the visitors' gallery had come out of morbid curiosity and a desire to see the harshest of sentences carried out. Transportation, yes of course, but from the snippets of conversation they heard, there would be much disappointment if they were denied the spectacle of an execution today.

Suddenly a loud voice declared,

'Silence in court!' and a hush of anticipation descended on the room.

A moment later the five judges emerged from a side door at the end of the room and took up their seats which were on a raised dais which ran along the end wall. They were a spectacle in themselves. All wore long black gowns and on their heads were voluptuous white wigs which hung down to their shoulders. The whole effect of these five elderly men, seemingly identical and all peering down in a superior manner at the assembled 'rabble' as they no doubt saw it, was intimidating enough for an observer. Goodness knows how it was to feel to the prisoners that were shortly to stand before them.

The jury was summoned, and twelve men filed in, taking up their seats on two benches ranged along the wall opposite the visitors' gallery. Some of them looked nervous and Susan assumed this whole experience was new to them. They were no doubt aware that lives would depend on the verdicts they would reach this day. Susan prayed they would be merciful to her Walter. He didn't deserve to be here, she thought, he was a good man who'd only got involved in this mess with the best of intentions; to help his fellow man. George was thinking much the same. He knew his brother to be an honourable man, if a little 'soft', and he didn't belong here, and certainly not on a rat infested ship that would carry him to the other side of the world.

After the jury were sworn in, the judge called out in a loud, authoritative voice,

'Bring forth the prisoners!'

One by one the men appeared as they mounted the steps from the cells below. They were instructed to stand in a raised area bordered by a low balustrade. Susan's heart leapt as she saw Walter appear. More than ever, she was convinced that he didn't belong here, yet here he was, and goodness only knows what will become of him, she thought. She fixed him with her gaze, willing him to look over to where she stood, but as he lined up with the others behind the low balustrade, his eyes were flicking from side to side, no doubt trying to absorb the reality of the scene before him.

It seemed that they were to be tried together as they were to be judged as being equally involved. This alarmed Susan and George, as it appeared there would be no special pleading for Walter. The fate of one was to be the fate of all. They now feared the worst. Surely, they wouldn't hang them all!? Susan gripped George's arm.

Each of the men in turn was asked to state his name and the parish from which he came. Some answered loudly, others mumbled their reply and were asked to repeat it. Before Walter's turn came, he finally scanned the visitors' gallery looking for a familiar face. His eyes met Susan's and his heart leapt. She smiled and nodded her head, affirming what she had already told him earlier. She was here and would wait for him, however long it took. Although unable to return her smile, he acknowledged it with a slight inclination of his head. Now he stood a little taller and when it was his turn to state his name he did so in a loud, clear voice,

'Walter Bangham, Madeley Parish.'

Next to Walter stood young Freddie Furlong. He looked tiny compared to the rest of the prisoners and was in distress. Walter managed to place a reassuring hand on his shoulder before one of the gaolers stepped forward and knocked it off. Susan's heart warmed when she saw Walter's act of kindness.

The boy mumbled his name and that he was from Coalbrookdale. The main judge called out,

'And what is your age, boy?'

'I'm fourteen years, sir,' Freddie responded.

The judge glanced from side to side, nodding to his fellow judges, and then called out,

'Very well. Continue!'

When all of the prisoners had identified themselves, the charge was read out by the Clerk of the court.

The counsel for the Crown set out the case against the men, then Edward Cludde was called to give evidence for the prosecution. He took his oath in a loud, cultured voice with his hand resting on a bible. As he was obviously a wealthy man and was also a magistrate, George felt that whatever he said, his words were likely to go unchallenged. It was obvious to everyone that every word he said would be accepted by the judges.

Cludde was asked to recount the events of the day of the riot, and he explained how he had read the Riot Act and given the statutory time of one hour for the mob to disperse.

The main judge then spoke up,

'And did they, disperse?'

'Some did, your Honour, but these men did not, encouraged by Charles Fox to stand their ground.'

'I see,' said the judge, 'Please continue.'

Cludde continued with his account, explaining that the remaining men had been arrested and incarcerated in Wellington lock up until their transfer to Bridgnorth for trial. The judge asked whether any of the men had expressed any remorse or regret at their actions.

'They did not, your Honour.'

'Thank you, Mr Cludde, you may step down.'

The judge now turned his attention to the men in the dock and finding Fox standing at the left hand end of the line, instructed him to take the witness stand.

Charles Fox stepped forward with his head held high. Overnight, after listening to nails being hammered into the scaffold the day before, something of a transformation had come over him. He had accepted that this day was to be his last. He knew he would be mounting the steps of the scaffold before the sun sank in the sky. If it was to be so, he would face it like a man. He believed, passionately, that all men are created equal and free, and deserved to have food in their belly and a roof over their head. The last thing he could do for the cause now was to show courage, to demonstrate that whatever they did to his body, his spirit was still free. He prayed fervently that the courage he showed in the face of death would inspire others to work for a better world for all, regardless of the bed in which they were born.

He was sworn in, saying,

'I swear by Almighty God to tell the truth, the whole truth and nothing but the truth, so help me God.'

'Ah, Mr Fox.' the judge then began softly but with a world of meaning.

'Yes, sir?' Fox replied.

'So, you were the ringleader of this riotous mob?'

'Sir, we were no riotous mob. We were simply a group of men intent on finding food for our starving families.'

'Enough, Fox. We need no righteous speeches here! The facts are plain. You had amassed a mob intent on marching to Wellington market to demand goods by menace, as you had done in other places on several occasions over the previous weeks. Can you deny it?'

'Sir,' Fox replied, 'I do not deny we were on the way to Wellington. We had declared as much, but I do deny that we were rioting. We were simply resting on Ketley village green when the militia arrived.'

Ominously, the judge hammered the bench in front of him to signal that there were to be no further arguments, and he instructed Fox to stand down from the witness box.

He turned to face the jury and proceeded to sum up the facts of the case as he saw them. He pointed out that there could be no doubt that these men had all been involved in riotous assembly and had refused to disperse when the Riot Act had been read to them. The verdict he recommended in all cases was to be 'guilty'.

Susan's gaze had been on Walter the whole time this was going on. He had been looking down at the floor, but at the sound of the word, 'guilty' he suddenly looked up. Their eyes met once again and in spite of what she was feeling, Susan managed to smile at him, inclining her head slightly. This time, he did manage a faint smile then once again squared his shoulders, ready to face whatever was to come.

Chapter 46

The judge instructed the jury to make their decision in the case of each defendant. It took them only five minutes in their huddle to signal that they were ready to pronounce the results of their brief deliberations. Each name was read to them, and the foreman asked to state what verdict had been agreed. The results were of course, a foregone conclusion. In each case the foreman called out 'Guilty!'

Each time the word was spoken the murmurs of excitement grew louder until, by the time Charles Fox's name was read out and he was pronounced guilty, the prospect of executions had raised the mood to fever pitch. Some called out 'Aye!', or 'So be it!' but others, visitors connected with the prisoners, such as Susan and George, were filled with horror as the reality of what may be about to happen finally sunk in.

The judge banged his gavel on the desk and called for silence, then looked directly across at the men ranged in the dock before him.

'You have been found guilty of riotous assembly by this jury of your peers. I now pronounce sentence upon you.'

He then read out their names one by one, and to each of them in turn he said,

'Transportation to America for a period not less than seven years.'

Some of the men received their sentence without any visible reaction, whether through disbelief or fortitude it was impossible to tell. Others were visibly shaken and some who had loved ones in the gallery shot frantic looks in their direction, looks that conveyed worlds of meaning, love, fear, regret, remorse, and an overwhelming hopelessness. Walter simply gazed at Susan and now he smiled broadly. So, his fate was sealed, but he was to live! The scaffold was not his destination on this day. Now he knew with certainty that he would one day return. He knew there would be horrors to face, but face them he would, knowing that she was waiting here for him.

Then it was Freddie's turn and as the judge read the sentence of seven years transportation, a woman who had been standing in the gallery called out,

'No! No! My son! Please your honour he's only a boy!'

Freddie was sobbing now, completely unable to contain his emotions, the tears streaking the filth on his face.

'Silence in the court!' the clerk called out, and the proceedings continued.

The judge finally came to the last name on the list. Charles Fox. He paused and turned to face the judge on his right, who handed him a square of black cloth. Everyone knew the significance of this, and the room fell silent as he placed the cloth on top of his wig. Fox struggled to contain the bile rising in his throat. The only outward sign of his fear were the white knuckles of his hands as he gripped the balustrade rail in front of him. Then came the words he expected, but dreaded with all his being,

'Charles Fox, because I am satisfied that you were the leader of this riotous mob, I sentence you to be taken immediately to the place of execution and to be hung by the neck until you are dead.'

The muscles in Fox's neck bulged as he struggled to control his emotions. The crowd was hushed now, each of them processing the words the judge had pronounced. A woman standing just in front of George collapsed in a faint, and Fox almost lost his composure as he saw his sister slide to the floor. George helped the elderly man who was with her to carry her out of the courtroom.

Susan had remained to watch Walter being led back down to the cells and as he was just about to disappear from sight he turned and smiled at her once more. She smiled back and mouthed the words, 'I love you' knowing that this would be the last sight they would have of each other until he returned. Then he was gone, and Susan let the tears flow at last.

The crowd was filing out of the courtroom, no doubt making for the scaffold outside the courthouse. They knew the death sentence which had been pronounced on Fox would be carried out immediately. Susan found George just outside the front door of the building. He told her that the woman who had fainted was Fox's sister and the man had been his father. He, of course, was distraught, but nevertheless determined to be with his son in his last moments, and they had made their way to the scaffold. Wanting the last image imprinted in her memory that day to be Walter's smiling face, and not the sight of Fox's execution, Susan said she had no wish to watch the spectacle and would wait for him at the inn.

In spite of his revulsion, curiosity got the better of George and he decided that he would stay and watch, if only so that he could relate what happened to the folks back home in Madeley. He found the woman he'd helped, standing with the support of her father, to one side of the scaffold. Within minutes, Charles Fox was led out. As he glanced up at the noose that was hanging down over a beam, he hesitated, but for only a moment, at the foot of the steps. A push in the back from the gaoler's pistol prompted him to move. At the top of the steps he halted slightly once again, but it was barely perceptible. As he stood on the platform the hangman stepped forward and placed the noose around his neck.

He looked down once to find the faces of his father and sister and smiled at them. Then he gazed out across the city and finally looked up to the sky, ignoring the crowd which had gathered to see his end. As he gazed upwards, the sun suddenly peeped out from behind the clouds, flooding the scene with golden sunlight. It was his last sight, as the hangman suddenly pulled the lever, the sandbag on the trapdoor dropped and he was snatched off his feet. His body, unwilling to die, flailed around for a minute or so before his life was snuffed out and he hung limply from the rope. Fox's sister let out a wail that seemed to come from the depths of her soul, her father trying to console her as he battled with his own emotions.

Some in the crowd cheered, some wailed in sympathy. George was sickened and turned quickly away. Before going to the inn to find Susan, he went back into the court building to ask whether he was allowed to see his brother. However, the clerk on the desk told him it wasn't possible, as the prisoners were to be placed on a trow immediately, to be taken down to Bristol.

Sadly, George left the building and made his way to the inn. He did briefly consider whether they should go down to the wharf to await Walter and the others being boarded onto the trow. In the end, he decided Susan had been through enough that day, and nothing could be gained by observing Walter's ultimate humiliation as he was herded onto the boat, no doubt shackled to the other prisoners.

He found Susan waiting by the waggon. She was composed, but her face was tearstained.

'Susan, I'm so sorry, truly I am,' he said, 'but he will return you know.'

'I know he will George. I've promised to wait for him and that's what I'll do.'

'Are you ready to go now?'

'I am,' she said sadly, 'there's nothing more to be done here.'

***

Walter and the others had been taken back to the cells after leaving the courtroom and were told they were to be taken within the hour to the waiting boat that would take them down to Bristol. Of course, they all heard the noise of the crowd as Charlie met his end, and they were shaken to the core at the sound. To a man though, there was some relief that it wasn't them on the end of that rope. Freddie had calmed down a little now and just sat in the corner, his body language signifying defeat and resignation. Walter once again placed a reassuring hand on his shoulder and Freddie glanced up, grateful for any human contact at that moment.

Walter briefly wondered whether Susan and George would be at the wharf to see them depart, but he fervently hoped they would not. It was humiliating enough to be led through the streets shackled to the other prisoners in front of strangers, let alone those he loved. He had said his goodbyes and that was that. Now he must look to the future and the privations he must soon endure, swearing once more that one day he would return.

Chapter 47

By the time George and Susan reached the Gorge, it was late afternoon. Before going on to Madeley, they called at Dale Coppice. George needed to tell Betty, and Will what had happened to Walter, and Susan had decided to stay overnight with her family. She desperately needed to feel her mother's arms around her and the comfort of home, before she could face the wider world.

As the waggon rumbled into the clearing, George saw Betty standing at the cottage door, as she had been doing for the last couple of hours, in spite of Will's pleading,

'Come inside lass! They won't be here any quicker with you catching your death on the doorstep!'

When she saw the waggon, her face fell. She had been hoping against hope that just maybe Walter would have been acquitted and would be coming home with them. It was fanciful of course. He was caught fair and square and now she knew he would be transported for seven years, or worse.

George jumped off the waggon and helped Susan down. She went straight to Betty and embraced her tightly, simply saying,

'Seven years.'

Betty's legs almost gave way and George stepped up to support her. Susan was too overcome with emotion to speak further, but turned to George, indicating that she must go to her parents, before striding across the clearing towards the Bly cottage.

George helped Betty to the cottage door and as they entered, Will looked up, and seeing Betty in a state of near collapse, assumed for the moment that the worst had happened. He let out a cry,

'Nay! Surely not! George?'

'No, Da, only Fox was for the gallows. All the rest got seven years in the Americas.'

'Thank God for that!'

Betty said nothing. Her mind was racing. Seven years! God only knows what dangers he would face in that time. She knew as well as any, that few ever made it back home. Apart from the privations, hard labour, and disease they must endure, they had to pay their own passage home and not many were ever able to do that. She had to face facts; she may never see her son again. She also knew that even if he did manage to return home, it was unlikely he would see his father again in this life. She knew her husband's health was failing. The weakness in his arm and leg were getting no better and she knew he wouldn't be able to carry on working. What would become of them she dreaded to think.

'Did you see him?' she asked George.

'We did Ma. He was in good spirits, relieved I think that he was to live after all! He sends you and Da his love and told me to tell you that he will be back.'

'Well, a lot can change in seven years,' Will mumbled sadly.

George looked at his father, who suddenly looked older. He hadn't realised before just how much all this had affected him.

Practical as ever, Betty's thoughts turned to feeding her family and as usual had a pot boiling over the fire. She insisted that George have supper with them before he set off to Madeley. The light was fading as he said his goodbyes and left the sad little cottage, assuring them he would help them as much as he could now that they had lost Walter's wages.

When Susan had entered the Bly cottage her mother, who had been sitting by the fire, sprang up and seeing Susan's red-rimmed eyes, feared the worst, taking her daughter in her arms saying,

'Oh love, I'm so sorry!'

Susan now finally gave way to tumultuous sobs, her whole body shaking, then realising that her mother probably thought Walter was dead, struggled to control her sobs until she was finally able to explain that Walter had been given seven years' transportation. As she spoke the words, a certain calmness came over her as she told her mother that he had promised to return, and she had promised to wait for him.

'Oh Susan, I'm so sorry love!' her mother declared.

'I know mother, but I know he will come back to me, and I will wait, no matter how long it takes. Walter Bangham is the only man for me, I will take no other.'

'You must stay here tonight love. You can't possibly go back to the 'big house' like this. I'm sure your mistress will understand, and you could ask George to call round to let them know that you will be there in the morning.'

'Well, you're right mother, I can't go back tonight, I need time to think about all this. It's been a terrible day, but at the same time, I am now surer of this than anything else: Walter will one day be my husband.'

At that moment, her father John arrived home from his work. Somehow, he had already heard about Walter's fate, and immediately and without a word, he enveloped his daughter in his arms, saying how sorry he was that it had come to this. He could have said a lot more, about how rash he thought Walter had been to get involved, but he knew that wouldn't help Susan right now, and kept his own counsel on the subject. He just held her until he felt her relax, then Susan and her parents sat quietly in front of the fire, each in their own thoughts, until George knocked on the door to ask if Susan was sure she would be staying at the coppice for the night.

She confirmed that she would and then asked if he would mind taking a message to the 'big house' to let them know that she would be back the following morning, which he gladly agreed to do.

As he made his way on the cart back down the hill to the river, his thoughts once again turned to his brother. He glanced at the water flowing swiftly by, knowing that at this moment Walter may well be on the same river somewhere, if he hadn't already arrived in Bristol. He sent a silent greeting to him, wishing him the strength to endure whatever may befall him and to come back home safely at the end of it.

As the trow left Bridgnorth, to add to the misery of Walter and the other prisoners, a steady drizzle had set in. As they had been ordered to sit down on deck, they were soon soaked to the skin. At least the rain might wash away some of this filth, Walter mused wryly. They had been given no opportunity to wash or change their clothes the whole time they had been locked up. They certainly made a sorry sight, looking every bit the convicts they had recently been judged to be.

Walter hunched up against the rain, trying not to think of anything, particularly home and Susan. Time enough for that later he told himself. He was simply trying to keep warm, shifting his position every now and then as the hard timbers of the deck caused his flesh to grow numb.

After what seemed like several hours, they arrived at the Gloucester docks where one of the militiamen who were accompanying them informed them that they were to be transshipped to a downriver trow, then he shouted at them,

'Right, you lot, on yer feet!' and poked the prisoner nearest to him in his ribs with the barrel of his gun, prompting Bill Cadman to drag himself to his feet, and as the chains tightened, one by one all the men did the same. Walter was at the end of the line and now a second militiaman shoved his gun between Walter's shoulder blades.

'Come on, get moving!' he called out roughly, causing Walter to stumble against the man in front.

The line of prisoners shambled along to the gangplank, then shuffled down to the dockside, which was bustling with activity. Scores of trows were lined up and eventually the prisoners arrived at a larger vessel moored further along the quayside. Wearily, they climbed the gangplank. Once on deck, their shackles were removed, and they were made to climb one by one down a wooden ladder into the hold.

The ship rested at anchor for the night. They were given some bread and water, the first food they'd had since leaving Bridgnorth Gaol. There were several planks of wood covered with sacking, which were apparently meant to serve as beds and they fell wearily onto them, relieved at that at last they were free to move around without the chains on their ankles. They were given the usual bucket to relieve themselves in, and as light faded through the metal grid above their heads, settled down as best they could to snatch some sleep. However, it wasn't easy to drive from their minds the thought of Charles Fox swinging at the end of the rope as the crowd cheered, and the faces of their own loved ones as they heard about their fate. In the end, sheer exhaustion gifted them a few hours' sleep, respite from the horrible scenes dominating their waking hours.

Walter was wakened as the first dim light percolated through the grille above his head, illuminating his grim surroundings and reminding him that this was the first day of his new life. His old life was gone. He knew that when he returned, and he was determined that he would, nothing would ever be the same again. He wondered for instance, if he would ever see his father again. He knew Will's health was failing and that he would probably be unable to continue working.

At that moment he felt a sharp pain in his leg just above his ankle, and there to his horror was a fat black rat trying to have a nibble at his flesh, where the shackles had grazed his leg the day before. He kicked it away with his other foot and with a squeal it scurried off into the shadows. Noticing a few bed bugs who had settled down to sleep on his clothes overnight, Walter jumped up, batting his clothes wildly to dislodge them. The other men began to wake up, disturbed by the commotion. One by one they went through a similar procedure, before following Walter over to the bucket to urinate.

After half an hour or so the hatch above them opened and one of the militiamen handed down several loaves, a pitcher of water and a wooden drinking vessel, telling them to share them out because it was all they were going to get.

Sometime later they felt the ship sway and then rock as it turned to join the flow of water making its way down to Bristol and the sea. Walter wondered how long they would be held there before setting off for America. He had heard tell that convicts could be kept for days or even weeks on a prison ship, until enough miserable human cargo had been amassed to justify the expense of the trip. He didn't allow himself to contemplate too deeply what a prison ship might be like. He'd thought Bridgnorth gaol was bad enough, but the night he'd just spent in the hold of this ship was probably a foretaste of the horrors that were to come, and he forced himself to push these thoughts from his mind. He'd find out soon enough, he told himself, no need to imagine it. In the event, it would turn out to be far worse than the images his mind could ever have conjured up.

Chapter 48

They arrived in Bristol in the late afternoon. As they were shambling along the dockside, fear and shame kept Walter's gaze firmly fixed on Freddie's feet, who was directly in front of him. He was sure everyone on the bustling docks must be staring at them, labelling them as 'criminal scum' or some such, and not for the first time Walter cursed his own impulsiveness for landing him in this mess.

They shuffled along to the far end of the dock, where they were herded into an old warehouse. It was dingy and virtually derelict, and the men wondered what on earth was going to happen to them here, away from public scrutiny. However, they were surprised to see several bowls of water ranged in front of them. Their shackles removed they were told to strip and wash themselves. They weren't too happy at being forced to strip, but were certainly grateful that they could now wash, for the first time in weeks.

They had seen their own clothes whisked away, no doubt to be destroyed, and were even grateful for the rough prison clothes they were handed, not least because they had not yet been infested with lice.

Still unshackled, their hands were tied, and they were roped together to be led at gunpoint to board a large rowing boat. They were rowed half a mile or so towards the open sea until they arrived at a dilapidated old sailing ship with tattered sails, that looked as though it would never travel the high seas again.

Walter concluded that this must be just a holding vessel, one of the dreaded prison hulks, and surely not the ship that would take him across the Atlantic.

Sounds of men shouting angrily emanated from the window-less openings in the sides of the vessel as they undoubtedly heard the rowing boat pull alongside. Along with the noise, there emerged a stench worse than anything Walter had ever smelt before. His stomach heaved and it took all his willpower to keep its meagre contents where they should be.

Their ropes untied, the prisoners were forced one by one to climb a narrow ladder running up the side of the ship. Weary and weakened by his weeks of confinement, Richard Corbett lost his footing and fell into the water and for one moment Walter thought with horror that his guards were simply going to let him drown. Desperate to live however, Richard managed to catch hold of one of the oars and was eventually dragged back into the boat where, after only a few minutes rest, he once again began to climb the steps, and this time, his instinct for self-preservation drove his feet higher and higher until eventually he reached the deck. Walter was by now standing on the deck, well aware of the horrors that awaited him beneath his feet.

As the men were lined up, the hatch to the hold was opened and the noise and stink from below decks amplified. Bill Cadman who was at the head of the line, visibly recoiled at the thought of descending into the foul blackness, but the guard waved his pistol in his face, snarling,

'Down you go matey!'

Bill knew he had no choice and nervously started to climb down the narrow steps into the hold soon disappearing from view. One by one the others followed. After the bright day-light, it took a little while for their eyes to grow accustomed to the darkness, and when they did, to a man they were horrified by what they saw. Down each side of this floor were iron cages, each one filled with prisoners. A passage ran the length of the ship between them. The cage on the left was packed with men and the one on the right, to Walter's horror, was filled with women and a few of them had a child clinging to their legs. How could they do this, he thought. This hell was no place for women and children.

Freddie was standing beside Walter and was visibly shaken by the sight of so much anger and filth. The convicts looked as though they hadn't eaten properly in weeks. Their clothes were dirty and hung from their emaciated bodies. Walter wondered whether they could possibly be shoved into this cage. It looked impossible to cram anyone else into it.

'Keep moving there!' came the rough cry above the din emanating from the cages, and the men were pushed along the passage to the far end, where another set of wooden steps descended to the floor below. So, they were to be housed on the lower floor! This one was bad enough, Walter thought. Could the lower deck be even worse?

As it happened, it wasn't yet as crowded as the upper floor. There were similar cages down each side of the ship, but these were half empty. Walter immediately realised this was a mixed blessing. Presumably they would be kept here until the cages were full, as the ship that would take them across the Atlantic wouldn't sail until there were enough prisoners in this ship to make the journey financially worthwhile. The fewer the prisoners already here, the longer they would have to endure it. It was just as well that none of them knew how long they would have to do so, or how grim their stay was to be.

Sleep was virtually impossible. There were no bunks, not even blankets to cushion the hard wooden floor. As the cages filled over the next days and weeks, predictably, conditions deteriorated. Food was scarce, consisting of thin gruel and dry biscuits, and they were constantly hungry, with a gnawing pain in the pit of their stomachs. Arguments increased as the numbers of prisoners grew. Eventually it was impossible to stretch out without encroaching on someone else's space. Rats and lice were numerous in the insanitary conditions. Being two floors below deck with only tiny portholes, the place was stiflingly hot and the air fetid.

The physical conditions, the hopelessness of his situation, the lack of sleep and complete absence of any comfort whatsoever, dulled Walter's senses to the point where even thoughts of home and his loved ones became impossible. If he indulged in such thoughts, he was plunged further into despair. It was easier to simply concentrate on getting through each hour in the knowledge that eventually this ordeal must surely end. He kept his eye on Freddie, who naturally gravitated to his side whenever possible. In fact he was coping surprisingly well. The natural optimism of youth seemed to be carrying him through.

The same couldn't be said of some of the other men, who grew more agitated with every passing day. It was obvious to Walter that they were unable to understand how they had ended up in this situation, frequently letting everyone else know what had brought them to it. Several angrily declared their total innocence. Another said that stealing a loaf of bread for his hungry family was no crime in the eyes of God, and how could it be right that they had now been left without support and no doubt now sent to the Poor House? Walter heard many sad stories over the next couple of weeks, but finally, their protestations subsided as hunger and weariness took hold and eventually, most of them hadn't even the strength to declare their sense of injustice.

Walter thought that maybe this was another reason why they were being kept in these conditions for some time before being transferred to the transportation ship. Weakened, starving men would no doubt be more compliant during the long and arduous journey to the Americas.

Finally, after what Walter judged to be about six weeks, although it was difficult to keep track of time, there was a commotion in the floor above with much clanging of iron on iron and the sound of many feet dragging across the boards. It became obvious that mercifully, or so they thought, they were being moved. The transportation vessel must be ready for them.

Walter judged that on this floor alone were about a hundred and fifty souls. If the same number were on the floor above, there would be around three hundred prisoners being placed on the ship that would take him across the ocean, and he realised that conditions aboard that ship were likely to be no better, and probably even worse, than those he had already endured on the hulk. Unfortunately, he was to be proved right.

It took the best part of the day to move the prisoners off the hulk. They took them in parties of twenty, presumably so that they could control them, although in truth most of them were too weak and weary to attempt an escape. When it came to Walter's turn, he made sure that Freddie went in the same group. After weeks of confinement and lack of exercise, Walter was amazed how much effort it took to climb the staircases up to the deck, but the feel of a fresh breeze on his face invigorated him somewhat. As they were climbing down the stairs on the side of the ship to board the rowing boat, one of the men who had been showing signs of madness brought on by the weeks of confinement and fear of what was still to come, suddenly let go of the ladder and threw himself into the water. Unlike Richard when they were boarding the hulk all those weeks before, this man had obviously made up his mind not to live and disappeared below the surface of the waters of the Bristol channel. He was never seen again.

After they had been transferred in rowing boats to the dockside, they were taken back to the warehouse and told to wash. This time unfortunately, there were no clean clothes to be seen. They were forced to walk in chains along the wharf in full view of the crowds of people, who paused from their business to watch them pass, some of them shouting obscenities at them, compounding their shame. One of the men unloading goods glanced down at the prisoners and Walter recognised him. He realised it was Henry Wood, from Madeley. He called out to him, saying who he was and was just about to ask him to pass on a message to Susan, when he felt the butt of the guard's gun across the back of his head.

'No talking!' the guard roared at him, then shoved the barrel of his gun in his back once more and Walter had no choice but to comply, devastated that he had been unable to get another message to Susan.

However, the man on the boat had heard his name and knew that he was one of the men who had been on trial at Bridgnorth some weeks earlier. He determined he would let George Bangham know that he had seen his brother at Bristol docks, although in truth, in the dirty and dishevelled state he was in, had Walter not cried out, Henry would never have recognised him.

After being herded along the wharf, they arrived at a three masted sailing ship that looked as though it may once have been a warship. Walter noticed that the name on the bow was 'The Lark'. It looked far too small to be capable of accommodating three hundred prisoners on a long journey. It was with foreboding that Walter and Freddie boarded the vessel and climbed down into the hold where they would spend the next couple of months of their lives, when disease would add to the horror of their lives as prisoners of the Crown.

Walter was relieved to see the conditions below deck were better than he had imagined. Of course, he reasoned, that was probably because the place was still half empty. Presumably it had also been cleaned out since its last occupants had been deposited in the Americas, and the hold filled with cargo for the return journey.

Here there were no cages, just rows of iron doors running along two sides of the upper floor and presumably the same on the floor below. So, they were to be confined in cells rather than cages and Walter at first thought this might be preferable. Several of the men, including Walter and Freddie were herded into one of them, and he now realised that this was to be no party. The cell measured about four yards square, and there were no beds. Once more they were to sleep on the bare floors. There was the usual bucket in the corner, mercifully empty for the moment. A small square opening in the side of the ship allowed light and fresh air to enter, which pleased Walter, although he was to curse it when the Atlantic gales found it in the weeks ahead. Further dim light percolated through the grille in the iron door.

He glanced round at the faces of his fellow residents. They were a sorry sight, with faces chalky white, their cheeks sunken and eyes bulging. No doubt he looked just as bad, Walter mused, thankful there were no mirrors where he might catch a glimpse of his emaciated self. Including himself and Freddie, a dozen men had to share the space, allowing little more than a square foot for each, barely room for sitting, never mind lying. No, this was to be no picnic.

It took the rest of the day to board the prisoners and the whole of the following day for provisions for the journey to be loaded into the hold below the lower floor. Finally, on the morning of the third day they felt the ship begin to move, swaying as it turned to face the west to sail along the Severn Estuary. Each man was now no doubt unable to banish thoughts of home and those they had left behind. After some time they felt the ship turn once more, realising that perhaps they were now leaving the Bristol Channel, one by one they clambered to their feet and gathered round the opening, eager to catch their last glimpse of England as the ship reached the open sea to face the Atlantic Ocean.

Freddie stood tall to see out of the window and remained there after the others had flopped down on the floor again. Stretching up as far as he could, he could just see the coast receding into the distance. Even though he had maintained his optimism up to this point, now the truth hit him hard. He may never see England or his mother again, and in spite of himself, tears began to trickle down his cheeks. Walter's heart went out to him, and he stood and put an arm across his shoulders. They remained like that until the rocky coastline had disappeared over the horizon and Freddie's tears had finally stopped, then Walter gently pulled him away from the window and settled him down on the floor once more.

For the first week or so emotions and therefore tensions, were high as the twelve men weighed each other up. As with any group thrown together in a confined space, there was always inevitably at least one who wanted to assert their authority to which some would succumb but also many who resisted. Two of the men apart from Walter and Freddie, had come from the Gorge. One was a coalminer from Broseley, Tom Leach, and the other a quarryman, Arthur Bentley from the Benthall Edge stone quarry. Walter was to be glad of those familiar faces in the weeks ahead.

As the ship sailed further on it began to pitch and roll in the Atlantic swell, and many of the men suffered badly from seasickness. Some days were worse than others depending how often the ship needed to tack into the prevailing westerlies. Already the conditions were miserable but weren't helped by several of the men vomiting and not always into the bucket. The personalities of the men began to emerge. A few were sympathetic, others angry, viewing their actions as inconsiderate which was of course, entirely irrational. The poor souls were in a dreadful state, which no one would enter voluntarily. After a week or so the men prone to seasickness were beginning to grow accustomed to the movement of the ship and everything calmed down. The episode had taught Walter much. He now knew much more about his fellow captives.

One particularly aggressive individual, Joel Cratcher, whose past demeanours found echo in the lines of his face and set of his chin, soon asserted control over a couple of pathetic looking younger men who had obviously decided it would be advisable to keep on the right side of him. It was sickening to watch them toadying to him, always making sure he had room to lie down while they squashed themselves together in the corner of the room. When the meagre food rations appeared they shared one serving while he enjoyed two. The rest of the men tried their best to avoid any interaction with him.

Chapter 49

After a few more weeks a routine of sorts had been established. They had one meal of gruel and dry biscuits about halfway through the day. Water was brought twice, morning and evening. Each morning one of them in their turn was made to carry the slop bucket up to the deck and dispose of its contents in the ocean. Every few days they were allowed up on deck for an hour or so and were given the chance to wash, undressed to the waist. Apart from that, their every hour was spent in the cell with no opportunity for physical activity and they all grew weaker with each day that passed. Thoughts of England and home faded as they used what strength of mind they still had left to endure each day.

It was about four weeks out that their lives suddenly got a whole lot worse. One by one they were struck down with dysentery and with no opportunity to clean themselves up properly, they were soon lying or sitting in filth. After a week or so, they were taken out of the cell and Walter and Richard, who so far had escaped the diarrhoea and were still stronger than the rest, were made to climb up to the deck to fetch buckets of sea water to swill the cell out. Little thought seemed to be given to where the water would end up which would presumably be in the floor below.

One of the young men who had been attending Cratcher had been suffering particularly badly, no doubt weakened by the fact he'd only been eating half of the meagre rations for weeks. The morning after the cell had been swilled out, his companion was unable to wake him. He had obviously suffered some kind of collapse during the night and was in a coma. By the end of the day his breathing had stopped. Without ceremony he was carried up on deck and slid off a board into the sea, as were several more, including three women and one child over the course of the next couple of weeks. By the time the infection had worked its way through the inhabitants of the ship, a further twenty souls had been tipped into the Atlantic.

Walter began to wonder whether he would even live to see America, let alone survive long enough to see home and Susan Bly, who he was sure would be waiting there for his return. Each day aboard The Lark brought new miseries to Walter and his fellow prisoners. The weather worsened as the journey progressed, the ship being frequently tossed about on the Atlantic rollers. The men were often thrown about inside the cell and with no furniture of any kind to hold on to, frequently found themselves being piled on top of one another or crashing against the cell walls. By now, rats and lice were their constant companions which, along with the constant hunger and lack of any exercise, made sleep for more than a few minutes at a time quite impossible.

One day, as he slouched against the wall of the cell, Walter realised that the sound of the wind had suddenly grown louder and was whistling through the porthole with added ferocity. Peering out, he could see that the sky was black, even though it was still only mid-day. Suddenly there was a blinding purple light illuminating the cell, accompanied by a loud cracking sound, and a thunderous roar of thunder which rolled around the sky. The ship seemed to be sitting back on its haunches and as he looked towards the bow through the porthole Walter was horrified to see a mountain of water rising up. He shouted out to the men to brace themselves as he realised there was only one way this could go. The ship was now climbing to the top of the huge wave and as it crested the top, seemed to shudder before plunging headlong into the trough. The men screamed in pain and fear as they were thrown around like rag dolls, tumbling onto one another and crashing against the walls of the cell. Screams could be heard from hundreds of mouths as the scene was repeated in each cell. God only knows what's going on up on deck, Walter thought. If the crew can't control the ship, we're all going down with her with no means of escape.

The Lark withstood the descent into the trough and in fact, somehow survived several more over the next hour or so before the storm began to subside, and they dared to believe that they might survive after all. However a couple of the men had been injured badly, Cratcher being one of them. His right hand was hanging limply at an odd angle, and he was scream-ing in agony. One of the colliers, Nate Black seemed to have sustained a heavy blow to the head and was lying unconscious on the floor. No doubt the scene was repeated throughout the rest of the two dozen or so cells on the ship.

There was much commotion in the corridor outside as the ship's surgeon began checking each cell to find out who might need his attention. Nate was carried off to be placed in the sick bay until he regained consciousness. As for Cratcher, he continued to scream while three men held him steady, and the surgeon aligned his hand and arm and strapped supporting splints round his wrist.

Desperate to gain some idea how much longer their ordeal might last, Walter managed to ask the surgeon where the ship was taking them and how long it might be before they reached land. Feeling some sympathy for their plight, the surgeon an-swered quickly,

'Chesapeake Bay and we should be sighting land within the next couple of weeks, God willing!'

Walter would have liked to ask further questions, but the surgeon quickly left, his skills being required elsewhere.

Cratcher now being injured, he became even more dependent on his little helper, who, having suffered his bullying since leaving port, saw his tormentor was now unable to fend for himself without help, and made the most of the reversal of roles, which was rather gratifying to watch.

The physical and mental condition of the prisoners, weakened after six weeks at sea and following their incarceration on the prison hulk in Bristol, was dire. It appeared to Walter that many of them were exhibiting signs of madness, and he perceived that probably included himself. His sleep was full of strange dreams of being deep in the ocean, obviously drowned but still able to see and think and feel. His waking hours were not much better. More than once he found himself hallucinating, thinking he saw the face of a huge rat staring at him through the porthole, teeth bared, ready to pounce, and once, the rat's face was replaced by Susan's. That's when he was sure he was going out of his mind.

Freddie was now little more than skin and bone, barely able to stand, and Walter wondered what on earth would become of him. He had heard from one of the prisoners who had served a previous sentence in America, that they were likely to be sent to work for settler families who would bid for them at some kind of auction. He couldn't imagine who on earth would bid for Freddie in his current state. He decided that if he had the chance, he would do his best to vouch for him as being a good worker, once he had rest and decent food.

It was actually two weeks and two days before a cry from above went up,

'Land ahoy!

In fact, it would be several days more before they were taken off the ship. For two days they found themselves passing thick forest along the shoreline. This must be Chesapeake

Bay, Walter reasoned. Of course, he had no idea how far they would sail before reaching their destination.

Chapter 50

If the actions of Cludde had been intended to quell further unrest, it had certainly worked, and by the end of November the district had settled into an uneasy calm. The situation was also helped by the fact that several of the landowners had cut the price of their corn to five shillings a bushel, and many of the landlords had reduced their rents a little to compensate. So the sacrifices of Fox, Walter and the other captives had not been completely in vain, which gave rise to some gratitude among the miners, quarry men, and ironworkers of the district, and many made contributions to a fund for their families. Of course, this could only help in the short term and as the men had feared, many of their wives and children were eventually sent either to Mine Spout Poor House, or to their home parishes for support. Even though Will was now unable to work, he and Betty avoided destitution after Walter left, as Joe had allowed them to live in the cottage rent-free and George made sure they had enough to live on. Also, the birth of Sally's third baby, who they named Walter, after his uncle, helped to lift their mood rather.

Susan continued her work as chambermaid at Harden House, trying to content herself with the belief that one day her lover would return. They had snatched just a few minutes of intimacy under the oak tree, but their love had been consummated and she knew she would never give herself to another man. If Walter never returned, she told herself, she would marry no-one.

For the rest of the year, life in Nailer's Row continued much as before. At the old furnace, Nat was a skilled mould maker and a valued employee earning good money by local standards. Joe had taken Walter's misfortune badly and he worried about his brother's health which had deteriorated since his son had been taken, to the point where he was no longer able to work, and he feared Will wouldn't be long for this world. He also felt his own strength ebbing away, and although Liz also noticed, neither of them referred to it openly, and Joe did his best to keep up with the workload at the furnace.

The success of the new process of making iron for forging at Horsehay meant there was more work than the furnace could cope with, and a second was now under construction. Ben was earning reasonable pay as an experienced furnaceman. Although he wasn't living at home, and lodging in one of the company houses, he still regarded the Nailer's Row house as his home, visiting as often as he could, and still making sure he contributed something to its upkeep. So the finances of the Bangham household in Nailer's Row were robust for the moment.

Liz was happily spending her evenings making items to welcome her first grandchild in the spring. She also did what she could to help her cousin Betty, taking her gifts of bread or vegetables whenever she visited Dale Coppice. She invited them to join them at Nailer's Row for Christmas Day, but Betty told her that George and Sally had insisted that they go over to Madeley Wood, and he was to collect them in the waggon a few days before Christmas. Liz had to admit she was rather pleased, as the house would be full enough.

For once, all the men were to have Christmas Day off and Anne had asked if Tommy Flint, the young man she'd recently been seeing could join the family. Elizabeth and Rod were also coming over for the day. It would mean a lot of work, but as always, Anne would help. One evening, as she planned the day, Liz was looking forward to having all her family together for once, but her heart went out to Betty. She would miss Walter so much, and she would not even know where in the world he was, or how he was coping mentally and physically with the privations he must surely be enduring. It's perhaps as well she doesn't know, she thought.

Only the weather could spoil the Christmas plans in Nailer's Row, and unfortunately it did exactly that. The snow arrived the day before Christmas Eve and Liz watched anxiously as it began to build up along the road outside the window. As Christmas Eve dawned a brisk breeze brought further snow and by Christmas morning the roads and tracks leading from Madeley Wood would be impassable in a trap, and in her condition, Elizabeth couldn't possibly walk through snowdrifts. Liz settled her mind to the fact that her eldest daughter and son-in-law would not be joining them. She wasn't even sure Ben would be able to put in an appearance. He could of course walk the few miles from Horsehay, so unless the drifts were very deep, hopefully he would make it.

Ben did in fact arrive at around eleven on Christmas Day, wet and weary, having battled his way through the snow which was still falling. He batted the snow off his clothes before entering the house, then took off his greatcoat and hung it behind the door before joining his father and Nat by the fire. Liz made more of a fuss of him than usual, grateful he'd made the effort to come.

'Couldn't have missed it, Ma,' he said, 'there's precious little in the way of Christmas cheer up at Horsehay. I'd rather be here than back there with four burly iron men and only bread and dripping to eat!' he added, laughing.

In spite of the snow and disappointment of not seeing Elizabeth and Rod, the family enjoyed the day. With three wages coming in there was plenty of food and ale, which was more than many of their neighbours were to see that day. When they had eaten, they sat around the fire just enjoying each other's company for once. Tommy Flint turned out to be a bright lad, if a little 'cocky', but he kept them entertained, if nothing else. Joe rather liked his spirit, and it was obvious Anne was besotted. I think we'll be seeing more of this young chap, thought Joe.

It turned out the lad lived just a few hundred yards up the road. His family had only recently arrived in the Dale. His father was also an iron worker who had been employed at another of the Darby works at Leighton, and after Christmas, Tommy was due to start labouring work at the Boring Mill across the road.

Over in Madeley Wood, Elizabeth and Rod had realised that journeying to Coalbrookdale through the snow was impossible and were spending the day with the Sheldons. Although disappointed not to be seeing her own family, Elizabeth was happy enough to celebrate with her in-laws. They lived just a hundred yards or so from their cottage in a good sized house at the end of a row which had been built many years earlier. Mr Sheldon, unusually, had had some education and was literate, and for many years had been employed as a clerk to one of the local landowners. When he was old enough, Rod's father made sure that his son was also educated. At twelve he apprenticed him to the same organisation. Once fully qualified, Rod found himself working for the newly formed Madeley Wood Company, in an office overlooking the Severn.

Rod had two brothers, but no sisters. It was obvious Mrs Sheldon enjoyed having another woman in the house, and she readily accepted Elizabeth's offer to help her prepare the food. She was a quiet woman, with a gentle manner. Elizabeth observed that there were little luxuries here and there, signs that this family had never had to scrimp and save. There were several stemmed glasses in the cupboard, along with half a dozen or so china plates decorated with pretty flowers. In the kitchen was an iron range with a large hotplate on top and an oven below. To one side of the oven was a roaring fire behind a hinged iron door. No need to be boiling a pot over the sitting room fire all day long, as her mother had had to do, Elizabeth mused.

Mr and Mrs Sheldon were involved in the Church of St Michael in Madeley, and they had insisted Elizabeth and Rod join them at the Christmas Morning service. This was a new experience for Elizabeth. The Banghams had never been particularly religious, and she had never attended church services on a regular basis. Of course, she and Rod had been married at St Michael's, but that wasn't what she thought of as a 'proper' service. She had to admit she had found it very pleasant that Christmas morning and the sermon by the Reverend Rowland Crowthorne rather inspiring. The singing was beautiful and the whole experience had been altogether uplifting. She told herself she must visit the church more often in future, particularly as she and Rod had made the decision that their baby would be baptised there. Elizabeth was struck by the peace she'd found in the church. There was something good here, she felt, in contrast to the rough and sometimes frightening world outside. Indeed, she was often uncomfortable just walking the streets alone these days.

As the various foundries and furnaces had expanded over recent years, there had been an influx of hundreds of workmen and their families. Many of them lived in the surrounding woods in their squatter cottages, but some of the employers had built rows of houses for their workers in the town. However, there were too few, and many of them, even though they were tiny, housed more than one family, each of which invariably had several children. Wages weren't high and there was much poverty in the tenements. Along with the poverty, unfortunately had come much drunkenness and rowdiness. No longer was Madeley Wood the peaceful village it had once been.

However, whether in Madeley Wood or Coalbrookdale, the Bangham families enjoyed a good Christmas that year, relieved that this year was nearly over and hoping that the next would bring better times. This wasn't so for Will and Betty of course. Will's health had been steadily declining, and all feared this Christmas may well be his last. George and Sally did their best to lift their mood, but to no avail.

Will in particular, had some idea what his son must be going through. He himself had voyaged across the very same ocean and knew its perils. He also knew that Walter's experience, travelling as a convict, not a paying passenger, would no doubt be much worse. He had also seen what would happen to him at his journey's end. He would be auctioned alongside the poor souls recently transported from Africa, to be treated little better than them when he reached his final destination, probably on a cotton or tobacco plantation. This was the knowledge Will was having to come to terms with, whilst also believing that it was his own impulsiveness that had driven Walter to take part in the protests. As the days passed, he sunk further into depression, sapping his very will to live.

Chapter 51

January saw more snow in the Dale, and Betty and Will struggled to get by without Walter. George visited as often as he could and brought them food and other supplies, but he wasn't always able to bring the cart because of the drifts across the track up to the coppice. He was glad to see that the Bly's also kept an eye on them, and in turn, when she could, Betty helped Fred out with the children.

Finally, the snows went, being replaced by day after day of dismal rain. The cold and damp did nothing for Will's health and he struggled to draw breath into his weakened body. Finally, at the end of February he came down with a bad cold which predictably turned to pneumonia. Betty was afraid his body was too weak now to fight it, even if he had the will to do so. Since Walter was taken, he had been in a deep depression, convinced his own impetuousness had caused his son's demise. Betty asked John Bly if he could possibly let Joe know how ill Will was, and the next day, being Sunday, Joe, and Liz both made their way up to Dale Coppice.

Joe had been shocked to get the news, knowing that Will must be bad for Betty to send for him, and when he saw him lying in bed, he was glad he had come. He'd seen his father go the same way and could see that Will would not last long. His skin was burning hot, and his breathing laboured.

'Will,' Joe said softly, 'I'm sorry you aren't feeling too good lad.'

Will opened his eyes at the sound of Joe's voice and smiled weakly.

'Good to see ye Joe,' he said quietly, and with some effort reached out his good hand to Joe. 'Promise me you'll look after Betty,' he went on earnestly.

'You'll look after her yerself lad,' Joe replied.

'Nay, we both know that's not true. This thing'll tek me Joe, like it took our Da.'

'Well, don't you worry about Betty, I'll mek sure she's tekken care of an' so will George, ye knows that.'

'I won't see our Walter agin i' this life an' I want you to tell 'im when he does come whoam, that I was sorry.'

'You have nothin' to be sorry fer Will. Walter's his own man and med 'is own decision when 'e joined t'protest, but I'll mek sure 'e gets thy message, just t'same.'

With that, Will settled back into the pillow and seemed more content, then exhausted by the effort of speaking to Joe, drifted off into a deep sleep. Joe turned, to see Betty being comforted by Liz. They had heard everything Will had said, and Betty knew he was ready to leave her. Liz knew it too and said she would stay with her that night.

After supper the two women spent the rest of the evening sitting with Will, who was now sleeping soundly. They chatted about Liz's parents John and Susan Spencer, who used to live in the cottage next door to the Banghams, and how kind they had been to take their niece Betty in when her first husband was killed and George only a little boy. Sadly, both of them were taken some years ago with a pox that had swept through the Gorge. Liz's brother Tom had moved away then, in search of a better life, but no-one now knew where he was. After that, the old cottage had been derelict for a while, until new squatters came in and claimed it.

Will stirred now and opened his eyes a fraction. With his good hand he indicated that he needed a drink, and Betty got up and put the cup of water to his lips, then lovingly wiped round his chin where it had trickled out of the corner of his mouth. Will sank thankfully back into the pillow and closed his eyes once more. Betty looked at Liz and sadly shook her head, knowing she wouldn't have him much longer.

In the event, Will lingered for another day before his body finally gave up the fight. Betty of course, was distraught. Within a few months her world had turned upside down, first losing her son and now her husband, leaving her with no means of supporting herself. The home she and Will had created would be taken from her along with her independence. Of course she knew George would take her in, but the thought of living on charity, even from her own son, was deeply upsetting, compounding the grief she felt at losing her beloved Will.

That night, word was sent to George and the next day he came with the cart to prepare Will's body for burial in Madeley. As he entered the cottage, he found his mother sitting staring into the fire, no doubt wondering how she could go on without Will. He knelt down beside her and placed his arm around her shoulders saying,

'I'm so sorry Ma, but he is at rest now.'

Betty broke down in tears and placed her head on his shoulder as she gave way to the grief and despair she was feeling. When her sobs had subsided, Will ventured,

'You will, of course, come and live with us now Ma. Sally's already making room for you. Let me take Da now and you can come back with me. I don't like to think of you here by yourself.'

'Nay lad, I want to stay 'ere with 'im until t'last. Do what tha needs to do, but don't tek him yet, until the burying day. Then I'll come with ye. I'll be ready then, but not yet.'

'Aye, I understand Ma. The funeral's arranged for Thursday so I'll do as you say and come back to collect you both then.'

Joe and his sons managed to get time off work to go to Will's funeral along with Liz and Anne. Dorothy, John, Elizabeth, and Rod, who all lived in Madeley Wood of course, were also there to support Betty. Her grief was compounded because her youngest son couldn't be with them and there was no way to even let Walter know that his father had passed away.

Liz was pleased to see Elizabeth looking so well. Her time could only be a matter of weeks away now she thought, as she looked at her standing beside her husband at the graveside. Gazing fondly at the pair she contemplated how as one life ebbs, another flows and so it goes on. After the funeral the Coalbrookdale contingent spent an hour with Elizabeth and Rod before setting off back home to Nailer's Row.

They had said their goodbyes to Betty at the burying ground as she was to stay with George. He said he would go up to the cottage in a day or two to collect the rest of his mother's things, and asked what Joe now intended to do with the place.

'I've not given it any thought yet George. I expect I'll have to find a tenant for it. There are plenty around who need a roof over their heads.'

A week after the funeral, Rod arrived on horseback outside the house to report that Elizabeth had gone into labour the previous day and had been delivered of a little girl. Apparently, it was thought that she was before her time, but the baby was well, if a little on the small side. Joe and Liz were delighted, Joe even more so when Rod told him that they were naming her Abigail, after Joe's sister. The christening was to be on the following Sunday at St Michael's in Madeley and of course, all were invited to come if they could.

Joe, Liz, and Nat were free as it happened to be the Sunday off for the menfolk. Ben, however, couldn't get time off as he'd already taken a day for Will's funeral the week before. Abigail's christening turned out to be a most solemn and meaningful service, of some length, conducted by the newly ordained priest the Reverend John Fletcher. Elizabeth in particular, seemed extremely moved by his words and Liz was a little surprised by that, as really none of the Bangham family had previously been interested in religion. However, Liz had to admit there was a certain magnetism in this man. He was rather young for a preacher, Liz thought, softly spoken with an attractive and hypnotic foreign accent. Softly spoken as he was, he could certainly ramp up his voice when he wanted to make a point of calling sinners to repent their sins. The whole experience left an indelible impression on Liz and along with Elizabeth, she felt she wanted to know more about this church and its preacher.

Little Abigail was of course delightful. Liz made the most of the few hours they spent with her, and as is always the case when a new baby arrives, everyone had an opinion as to whom she resembled most.

Spring came early that year and the valley bloomed with every kind of wildflower along the hedgerows and in the woodlands. It was a great relief after those damp and dreary days folk had endured during February, and the cold winds blowing along the valley towards the river throughout March.

Anne and Tommy were rarely apart and in fact Joe began to worry that they seemed to be seeing too much of each other, to the exclusion of everything and everyone else. He said as much to Liz one evening as they were waiting for Anne to arrive home after visiting the Flints for supper.

Liz said nothing but looked uncomfortable.

'Have you got something to tell me Liz?' Joe asked, with the uneasy feeling that it might be something he'd rather not hear.

'Well, I think we'll all be seeing more of Tommy Flint in the future,' Liz said quietly, casting a knowing look in Joe's direction.

'No, you don't mean? She's little more than a child. Are you telling me she's expecting a little-un?'

'Well, we're not absolutely sure yet, but it does look that way.'

'Good God Liz! What does she think she's going to do about it? We can't bring up another little un at our time of life.'

'As soon as it's certain, Anne said he's going to come and ask you to give them your blessing.'

'Well, I have to say I'm shocked. I thought our Anne had more sense!' Joe exclaimed loudly.

'I don't think sense comes into such things, does it?' Liz replied with a smile. 'I've been thinking,' she went on, 'As your cottage is still empty since Betty and Will left, perhaps they could live there?'

'Got it all worked out, haven't you Liz Bangham?' Joe said, in a more conciliatory tone and with a hint of a smile playing around his mouth.

'Two grandchildren in one year!' Liz exclaimed, 'I must say it's the last thing I expected, but it will be welcome, none-theless.'

Six weeks after this exchange Anne and Tommy were mar-ried at Buildwas Church as Liz and Joe had been all those years ago, and in spite of the circumstances, it was a joyous occa-sion. Tommy had nervously asked Joe for his daughter's hand a month earlier. They looked painfully young as they walked down the aisle, far too young for the responsibility of raising a child, but there it was, they had made their bed Joe thought, now they must literally lie in it. Joe had told them they could have the cottage in Dale Coppice rent-free until they got them-selves on their feet. Tommy's parents had helped to furnish it for them, and Liz found some sheets and a blanket for the bed. Betty had left behind some household items that weren't needed by Sally and George, so all in all, they just about had all they needed to begin their life together.

In Nailer's Row, life soon got back to normal although Joe in particular was finding the work at the furnace increasingly difficult. Liz was kept busy visiting Elizabeth and the new baby whenever she could. There was plenty of work producing the moulds for steam engine parts and other cast iron items as Nat continued to improve his skills.

Anne and Tommy Flint settled into their married life, and all went well with the pregnancy. They expected their baby to arrive just after Christmas, but in the event, she went into labour on the 20th of December, and was delivered of a healthy daughter, who they named Jane. Everyone was delighted of course, and Christmas that year was made all the more special with the arrival of a new baby.

Chapter 52

Ben could barely recognise the Horsehay works now. When he had arrived a few short years earlier, it had been a small settlement, the site of a disused mill. Now it had been transformed into a bustling industrial area with two furnaces roaring away day and night, and every manner of accompanying activities being undertaken by the vastly increased number of workers.

There were now people everywhere. From the few tens that were on site when Ben had arrived, their number had swollen to several hundred, mostly accommodated with their families in squatter cottages scattered around the area. The second furnace had been blown in on the 5th of May, and what an event that had been! A picnic had been organised and waggon loads of beef, veal, hams, plum puddings, and beer arrived from Sunniside, and over three hundred workers and their families were fed that day.

It was several weeks since Ben had been back to Coalbrookdale to visit Joe and Liz. Work at the two Horsehay furnaces had been relentless, and he had been unable to get the time off. However, he'd received word from Nat that Liz was unwell and that he ought to come home as soon as possible. He knew it must be serious, because his mother wasn't given to dramatics and wouldn't have allowed his father to send for him for something trivial.

As he approached the valley, he could already see the red glow of the furnaces in the evening sky, looking for all the world as though a spectacular sunset was developing over the brow of the hill in front of him. Of course, he knew this was no sunset, and as he rounded the last bend in the road, there it was in all its glory; Coalbrookdale. The works had been expanding for years of course, but as always, he was surprised once more at the sight of the fires issuing from the furnace mouths, and the sounds of industry now resounding in his ears; the roar of the fires, the shouts of men and the rumble of loads of ironstone, coke and lime being rolled along the wooden bridge to be tipped into the mouths of the furnaces, and the thump and suck of the steam engine pumping water back up into the upper pool to be re-used once more to power the bellows at their base.

As he strode further down the valley, he passed the forges and the foundries. Here there were other sounds, the thump thump of the hammer pressing out the wrought iron to be made into all manner of goods and the ring of metal on metal as it was hammered into shape. He hurried on, eager now to see his parents and to discover how things were with his mother.

It was almost dark as he arrived at Nailer's Row and lifted the latch on the front door of the house where he'd lived most of his life. He found his brother Nat and his sister Anne sitting in front of the fire, but his mother and father were nowhere to be seen. He took one look at Nat's face and knew something serious was afoot.

'Where's Ma, Nat?' he asked, with some trepidation.

'Ben, I'm so glad you came. It's not looking good.'

'What's happened? Nat? Anne?'

At this, Anne threw herself at him, burying her head in his shoulder and sobbing quietly.

'Now now lass, tell me, what is it?'

'You'd better go upstairs to 'er Ben,' Nat said. 'Pa's with her. She collapsed suddenly yesterday, and since then she's been struggling for breath. We don't know what's wrong with 'er but she's not getting any better. See for yerself lad.'

With that, Ben gently put Anne aside and hurried up to the front bedroom where he found Joe kneeling beside the bed holding Liz's hand up to his lips, with tears silently tumbling down his cheeks. His mother's eyes were closed, and she looked pale. He was terrified that he had arrived too late, but as he strode across the room, she heard his footsteps and opened her eyes.

'Ben!' she said, weakly. 'You came.'

'Of course I came.' he replied quietly. 'How are you feeling now Ma?'

Liz didn't reply, indicating with a slight movement of her head from side to side that she was too weary to answer him, but he didn't need to hear her words, he could see for himself that she was gravely ill.

Joe looked up at Ben with anguish in his eyes. He felt helpless and afraid. He had spent most of his life with Liz. She had been his rock in the bad times and his companion when life was good. He knew she was in mortal danger, and he couldn't contemplate life without her.

At that moment Liz arched her back and cried out in pain, clutching her heart and then Joe and Ben knew what was wrong. Her heart was failing and there was nothing they could do about it. She gradually relaxed as the pain subsided, but they knew it would be back and Ben shouted for the others to come up to join them, knowing the end wouldn't be long in coming.

So it proved, and it was in the early hours of the morning that Liz suffered another attack. This time it was stronger and longer and she gripped Joe's hand as the pain intensified, digging her nails into his palm until suddenly he felt her hand relax and he knew she was gone. His beloved Liz had left him, and he collapsed, sobbing over her lifeless body.

Anne too, almost slid to the floor until Nat drew her to him and held her close as the tears flowed. As he saw his father's grief take hold of him, Ben felt as though they were intruding and suggested they leave them alone for a while. They sadly made their way downstairs and Nat gently led his sister to the chair by the fireside, then after Ben had added coal to the dying embers, the three of them sat quietly, trying to comprehend what had just happened.

After an hour or so, Nat and Anne went back upstairs to see how Joe was doing. They found him still prostrate over their mother's body. Nat went over to him, saying,

'Come on Da, come downstairs now, there's nothing more to be done here and Anne will see to Ma for now.'

Reluctantly Joe allowed himself to be led to the door of the room and with one last lingering look at his wife, slowly descended stairs. Anne remained and with tears streaming down her face she gently straightened her mother's body out and closed her eyes, then she kissed her on the forehead pulled up the sheet to cover her face. She knew they would send for Elizabeth tomorrow, and together they would wash their mother to prepare her for the undertaker.

Three days later Liz was taken to the Buildwas burying ground to be placed in a new grave close by her parents. Joe was in a daze throughout the day of the funeral. He felt completely lost without his Liz. Utterly without direction. If it hadn't been for his children, and Elizabeth in particular he would have given up and may well have taken his own life to be with Liz. However, the sight of his two little grandchildren gave him the strength to carry on. Abigail and little Jane were both thriving, and Joe knew that however hard it was, life had to go on. Liz would have told him that he owed it to them to be with them as long as he was able.

However, it would not be long before Joe got his wish to join his wife. He knew his strength had been failing for the last few years but had battled on because Liz needed him to provide for her. Once Liz had gone, the incentive to carry on diminished and it became so much harder for him to motivate himself to battle through each day at the furnace. It was on one cold and misty October morning, just a month after the birth of Elizabeth's second child, also Joseph, that Joe Bangham, wearily climbing the steps leading to the furnace top, missed his footing and staggered backwards. He may have survived the fall had he not broken his neck as he hit the hard concrete ground at the foot of the steps.

They sent for Nat, who was working at the Old Furnace and together with Joe's workmates he carried him home to Nailer's Row. Three days later, once again, his children gathered at the Buildwas burying ground to grieve, this time for their father. Joe's death coming without warning hit them even harder than their mother's. They felt utterly bereft. If Liz had been the heart of the family, Joe had been its strength and without them both they felt rudderless. He was laid to rest united in death with his beloved wife.

As Nat was walking away from the grave, he glanced at the headstone on the grave next to Joe and Liz's. He had noticed it when they had been burying his mother, and now he read the inscription once again. It read 'Abigail Bangham, beloved mother of Michael Bangham' and he remembered how upset his father had been to read his sister's name there. Now another name had been added, 'Margaret Bangham'. Nat was sad to see that his Aunt Margaret must have recently passed and was even sadder to realise that his father had known nothing about it.

It had been ten years since they had gathered to lay Aunt Abigail to rest, and they had seen nothing of the Bridgnorth Banghams since that day. He knew their lives had taken a different path than their Coalbrookdale cousins, but still, he was surprised that no one had thought to tell his father about the death of his eldest sister. These thoughts were running through his head as he glanced around at his siblings and the realisation dawned on him that as the generations pass on, families drift apart, and he knew that with Joe and Liz gone, eventually the same thing would happen to this family. It was the end of an era. The last of the 'glue' holding the Bangham family of Coalbrookdale together was gone, and before long each of them would go their own way. Of course, they still supported one another when needed, but it was never to be the same again.

Chapter 53

Anne and Tommy had settled down in Dale Coppice, and now had a little boy, Benjamin, who was born one January morning in 1760. They were happy enough, the only cloud on the horizon being Tommy's fondness for drink. Anne told herself it was only natural for a man to want to satisfy his thirst after a hard day at the Boring Mill, and she suppressed the nagging concern that was forming at the back of her mind.

Since Elizabeth's first encounter with the Reverend John Fletcher at Abigail's christening, she had given much thought to the scriptures. Her mother in law had given her a bible and she read it avidly at every opportunity. Losing both her parents in quick succession had only intensified her spiritual yearning to find meaning and purpose in her life. She found herself drawn more and more into the life of the church, and now regularly attended Sunday services.

To Elizabeth's delight John Fletcher became the permanent Vicar of Madeley and she never missed an opportunity to hear him preach. One Sunday shortly after Joe's death, while still grieving, she was deeply affected by his call to all who believed, to come forward and profess their faith. A force beyond her control prompted her to stand and walk to the front of the congregation along with several others who were also called by the power of John Fletcher's words. They all knelt before him and acknowledged their sins and their love of God and he blessed them one by one, welcoming them into the congregation of Saint Michael's church. From that day on Elizabeth's faith never faltered. After having Abigail she had had to give up her teaching position, but she became a Sunday School teacher, encouraging many of her ex-pupils and neighbours' children to join her classes.

Betty had settled down in her new life in Madeley with George and Sally and her grandchildren John, Alice and little Walter. She missed Will greatly, of course, but had to admit that her life was considerably easier. She had no money worries as George's business was going from strength to strength. He was mainly supplying the rapidly expanding middle classes with items of furniture and had gained a reputation for the quality of his work. As the business grew, George extended the house, adding two more rooms, one on the ground floor as a sitting room, with a bedroom above for his mother.

Of course, thoughts of Walter were never far from her mind. It was four years since he had been taken, so he was over half-way through his seven-year sentence. It was hard for Betty, not knowing where in the world he was or how he was coping with the harsh life he must be living. Occasionally she saw Susan Bly at Madeley market and always stopped to have a chat with her. Betty was comforted to see that so far Susan had been true to her word. She was still working at Harden House and showed no sign of getting involved with anyone else, seemingly still determined to wait for Walter's return.

One day there was a loud knocking on the front door and as Sally was out at the time, Betty opened it to find a man standing there. She thought he looked vaguely familiar but couldn't put a name to him. He introduced himself as Henry Wood, from Madeley, and he said he brought news of Walter Bangham. Betty's heart leapt at the sound of her son's name, and she invited Henry in.

'Please, come in – what news do you have of my son? We've had none for nigh on four years. Do you know where he is?'

'Well, Mrs Bangham – I'm assuming you are his mother?'

'I am,' Betty assured him.

Henry continued,

'I only know where he was four years ago. I work on the Bristol docks, and I saw your son being boarded on a ship bound for America.'

Betty couldn't hide her disappointment that the news he brought related only to the time Walter was taken and was not more recent.

'I'm sorry it's taken me so long to give you this news, but I live and work in Bristol and rarely travel up to Madeley. I only come now because my mother is gravely ill.'

'I'm so sorry to hear that,' Betty said, 'but have you any other news of Walter? Do you know where in America he was being taken, and where he is now?'

'I did make enquiries as to where the ship, The Lark, it was, was bound for and was told that it was sailing to Annapolis in a place called Chesapeake Bay, so I assume that would have been the place Walter would have been landed. As to where he is now, I'm afraid I have no further news of him, but I felt I should at least let you know where he was sent to in the first place.'

Betty thanked him profusely, saying,

'Well thank you for telling me Mr Wood, and it does give me comfort to have an idea where he is.'

She offered to give him something to eat and drink, but he insisted that he must be getting up to Madeley to see his mother as he had come straight from the river to give her the news before carrying on to the family home.

'Well, I 'ope you find her improved Mr Wood, and thank you again for bringing me this news.'

With that, she showed Henry out and watched him striding off up the road, then throwing her shawl around her shoulders, hurried to the workshop to tell George the news. He was pleased, of course to have any word of his brother, but like Betty, was disappointed that it wasn't about more recent events.

Nat, now a valued and skilled mould maker had been allowed to keep the house in Nailer's Row and the tenancy was transferred to him after Joe's death. One Sunday, he was tending the vegetable plot behind the house when a woman's voice called out to him,

'Praties are lookin' good!'

Startled, as he hadn't noticed anyone emerge from the other houses in the row, he looked up and found a young woman standing in the doorway of the Lavin's place two doors down. She stood with her hands on her fulsome hips and was grinning widely at him. Her long black hair hung down around her shoulders and even at this distance he could see the twinkle in her bright blue eyes. The sight of her affected Nat in a way that no other woman had done before. He flushed and to his consternation, could only manage to mumble rather limply,

'Oh, err, yes.'

She stepped over to him saying,

'I'm Mary by the way,' she stated confidently, I'm staying with me aunt an' uncle.'

'Oh, well I'm Nat,' Nat replied rather woodenly but at the same time, wanting to know more about this vision of loveliness standing before him, but utterly unable to think how to go about asking her. Sensing his discomfort and well aware of the effect she was having on him, Mary smiled broadly then went on in a lilting Irish brogue,

'I know who you are Nat Bangham. I'm Mary Lavin, from Wrockwardine.'

Nat began to relax a little. Planting his spade in the ground, and deciding his digging was over for the day, he gave his full attention to Mary Lavin.

'Well it's good to meet you Mary Lavin,' he said with a smile, then ventured, 'Will you be staying long?'

'Maybe. I'm hopin' to find work here. There's not much to be had in Wrockwardine Wood.'

'Well, there's plenty round here, but much of it hard for a woman. What sort did you have in mind?'

Mary stood tall and spoke decisively,

'I don't intend to be picking coal from the tips, I can tell you that, or labouring in the Boring Mill for that matter!'

'No, I'm sure you'll find somethin' better.' Nat assured her. 'There are plenty of people goin' up in t'world, who might be looking for some 'elp around t'house. Mebbe that would suit?'

With that, Mary turned away and with a toss of her head, told Nat not to worry about her, she would find something suitable before long, giving Nat the feeling that he had pushed the conversation too far. He'd only just met her and already he was suggesting he knew exactly what she should do with her life! A minute later she had disappeared into the Lavin's house, leaving Nat cursing himself for presuming too much. Why had her presence caused him to completely forget the norms of polite conversation? This was a new experience for him which left him bewildered.

After that, Nat found himself making excuses to spend time on the vegetable plot in the yard whenever he could, in the hope that Mary Lavin would reappear, but two weeks passed and he began to think she had gone away, never to return. He had the uncomfortable feeling that their meeting had been a crossroad in his life and somehow, he had taken a wrong turn, and now it was too late. He may never see her again.

However, the following Sunday, as he was relaxing in front of the fire smoking his pipe and gazing out of the window, suddenly, there she was, striding past the window, making for her aunt's house. His heart skipped a beat, he jumped out of his chair, and without thinking opened the door and called after her as she reached the Lavin's door.

'Mary!'

She swung her head round to face him, smiling broadly.

'Nat Bangham!' she called out, as if surprised to see him standing there at his own doorway, but of course, knowing that walking in front of his window may well precipitate precisely this reaction.

Nat enquired whether she had managed to find work and it turned out she was to be a kitchen maid in the home of the Foundry Manager, just a little way up the valley. Nat was delighted and was now determined that he would not 'lose' her again.

Mary wasn't living in at the Foundry Manager's house and continued to stay with her aunt and uncle in Nailer's Row. She and Nat spent every hour they could together that summer, getting to know one another. Mary told him that she had been born in a little village near to Cork, in Ireland. Her family had been working the land but had been evicted when the landlord had decided to build a new mansion for his family. Mary's father Michael Lavin, unable to find work and a home for his family had moved to Shropshire, where his brother was working for the Darby's. He had heard they were needing miners in one of the newly dug mines in Wrockwardine Wood. That had been ten years ago, when Mary was just ten years old. She had three sisters, of whom she was the eldest, and two older brothers. Life hadn't been easy since they arrived from Ireland, she told Nat, and she and her sisters had done whatever they could to earn a few pennies, whether it was working on harvesting crops, or picking coal on the coal tips, and both her brothers had gone down the mine with their father. Now, she told him, she was determined to move up in the world. No more would she pick coal to survive and had decided that going into service, where she could work her way up and be involved in a better way of life, offered a more promising prospect.

Nat began to understand Mary's rather feisty nature. Along with her family, she had had to fight to survive, doing what was needed to keep the family afloat. Not only had this given Mary strength of character but had also cemented her family together by their common endeavour. He knew she would give the same effort and commitment to her relationship with him. By the end of the summer, Nat was certain that he wanted to spend the rest of his life with this woman.

On the one Sunday in the month she had off from her work at the Foundry Master's house, she always went home to visit her mother and father in Wrockwardine, and Nat began to join her whenever he could. They made him very welcome, and after the lonely months spent in Nailer's Row since Liz and Joe had passed away, Nat found much joy being part of a family once more.

He finally proposed in the middle of an April thunderstorm. They had been out for a walk up towards Dale Coppice when the first bolt of lightning struck, and the rain began tumbling down in sheets. They ran as fast as they could to Nailer's Row, and stumbling into the room, they fell, laughing, and soaking wet, into each other's arms. Their embrace soon progressed into something more intimate and finally, after the desire which had been building up in both of them for months, could no longer be resisted, their love was consummated there and then. After their passion was spent, they lay together in utter contentment, with a feeling of fulfilment, and with lightning still flashing through the window and thunder rolling around the Gorge, Nat asked Mary to be his wife.

Chapter 54

On Nat's next day off, they made their way up to Wrockwardine for him to speak to Mary's father, to ask for his daughter's hand. This was largely a formality as Michael had grown fond of Nat over the last months, as had the rest of the family, with the exception of Mary's eldest brother, Patrick. He had largely kept his distance, while always demonstrating to Nat how close he was to Mary, bringing up shared memories or enjoying some private joke with her in the knowledge, or so it seemed to Nat, that he would be excluded from the exchange. It was obvious that Pat and Mary had been very close growing up. It seemed to Nat that Pat resented his closeness to his sister.

Mary and her mother Kate disappeared into the scullery to prepare some food, where they chattered excitedly about the prospect of the wedding. Mary told her that as Nat already had an established home for the two of them, there need be no delay. Kate and Michael insisted that they would make all the arrangements at St Peter's Church, Wrockwardine. It was agreed that, if possible, the wedding would be arranged for 14th May.

The week before the wedding Nat visited Dale Coppice to invite Anne and Tommy to the celebration. When she opened the door, he was shocked to see that she had a nasty looking bruise round her right eye, extending down to her chin.

'Our Anne!' he began, 'What on earth 'as happened to you?'

Trying to hide her face by turning away from him, she replied, 'It's nothin' our Nat.'

'Well it don't look like nothin'!' Nat exclaimed. 'How did it 'appen? 'As 'e struck you?'

'O' course not!' Anne reassured him, saying that she had merely slipped and fallen against a log in the woods.

'Well, if yer sure,' Nat went on, 'but if ever 'e does, you let me know, right?'

'Anyway, thanks fer invitin' us to t'wedding an' I do hope you an' Mary will be 'appy, but I don't think we'll be comin'. I'm sorry Nat.'

With that she had stepped forward and hugged him, holding on slightly longer than necessary, and Nat held her tightly, trying to silently reassure her that he would indeed be there to offer her protection, should she ever ask for it.

After Nat had gone, Anne sunk down in the chair by the fire and let the tears fall. She felt fearful and defeated, knowing that her life, which had once held so much promise, was not going to be a happy one. Tommy's drinking was getting worse by the week. Each payday now, he would stagger home drunk and with his pockets half empty. If she complained about lack of money, or his drinking, more often than not, he replied with his fists. She missed Liz, with whom she might have confided, and felt dreadfully alone.

At that moment, little Benjamin began to cry loudly, demanding to be fed and Jane, who had been playing in the dirt outside the front door ran in, and seeing her mother in tears rushed to her side silently placing her head on her lap, trying in her little way to offer her comfort.

Anne stroked her hair fondly, reassuring her that she was alright, then stood and picked Benjamin up, cuddled him, then put him to her breast. With that, she smiled through her tears, hugging her children to her, the only shining lights in her miserable existence.

Nathaniel set out from Nailer's Row on his wedding day as the sun was climbing in the sky. He had arranged to ride on one of the horse-drawn Darby waggons which ran up the railway track to the Ketley ironworks, usually loaded with iron ore or other raw materials. He knew it would pass through Horsehay, where Ben had arranged to join him. From Ketley they would walk the last few miles to Wrockwardine.

Thankfully, the day was fine, and they were in high spirits as they strode up to St Peter's church, where Mary and her family were waiting to greet them. The bride looked as beautiful as any bride should. She wore a corn poppy blue dress trimmed with white lace. Her dark brown hair was piled on her head and trimmed with flowers. Michael Lavin was bursting with pride as he escorted her down the aisle, fighting back a tear or two as he handed her over to her future husband. Nat thought he would die of happiness, which was tinged only with the regret that his parents weren't there to witness his marriage. He was sure Liz would have loved Mary as much as he did.

After the service all the family congratulated them warmly. Even Patrick made an effort to say that he wished them well. Over the months he had got to know Nat better, and now had a grudging respect for him, seeing that he was genuinely in love with his sister and that she reciprocated his affection.

The wedding breakfast was held at the Lavin's cottage in Wrockwardine, and it was altogether a joyous occasion. Afterwards, Mary's uncle, also Patrick Lavin, and his family, with whom she had been staying in Nailer's Row, had borrowed a horse and waggon to attend the wedding, and now offered to take the young couple back to Coalbrookdale. There was much embracing and not a few tears as Mary said goodbye to her parents and siblings, knowing that this would no longer be her home. She promised to come back often to visit them all, but everyone knew that it would never be the same again.

Ben shook Nat warmly by the hand and the brothers embraced, also knowing that things must now change. Ben could no longer regard Nailer's Row as his home. It was Mary and Nat's home now and he realised that he must finally make his own way in the world. As he strode along towards Ketley, he determined that it was high time he also found himself a wife, and he would make a conscious effort to do so.

There was some consternation among the Madeley Wood Banghams when they heard about Nat's marriage to Mary. Elizabeth in particular was upset that she and Rod had not been invited. She had always been close to Nat and now that their mother was gone, she felt that as his eldest sister, she should have been there. The day after she'd heard about it, she visited Aunt Dorothy at the schoolhouse to give her the news.

Dorothy was also disappointed that she and John had known nothing about it, but in any case, she knew she was getting rather too old to be journeying along the rough tracks in the trap. However, as she said, it would have been nice to be asked! After talking it through, they eventually agreed that things change, people move on, and families grow apart over the years. That's just the way it was, and sadly, their connection to Coalbrookdale had just become more tenuous.

Elizabeth was always happy to visit the schoolhouse. She had spent many happy years there. Helping Dorothy and John; teaching the little ones to read and write. Of course, when Abigail was born John insisted that she stay at home to look after the baby. It seemed a lifetime ago that her father Joseph had brought her to Madeley to live with her aunt and uncle to help out with the housework and caring for their new baby. She had been just fourteen then, and she was shocked to realise that was over twenty-three years ago. Her own children were now growing up fast. Abigail was five years old, and her little brother Joseph was going on three, and chattering away. She wondered how her mother-in-law was coping with them. Mrs

Sheldon had offered to look after them while Elizabeth visited her aunt. They could be a handful though, and her mother-in-law wasn't getting any younger.

Elizabeth had felt that her aunt had been a little distracted throughout the afternoon and asked her if there was anything wrong. Dorothy admitted she was rather worried and went on to say,

'I do have quite a lot on my mind to be honest Elizabeth. As you know we have lived here all our married lives, but now we may have to leave our lovely home.'

'Oh I'm sorry to hear that aunt whyever is that?'

Dorothy went on to explain how, now that they were both approaching seventy years old, she and John had decided to retire from teaching at the Charity School. Unfortunately that meant they would have to find somewhere else to live, as the house was for the use of the schoolmaster. John had been teaching at the school and also for many of the more affluent families in their own homes, for over forty years. He and Dorothy had been married shortly after he had taken up his post.

Elizabeth told her that she would speak to her father-in-law Mr Sheldon, who had several properties for rent in the area. She said she was sure he would help if he could, which put Dorothy's mind at rest for the moment.

Elizabeth said she really would have to be going but promised to speak to her father-in-law as soon as she could, and embracing Dorothy warmly at the front door, she turned and strode off down the hill towards the river and home. She collected the children from the Sheldons' house and hurried home to prepare the supper for when Rod arrived. She liked to have his food ready to place on the table as soon as he arrived home. He had been working his way up in the Madeley Wood Company and was earning good money. Life was good for their little family. In fact, life had been more fulfilling for Elizabeth since she joined St Michael's Church. She loved running the

Sunday School, and her greatest joy came from listening to Reverend Fletcher. Other preachers came from time to time, but none moved her soul the way he did. He always seemed to have relevant words to speak directly to everyone in the congregation, regardless of their circumstances. More and more people turned up each Sunday as word spread about this remarkable man and the message he brought, which was one of hope in a dark world, and it surely was a dark world for most people at the time.

Work was hard, and living conditions for many were dreadful and precarious. Housing was scarce and often inadequate, with many families sharing a couple of rooms. There was much drinking and carousing among the men as they tried to escape the drudgery of twelve or thirteen hour days, which in turn, meant that many women were being expected to raise their children in virtual destitution.

Elizabeth understood how lucky she was to have married into the Sheldon family. They could be said to be middle class. Her father-in-law had worked and studied hard and made sure his children did the same. She was proud of what her husband had achieved and grateful that she and the children were benefitting from his industriousness. In return, she saw it as her duty to care for and support her husband as he continued to provide for them, so that they could go on nurturing their children so that they would enjoy even better lives. She did, as always, remind herself not to be smug about her good fortune. She had seen enough of life to know that everything could be taken away in an instant if a wrong decision was taken. Not for the first time, thoughts of Susan Bly and her cousin Walter crossed her mind. What a tragedy that had been, and she wondered if he ever would return to claim his bride.

She knew Rod would be home within the hour or so and busied herself washing the children and dressing them in their nightclothes, then set about preparing the food. Every evening, after eating supper with their parents, the children would spend an hour or so with their father, who would read to them, or play little games with them before carrying them up to bed. Tonight was no exception and Elizabeth followed them up the stairs, helped them to say their prayers and tucked them lovingly into bed, planting a kiss on each little forehead and telling them to 'sleep well'.

Now, as she sat opposite her husband with the children asleep upstairs and the fire blazing in the hearth, Elizabeth felt utterly content with her life, and silently prayed that nothing would ever come along to spoil her happiness. At the same time, she understood that such things could never be taken for granted.

No one knew that better than Betty Bangham, living four doors down. Her life in Dale Coppice with Will and Walter had changed in an instant when, encouraged by Will of course, Walter had taken the decision to join the food riots. She felt that her life had really stopped the day Walter was taken and would only restart the day he strode back into it. So, as Elizabeth was contentedly sitting by the fire, contemplating her good fortune, Betty's thoughts were all for her youngest son, as she wondered sadly if she would ever see him again. She often tried to imagine what Chesapeake Bay was like. It sounded like a pleasant place, and she prayed to God that it was.

Chapter 55

Nat and Mary had settled down well to their new life together. They were well suited, and Mary's sense of humour ensured that Nat didn't take himself too seriously, as he had always had a tendency to do. She teased him mercilessly at every opportunity. At first, he was defensive, but it wasn't long before he began to rather enjoy it and to see that it was good for him to laugh at himself from time to time. Life was good and even better when Mary announced that she was expecting their first child and that it would be due in early spring of the following year.

Once she was sure, she was eager to tell her parents that they would soon have their first grandchild, and she and Nat made their way over to Wrockwardine. Michael and Kate were of course pleased at the prospect of a grandchild and her mother made a great fuss of Mary. She insisted that as Nat's parents were no longer around, she should come to Nailer's Row when the time came so that she could look after Mary and the child for a few weeks. Nat wasn't too keen on the idea but had to admit that with him out at work all day, it would be wiser for Mary and the child to have his mother-in-law staying for a while. He had seen too many infants, and mothers for that matter, perish within days of the birth of a child. So it was agreed that Kate would be sent for when the time came.

It was a warm July evening as they made their way back to the Dale. As they strode along arm in arm, they were happy and full of hope at the prospect of bringing this new life into the world. Like all new parents to be, they wondered whether it would be a boy or a girl, but above all just hoped it would be healthy and brought safely into the world.

The sun had almost set by the time they arrived at Nailer's Row, but although they were weary after their long walk, Mary insisted that she must call in at her aunt and uncle's house to give them the news before they heard it from someone else. They had been good to her, giving her a home while she had been working at the Foundry Managers' house before her marriage to Nat, and she looked on them as 'second parents'.

When they knocked on the Lavin's door it was Bridie who opened it.

'Why, cum on in!' she said in her broad Irish brogue. 'We've bin wunderin' where you two have been, you'd visitors today and sure, we didn't know where you'd got to.'

'Aunt Bridie,' Mary said quickly, 'we've been up to Wrockwardine to see mother and father.'

'Oh! Is somethin' wrong, is someone ill?' her aunt quickly asked, with a note of alarm in her voice.

'No, not at all, aunt. Just the opposite actually.'

Mary glanced at Nat who nodded his agreement that she should tell her aunt and uncle their news.

'We went to tell them that they're going to have a grandchild,' Mary announced.

At this, Bridie threw her hands up in the air declaring,

'Lord luv us! That's wunderful news to be sure!'

She stepped forward and threw her arms round her niece, kissing her on the cheek, then did the same to Nat, who was grinning broadly. Patrick, who had been in the kitchen, hearing his wife's pronouncement, now stepped into the room saying,

'What's that then?' he queried, glancing at each one of them in turn.

'These two are to be 'avin' a little 'un Patrick! I'nt that grand?'

Striding across the room he took Nat's hand in his and shook it warmly.

'Congratulations lad,' he said with much feeling, 'That is grand, to be sure!'

'Thanks Patrick,' Nat responded. 'We couldn't be happier.'

'Well, this deserves a celebration,' Patrick declared, as he stepped over to the cupboard and took out the bottle of whiskey he'd been saving for a special occasion.

As he was pouring them all a tot, Nat remembered that Bridie had mentioned they'd had visitors while they were out, and now asked her who had called on them.

'It was your brother Ben, lad, and he brought someone to meet you,' she told him.

'Who was that Aunt Bridie?' Mary asked.

'Well, he brought a young lass, a Mary Nicklen from over Ketley way, I think she said!'

'What? We didn't even know he was courtin'.'

'She seemed nice enough. She's called Mary Nicklen,' Patrick told them, 'and they seemed happy in each other's company, to be sure!'

'I'm right sorry we missed 'em,' Nat declared, 'I've bin 'opin Ben would find 'isself a wife an' settle down.'

'Well,' Patrick went on, 'Ben said to tell you he'll be over again on his next Sunday off.'

One Sunday morning a few weeks later, Ben brought Mary Nicklen to meet them and to tell them that they were engaged to be married. Mary and Nat were pleased to hear their news and eagerly shared their own. Ben was delighted to know he was to have another niece or nephew.

Mary Nicklen was fair haired and, while you couldn't say she was beautiful, she had an open, pleasant face and ready smile. From the way she looked at Ben she was obviously smitten.

Ben surprised Nat and Mary by how attentive he was to her. It seemed completely out of character to them; not the rather self-centred young man he had always seemed. What a difference a woman could make to a man, Nat mused as he watched his brother fussing around her.

Mary Nicklen was pleasant enough and Mary liked her. It would be good to have another sister-in-law, and who knows, cousins for her own children as they came along. Of course she already had Anne, but somehow, she never seemed to want to have much to do with them. Mary wasn't sure why, but she always seemed rather guarded in her conversation and never invited them up to Dale Coppice. As for Nat's sister Elizabeth, she never visited Coalbrookdale and Nat never seemed inclined to visit her. Mary suspected that he felt she was rather too far above him socially now, and didn't want to remind himself of the fact, for which she couldn't blame him.

However, Ben and Mary had other news to share with them. Nat knew that Ben had always been fascinated to hear about his Uncle Will's time in the New World, and he had often confided to Nat that one day he would go and find out for himself whether a better life could be found there. So, it came as no great surprise when Ben declared that once he and Mary were married, they intended to try their luck in America. His eyes were shining as he reminded Nat that Will had often told him that settlers were given land and if they were prepared to work hard, fortunes could be made. He took hold of Mary's hand as he said,

'Mary's with me on this, aren't you lass?'

'I am love, the sooner we can get away from here and see something of the world, the better.'

Nat was of course, disappointed that his brother wanted to go to the other side of the world, and if he was honest, felt rather hurt that he should want to leave his family behind, but he knew that, if it meant so much to him, he would have to follow his dream or forever regret it.

'Well, lad,' Nat told him, 'I wish you well, but yer'll be missed 'ere, and no mistake.'

'Thanks Nat, but tha knows 'ow long I've bin thinkin' about this. It's somethin' I 'ave to do, and now I've found Mary, it's t'reet time for us.'

So they all began, each in their own way, to prepare for the changes that would come to their lives over the next few months.

When Ben had heard the news that Walter had been taken to a place called Annapolis, he secretly decided that that is where he would head for when he finally fulfilled his dream of seeking a new life in America. As he now set about planning the journey, he wondered how he might be able to find out more about the place. He decided that perhaps his aunt Dorothy's husband John, the schoolmaster, may know something about it. One Sunday, he made his way over to Madeley Wood to speak to him about it.

They were pleased to see him, but wondered what could have prompted this rare visit. When he explained his mission, John said he had an atlas which showed places in America and quickly took it down from the bookcase. Ben was impressed how quickly John navigated the pages and in no time was pointing at a large inlet on the coast of a huge landmass marked as America. Ben was astounded at the size of the place, particularly when John pointed out England on the other side of the Atlantic, which looked like a tiny island in comparison.

Looking more closely at the inlet, Ben could see the name of it, which he struggled to read, but which John read as Chesapeake Bay.

'And here is Annapolis,' he went on, pointing to an area to one side of the Bay a short distance inland, away from the Atlantic Ocean.

Ben spent another hour or so with them, Dorothy producing a plate of scones and glass of ale for them to enjoy while he told them the news about Nat and Mary's expected child, and about his coming wedding to Mary Nicklen and their plans regarding emigration to the New World. Finally he thanked them both, then announced that he must be leaving, as he had a long walk back to Horsehay before nightfall.

As he strode off over the hill to Coalbrookdale, he contemplated his next move. He knew that the Company had some connections with America, both through the trade but also with other Quakers. There had been talk that the Darbys had even visited them. Ben wondered if he could find a way to speak with Mr Reynolds, who may be able to at least give him some idea whether this Annapolis might offer him some prospect of employment. If there were ironworks there, maybe he could find work fairly easily, as he had years of experience of working the furnace. Although determined to get out of the iron trade eventually, Ben realised that having work as soon as they arrived would give them time to save money in preparation for getting their own land and he also wondered if Mr Reynolds might be able to give him a letter of recommendation which he was sure would greatly improve his prospects of finding a job.

The following week, Mr Reynolds paid his usual weekly visit to Horsehay. After spending time with the Works Manager, he always found time to make his way round the works to talk to the foremen, and Ben took his chance to speak with him about his plans. Although a little taken aback by Ben's announcement that he intended to emigrate, but impressed by his ambition for a better life, Mr Reynolds felt inclined to help him if he could. He told Ben that there were indeed 'connections' between Shropshire and Annapolis, and he knew of several ironworks in that area, from whom they had bought pig iron in the past. He thought they were probably always looking for skilled workers, and although he said he would be sorry to lose such a good worker, offered to write Ben a letter of introduction when the time came. Ben thanked him profusely, even forgetting himself by offering his hand, which Mr Reynolds shook warmly but with a wry smile on his lips.

Always having had emigration at the back of his mind after years of listening to his Uncle Will talk about the opportunities to be found in the New World, Ben had been saving what he could for some time, and along with a little money Mary's parents had offered to give them as a wedding present, he figured they would have enough to pay their passage – steerage of course, which would be hard, but spending more on the journey would leave them with nothing when they arrived in America. He was hoping that the letter of introduction would help him to get work immediately, although he knew he would have to work for a period before being paid, and they would need something in reserve until then.

Meanwhile, Mary was busying herself getting ready for the birth of their child. All seemed as it should be with the pregnancy. Bridie insisted that she would attend her at the birth until Kate could be sent for as 'babes ne'er cum as planned, for sure!' she declared.

As it happened it was just as well that Bridie was on hand because Mary went into labour one dark February night when the snow lay several feet deep across the tracks, and it was impossible to think of sending anyone to fetch Kate. Fortunately Nat wasn't on the night shift and was able to help Bridie, finding her whatever she needed as his wife battled her way through a painful labour.

Finally, as dawn was breaking, he heard the wonderful sound of the baby's first cries and rushed up the stairs to meet his child. It was a boy and Nat was overjoyed. He had a son! Mary was exhausted but happy as she lay with the child in her arms.

They had already decided that if it was a boy, they would name him after Mary's grandfather, Thomas.

Kate finally arrived a week later after the snow had largely disappeared, happy to meet her grandson but rather put out that she had been unable to be at his birth. Still, she had to admit, it was good that her sister-in-law Bridie had been able to step in to help Mary. She stayed for several weeks, getting to know her grandson and helping Mary with the chores.

Little Thomas was a fine, healthy boy and Mary soon regained her strength and was revelling in motherhood. Kate would happily have stayed longer but after four weeks decided that she must return to care for her own home and Michael.

Chapter 56

As the months of 1762 wore on, Anne sank deeper into despair. Tommy showed no sign of trying to control his drinking or his temper. More or less on a weekly basis now, Anne had to feel his fists, usually aimed at somewhere that wouldn't be seen by anyone else, mainly her stomach, or chest. After one particularly vicious attack on her, seeing her mother being hurt, Jane had started crying. Tommy had shouted at her to be quiet, and when the child predictably cried all the louder, he had struck her across the face, and she screamed in pain. That was the moment Anne knew she would have to do something. But what could she do?

She knew if she told Nat or Ben, they might literally kill Tommy, and she would lose not only her husband but her brothers too. In any case, she didn't want him killed. He could still be a loving husband when he wasn't in drink. He was always full of remorse the day after hitting her and swore he would never do it again. But come the next payday it would happen all over again.

She wished her mother was still alive. She would have known what to do. Then she thought of Elizabeth, her eldest sister. She was sure she would help her if she could and decided that she would take the children and make her way over to Madeley Wood the next day.

As soon as Tommy left for work the following morning, she washed and dressed the children and gave them their breakfast.

With Benjamin wrapped tightly to her using her shawl and holding Jane's tiny hand, she set off over the hill to Madeley Wood. It was slow going, but eventually they descended the path towards the town. As she walked along the main street, she noticed her cousin George standing outside his workshop. Not really wanting to see anyone, she tried to hurry by, but he called out to her as she passed,

'What brings you here Anne. You've never walked from the Coppice, have you?'

'I 'ave George,' she replied.

'That's a long, hard walk with a little one in tow!'

'It certainly is, but I needed to see our Elizabeth an' 'ad no choice.'

Then Anne thought about Walter and asked George if he had heard any news from him.

'Not a thing Anne, but his seven years is nearly up now, so we're all praying for his safe return soon.'

'Well it was an awful business, an' I can't begin to think 'ow poor Aunt Betty, Uncle Will and Susan coped wi' it all, and yerself, too, o' course George!

'Aye, well, we're all just living in hope that somehow he'll find a way to come back to us.'

'Well, I'd better be going, goodbye George,'

As George watched her trudging up the street, he was sure all was not well with her. Why had she walked all the way to Madeley Wood with the little girl and a babe in arms, he wondered.

The climb over Lincoln Hill had worn Anne out and she was eager to get to Elizabeth's. At the same time she was a little apprehensive about the reception she might receive, and also of Elizabeth and Rod's reactions when she told them about Tommy's ill treatment of her. In truth she felt ashamed; that she had somehow let this happen to her.

All this was going through her head as she approached Elizabeth's house.

As Elizabeth opened her front door in response to a rather timid rat-a-tat on the knocker, the sight that greeted her was the last thing she expected. Her youngest sister was standing on the doorstep looking old beyond her years and utterly weary, with her shawl wrapped around young Benjamin, and with little Jane clinging to her mother's skirts.

'Anne! For goodness' sake, come in child!'

Elizabeth still thought of her youngest sister as a child, and all the more so as she stood there looking so tired, sad, and vulnerable. Anne almost stumbled across the threshold as Elizabeth lifted Jane in her arms. As she did so, she removed the child's bonnet and was horrified to see the bruise on the side of her face. Jane struggled and cried as she wasn't familiar with her Aunt Elizabeth, who had to ignore her cries as she ushered her sister to the chair at the fireside.

'Sit yourself down there Anne, you look as if you could do with a rest!'

Elizabeth could see that Anne could barely speak and was close to tears. She was full of questions, but realised they would have to wait until she had made sure that her sister had gained some comfort in front of the fire. Jane was still crying, and Elizabeth set her down beside her mother, then gently took the baby so that Anne could take the child on her knee to comfort her.

After a few minutes all seemed calmer and Elizabeth ventured,

'Anne, what is the matter, love? You wouldn't have walked all this way for nothing. Tell me, what is it?'

At this, Anne finally began to cry, then silently, she unbuttoned her blouse to reveal an ugly black bruise. Seeing this, along with the bruise on the child's face, Elizabeth began to understand what all this might be about.

'Did he do this to you?' she asked Anne, who silently nodded.

'And on Jane's face too?' Elizabeth went on.

'Oh Elizabeth, I don't know what to do,' Anne gushed. ''e just don't stop. Week after week, it's the same every payday. I'm so shamed! An' now 'e attacked Jane, just because she cried to see me hurting, and I knew I 'ad to do somethin'.'

She was sobbing now, all the months of humiliation and shame pouring out of her. Without a word, Elizabeth knelt down beside her, still holding the baby, and put her arm around her sister's shoulders to offer her some comfort. They remained like that for some minutes until Anne's crying ceased. Suddenly young Benjamin began to wail, demanding to be fed.

Once Anne had settled him to her breast and seemed much calmer, Elizabeth ventured,

'How long has this been going on our Anne?'

'The drinkin' started just after Jane was born, but 'e wasn't violent at first. Then after Benjamin came along, 'e drank more and more and got more angry and violent wi' me. But 'e never hurt the children 'til now.'

'Oh love, I'm so sorry you've had to be going through this alone. You should have come to me sooner.'

'I couldn't, Elizabeth, I've been so shamed!'

'Why on earth should you be ashamed Anne? He's the one in the wrong, not you! So, what would you like to do about it? Do you want to leave him?'

'No!' Anne replied vehemently. 'I just want it to stop! 'E can be very lovin' most times, but when 'e's in drink 'e changes. 'E gets so angry if I complain about 'im spending 'is wages on drink, but what am I do? We have t'little ones to feed and clothe now.'

The mention of the children brought more tears which trickled slowly down her cheeks. Elizabeth realised that there were no simple answers to this problem.

'Well, stay here tonight anyway. Give yourself some time to think about what you want to do.'

Anne looked horrified at this suggestion, insisting that she must go home as she hadn't left word for Tommy as to where she'd gone.

''E'll be worried sick when 'e gets home and finds us gone.'

Elizabeth was thinking that it might make him realise that he was risking everything by his behaviour but realised that Anne wasn't yet ready to give up on him. The best she could do was to be there for her whenever she needed someone to confide in. Meanwhile, she would discuss it with Rod, to see what, if anything, they could do to help them. If Tom really loved his family, maybe there was a way to make him see sense. She silently prayed to God to show her how she might be able to help her sister.

As it seemed Anne was determined to return to Dale Coppice, Elizabeth insisted that they should eat first. She disappeared into the kitchen to prepare something and while she was gone, Anne glanced around the room. What she saw made her feel a little envious of her sister. This was a real home, full of nice things.

There was a small piano against one wall and a sideboard with drawers and a mirror standing on top. There were china ornaments on the mantel above the fireplace and pictures on the wall. One in particular drew her attention. It bore a religious image of a man, who Anne presumed to be Jesus, as there was a halo around his head, and he was holding up a hand, palm forward, presumably in blessing. Anne realised for the first time, just how involved Elizabeth was in the church. However, there was something comforting in the image and Anne wondered if maybe she could find help there for her own troubles.

As Anne was thinking about the picture Elizabeth returned with some bread and cheese for the two of them and milk and a scone for Jane, who was now playing happily with an old rag doll of Abigail's. When they'd eaten, they sat awhile chatting about family business. Glancing once again at the picture of Christ, Anne asked Elizabeth about the church and whether she thought it may help her. Pleased that Anne had raised the subject of the church she gladly explained how the Reverend Fletcher, through his words, and she believed, the power of the Holy Spirit, had turned many men away from drunkenness. She had seen with her own eyes the changes that this had wrought, their whole lives and those of their families had been transformed from misery to joy. She was sure Tommy could be helped in the same way.

Anne listened politely but she was doubtful that Tommy would be in a mood to listen. He'd never shown any interest in religion before, and nor had she, for that matter. However, she filed the thought away at the back of her mind. If Tommy really showed that he wanted to change, maybe she would suggest that they could go together to listen to the Reverend Fletcher.

Finally, Anne said she ought to be getting back home, so that she could prepare Tommy's supper before he arrived. With some reluctance, Eliabeth said if she was sure, she would pop along to the Sheldon's to see if someone could take her back home in the trap.

'I am sure Elizabeth,' Anne insisted, 'I want to go home. I'll just have to find a way to get him to stop.'

'Well, you know now, I'm always here for you if you need me,' Elizabeth replied, giving her sister a hug. Then wrapping her shawl around her shoulders, she stepped out of the front door and made her way along to the Sheldon house.

She was back within minutes to say that Mrs Sheldon had asked Jack Black, their groom, to take them over to Dale Coppice and he would be bringing the trap round in a few minutes.

'That's kind of her,' Anne murmured as she got the children ready for the journey home, 'and thank you so much Elizabeth, I do feel much better now, to know I have your support.'

Jack Black arrived outside the front door, and the sisters parted with more displays of affection, even Jane now allowing her aunt to plant a kiss on the top of her head before helping her to climb into the back seat of the trap.

Jane was excited at riding in a trap, which was a new experience for her, and a rare one for Anne for that matter. Within half an hour they pulled into the clearing in the Coppice and Jack deposited them outside the cottage door.

'Thank you so much,' Anne said, 'it was kind of you to bring us 'ome.'

'No trouble at all Ma'am,' Jack replied politely, touching the peak of his cap as he did so. Anne was rather taken aback by this expression of respect, being totally unused to such displays of deference being directed at her.

The afternoon was wearing on and Anne set about stoking up the fire and hurriedly preparing supper. She just about managed to finish when the sound of the latch told her that Tommy was home.

He strode in, in his usual jaunty manner, declaring,

'How's my best girl then?'

He scooped Anne up in his arms and kissed her on the lips. She didn't resist but didn't respond either, although he didn't seem to notice. He said nothing about what had happened the day before. His capacity to completely block out any memories of his displays of violence always amazed Anne. However, it was obviously not so for young Jane, for when he went to pick her up, instead of running towards him as she usually did, she cowered away from him, holding the side of her face. Then, he remembered.

'Did I do that Anne?' he asked incredulously.

'Aye, you did, and this,' she added unbuttoning the top of her blouse to expose the deep blue bruise on her chest.

'Oh my God! I'm so sorry love! I don't know what must 'ave come over me.'

Anne pondered whether to say something about the drink, hesitated and then buoyed up by having spoken to her sister about it, went on,

'You know what came over you Tommy. As always, it was the drink. You would never do this to us without the drink. Please, Tommy, you must find a way to stop. We can't take much more of it.'

With that, Tommy sank down in the chair before the fire with his head in his hands.

'I don't know how to stop, love. I do try, but when I have one, I need another and another and I forget everything else and just want the next drink.'

'Well, I went to see our Elizabeth today. I needed someone to talk to Tommy,' she told him with some trepidation.

'What?!' he cried out angrily, jumping out of the chair. 'You mean you told her what I'd done?'

Anne flinched at his anger but stood her ground.

'I 'ad to do somethin' after what 'appened to Jane. Something will 'ave to change Tommy.'

He glared down at her now, his fists clenched threateningly by his side.

'You 'ad no right, Anne!' he shouted.

Little Jane ran to her mother, fearing what her father would do next and she clung to her mother's skirts. Pulling the child's head towards her Anne went on, emboldened by her need to protect her children,

'You're wrong Tommy, I 'ave every right to seek help. When you struck Jane as you did, you lost any right you 'ad as far as I'm concerned.'

Tommy was taken aback by Anne's reaction. She had never stood up to him before and he wasn't sure how to deal with it. He stood stock still, fists still clenched and the muscles in his neck bulging as he wrestled with himself. Part of him was demanding that he quell this rebellion in his own house by whatever means he had, which in reality meant using his fists once again. On the other hand, his conscience was telling him she was right and without the drink in his system he was able to listen to it.

Anne watched with foreboding as he wrestled with his feelings. This was a new experience. She had never had the strength before to confront his behaviour so directly. She pulled her daughter closer to her while she waited to see which way things would go. After what seemed like minutes but was probably seconds, she saw his shoulders suddenly sag, and she knew that, for the moment she and the children were safe.

Tommy had tears in his eyes now as he pleaded with her once again to forgive him, and promised as earnestly as he could, to stop drinking. Anne was pleased he'd backed down but knew that there would still be a long fight ahead of him, and her too, if he was to stay off the drink.

However, she now knew she had the strength to help him to fight it, and for the first time she had some hope that together, they would be able to beat this curse that had fallen on their family.

Chapter 57

Late 1762

On the other side of the world, Walter opened his eyes, and remembered once more, how far away he was, in both time and space, from his home in Dale Coppice and the people he loved. He thought particularly of Susan. He had relived those precious moments under the oak tree countless times over the years, and the feelings the memory evoked were as real now as they ever were. For a moment, he wondered as he always did, whether she had waited for him as she had promised. It was nearly seven years since that fateful day when he had left the Boring Mill to join Charlie Fox and the others, called to action by the sound of the horns as they marched up towards the Darby works. That was a long time in a young woman's life, and he knew it was possible she may have found someone else. Then as always, he consciously dismissed the thought. He couldn't allow himself to doubt her. She had been his motivation to survive many times over the years, through the dreadful sufferings he had endured on the prison ship, and the long days of toil at the Baltimore Iron Works where he had finally ended up.

The nightmare of the horrors aboard the prison ship was never far from his thoughts, nor was the shame of being auctioned to the highest bidder like a piece of meat. However he pondered, in the end, he had been lucky, if that's what you could call it, to be 'bought' by the agent of the Baltimore Iron

Works. Unfortunately, Freddie Furlong hadn't been so lucky and was bought by the overseer of a sugar plantation, who looked as though he would enjoy inflicting pain on his unfortunate prisoners. Walter has never forgotten the look of terror in Freddy's eyes as they dragged him off to goodness knows where. He had never seen him since that day and often wondered how he had fared.

At least at the ironworks it was work Walter was familiar with, and the fact that he possessed some skills in the trade had given him advantages over his fellow 'indentured servants' as they called them. The Quaker owners of the works were better masters than most and treated their 'servants' reasonably well.

Sadly, the same couldn't really be said for their African slaves, who numbered around a hundred and fifty. Walter observed that their lives were dreadful, and their living conditions positively inhuman. They mainly worked on the tobacco plantation, but some of them were sent down the coalmine, spending fourteen hours a day digging at the coalface, even children of five or six. Others were set to breaking ironstones to be tipped into the top of the furnace. The women were expected to work as hard as the men on the tobacco plantation, even when they were heavily pregnant or nursing their infants, which they carried to the fields strapped to their backs.

After the day's work was done, as Walter lay on his straw mattress, he could often hear strange rhythmic drumming sounds emanating from their huts, accompanied by mournful songs, no doubt sung to remind them of their home from which, if the stories were to be believed, they had probably been snatched away.

Over the years he had witnessed cruelty beyond imagination, and he could never understand how his owners could treat his fellow prisoners with a degree of compassion but seemed incapable of doing the same for the Africans. In the end he concluded that the company owners just didn't regard the slaves as human beings at all, and that appalled Walter. He also observed that this state of affairs was in no way exceptional. It was repeated in all of the plantations, mines, and workplaces around the area, and as far as Walter knew, in every part of the American continent, and it sickened him.

Walter had a few months of his sentence to serve and was as determined as ever to make his way back home once it was finished. The Baltimore Company used a system known as 'overworking' and if a man worked hard and produced more than his expected quota, he was paid overtime in extra tokens which could be spent in the Company shop. Walter had chosen from the first, to save up all his tokens and he judged that if he could exchange them for dollars, he would have enough by the time he had served his sentence, to pay for his passage back to England, even if it was only steerage. It must be better than travelling as a prisoner, he mused. He was a hard worker which was appreciated by the overseer Mr Roberts, who it seemed had developed a certain respect for him. Walter felt sure Mr Roberts would ask the Company owner to change his tokens into cash when the time came.

He roused himself now as the overseer struck an iron ring hanging in the yard, with an iron bar, the signal for the workforce, whatever their tasks, to be on their feet and ready for work. The sun was still below the horizon, merely creating a glow in the eastern sky, as Walter hurried over to the waterbutt, bared to the waist, to wash himself. The 'servants' had a small hut where they gathered to eat their meagre meals. Breakfast was watery porridge with, wonder of wonders, a little honey.

After the years he had spent here he knew precisely what to do next. His duties involved overseeing the charging up of the furnace and he hurried over to it now, climbing the steps to the platform above the charging hole.

From his vantage point, he watched sadly as the Africans, old and young, trudged slowly away from their huts. They already looked weary, and the day had barely begun. Their food, if it could be called that, was served to them in the open air, rain, or shine, ladled onto crude wooden 'plates' from a huge cauldron boiling over an open fire. It consisted of a grey 'mush', which didn't resemble any food Walter had ever seen. There was no variation in their diet and the whole procedure was repeated as the sun disappeared from the western sky, when they staggered back exhausted, from their daily toils. Of course, they soon learned to eat it and say nothing, as any suggestion of a complaint brought the overseer's whip down across the back of the unfortunate wretch who dared to ask for better food.

Later that evening, when the Africans had arrived back in the yard after toiling in the hot sun, and were lining up to receive their meagre rations, one child, ten or eleven years old, was brave enough to ask for more to eat. Instantly his wooden platter was knocked from his grasp, spilling its meagre contents onto the ground. A tall African, who had been standing in line behind the boy, suddenly bellowed and tried to grab the arm of the overseer who had done it. Walter realised he must be a recent arrival. Not only was he still fitter than many of the others, but it was obvious that he hadn't yet learnt the rules of this cruel game. Walter cringed, knowing what must follow.

Immediately, two or three of the overseer's lackeys rushed at him, dragging him kicking and screaming to the ground. He was strong and fought as if his life depended on it, which, unfortunately as Walter knew, it may well do. It took six men in all to hold him down long enough to truss him up with ropes until finally, he was unable to move his arms or legs. Even so, the muscles over the whole of his body still strained against his bonds, and he continued to roar and writhe about, until one of the overseers picked up a rock and crashed it against his head, and finally he lay still.

They dragged him to the dreaded lock up, a structure about four feet high with no windows, just a strong iron door. They threw him in, still trussed up, and slammed the door shut. The rest of the slaves were cowering, knowing that if any-one objected, they would suffer the same fate. The overseer bellowed to them to keep moving and the line began to move once more.

It was in the middle of the night that a low moan began emanating from the lockup. The African had obviously re-gained consciousness, finding himself in complete blackness and trussed up like a turkey. Ignoring his moans, they left him there for the rest of the night and the whole of the next day. Walter noticed that by mid-day there was no longer any noise coming from the lockup and feared the worst.

As the Africans were once more lining up for their food, wanting to impress on them all what would happen if any one of them should defy their masters again, the overseers finally opened the lock up door and dragged the African out. To every-one's horror, he was lifeless. The blow to his head and twenty four hours trussed up in the blackness through the heat of the midday sun, without water and unable to move, had been too much for even his strong frame and indomitable will. He had given up the fight and was gone.

When the other Africans saw that he was dead, a low moan began to rise from them, and a ripple of angry murmuring grew until one of the overseers raised a whip and brought it down on the nearest back. It was a woman, and she screamed. The rest fell silent and moved back into line.

Walter couldn't help but be angry at this treatment of a man who had simply objected to the child's food being thrown to the floor. He thought about the reason he himself had joined the riots. He knew what hunger was, but seeing the way these souls were treated, he realised his life in Dale Coppice could have been a whole lot worse.

They removed the ropes, presumably not wishing to waste them. As they did so, Walter expected the man to be stretched out, but he must have been dead for some hours as his body and limbs remained folded tightly, and the lifeless man was carted off just as he was, probably to be thrown into the creek, which Walter had witnessed more than once before.

This was a cruel place, Walter thought as he watched them carry the African away. He was more determined than ever to forgo any small luxuries he might have bought with his tokens, and to save them up to buy his passage home as soon as he could. His father had often talked about the way slaves were treated in this land, but until witnessing it for himself, had never realised just how brutal it was. He knew that there were people in England trying to bring an end to this ghastly practice, and he determined that when he did get back to Shropshire, he would do what he could to bear witness to the horrors he had seen with his own eyes.

Chapter 58

1763

Walter opened his eyes and in the dim light of dawn seeping into the room from around the edge of the piece of hessian that served as a curtain, he observed his fellow prisoners still sleeping on their straw mattresses. They were a rough bunch, but over the years they had formed some kind of a bond. They were all in the same situation, far from home and loved ones, and their mutual need for companionship had brought them together. Unexpectedly Walter had to admit that he would be sorry to leave them. However, this was a fleeting thought, banished by the excitement of the prospect of seeing home and more particularly, Susan Bly, once again. His faith in her had never faltered and he was still convinced that she would be awaiting his return.

He had been eager to leave for home ever since his seven years indenture had been completed a couple of months earlier. He knew that shipments of pig iron had occasionally been sent from Baltimore over the Atlantic to the port of Bristol, and for some time had been hopeful that if a consignment was due to leave, perhaps he could work his passage home. He knew they had been producing pig iron bound for the English iron trade for some weeks and with rising excitement, had asked Mr Roberts if it was bound for Bristol. Mr Roberts confirmed that it was indeed, although it would be a couple of months before the shipment was ready. Walter had tentatively suggested that he would be prepared to work his passage home on the ship if Mr Croxall, the Company manager would allow it.

Walter had been a good worker and had earned the respect of his employer, who had agreed to speak to the ship's captain as soon as it arrived, and if there was a need for an additional deck hand, he would suggest they take Walter. Furthermore, Mr Croxall had agreed to convert Walter's tokens into cash. He was delighted. He would not be going home empty handed and would have some money to begin his life with Susan and to help his parents.

So the day had finally arrived. The last couple of months since he'd heard about the shipment had dragged by. Then, a week ago, the cargo ship The Venturer had arrived and Mr Roberts had confirmed that the captain had agreed that Walter could join it on the return journey to Bristol. Walter was ecstatic. He was finally going home!

For the past couple of months, he had continued to work, and no longer a prisoner, had been paid the going rate. He had used the money to buy second hand clothes. He was going home a free man and was determined to look the part. At the sound of the wake-up call ringing out, he jumped up out of bed and hurried outside to take a dip in the creek. Then he quickly dressed in the breeches, shirt, and jacket. Having worn only prisoners' clothes for seven years, he savoured the feeling of being a free man.

Picking up the bundle of his possessions he stepped out of the hut into the yard. He observed the too familiar, depressing scene of the Africans lining up for food, and once more swore to himself that when he was home, he would do whatever he could to make people aware of their plight. He had to admit though, that their lives were very slowly getting better, the quality and quantity of their food had improved of late, and there were rumours that soon they would be allowed to marry, and some provision was to be made for them to live in family groups. But these were mere rumours and somehow, he doubted it would ever happen.

After eating a hasty breakfast he said goodbye to his companions in the prisoner quarters then spoke to Mr Roberts who was in the yard overseeing procedures, to thank him for his help. The last of the pig iron shipment was being loaded as he strode towards the dock and his new temporary home aboard The Venturer. It was a three masted sailing ship that looked rather different from the one that had transported him to Chesapeake Bay. This ship was longer and narrower and looked to Walter as if it might be built for speed, which pleased him greatly. The thought of weeks at sea facing the dangers of the Atlantic storms, were rather daunting, and anything that shortened the journey was to be welcomed. He hoped fervently that the conditions aboard her would be better than those he had encountered on The Lark.

In fact, much to Walter's dismay, they were in many ways little better. Of course, they were not crammed into cells, but the crew of fifty men slept in hammocks strung between beams along the middle deck and they were close together with no privacy, the only exceptions being the Captain and the other officers, who were housed in cabins. Sanitation was provided by the usual buckets, each one shared by at least ten men. In contrast to his previous experiences though, the food was reasonably plentiful, if a little boring, consisting mainly of a dry biscuit they called hardtack, salted beef, and beans, with the occasional piece of dried fruit. Understandably, fresh water was at a premium and they were given their ration twice a day.

Walter had to quickly learn new skills, his only previous experience of life aboard a sailing ship being that of a prisoner confined below decks most of the time. After the years of hard labour at the furnace he was strong and reasonably fit, so he was able to cope well with the long hours hauling the sails and other duties. At least having plenty to do made the days pass quickly, unlike the endless hours he'd spent without hope during the weeks he'd been incarcerated on The Lark.

However, when they finally left the relative shelter of Chesapeake Bay and sailed out into the Atlantic Ocean, the weather deteriorated rapidly. As they sailed into the first storm a couple of days later the cry of 'all hands on deck' was heard throughout the ship and Walter understood why. Experiencing Atlantic storms confined in the cell in the bowels of The Lark, being crashed against the walls and fellow prisoners had been terrifying. However as he was about to discover, to be on deck fighting to control the ship, while being lashed by a force ten gale would terrify him even more. As the ship climbed to the top of a particularly huge wave rearing high above them, he held his breath as he knew what would follow. He felt the familiar shuddering of the ship as it struggled over the peak of the wave, and the First Mate shouted desperately,

'She's going over! Hold on!'

Walter threw his arms around the nearest stanchion, holding on with all his strength as The Venturer plunged headfirst into the trough. One unlucky deck hand had failed to hold on to anything and Walter watched in horror as the oncoming wave broke over the deck and snatched the man away. One second, he was there and the next he was washed away into the Atlantic. Walter knew there was no chance of saving him. He was gone forever.

After what seemed like hours the storm abated, and the crew began to take stock of the damage. Below decks it was awash with the water that had poured through the gratings as wave after wave had washed over the ship. Many men were set to bailing it out, and then mopping up the residual mixture of sea water and night soil which had spilled from the upturned buckets. Thankfully, Walter was given other tasks on this occasion, although he wasn't so lucky when subsequent storms hit the ship. Finally, after several weeks the weather suddenly, it seemed, changed completely. Now the problem seemed to be a lack of wind, not too much of it, and for a couple of days, the sails hung limply against the masts, and they were virtually becalmed.

Realising that he must be over halfway towards journey's end at Bristol, Walter was impatient now. How unpredictable this ocean is he thought, as he lay in his hammock in the fetid air below deck. However it did give him time to think. He was a little apprehensive about what he would find at home. Would his father still be alive? He had known when he left that Will was ill. What would have happened to his mother if Will had passed away? Probably George would be taking care of her. And what about Susan. He hardly dared to think about her now. Believing she was waiting for him had been the main reason he'd survived the worst of the horrors he'd suffered. He felt he wouldn't be able to bear it if she had found someone else.

Finally after two days and nights he woke to feel the motion of the ship under sail, and apparently moving rapidly along. As he climbed up onto the deck, he was pleased to see that the sky was blue with just a few white clouds scurrying along on the westerly breeze that was carrying the ship along at a fair pace. He overheard one of his shipmates asking the First Mate how long he thought it might be before they would see England and was delighted to hear that with this fair wind behind them, they may make landfall within the week. This was good news indeed.

He knew that once he landed in Bristol it would be an easy matter to find a vessel heading up to Gloucester, and from there he would catch an upriver trow to the Gorge. His excitement grew with every day that passed now. It seemed that all the hurt and horrors of the past years had melted away, leaving only joy at the prospect of seeing his home and loved ones once more.

Finally he was swilling the deck one morning when a cry of 'land ahoy' was heard from the Crow's Nest. The English coast had been sighted. A rousing cheer went up, as to a man, the crew expressed their relief that this journey was nearly over. They anchored for a couple of hours just outside the mouth of the Bristol Channel to await the turn of the tide.

Tears sprang up in many an eye as with sails unfurled and flags flying, they were finally riding the tide up the estuary towards Bristol, savouring views of England on the starboard side and Wales on the port side. Against all the odds Walter had survived and made it back to his homeland. Not many would have expected it, as few prisoners who were transported across the ocean ever returned, and he silently thanked God for it, even though he had never been particularly religious. Within a day he would be sailing up the Severn to the Gorge, home, and Susan!

Unbeknown to Walter, his cousin Ben and his new wife were also aboard a sailing ship. The Adventurer, sailing in the opposite direction, having left by the outflowing tide was at that very moment heading westwards into the Atlantic Ocean. Ben and Mary had been married just four weeks before setting off on the epic journey to their new life. They had stood on deck watching the English coastline disappearing over the horizon, full of hope, yes, but also fear of what they must face before reaching the New World with all its opportunities.

Ben had been gleaning some knowledge of the conditions aboard settler ships, and the hazards of sailing into the prevailing winds of the Atlantic, and he was under no illusion as to the privations and possible dangers that awaited them. Well, here they were, Ben mused as he stood beside his wife staring at the empty horizon. For better or worse, that's what they had promised each other just a few short weeks ago, and now whatever should befall them, they would face it together. He glanced at his wife and noticed a tear trickling from the corner of her eye. No doubt she was thinking about the loved ones they had left behind, and whether they would ever see them again. He put his arm around her shoulder and gently drew her to him but couldn't find words at that moment to comfort her as his own feelings almost overpowered him.

Their families had given them a good send off, even though many tears were shed. Everyone knew that few people ever returned from America, and that this was likely to be their final farewell. Some couldn't understand why they had made the decision to journey into the unknown, far away from everyone and everything they had ever known. Others were slightly envious, realising that they would personally never find the courage to do such a thing.

Chapter 59

The docks were bustling as The Venturer pulled alongside. Waggon loads of goods to be loaded onto the ships were trundled along the cobblestones. Lines of passengers, men, women, and children were lining up at the various gangplanks, ready to board the ship that would carry them across the ocean. Other ships were being unloaded, with scores of seamen carrying heavy boxes or rolling barrels down to the waiting waggons on the dockside. As Walter surveyed the scene, memories flooded back of that terrible day nearly eight years ago now, when, along with his fellow prisoners he had been herded in chains to be thrown into the hell hole they called 'The Lark'.

He remembered how he had dreaded boarding that ship, but that even in his worst nightmares he could never have imagined what he would face in the weeks ahead. He quickly shook his head as if to drive out the memories and strove to concentrate on the future instead. The past was dead and gone, he told himself, now he could look forward to picking up the pieces of his old life, seeing his family and of course, his beloved Susan Bly.

After leaving The Venturer, he found the shipping office and enquired as to whether any of the ships being loaded were bound for the Gloucester Docks. He was told by an officious looking clerk that the trow, Lucky Lady, would be travelling upriver on the next incoming tide, to take a load of pig-iron which was eventually bound for the Severn Gorge. Walter couldn't believe his luck and hurried along to find the vessel and found the skipper, enquiring if he could join them.

The captain of The Lucky Lady was agreeable, and they negotiated a price that suited them both. Walter soon found a suitable space below deck to stow his belongings. His needs were few, accustomed as he was, to enjoying little or no comfort. He was simply glad to be beginning his journey back to Dale Coppice. After buying some food and drink from a street seller on the wharf, he returned to the ship and settled down for the night.

He was awakened at first light by the gentle swaying of the boat as it picked up speed, heading inland. Walter climbed up on deck and was glad to see that they had already left the port and were making good progress. Asking one of the deckhands when he expected they would reach Gloucester, the man replied,

'Noon at the latest mate if we can keep up this speed.'

Walter settled down in a corner of the deck now to watch the English countryside slipping by. He was happy to notice the wonderful autumn colours of the forests of oak, elder, and ash reaching down to the water's edge in places. He hadn't realised until now, how different the landscape of Chesapeake Bay had been. The weather had been hot and humid, and the vigorous vegetation was always struggling to encroach on any spare piece of open ground. He supposed that when he had arrived there, he hadn't been in any fit state to notice much of anything and had subsequently tried his best not to think too much of the land he had left behind. Now that he was home, he allowed himself the luxury of wondering at the beauty of it and swore to himself he would never leave it again.

As predicted, the sun was at its zenith as the Lucky Lady drew up alongside the dock in Gloucester. Thanking the captain, Walter disembarked and strode along to the section of the wharf where the upriver trows were being loaded. He knew that some of them may well be heading up to Shrewsbury and passing through the Gorge on the way. He was overjoyed to see a familiar name on one of the trows. It was the Severn Lady, belonging to Owner Blake. They were loading a shipment of iron pigs no doubt bound for the Coalbrookdale forges. On enquiring when the trow was due to leave, and being told it would be several hours before they would be ready, he negotiated a fare with the trowman for him to travel with them to the Gorge, then left the ship to find refreshments at an inn alongside the docks.

After enjoying a hearty meal and ale to wash it down, he enquired if he might find somewhere to wash and change his clothes as he had been travelling for some time. For a price, the innkeeper showed him to a room that he could use and brought hot water for him to wash. Walter felt quite the gentleman as he stripped, washed, and dressed in new shirt, breeches, and coat he had brought with him all the way from Chesapeake Bay, saved carefully for his homecoming. He was determined that when Susan set eyes on him, he would bear no resemblance to the filthy, dishevelled creature she had bade farewell to all those years ago. . He tied his hair back in a ponytail and surveyed himself in the mirror on the wall. He hadn't actually enjoyed the luxury of observing himself in a mirror since leaving Dale Coppice and was surprised at his reflection. He looked older of course, but his shoulders seemed broader and his waist narrower. His skin was brown and his hair lighter than he remembered. Overall, he was highly satisfied with what he saw. Picking up his bag he strode out of the room, ready now to face the future that awaited him.

Making his way back to The Severn Lady, he was soon on board and eagerly awaiting its departure. He was told that they would only travel as far as Bridgnorth that day, and tie up there for the night, sailing on to the Gorge at first light, and should, with plenty of water in the river and a fair wind, arrive there by mid-day. Walter was disappointed that this meant another day's delay before reaching home, but he knew there was nothing to be done about it.

So it was, that at noon on the third day after arriving in Bristol, he was almost overcome with emotion as he saw for the first time in eight years, the familiar outline of the Gorge. Within ten minutes the Severn Lady slid into the wharf at Dale End and in no time at all he was striding up Lincoln Hill, eager to reach Dale Coppice to see his mother, and maybe his father, although he had long ago prepared himself for the possibility that he may have passed away in his absence.

When he arrived at the Coppice, he was relieved to see that little had changed there. He glanced fondly and longingly at the Bly's cottage, but not knowing yet how things were with Susan, he decided he would first go to see his mother. He strode up to the cottage door and without knocking, quickly lifted the latch and entered. He was shocked to see, not his mother or father sitting on the settle, but a young woman with two children at her feet.

Anne looked up quickly as Walter entered, then jumped up and declared,

'What... Who... Who are you? What are you doing in my house?'

'Your house? What do you mean, where is my mother?'

'Oh, my goodness,' Anne exclaimed, 'You're Walter! I didn't know you!'

'Oh, now I can see it's you Anne! What are you doing here? What's happened to mother and father?'

'Oh Walter, it's good to see you back but a lot has 'appened since you left us, and not all of it will be good news for you I'm afraid. But come in and set yourself down and I'll tell you all about it.'

'Thanks Anne, but I can't sit down, I need to know what's happened to them, are they both passed away?

'Oh Walter, I'm sorry to tell you that yes, your father did pass away, not long after you left. It was the pneumonia that took 'im in the end.'

'And what about mother? Where is she?'

'She's well Walter, as far as I know. After your father passed, George took her to Madeley Wood to live with them. Oh goodness, she'll be beside herself when she sees you've come home to her!'

'I must go to her straight away Anne, but first I must call at the Bly's cottage to get news of Susan. I don't suppose you know if she's still in service at Harden House Anne?'

'Well, I believe so as she comes to visit her mother and father every couple of weeks still.'

Walter's heart leapt in his chest. Dare he hope that she had waited for him just as she'd promised?

'But Anne, what are you doing here, and with these two little ones?'

'Well, Walter, I'm married now, to Tommy Flint, and after your mother left, father let us have the cottage, so here we are!'

'Well, I'm glad to see you settled and making good use of the old place Anne. Anyway I must be off now, and I'm sure I'll be seeing you soon. Tell your Da that I'm back when you see him.'

Anne's face clouded over as she told him that both her mother and father were gone, taken within a year of each other.

'Oh, I'm so sorry to hear that, Anne. There have been too many changes since I left. How are Nat and Ben?'

'Well, Ben left over a week ago, with his new wife, bound for America. I believe their ship was to sail from Bristol four days ago!'

'What? Noo! It's just three days since we landed at Bristol! Their ship must have passed by ours while we stood off waiting for the tide! Well they've got a long hard journey ahead of them, and no mistake, but I would have liked to have seen them before they left, I could have told them a thing or two about America, that's for sure. Although on second thoughts maybe it's as well that I didn't, they'll find out soon enough for themselves.'

'And Nat is married to Mary Lavin and still in Nailer's Row. They have a son, Thomas, and seem well settled.'

'Well that's good news at least, I hope to see them soon Anne, but now I really must be on my way.'

They embraced, a little awkwardly after not seeing each other for so many years, and then Walter left and strode over to the Bly's cottage to enquire after Susan.

Walter stood for a moment or two outside the door to the Bly's cottage. The time had finally arrived when he would find out whether Susan had been as good as her word. What if she had moved her life on with someone else? How could he stand it? Well, he thought, there's only one way to find out and knocked sharply on the door.

Susan's mother Grace opened the door and after just a moment's hesitation, threw her hands up in the air, declaring,

'Lordy! Walter! You're a sight to behold for sure! Come in lad and set yourself down by the fire!'

'Thank you, Mrs Bly, but I can't stay, I've just found out about Da, and mother being in Madeley Wood with George, and I must go to her straightaway, but I had to find out about Susan.'

'O'course, you did son,' Grace replied, 'Well, you don't need to worry, she's never doubted that you would return. She'll be overjoyed to see you now, and looking so handsome, if I might be so bold!'

Walter was grinning now, happy at last and daring to hope that his dream of a life with Susan may finally come to pass.

'Is she still at Harden House?' he enquired quickly.

'She is Walter. So off you go now to your mother and then to find Susan, and God bless you both, lad.'

With that, Walter took the liberty of kissing Grace on the cheek, which startled her slightly but nevertheless caused her to preen a little. Then he turned on his heels and headed off down the track that would take him over the hill to Madeley Wood.

Chapter 60

Running most of the way Walter arrived at the main street through the village in about twenty minutes. He noticed that unlike the Coppice, this place had undergone quite a lot of change since he'd last seen it on the day the protestors had made their way up to Madeley market. That seemed like a lifetime ago now. One or two familiar faces nodded at him as he passed, although he couldn't have put a name to any of them.

Finally, he found George's workshop. As he entered, he was surprised to find several men working at various pieces of machinery. It was obvious that his brother's business was thriving. There were several part-finished pieces of fine furniture around the place, obviously bound for grand houses, certainly not for any squatter home.

Walter asked one of the men if George was around and was told that he could be found in his office in the house next door. The tall polished wooden door on the house next to the workshop reinforced Walter's feeling that George's business was doing well, and he excitedly knocked using the impressive cast iron door knocker, expecting to see his mother opening it. However, he was slightly disappointed when it was opened by a young woman he had never seen before.

'Hello, sir,' she said, 'Can I help you?'

Realising that this must be a parlour maid, or some such, and said he had come to see Mrs Betty Bangham.

'Who shall I say is calling sir?' she asked politely.

'Mr Walter Bangham, Mr George Bangham's brother,' he replied, rather annoyed at all this formality.

'Oh!' the maid went on, obviously rather embarrassed, 'Please come in sir and I'll tell the mistress that you're here.'

The maid disappeared into one of the rooms off the hall while Walter waited impatiently behind the front door. This was not the welcome he had imagined. Within a couple of minutes, the door to the room opened and Sally stepped out, smiling broadly and declaring,

'Why, Walter, we had no idea! How? When did you get back?'

'It's a long story Sally, but it's good to see you. Is mother here?'

'She is, and she's going to be overjoyed to see you home again. But look, do come in here,' she said, gesturing to the open door of the room she had just left, 'and I'll go and fetch her.'

Walter stepped into the room which as he might have expected was full of fine furniture, no doubt built in the workshop next door. There was a handsome fireplace with a welcoming fire in the hearth.

'Please, Walter, do sit down,' Sally instructed, 'I'll go and find your mother, and George, of course.'

While he waited, Walter glanced around the room at the fine china ornaments, the shelves full of books, and the pictures on the wall, and once again realised that George was moving up in the world, and he was glad for him.

A few minutes later there was the sound of several footsteps in the hallway and Betty burst through the door. Walter jumped up and seeing her beloved son standing there, Betty couldn't speak, she simply opened her arms wide as he rushed across the room and threw his arms around her, saying,

'Mother, it's so good to see you!'

Overcome with emotion, still Betty couldn't speak, but simply clung to her son with tears rolling down her cheeks.

Eventually, after a minute or two, she gently pulled away and stood back to look at him. She had so many questions running through her head but knew there would be time for them later. For now, she just wanted to bask in the knowledge that the son she thought was lost, had come back to her.

'Well, I can't tell you 'ow good it is to see you standin' 'ere. I 'ardly dared 'ope it would 'appen, yet 'ere you are!' she said softly, the tears starting up in her eyes once again.

Sarah stepped forward saying,

'Betty, Walter, come and sit by the fire and I'll fetch George. He's going to be thrilled to see you, Walter.'

Mother and son sat down on the sofa by the fire and Walter placed an arm around his mother's shoulders as they both just enjoyed each other's closeness. For the moment words were unnecessary, they would come later.

After a few minutes, the door opened, and George stepped into the room, declaring,

'Walter! By, it's good to see you!'

Walter stood up and the two brothers embraced, clapping each other on the back.

'Well It's good to be back!'

'We'll want to know all about it, I'm sure you've got many a tale to tell us, but we should think about practicalities too. You'll need somewhere to stay as Anne and Tommy are living in the old place, and you must stay with us until you get sorted out.'

'That's kind of you George, and I'd be grateful for it, although I hope it won't be long before I'll need a home of my own.'

Walter smiled at his mother, who smiled knowingly back, saying,

'You may be right son. That young lady of yours is still waiting as far as we know. She's still in service at Harden House and I've heard no mention of anybody else on the scene.'

'I must go to her, before she hears about me from anyone else,' he announced.

'Of course,' George replied, 'but you've had a long journey, perhaps you'd like to take a wash and change of clothes – I have some you can use. You want to make a good impression after all these years away.'

Walter smiled, 'Do I smell so bad?'

George also smiled and simply said, 'Yes! Anyway give me a few minutes to organise a bath for you and find some clothes.'

'A bath! Good grief George, you certainly have moved up in the world! Whoever thought of a Bangham having a bath!'

'First time for everything, little brother!' he replied, throwing the words back to him as he left the room.

Then Will turned to Betty, saying,

'I was so sad to hear about Da, Mother. I could see he wasn't well when I left, but what happened, exactly?'

'Oh Walter, he was so poorly after you'd gone, and he just hadn't the will to fight it. He blamed himself for what happened to you, you know.'

'What? No, he shouldn't have done that. It was my decision to join the protest, and no one else's.'

'I know, and I tried to tell 'im as much, but whatever I said made no difference. O' course 'e knew better than anybody what suffering you would be facin', and I think that's what preyed on his mind. How was it, really, son?'

'Well, it's over, and for now I don't even want to think about that Ma.'

'No, you've got to sort your life out 'ere now, and 'opefully marry that young lady o' yours.'

Just then they heard George summoning Walter to go upstairs as everything was ready for him. He embraced his mother once more then made his way up the staircase in the hall. In the bedroom at the front of the house he found George laying out some clothes for him on the bed and in front of the fireplace stood a bathtub filled with steaming water. George left him to it, saying,

'Take your time Walt, I'm sure Sally will have some food prepared when you've finished and then you can go and find that lass of yours!'

Half an hour later he was bounding down the stairs and into the parlour but finding it empty went in search of the others. He found them in the dining room, just about to sit down at the table which was already set with china cups and saucers and shiny knives and forks.

'Walter! Well, I think it is,' quipped George.

Walter grinned, saying that he must have a bath more often, it had been grand. He had also washed his hair and it was still wet, but he'd tied it into a ponytail. The clothes George had found for him were slightly large, but smart nonetheless and he looked quite the gentleman. Betty glanced at her sons and was proud of them both. If only Will had been here to see this day.

The maid came in with bowls of cold beef, potatoes and vegetables, and Sally served them each in turn before sitting down next to George. The children, John, Alice and Benjamin had joined them and seemed slightly in awe of this stranger who had been made so welcome in their home. He was introduced to them as their uncle Walter and then they understood; they had been told about him many times over the years and that he might one day return.

Walter could see they were growing up to be delightful children. John and Alice had only been little when he left and Benjamin not yet born, but he could see that they were bright children and were being well brought up. It was obvious that given George's successful business and the education they would undoubtedly be given, they would all do well in the world. He determined that the same would happen for his own children if he was fortunate enough to have any, at which point his thoughts as always turned to Susan and although he had only just finished eating, he declared that he really must be going.

Betty, Sally and George all smiled broadly and George said,

'Of course you must. Off you go, and good luck!'

'Thanks,' he said, standing quickly, 'but I hope I won't need any!'

Chapter 61

The light was fading as he strode up the hill towards Harden House. His heart was pounding and not only from the exertion of climbing the hill. His excitement grew with each step. He had waited so long for this moment, and now it had arrived he was afraid it wouldn't work out as he had dreamed it would. Would Susan still feel the same as she did that day under the oak tree? Had he been magnifying the importance of that moment of intimacy to sustain himself during the long years of hardship and deprivation? As he reached the back door of Harden House he hesitated for a moment before knocking.

After a minute or so the door opened by a young girl who, from her appearance was the scullery maid. She was very young, maybe twelve years old or so and didn't seem to know what to say. Walter helped her out by asking to speak to Miss Susan Bly.

'Just a minute, sir,' the girl replied and disappeared through a door to the left. He heard her telling someone that there was a man at the door asking for Susan Bly. He also heard a woman saying impatiently,

'What on earth does he want, coming here at this time of day.'

The door was opened by a large woman whose frame almost filled the doorway as she stood there, wiping her hands on her apron.. She looked rather intimidating, but her attitude softened slightly when she saw a handsome young man who looked rather prosperous standing in front of her.

'What's this then? You want to speak to Susan? May I ask what business you have with her?'

'I need to speak with her urgently, please mistress, it is very important.'

Something about the earnestness in his voice and his eyes convinced the cook, and she said,

'Alright then, who shall I say is calling?'

'Please mistress,' he replied, 'I would prefer to surprise her. Could you just give her a message that a friend needs to speak with her?'

With a 'Hummmph' the cook plodded down the hall and opened a door on the right. He could hear her speaking to someone in the room, and from what she was saying it could only have been Susan. His heart leapt as he heard her voice asking who it was. The cook told her he wouldn't give his name, but it was a young man, and a handsome one, at that.

Then Susan was standing there, in the corridor, not twenty feet away. His heart was thumping in his chest. She looked every bit as lovely as he remembered. He was as tongue-tied as that first time he saw her walking out of the woods, no longer the little girl he used to play with.

'Susan,' was all he could manage, but it was enough.

'Walter!' she declared, and as she hurried towards him all his doubts disappeared and he opened his arms wide to receive her, oblivious of the cook's 'Lordy me!' as they held each other tightly, the years of separation rolling away now. They were together again, and both swore to themselves that they would never again be parted.

For a full minute they stood like that. Walter could feel Susan trembling with emotion. Then he gently lifted her chin and kissed her softly and lingeringly on the lips. Then, suddenly becoming aware of the cook, standing behind Susan with mouth open, he gently whispered in her ear,

'When can we meet, properly.'

'This Sunday is my day off and I'll be going up to visit ma and da. Meet me at the gate at nine,' she replied.

As Sunday was two days away and seemed like an eternity to wait, it took considerable effort on both their parts to release themselves from their embrace, but the sound of the cook clearing her throat reminded Walter that this was neither the time nor place to linger longer. He gently pulled away and kissed her lightly on the forehead.

'Until Sunday then,' he whispered, smiling down at her.

She looked up with shining eyes and repeated, 'Until Sunday.'

Then reluctantly, she turned and walked back down the corridor. Walter watched her go until she reached the door of the room, where she turned and gave him one of her wonderful smiles before disappearing into the room.

'Well! I can see why you had to see her, lad!' ' declared the cook as she opened the door to let him out.

Walter beamed at her, thanking her for her help, then strode off into the night.

He felt as if a great weight had been lifted from his shoulders. All those years of longing, wondering whether she would be feeling the same, hoping that when he returned, she would be waiting for him, had now disappeared. Now he knew that Susan Bly had remained true. The years of misery were behind him and only happiness stretched ahead. Whatever the trials they would have to face, they would face them together.

When Walter arrived back at George's house, he went to find his mother who was sitting in front of the parlour fire. As soon as Betty looked at his face, she knew his mission had been successful, but nevertheless, wanting to give him the chance to tell her, asked,

'Well son? How did you get on?'

'Oh Ma! I can hardly take it in. She's waited all those years for me to come home! And Ma, she's as beautiful as ever.'

'That's wonderful son,' Betty replied, beaming.

'O' course, we couldn't say much there, but as this Sunday's her day off, she's going to see her Ma and Da and I've said I'll meet her at nine up at the House, but it seems hard to have to wait another three days before we can be together properly.'

'After eight years apart son, three days'll soon pass, you'll see.'

Of course, two days actually seemed like another two years to Walter and Susan. He decided to spend some of the time visiting his cousins in Coalbrookdale. On the Friday afternoon he made his way over the hill to call on Nat and his wife Mary, who he had not yet met. He arrived at Nailer's Row in the middle of the afternoon. Knocking on the front door but getting no answer, he made his way round to the yard at the back of the row, and there he found a young woman he assumed was probably Mary, hanging out some washing, with a little child of about eighteen months toddling around her.

'Hello!' he called out.

She turned and saw a young man, well-dressed and tanned with sun-bleached hair tied back in a ponytail, standing at her gate.

'Hello,' she replied, 'I'm sorry, do I know you?'

'Well, I'm guessing you're Mary, my cousin Nat's wife?'

'Oh, you must be Walter! Sure, we heard from one of the bargees that you were back!' she replied in her soft Irish brogue that Walter found very pleasing to the ear

'I am, and I was hoping to see Nat, and meet yourself too, of course!'

Then scooping up her son she stepped across the yard and opened the gate, declaring,

'Well, do come on in!'

She led Walter through the back door of the cottage and set the boy down on the rug, then turned to Walter.

'Nat's at work but he'll be home by six. He'll be glad to see you Walter, I hope you can stay and have some supper with us?'

'Thanks Mary, that will be grand,' then glancing down at the child, went on, 'So, this is Thomas?'

'It is Walter,' she replied, ruffling the child's hair fondly as he grinned broadly at his mother.

'Well, there's no mistaking he's a Bangham, Mary. He's the image of his father.'

'Come into the front room, I've got a good fire on, so set yourself down. I'll get us a drink.'

The child toddled off after his mother as she went back into the kitchen and Walter was left alone. The fire was blazing brightly and glancing around, he could see the room was full of little touches, there were china ornaments on the mantlepiece and on the windowsill. A white cloth trimmed with lace, presumably made by Mary, covered the table The rag rug was bright and colourful, presumably newly made. There were lacy curtains at the window, they too probably made by his cousin's wife. Altogether it presented a cosy picture if not one of affluence. There's a lot of love gone into creating this home, and if Susan and I can create one as comfortable and welcoming as this, life will be perfect, he thought.

Mary and Walter spent an hour or two catching up with the events of the past eight years. She told him that she hadn't met Nat until after his Ma and Da had passed, so she couldn't tell him much about how it came about, but she knew Liz's death had been sudden, within a few days of her becoming ill. Joe however, had died because of a tragic accident, when he had fallen down the steps at the furnace and broken his neck.

Walter was shocked. He had always loved his Uncle Joe.

'That's terrible Mary.'

'It must have been,' she agreed, 'I know it hit them all hard.'

'And I believe I just missed seeing Ben and his new wife? Their ship bound for America must have passed mine as we stood off the Bristol Channel, waiting for the tide.'

'Yes, that's a shame. No one could believe it when Ben told us he intended to settle in the New World. I think he was swayed by the promise of a piece of land of his own.'

'Well, they've a lot of struggles and hardships ahead of them, I hope they know what they're taking on,' Walter said, 'although I know father had told Ben all about that over the years.'

'Yes, I believe he spent some time in America?'

'Not really by choice,' Walter replied, 'but that's a long story. Anyway, how's our Nat? Still working as a mould maker at the old furnace site?'

'He is. It's hard work, like everything round here, but as a skilled man he gets decent pay. The Coalbrookdale Company are decent employers, and they gave Nat the lease to this place after Joe died.'

'Well, I must say, you've made it very comfortable, Mary.'

After an hour or so, she said she must start preparing supper, and Walter spent a pleasant hour playing with his little cousin Thomas, who turned out to be a pleasant and responsive child. With a promising smell emanating from the kitchen, Walter began to feel hungry. Finally, the latch on the door rattled and Nat appeared in the doorway.

'Oh my God!' Nat declared, 'Walter!'

Walter sprung up and embraced his cousin as he stepped into the room.

'Good to see ye!' Nat went on.

'Good to be here, I can tell ye,' Walter agreed.

'Well, I must say, you're looking well, if a little older, like us all!'

Mary came in and strode over to Nat to receive his customary peck on her cheek.

'Hello love,' he said. 'I hope you've been looking after this cousin of mine!'

'She certainly has,' Walter interjected.

'Well, supper's nearly ready, so get washed up Nat and I'll bring it out.'

Nat disappeared into the kitchen to wash his hands and face while Mary proceeded to lay plates and glasses of ale, inviting Walter to come and sit up at the table, then returned to the kitchen, presumably to fetch the food. It was Nat who reappeared carrying a large pot of delicious smelling chicken and vegetable stew.

Little Thomas continued to play around on the floor at their feet while they tucked into their supper served with chunks of bread. Walter declared that it was literally the best meal he'd eaten in eight long years and Liz beamed at the compliment. As they ate, Walter said how sorry he had been to hear about Liz and Joe.

'Aye, it was a hell of a shock I can tell you, particularly Da going like 'e did. I think that's one reason our Ben decided to leave you know. I think 'e thought about Da toiling all those years at that confounded furnace that in a way, did for him in the end. 'E was determined to see something of the world that Da never had the chance to, and I think he had a point, really.'

'Well, I hope you're not thinking the same Nat Bangham!' Mary interjected, 'Because if you are, you'd have to go without me!' her smile softening her words.

'Nay lass!' Nat quickly replied with a grin. 'Either I'm not as foolish as our Ben, or I just don't have the guts to do it.'

'Well speaking as one who knows a bit about America and the journey to get there, I think you're wise to stay here. For all its faults, there is no place England, and particularly the Gorge.'

Nat enquired about Aunt Betty and George and Sally and their family.

'Business is doing well by all accounts. In fact I'm hoping he might find me work. I don't want to go back into iron making, after the eight years hard labour I just spent on top of a furnace.'

'I don't blame you Walter, I wish I had some way out of it, so if George can take you on, good luck to you.'

'Well, from what I've seen in the past day or two, business round here is booming! There seems to be a new furnace around every corner. I hope some of the proceeds are spread out a bit, like, and not staying in the owners' pockets.'

'Not much changes in that direction Walt. The Darbys still prosper more than ever, although they've had their share of grief, what with Abraham passing a couple of months back. His son-in-law Reynolds has taken over for now as young Abraham's still a child. But Reynolds is capable enough and a fair manager so I guess it could be worse.'

After a short pause he changed the subject by asking, 'Have you seen anything of Susan yet?'

At the mention of Susan, Walter felt his face flush, and hoping that Nat and Mary hadn't noticed, quickly replied,

'Yes, I saw her yesterday and am meeting her on Sunday, on her day off.'

'Well,' said Nat, 'I had heard she was still up at Harden House.'

'She is, and I can hardly believe it, after all these years.'

Mary glanced from one to the other questioningly, but Nat hadn't missed Walter's blushes and realised that this was a sensitive subject, so looking at Mary he just gave a slight shake of his head, indicating that he would explain later. Nat quickly changed the subject by asking whether Walter had seen anything of Elizabeth. He said he hadn't but intended to call on her the next day.

They chatted on for some time after supper, until Walter declared that he had to be getting back over the hill, then took his leave, revelling in the statement that he 'would see them all again soon'.

Chapter 62

As Walter walked quickly up the track leading back to Madeley Wood, he indulged once more in thoughts of Susan. In two days he would see her again and after visiting the home that Nat and Mary had created, was already planning how he could achieve the same for her. Would he, could he, go back to ironworking? It was the last thing he wanted to do. He'd had enough of it after the gruelling years spent at the furnace in Baltimore. After talking to Nat the idea of possibly working for George was solidifying in his mind. He had never tried his hand at carpentry but knew he was a quick learner. Surely, he would be able to make himself useful. He determined to speak to George about it once he and Susan had discussed it and decided where they wanted to live.

He was up with the dawn on the Sunday morning. This was the day he'd been living for. After he'd washed and dressed, he went downstairs and found that his mother was also up and about. She had prepared him some porridge for his breakfast. He really felt too excited to eat but as she had made the effort of getting up early to make it, he forced himself to eat. Then, when he was ready to go, Betty embraced him saying,

'Good luck lad, although, I don't think you'll need it. I think we all know you two were meant to be together.'

'Thanks Ma,' he replied, and grinning down at her kissed her lightly on the top of her head.

As he strode up the track towards Harden House, hazy sunshine was just beginning to fight its way through the constant smog that hung about the Gorge. This was something that Walter had noticed since he'd arrived in Madeley Wood. He assumed rightly, that it was caused by the huge increase in the number of furnaces in the Gorge since he'd left. It seemed like a new one had appeared round every corner, all spewing out smoke and sparks into the once fragrant air, and acrid fumes, which caught the back of the throat with each breath.

As he arrived at the back gate to Harden House, the church clock was striking nine. Susan wasn't there, and still hadn't appeared as the clock struck the quarter hour. He was beginning to worry that something had prevented her from coming. He knew it would be unusual for a servant not to be allowed their usual day off. However, after their brief encounter earlier, he didn't doubt her intention to meet him, and so he waited patiently either for her to appear or send him a message that she wasn't able to come. He had just about given up hope of seeing her that day, when the back door of Harden House opened, and Susan stepped hurriedly out and almost ran down the path towards him.

She threw herself into his arms, oblivious as to who might see.

'I'm so sorry,' she blurted, 'I just couldn't get away. Madam decided she wanted her hair dressing, as she had to visit a sick friend this morning.'

'Don't worry love, you're here now and that's all that matters.'

'I was afraid you might have gone.'

'Nay I've waited eight long years for this Susan Bly, and I would have waited eight more!'

She smiled up at him and reached up to kiss him lightly on the cheek, then hand in hand they turned and walked down toward Madeley Wood.

'So, shall we make our way up to the Coppice right away?' Walter asked her.

After a moment or two she answered,

'I would like to go up to Ma and Da's, but perhaps we could first take a walk in the woods?'

She gazed up at him, her eyes shining and full of longing, and he understood perfectly what she was telling him. They strode quickly past George's house, not noticing Betty, who was sitting by the window, watching for them to pass. She had an inkling where they might be heading and she smiled indulgently as they swung by, making for the path over to Dale Coppice.

After a hundred yards or so, they did turn into the path leading up to Lincoln Hill. Twenty minutes later, their feet had taken them to the one place on earth that was theirs, and theirs alone. They were deep in the woods, and Walter was sure they wouldn't be disturbed. He was determined that this time it would be no hurried affair. He took off his coat and laid it on the earth beneath the tree.

For a few moments they lay together side by side, gazing up at the branches of the magnificent oak, just holding hands with mounting passion. Walter turned on his side and leaning on one elbow, gazed down at her. Slowly, he bent his head and kissed her gently on the lips. She moaned slightly and her lips responded. Their kisses grew more urgent, until finally she reached up and pulled him towards her and he positioned his body above hers. By unspoken mutual consent they were determined to savour this moment that they had waited for, for so long. This was to be no hurried fumbling, and they lovingly caressed each other, needing more than anything to express their love. This time, when he entered her, it was gently. They began to move in unison and slowly, deeply, their passion rose until they trembled on the peak of the wave. There, they hovered for a delicious moment until the final release came, and they tumbled headlong together into pure ecstasy. It was the sublime fulfilment of all the long years of yearning.

They lay like that, still conjoined, for some minutes, totally as one, until finally he withdrew and lay down beside her. She laid her head on his shoulder while he stroked her hair. They declared their undying love for one another, this time in words, promising that nothing on earth would ever part them again.

'I think we need to speak to your ma and da, love,' Walter stated with conviction.

'Yes love, I think we do,' Susan replied, tilting her smiling face up to him and planting a lingering kiss on his lips.

'We'd better go now then, I guess your Da will be at home today as it's Sunday.'

'He will,' she replied, kissing him again.

After lingering a little longer to savour these precious moments together, they stood up, and arm in arm made their way along to Dale Coppice, secure now, in their love, and sure of their future together.

They were married at St Michael's Church, Madeley, on the last Sunday in June. Walter and Susan wanted no fuss. Their wedding was to be only about their love for each other and they insisted that it was a modest affair, with just witnesses and close family in attendance. After the ceremony and a meal at George's house, the couple retired to their rented cottage at the other end of the row, that Cousin Elizabeth had secured for them.

Later that evening they sat in front of their own hearth with a cheerful fire supplementing the candlelight and illuminating the sparsely furnished room. As Susan glanced around, she was content. Finally she had a home of her own. Everyone had been very generous, George providing the settle, table, and chairs, and for the bedroom, a bed and bedding chest. Sally had managed to find a few pots and pans and Betty had given them some items of household linen she had brought with her from the Dale Coppice cottage for just this occasion, always convinced that Walter would one day return to claim his bride.

Susan had been grateful of course, for all the gifts, but the thing that she was most proud of was the small sideboard given to her by the mistress up at Harden House, in gratitude for her years of service. Made of a rich, dark wood, it was a thing of beauty in Susan's eyes, polished over the years until it shone. Her years working at the House, surrounded by beautiful items had given her an appreciation of the finer things. She knew the sideboard well of course having seen it many times as she went about her business up at the house. She also knew that it had been a redundant piece after the mistress had organised the refurbishment of the drawing room. Nevertheless, she reasoned, the mistress had no need to give it to her, and she was grateful that she had been thoughtful enough to do so. She was determined that it wouldn't be the only furniture of quality to grace their home. As Walter was now working for George and learning the carpentry trade, she was sure it wouldn't be long before more fine items of furniture would start to appear.

Over the next few months they settled down to married life and it was in the autumn that Susan announced they would be having a little one in the following summer. Walter was beside himself with joy and the anticipation of becoming a father, and they felt their happiness was complete.

The only cloud on Walter's horizon were the thoughts and memories that came to him in the middle of sleepless nights. The horrors of the prison ship and his own privations at the ironworks were fading, it was true. However, the memory of the Africans singing their songs of home at dead of night grew ever more insistent. The images summoned up in his mind of the horrors they daily endured, stirred in him something that he had felt once before, as the horns sounded summoning him to join the Levellers, the same sense of injustice that nagged away at him, demanding that he join them. Increasingly, he became aware that he would only find true contentment in his life here if he could do something to help bring about change for them.

He hadn't said anything to Susan about all of this, but eventually he knew he must do so. They had no secrets, except this one. Understandably he had not wanted to tell her much about what had happened to him and what he'd seen in America. It was a chapter in his life that was now closed, and he didn't feel inclined to re-live it in words. However this conviction that he must do something, however little, to help the Africans, or at the very least, to bear witness to what he had seen, was growing every day and he knew the time had come for him to share it with Susan.

One evening after supper he tentatively broached the subject.

'I've never told you much about what went on in America love, because to be honest, I didn't want to remember it myself.'

'I know love,' Susan replied, 'and I never asked you about it as I knew you would tell me if and when you felt the need.'

He smiled fondly at his wife, grateful for her patience and understanding, then he began to tell her his story. Of course, he spared her many of the more horrific details about his own experiences, but even so, he could see the pain in her face as in her mind, she put images to the words he was speaking, realising that they were so much worse than she had ever imagined.

'Walter love, I had no idea!' she told him as he paused before moving on to the main revelation he was coming to; the Africans.

Now, staring at the fire, he told her their story, of how they had been stolen away from their homeland in Africa, separated from everyone and everything they loved, and transported in conditions you wouldn't keep an animal in, to a strange land where they were auctioned exactly like the animals that were sold on market day in Madeley. Now he glanced up at Susan and could see the tears glistening on her cheeks in the firelight and loved her more than ever.

'But that was only the beginning for them,' he said quietly and went on to tell her about the branding of their flesh as though they were cattle, their long days of toil with little food, the beatings into submission for anyone daring to object. He told her about their songs of longing for home, the look of fear in their eyes whenever the overlooker glanced their way, the separation of children from their mothers, to be sold on to other estates.

Finally, he came to the story that haunted him most; of the African who was thrown, trussed up like a turkey into the dreaded lock up and left to die in agony. The feelings of guilt he had borne since that day now welled up in him, and tears sprang up in his eyes. Susan, seeing the emotion in his face, reached across and placed a reassuring hand on his arm. He confessed to her that he had always felt that he should have done something to help the man. He had been aware through-out that long night that he must be dying but closed his ears to the moaning emanating from that dreadful place and did nothing.

In reality, he told her, there was little he could have done and whatever he had tried to do, he would have doubtless found himself thrown into the hellhole along with the African, as well as adding years more to his sentence.

'Oh Walter, love, that's a dreadful burden you've had to bear,' Susan declared.

'Nothing compared to what those poor people endured and still are enduring every day, love.'

They sat quietly now, staring into the fire, each in their own thoughts, until Walter spoke again,

'But you know, love,' he began, 'even though I couldn't help the African, maybe I can do something to tell his story and make people in England realise how dreadful the practice of enslaving human beings is. Surely as a Christian country there should be enough good people who would be willing to listen and to try to bring about change.'

'You are a good man, Walter Bangham, and if there's anything I can do to help you do that, I will gladly do it.'

Chapter 63

Over the next few months, Susan and Elizabeth struck up a firm friendship, finding much in common. Susan having been in service for so many years had grown accustomed to being surrounded by the fine things, and as lady's maid had enjoyed a certain status. She was determined that her child would have an education and be given the best possible chances in life. Living with Dorothy and John at the schoolhouse and later becoming a teacher, Elizabeth also understood that education was the route out of poverty. Marrying Rod and joining the Sheldon family had reinforced this belief. She had seen how Mr Sheldon had ensured that his children had had the best education he could afford, which in turn, had enabled her and Rod to build the comfortable life they enjoyed, and she was grateful for it every day.

Walter continued to discuss with Susan how he might find a way to expose the treatment of the Africans in America. He knew it wouldn't be easy. People would find it hard to believe what was happening on the other side of the world. He had discovered that many of the plantations were owned by English people, most of whom never saw with their own eyes what went on there. It seemed that as long as money was being made, they were able to convince themselves that their 'workers' were living comfortable lives. As he knew only too well, nothing could be further from the truth, and he was determined to try to open their eyes.

As the sun was rising on the 1$^{st\,of}$ June 1764, their little boy was born, whom they named William. He was a fine healthy baby and life was good for Walter and Susan. As for the promise he'd made to himself that he would bear witness to the miseries he'd seen in America, at every opportunity he told the story of the Africans. Of course, these opportunities were fairly limited as his circle of acquaintances was small in Madeley Wood. However, Elizabeth suggested that he might like to speak at one of the prayer meetings that she and John were now holding on a regular basis in her home. Although nervous of speaking publicly, he knew if he was to fulfil what he now saw as his duty, he could not refuse.

When the day came, he and Susan arrived at Elizabeth's to find the room packed. Most of them were strangers to him, a few he knew by sight and one or two he knew well. He was surprised to find them here. He had no idea how popular this new kind of meeting was becoming. Previously, religious meetings had been limited to church services. This was very different, more informal, but exciting. It was obvious that the people were full of joyful anticipation. He'd always found church services austere and frankly quite boring. This was very different, if they were keen to hear what he had to say about a subject not often spoken about, he thought, they must be keen to learn.

After a few prayers were said, for anyone who didn't know him, Elizabeth introduced Walter, explaining that he had come to talk to them about the plight of the enslaved people in America. Walter stood up nervously, a little unsure where to start. In the end he decided to fully explain how he had come to be in America, which of course meant explaining that he had been transported, and why. As it happened most of the people there were well aware of the events of nine years previously, and he was pleased to feel no animosity regarding the circumstances that had taken him to the New World.

Once that part of his story was concluded, Walter paused and taking a deep breath, began to talk about what he had witnessed of the lives of the workers on the tobacco plantation and in the ironworks. He could tell from the expressions on the faces around him that what they were horrified. It was obvious that this was all news to them, and they were utterly shocked, particularly when he talked about the African who had tried to help the child and who had to die for his efforts. Several of the ladies had tears in their eyes and when he had finished the room was completely silent for several moments, as they all struggled to process what they had just heard.

Then, several of them began to question Walter. Some wanted to know whether they were allowed to have families, or what other kinds of punishments were meted out and for what, and still others asked about the children and how they were treated. Finally they wanted to know how they could help. Walter explained that the best, and really, the only way to help was to work towards bringing about the end to the system of enslavement. He went on to explain this wouldn't be easy. It had been going on for centuries and many of the aristocracy, the landed gentry and even the company owners were deeply involved in it, owning slaves even though they had never set eyes on them, knowing them only as names on a ledger.

The meeting concluded with more prayers and afterwards, several people came up to shake Walter's hand and say that they would be glad to help to spread the word about what they had just heard. Overall Walter was pleased that he had been able to give voice to the Africans' stories and that people were willing to join him in his mission and the load on his conscience had eased a little. As Susan had watched Walter standing in front of the meeting speaking passionately on this matter that was so close to his heart and knowing that public speaking hadn't come naturally to him, she was proud of him.

Over the months and years ahead, Walter took every opportunity to recount his stories and eventually he joined the growing anti-slavery movement. He often reflected on the life journey he had travelled since that day at Ketley when he was taken by the militia. In so many ways it had been a terrible journey. Apart from the physical and mental trials he'd had to endure, it had meant years away from the woman he loved. However, in the end he had found purpose in it. Working for the end of the enslavement of other human beings had become his life's mission and if he hadn't been transported to America, he wouldn't even have known that such dreadful cruelty and injustices existed.

Chapter 64

Nat and Mary had managed to build a good life, by the standards of the day. Nat was earning good money as a skilled mould maker and Mary was an excellent manager, growing most of the vegetables they needed in the plot behind the house, and skilfully sewing clothes and household linen. Thomas was four years old and a bright lad. They hoped to have more children, but it just hadn't happened as yet. Nat still worried about Anne and visited her as often as he was able, but he had seen no other outward signs of ill-treatment by Tommy, and she never complained of any. He missed Ben greatly and often wondered where he was and whether he had found the life he'd dreamt of.

One evening when he arrived home from his shift, he found Mary in a state of great excitement.

'You'll never guess what, a letter arrived today!'

'A letter! Who on earth would be sending us a letter?

'Well, it was brought by a bargee who had been making a delivery to the works. Apparently, someone at the Gloucester Docks had given it to him, knowing that he was bound for the Gorge, as it's addressed to you as you can see.'

She handed him the letter and he could see his name and 'Nailer's Row, Dale End, Coalbrookdale' written on the front of the folded sheet.

'Well, bless me! I wonder if it's from Ben. I can't think who else would be writing to me.'

They sat down on the settle and Nat carefully broke the seal and opened it up. His reading skills were not good, but he eagerly looked to the bottom of the letter to find out who had sent it and was thrilled to see his brother's name.

Mary's reading skills although limited, were rather better than Nat's as her old employers, in the interest of the smooth running of the house had ensured that all staff had some basic tuition in reading and writing. Nat handed her the letter, and she began to slowly read out loud.

Ann-ap-ol-is, May 1765

Dear Nat and Mary,

I am trusting that this letter will reach you. I am handing it to a crewman on a ship destined for Bristol, who has agreed to send it on to you.

I write to tell you that Mary and I are well, although I confess the journey and the years since have been hard. I have been working at an ironworks in Annapolis on the Chesapeake Bay. There is much work to be had here and the place is growing fast, but I didn't come to America to work with iron. As you know, I came to find land of my own and as I now write we are finally about to leave this place to join a waggon-train of settlers moving west, to claim a piece of land. I know not when I will be able to write to you again, but I want you to know as we set out on this journey, we do it in the hope of a better life. I trust that you and Mary and all the folks in the Gorge are well. I think of you all often and cannot deny that I do miss Shropshire, but we have made our decision and it's now up to Mary and me to make the most of it and build our lives here. Please pass on this news to Mary's family.

One day I hope to see you all again, but until then take care of one another and think of us often.

With fondest love

Benjamin Bangham

For some moments after Mary had finished reading, Nat sat staring into the fire, then said quietly,

'Well, it's good to hear that they are well, or at least were when Ben had this letter written, which was six months ago now. Goodness only knows where they finally settled, and sadly we may never know.'

'I know love, it's hard, not knowing, but we just have to get on with our own lives, don't we?'

It was a just couple of months later that Nat came home with news of his own that would change those lives forever.

Mr Reynolds had sent for him to tell him he was expanding the Ketley Ironworks and needed another skilled moulder to work there. He wanted Nat to move to Ketley, some five miles to the north of Coalbrookdale. He said there would be an increase in his wages and a house for his family, but they would need to move from Nailer's Row within the month. Nat had been shocked but knew he had little choice but to accept, although he couldn't imagine what Mary would think of the idea of leaving their little home that she had so lovingly created. Neither would she be happy to leave her aunt and uncle, although Ketley was nearer to Wrockwardine and her own parents. In the event he thanked Mr Reynolds for the opportunity and said he would begin to make arrangements to move his family to Ketley.

It was with some trepidation he entered the house that night, not being sure how Mary would react to the news. In the event he was right to be nervous. She was shocked and initially even rather angry at this proposed disruption to their settled lives, telling Nat that it wasn't right that the Company could dictate their lives in this way.

'Well love,' Nat began, 'they do already control our lives, owning the roof over our 'eads and payin' my wages.'

'I know,' Mary replied, 'but it's not pleasant to be reminded of it.'

'I know it will be hard to leave our home here and you'll miss your aunt and uncle, but Ketley will be nearer to your Ma and Da don't forget.'

'That's true,' Mary replied, 'and I know you're right, we have no option other than to make the most of it I suppose. When do they want us to move?'

Mary's Irish eyes flashed again when he told her they had to move by the end of the month, and she proceeded to bang about the place for a while until she finally became resigned to the idea and began to plan what she would need to do to prepare for the move.

It was just three weeks later that the waggon and driver provided by the Company, turned up outside Nailer's Row. Nat had been given a couple of days off to move his family and belongings to their new home in Ketley. Mary's uncle Patrick helped him to load everything on the waggon. Her Aunt Bridie had packed a loaf of bread and a ham hock for them to take with them so that they would have something for supper when they arrived. Finally, everything was piled on the waggon and after hugs all round and a few tears from Bridie, Mary climbed up beside the driver and Nat handed Thomas up to her.

Nat, who was finding it hard to leave this house which had been his home for most of his life, stepped back inside to take one last look around. He checked the bedrooms, supposedly to make sure nothing had been left behind, while in reality, he just wanted one last look, remembering his Ma and Da, Elizabeth, Anne and Ben and their lives together within these walls.

The impatient neighing of the horse outside brought him back to the moment, and he knew it was time to go. Now he hurried down the stairs and out of the door without a backward glance, locking it as he went.

Half an hour later, after Nat had dropped the keys to Nailer's Row in at the Company office, the waggon finally took the road towards Horsehay. The last of the Banghams had left the Dale.

The Machine

It came from nowhere, an image in the mind
Innocent and beckoning bountiful and kind
It gave the world a promise of work and jobs and hope
Of riches yet undreamt of and freedom from the yoke

Soon it needed factories in which to multiply
All power devouring being, it grew and drew us, why
We gladly came in millions like lemmings to the edge
Chasing dreams inspired by greed but we betrayed ourselves

We fed it with our bodies and still it craved for more
We sacrificed our minds to it, our very will it broke
For fifteen hours each day we fed its hungry mouth
Our bodies wracked and broken, too late we saw truth

This thing we had created from somewhere in the mind
Was a reproducing nightmare, how could we be so blind
We'd had the world to live in, the sunshine and the rain
A life we'd lost forever which would never come again

Marilyn Freeman,

Map of the Severn Gorge

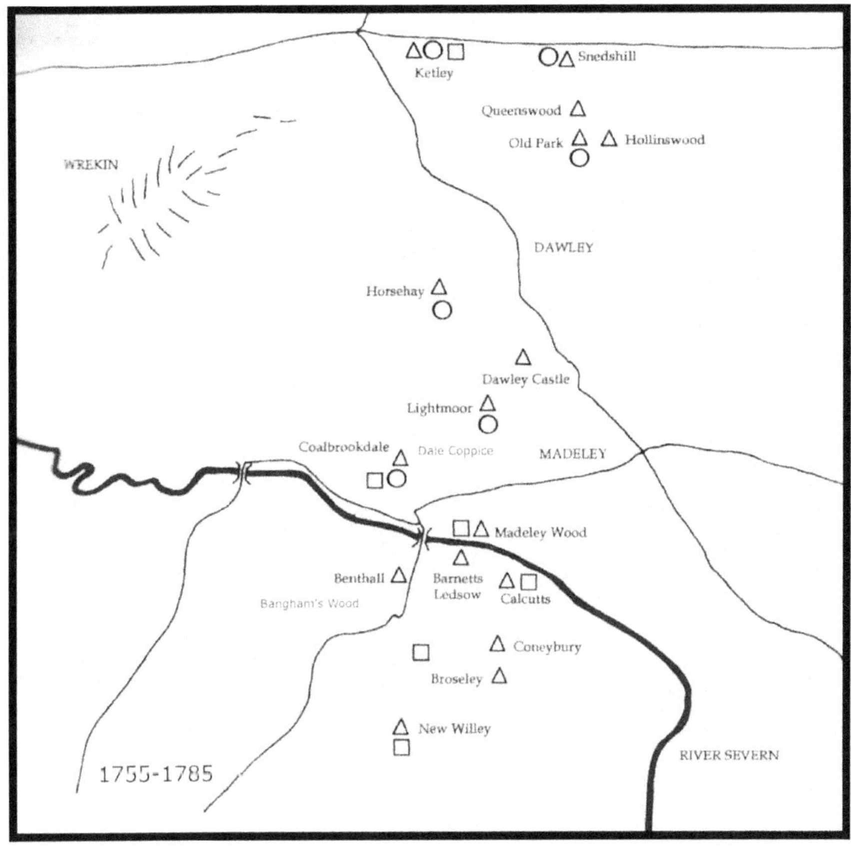

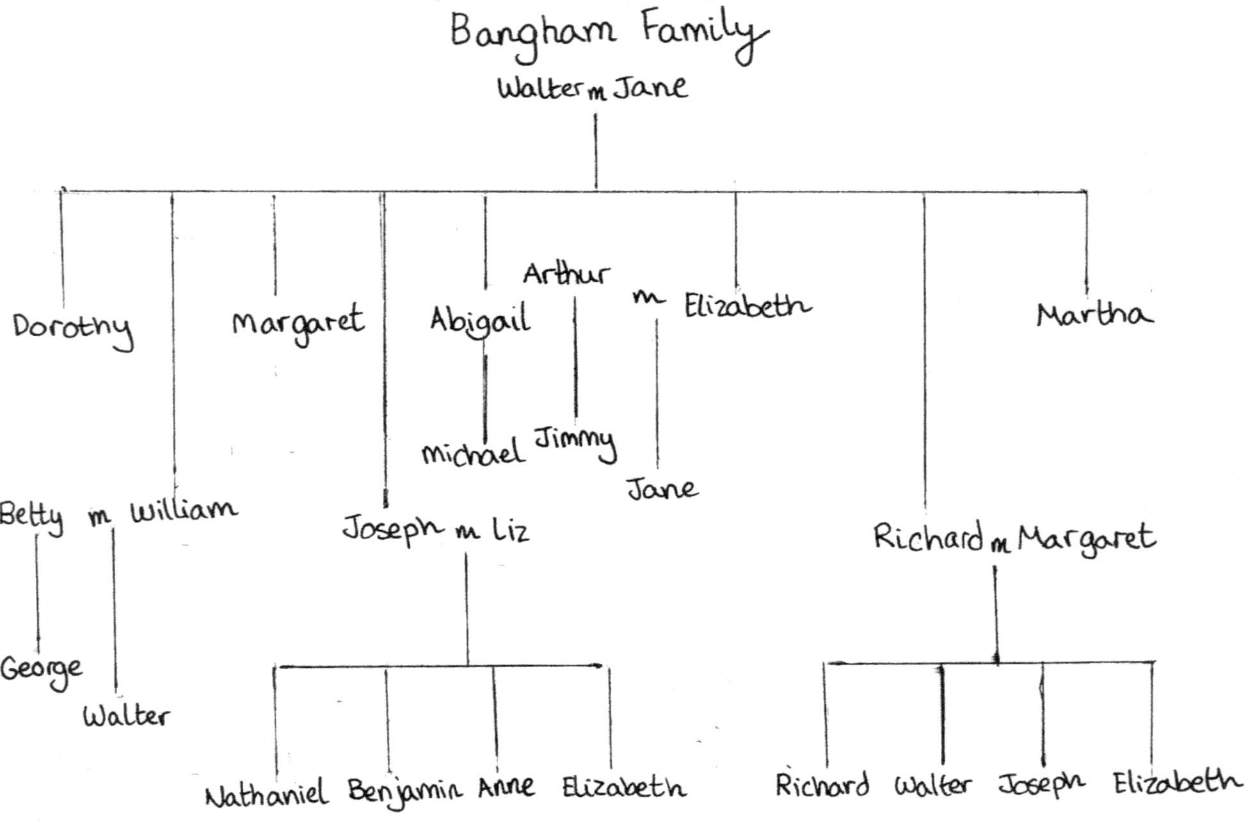

Bangham Family
Walter m Jane
Dorothy
Margaret
Abigail
Arthur m Elizabeth
Martha
Betty m William
George
Walter
Joseph m Liz
Michael Jimmy
Jane
Nathaniel Benjamin Anne Elizabeth
Richard m Margaret
Richard Walter Joseph Elizabeth

MARILYN FREEMAN

Meet **Marilyn Freeman**, a woman whose journey through life reads like the pages of a compelling novel. Born in the industrial town of Oldham, England in 1946, Marilyn initially forged her path as an Industrial Chemist, delving into the intricacies of science. However, her story took a captivating turn when she partnered with her husband in a successful venture manufacturing high end toiletries.

After a fulfilling career in business, Marilyn found a new calling upon retirement. Driven by a deep-seated empathy, she transitioned into the realm of counselling, becoming a person-centred counsellor. Her compassionate nature led her to volunteer in bereavement counselling, offering solace and support to those navigating the difficult journey of loss.

In the later chapters of her life, Marilyn discovered a passion for storytelling. Four years ago, she embarked on a writing career that has seen the publication of four novels. Three of these novels belong to the captivating genre of family mystery and suspense, highlighting Marilyn's skill in crafting tales that grip the reader's imagination.

The latest addition to Marilyn's literary repertoire is a historical novel, a departure from the mysteries that defined her earlier works. This novel, rich in detail and steeped in the tapestry of history, draws inspiration from Marilyn's own ancestors. She weaves a narrative that explores the profound impact of seemingly inconsequential decisions, echoing through the corridors of time with sometimes tragic consequences.

Marilyn's fascination lies in the intricate dance of characters within her stories. She delves into the complexities of human relationships, unearthing the profound repercussions of choices that resonate through generations. In her writing, she skilfully navigates the twists and turns of familial ties, unravelling the mysteries of the human heart.

Other Books by the Author

Karma: A Mystery in Paris
Love Ties: An Unbroken Bond
Secrets and Lives
Coalbrookdale (which comprises Part One of this book)

All the books are available from the main online bookstores including Amazon, as a printed book, Ebook, or audiobook.
Website: www.spellbrooktales.com